"So much Gnostic and sub-Gnostic nonsense has been written about Mary Magdalene that it comes as a relief, as well as a pleasure, to read Christine Sunderland's novel. Unlike many other popular writers, she is well aware that truth is often stranger than fiction—and much more fascinating. Accordingly, though the plot of her book is indeed fictional, Christine has throughout based it on the most reliable evidence and writes from an orthodox point of view, weaving complex material into a gripping tale surprisingly easy to read. One that takes us not only to Provence—where lies the heart of the mystery—but on a guided tour of several of Rome's most inspiring churches."

    MICHAEL DONLEY, PH.D.
    Author of *Saint Mary Magdalen in Provence, The Coffin and the Cave* (Gracewing, 2008)

"*The Magdalene Mystery* has history, intrigue, romance, and predatory Internet behavior. It is an up-to-date mixture that intertwines past and present in Christian life and practice. Where else can you see a single parent and a theology professor compete with a cyber-predator to find a manuscript revealing the real Saint Mary Magdalene? It made me yearn to visit Rome again!"

    PAUL S. RUSSELL, PH.D.
    Author of *Looking Through the World to See What's Really There: One explanation of the first step towards religious belief* (AuthorHouse, 2004)

Novels by Christine Sunderland

* * *

THE TRILOGY
Pilgrimage
Offerings
Inheritance

Hana-lani

The Magdalene Mystery

THE MAGDALENE MYSTERY

CHRISTINE SUNDERLAND

OAKTARA
www.oaktara.com

The Magdalene Mystery

Published in the U.S. by:
OakTara Publishers
www.oaktara.com

Cover design by Yvonne Parks at www.pearcreative.ca
Cover image © 2013 by Christine Sunderland
Author photo © 2007 by Brittany Sunderland

Copyright © 2013 by Christine Sunderland. All rights reserved.

Cover and interior design © 2013, OakTara Publishers. All rights reserved. No part of this publication may be reproduced, stored in a retrieval system, or transmitted in any form or by any means without the prior written permission of the publisher. The only exception is brief quotations in professional reviews. The perspective, opinions, and worldview represented by this book are those of the author's and are not intended to be a reflection or endorsement of the publisher's views.

All Scripture quotations are taken from the King James Version of the Bible. Public domain.

ISBN-13: 978-1-60290-126-1
ISBN-10: 1-60290-126-0

Printed in the U.S.A.

Acknowledgments

I wish to acknowledge with extreme gratitude:

The many friends, family, and clergy who read early and late drafts and encouraged me.

Dr. Michael Donley, author of *Saint Mary Magdalen in Provence, The Coffin and the Cave* (Gracewing), who advised me on the Magdalene traditions in Provence, proofed and corrected the manuscript with detailed precision, and has provided immeasurable support in this project.

The Rev. Dr. Paul S. Russell, Dean of Saint Joseph's Theological Seminary, Berkeley, who advised me on the history of New Testament scholarship in the last sixty years and graciously read early and late drafts.

A lovely English nun in Rome who cannot divulge her name or her order, but whose enthusiasm for the project buoyed me along on a tide of happiness as she read the manuscript to verify my accounts of Roman churches and rituals.

Editor Margaret Lucke, who tackled structure, character, plot, and theme and gave me invaluable suggestions to make the book better.

Ramona Tucker and Jeff Nesbit of OakTara, who continue to have faith in my work.

My dear husband, Harry, who reads my manuscripts with great devotion and advises me on the truth of real-life situations. He is a true-hearted companion in my journey through time.

"Thou shalt not bear false witness against thy neighbor."
EXODUS 20:16, THE NINTH COMMANDMENT

*

"The first day of the week cometh Mary Magdalene early,
when it was yet dark, unto the sepulchre,
and seeth the stone taken away from the sepulchre."
JOHN 20:1

Prologue

Roma

IN THE FADING LIGHT FATHER KEITH GILBERT BENT OVER THE PAGE, reading his words with care. Soon it would be time for Vespers, and the yearnings of hours past would return, the echoes of other bells and other chants, the flicker of flames before ancient altars, here in Rome and throughout Christendom. Soon one of the postulants would help him to the chapel, and Father Gilbert would be grateful.

The old priest knew he must finish this letter to Kelly, the child he had neglected and for whom his heart ached. Others had typed much of it—but he must add his own script.

May 9, 2010
My dear goddaughter,
 If you are reading this, I shall be with our heavenly Father.
 From this great distance, from this historic and holy city of Rome, I have watched and prayed for you. Your parents' death was a great loss. They were like my own children.

Images of Martin came to him. The young academic had visited Saint Mary's with his Katherine, looking for a suitable site to be married. In the process of marriage counseling, it was not long before Martin was converted—"fell in love with God," as he often said later. Katherine renewed her faith, returning to her roots, she claimed. They were received by the Church, and Father Gilbert blessed their marriage vows. Martin drank up the faith like a traveler in the desert. He served as acolyte at the altar. Katherine, too, with her serious dark eyes, learned quickly, eventually teaching Faith Formation classes. Then Kelly was born, such a joy to everyone. They had waited so long. They had prayed so many prayers for a child.

Father Gilbert studied the letter to his goddaughter.

 You have been always in my prayers. You are intelligent, but do you use the mind that God has given you? Do you know what you believe? Do you know *why* you believe? Do you understand truth, and how one finds it? Today many authorities will compete for your allegiance. Indeed, the creed of emotions has supplanted rational thought, so that truth and reality are vague and wispy things.

He asked himself, *Is this too much—too heavy a beginning?* But he continued.

> Kelly, a great weight has been on my heart. I feel responsible for your parents' death. If they had not been with me, if they had not been involved in my work on the Magdalene, they would not have died. My grief at times is overwhelming.
>
> I vowed to finish the work they died for. I continued the research. I increased funding and staff for the newsletter we founded, *Opus Veritatis:* the telling of the truth, the correcting of the lies, the making straight the crooked paths weaving through arts and letters, those half-truths that pollute the minds of the young and vulnerable. It was—and is—our great work, to fearlessly set the record straight.
>
> Now, with this letter, I re-own my duty to you, for *duty,* defamed as the word is today, is the conscience and discipline of love. I pray I am not too late.
>
> I believe my hour to meet our God is near, to see his face at last, not merely to hear the melody in time but to sing with his angels and saints. My body is decaying. I gladly relinquish it and look forward to my new and resurrected one.
>
> I recall that you like mysteries, and with this letter I challenge you. To be sure, all life is a mystery, as is the Holy Trinity: God the Father, God the Son, and God the Holy Spirit. Our world is charged with God's grandeur, as the poet Hopkins said, for it is full of mystery and miracle. But the mystery of which I speak is more of a personal quest, with a true grail to be found.
>
> I have been studying the early Church, those first centuries of Christianity. Many writers are interested in Mary Magdalene, the sinner and saint, said to be the woman with the jar of ointment who washed the feet of Christ, the woman with the seven demons from Magdala. She has been known as many Marys, but who was she really?
>
> I have traced her through the centuries and have recorded my conclusions. Your quest is to find this writing, the work of my life. For the story of the Magdalene is the story of the first-century Church. And the story of the first-century Church is the story of Jesus and his

resurrection. It is a story that gives the modern world reason to believe.

Should you solve this mystery, not only will you receive your legacy, but you will hear the Magdalene's melody. And I pray the tune will touch your heart and soul as it has touched mine.

Do you accept my challenge, Kelly? If you do, then come to Rome, to the Church of Santa Susanna. Ask to see my associate, Father Fitzroy. He shall give you your first clue.

To begin, you must solve the following puzzle. The answer will gain your audience with Father Fitzroy. Also contact Dr. Daniel C. Weaver in Berkeley, a professor of New Testament Studies, a member of Saint Mary's. He will help you. Show him this letter.

May God be with you, and one day, may you see Our Lord face to face.

With all blessings and love,
Until we meet in heaven,
Your Godfather Gilbert

PSLESDRCEEAOT

Not a deed,
Nor a rhyme,
It tells of a seed
That grew in time.

It holds the heart
And calls the mind,
But is only a part
Of a greater find.

From ancient of days
It ruled the soul
And led to praise
As bells did toll.

His chest aching, the old man reread the letter and said a short prayer. His fingers shook, and he struggled to control them as he scrawled his name, jerking the letters across the page. He folded the thin paper, worked it into an envelope, and sealed the triangular flap with wax, a dove above a heart, the emblem of his order, *Opus Veritatis*.

Relieved, he turned to the open window and gazed over Rome, massaging his chest. The evening was drawing near, the day ending, and the bells of the city clanged. The light in the room in the *monastero* was dimming, and already he could hear men and women chant the Psalms in the chapel. He focused watery eyes on the envelope and scratched the address: *Kelly Ann Roberts, 618 Oak Grove Road #15, Walnut Creek, California 94595, U.S.A.*

The wooden crucifix on the wall had always given him strength and now he waited upon it. He folded his hands, closed his eyes, and rested in the image. Then, full of certainty, he opened his eyes and made the Sign of the Cross over his head and heart.

Father Keith Gilbert reached for his cane. He pounded the wooden floor twice and watched the door, waiting for the postulant.

1
Kelly

THE DREAM SHE DREAMED WAS ETHEREAL, pulling her higher and higher, as if wings fluttered beneath her hands and arms, and although she felt fear, it was a fear promising happiness.

And so Kelly Ann Roberts climbed, rooted on earth, each step leaden, as she watched for boulders and tried not to glance down. The cliff face offered footholds, shallow ledges in the massive wall of rock, but there were also shiny surfaces, slippery, deadly. She focused on the stone and the ascent, and when she glanced up, more sky breathed upon her, changing from brilliant blue to deep and starry like a Van Gogh painting.

As she climbed, she heard a distant melody, feather-light and in a major key, or was it minor now, weaving through her, louder with each step, a harp or a violin or a piano. She climbed, full of fear and hope and wonder....

*

Sensing the dream slip away, Kelly tried to hold it close, but failing, sat on the edge of her bed and willed its return, failing again. Nevertheless, she carried with her through the early morning both the fading memory and an increased longing, as she woke her son, helped him dress, and prepared their breakfast. Would that she could return, re-enter the place where she had been, but soon she was rinsing cereal bowls, positioning them in the dishwasher, and the sweetness, the music, was gone.

More important matters faced her this Saturday in May, matters of loss, matters of death. As she dressed for her godfather's funeral, she drew her heart and mind together to meet the coming hours. She knew she would mourn Father Gilbert, not as she mourned her parents, but as someone who was part of her history, and she would have to face this loss. She supposed this was the purpose of funerals, to help with the facing. She hadn't seen him in many years, but he had kept in touch with cards at Christmas and Easter and occasional lengthy letters. Only last year he sent her a colorful, gilded icon, and she found it comforting to place it near the door, blessing her going out and coming in. Yes, the funeral would make sense of it all.

For now she chose her clothes carefully, deciding on a conservative black blazer from her days at the bank, a cream camisole, and a heather gray pencil skirt. As she reached for pearl earrings she could hear five-year-old Matt playing in the next room, making grating noises for his trucks—the front loaders, the mixers, the forklifts, the graders—and the sounds soothed her. Not for the first time she wished there was a father in Matt's life, but she had no regrets that she chose to have the baby.

Kelly loved her son more than she loved herself. She often thought it was them against the world, although the melodrama—and the triteness—of the phrase annoyed her. *She* was better than that, doing what must be done and not wanting praise or pity, but at the end of the day, after bath and story and prayers and a snug tuck-in of the worn sheets under the soft mattress of her child's bed, she would scrutinize her pinched face in the tarnished bathroom mirror and feel so lonely, so scared. She had turned thirty last week, and as she soberly reflected on the passage of the years, decided she had more dark nights than bright days, anxiety shadowing her. Above all, she wanted to be safe, and safety was never quite within her reach.

Working for the bank, she had felt safe, at least financially, but since the layoffs her monthly bills had eaten into her small savings. How would she ever make ends meet? Her English degree hadn't helped her with employment, and she had worked hard for that BA. She had applied to other banks and businesses, but with no luck. Her apartment in Oakview Gardens was the cheapest she could find. Where would she go if she couldn't make the rent?

Kelly stepped to the small window of her bedroom and peered through the mini-blinds, angled discreetly, to the neat beds of oleander and juniper, trying to calm her approaching panic. What would become of her? She turned to the bureau and the instant photo taken in the booth at the mall. She and Carter were happy, joking that day, making silly faces at the quickly shooting camera. Why didn't he want to get married? She had been in love with him, or so she thought. Evidently, he had not been in love with her.

She had led a quiet life, homeschooled and bookish, and perhaps, looking back, was somewhat sheltered from the real world. But to Kelly, sex meant love and not lust. Sex meant marriage and family. When she brought up the question of their future, Carter's eyes had shifted away. Into his silence she poured her urgent demands, hating the shrill sound of her voice. Within the month he was gone, and she steeled herself to not return his calls, calls that never came.

He had been her first love, her first intimacy, her first heartbreak. Before

Carter, she had refused guys again and again, recalling her mother's moral admonitions and dreading disease. With Carter and his smooth way about him, she felt comfortable. She trusted him. Yet, in spite of his tenderness, he was often distant in his lovemaking, as though they engaged in a delicate sport where timing mastered the moment. The experience was a mistake she did not repeat and promised herself not to repeat in the future.

When she discovered she was pregnant, Carter had urged an abortion, but once she saw the ultrasound, she knew what she would do. The tiny arms and legs moved to the thump of the baby's heartbeat. She could see the head, the eyes, even the genitals. The volunteers at the pregnancy center helped her through the remaining seven months, offered adoption services and follow-up care. When she decided to keep her baby, they encouraged her to go back to church, to find a support system, since she had no family nearby. She had never looked back, never second-guessed her choice. Today, she could not imagine life without her child. She could not think of breathing without her son, Mathew Michael Roberts.

With her index finger she nudged her tortoise shell glasses higher on her nose and eyed a polka-dot scarf, then thought better of it, for she *was* attending a funeral. Did one wear such decorative things to funerals? She recalled her parents' funeral ten years earlier with a too-familiar pain.

Kelly twisted her long thick hair into a bun, securing it with pins. "Matt, use the bathroom, honey. We need to get going, or I'll be late." Where had she put her godfather's last letter?

"Will Josh and Ethan be at Andrea's?" Her son's voice rose with interest.

She checked the desk drawer, pulled out the tissue envelope with the Vatican postage, and slipped it into a side pocket of her handbag. "They should be, since they live there now." How did Andrea manage, having custody of her grandsons, and at her age? But Andrea always managed, and once again Kelly was grateful for the friendship of this elderly widow who lived next door and loved children.

Kelly heard the toilet flush, and her son, stooped under a backpack crammed with trucks, joined her in the hall. His eyes were serious, she thought, as though mapping the afternoon with his friends. She glanced at her watch and checked the front room. TV off. Lights off. Sliding glass door locked with metal bar in place.

She eyed the open kitchenette. Nothing appeared to be on. Lady Jane, their black-and-white longhair, lapped water from a dish near the fridge. Laddie, their red tabby, slept soundly on the worn armchair near the window, basking in a pool of sun. The room with its familiar furnishings encouraged her with a sweet sense of belonging, as though ensuring her return. *Home*. As she gazed at the bookshelves, she recalled Andrea's novel, found it, and slipped it into her bag.

Moving toward the door, she saw that Father Gilbert's icon tilted a bit, and she straightened it. Nancy from church had explained it was called "Trinity." The image depicted three angels who, in the form of men, visited Abraham, but Kelly could not recall the Old Testament story. Even so, the gilded image intrigued her, and she wondered for not the first time whether angels existed, or whether they were the product of wishful thinking as some claimed. For that matter, had Abraham ever existed? Her anthropology class had dismissed these "holy tales" as cultural phenomena created by society's psychological needs. Even so, the colorful painting on wood glowed with reassurance, as though beauty and form were enough. Could she hold onto beauty and form? Could she trust them?

Matt grabbed the edge of her jacket and pulled down hard. Taking his small hand, she opened the front door, stepped into the morning light, turned, and carefully fitted her key into the lock. The bolt slid, clicking hard into the jamb.

They followed the path to Andrea's and, as Kelly expected, her neighbor greeted them with an open smile and crinkly blue eyes. She wore a plaid apron tied loosely over blue jeans and dusted with flour, and was sliding her fingers down the fabric, drying them. Her gray hair, feathered short, reminded Kelly of the British actress Judi Dench, whom she greatly admired, and Andrea did indeed have the classic face of a star—the high cheekbones, the sculpted nose, the wide smile. She must have been stunning when she was younger, Kelly thought, although today she simply looked tired. Kelly hoped she wasn't adding to Andrea's already heavy load, and thought once again how much she appreciated the babysitting co-op in her apartment complex. She would babysit Josh and Ethan soon. She would repay her.

"Something smells good." Kelly stepped into the apartment, a reverse floor plan of her own. But here, Andrea's earlier life with Mr. Fairchild filled the room. The worn antiques were pleasingly old-fashioned: mahogany tables, Queen Anne chairs, damask slip covers, silver-framed mirrors, Impressionist prints enhanced with oils, cameos arranged on a roll-top desk. Recognizing Vivaldi's *Four Seasons* playing, Kelly was eased by the ordered tempo.

"Bread. Yeast rolls. The boys love 'em." Andrea turned to watch Matt as he ran to the back room to play with her grandsons.

"Everyone loves them." Kelly laughed and handed her the novel. "And I loved *this*."

"I thought you would! *Children of Men* is amazing. Popped my socks right off! Can you stay for a bit? A little coffee? A cinnamon bun?"

Kelly shook her head with true regret. "I wish I could, but I can't. I'm late already." She set her purse on an ottoman and searched inside for a slip of paper. "Here's my number, the church number, the doctor."

"I have all that."

Kelly nodded. "I know, but just in case, I'll set it by the phone. And here's Matt's asthma medication and inhaler." Her heart clutched when she recalled Matt's brush with death last year, across the street in the field of mustard grass. Who knew he was asthmatic? And how quickly it had come on—one, two, three hours and his lungs had filled with liquid. His eyes had swollen shut. His stomach had cramped in pain. She drove like a madwoman to Emergency, where they pumped him with an intravenous solution. Within weeks they found he had multiple allergies, but mainly to grasses, and Kelly worried how she would keep a boy away from lawns, from parks, from yards. Was such a thing possible?

"Right." Andrea peered at her with extra encouragement. "Now don't you worry. He'll be fine. Everything will be right as rain."

Her friend's truisms wrapped Kelly like a soft shawl, and she found Matt and hugged him. "I'll be back soon, sweetie. You be good for Andrea."

He wriggled from her grasp and returned to his friends.

She checked to see that her cell phone was on and slipped out the door, waving to the elderly woman, grateful for the invisible thread connecting them, a thread that unwound slowly as she drove away, her heart sinking with each mile. As she turned onto the freeway, she checked her gas gauge, usually hovering around the quarter mark. While her Taurus got good mileage, she rarely had enough cash to fill up the tank and she was trying to save her credit card for emergencies. She eyed the dial: enough for Berkeley and return.

She glanced at the envelope peeking out of her handbag on the passenger seat. Father Gilbert had said to contact Daniel C. Weaver, a professor who attended Saint Mary's, but neglected to give her a number. Kelly hoped he would be at the funeral. Searching her memory, she couldn't recall him. The letter was intriguing, but surely there was another way to receive her inheritance. She couldn't afford to go to Rome, she couldn't leave Matt, and she couldn't take him with her. But her godfather had written that she would greatly benefit from the trip, and she could sure use the money.

2
Lester

IT WAS EARLY SATURDAY MORNING, the week after final exams, when Dr. Lester Sansby of Berkeley University made his monthly visit to Peoples' Park, not far from his office on campus. It was a visit that disgusted him, but it was a necessary one. His middle-aged body demanded it, his work required it, but most of all he deserved it.

The park was quiet at this hour, but, as always, the usual detritus and garbage, sleeping bags and staring lumps of humanity forming dirty heaps, littered the tree-shaded area. He found his contact, who called himself Zebediah the Great, and made the deal quickly. Relieved, he left with a fair supply of pills in an innocent zip-lock bag, and gave thanks once again for Berkeley's easy access to all manner of lifestyles, including the availability of the occasional recreational or pharmaceutical drug. He picked up a bagel and a large coffee at Starbucks and, as he passed his athletic club, considered swimming a few laps later in the afternoon. One way or another he needed to keep the previous evening at bay. His office usually steadied him, as did the pills, and he still had student grades to file for the spring semester. Saturday was always a good day to catch up.

Entering his office, Lester turned and locked his door; then, with a quick, practiced movement, he placed a pill on his tongue, threw his head back, and swallowed. He secreted the bag in a far recess of his desk drawer, reclined in his chair, and turned on his laptop. Soon he was surfing his Internet sites, posting a comment here and reacting there, chuckling with self-admiration at his great gift of directing the debate. His words flowed, so many of them, paragraph after paragraph, sliding down the screen. After clicking *Publish* the fourth time, he took a break. He tapped and lit an unfiltered cigarette and sipped the last of his now-cold coffee. Walking to the window, he opened it and looked out to the Student Center. He exhaled a smooth stream of smoke, outside, where it was allowed. The campus smoking ban was absurd, he fumed to himself, but so far no one had complained.

Near the window, his cockatiel, Freedom, swung jauntily on her perch in her cage, cocking her gray-and-white head toward him with its pretty orange-spotted cheeks, an action Lester liked to think meant curiosity, but probably only meant acute observation. Her topknot was erect, which according to the avian vet, meant she was particularly alert. Freedom had been his brother's bird, inherited when Dalton left California. It seemed to Lester that, when he cared for Freedom, he cared for poor Dalton too. He even had taken to bringing the bird to the office with him. She was friendly. She liked him. His female acquaintances enjoyed his bird as well. Freedom broke the ice in a satisfactory manner.

He tapped the cage and peered in. "Hi, Freedom, miss me?" He refilled her food and water buckets. "Sweet Freedom." She moved from foot to foot and let out a loud squawk, shaking her head at him like a dog emerging from a lake.

He inhaled his cigarette deeply, welcoming the harsh heat of the tobacco, as he watched a group of students demonstrating, waving placards, shouting slogans. But his mind returned to the previous evening, hearing again Mandy's high whine, her last words: *You greedy, horny old man. You need to grow up.* Then the door had slammed in rejection.

She, he thought now, gazing unseeing at the protest, needed to grow up, face the reality of their open society coming of age. *She* needed to face not getting an A in his Humanities class. Face a change of major. But she was gone, and he could only feel relief that he needn't lie anymore, that the other co-eds who shared his bed would not prey upon his conscience as she did.

Such twinges, he knew, were merely leftovers of an indoctrinated moral sense. They were a remnant, an echo, a shard of his former Judeo-Christian conscience, drilled into him by irrational parents with medieval mindsets. Such a moral imperative was, he judged, in no way logical. He need neither fear nor heed it. It was pure superstition to claim love demanded commitment. Love was lust and lust was the natural function of man, or woman as the case may be. Man was clearly no more than an evolved ape. Why not face the facts and enjoy the implications? Life was short.

As he mused on the little tramp's tantrum, hearing again the door slam in its conclusive, however trite, finish, he watched the demonstration outside with a rising irritation that soon flared to anger. He clenched his fist and stubbed his cigarette in the ashtray, shoving it down with a hard, brutal movement. How dare they! How dare these fresh-faced instructors and spoiled-brat students complain about such trivia! Lester read the placards, the usual vapid stuff: *No more cuts! Keep tuition down! Free the university!*

The protesters were relatively quiet, marching in a loop, and bore little resemblance to the protesters of the sixties, of whom he was a proud alumnus.

At least those protests had some guts, he thought. And they had real issues at stake, like the war, the draft, American imperialism, real future-of-the-world stuff. Today it was *save the trees* and *slow food* and now they whined about tuition raises. *Please.* This university was still the best bargain in the free world, and the professors were way underpaid.

He checked his watch and lit another cigarette. He needed to prepare for his summer-session class, Comparative Religions, but that could wait until spring grades were filed. His notes were comprehensive, and the class wasn't scheduled until late June. It was one of his favorite courses, analyzing the subjectivity of belief, the impossibility of truth. He eyed his laptop, the keeper of his numerous Internet sites, full of ripe bodies and unripe minds, then from the edge of his vision noticed the family photo staring from the file cabinet. He reached for it nervously.

His mother, father, younger brother, and himself, around twelve, he thought, posed in a formal portrait faintly colorized. He turned it face down. He didn't like his parents watching him online, blogging or checking his porn network, although he knew their photo was merely a piece of paper and their scruples were not his. They couldn't touch him, now that they were in the rest home and rarely coherent, but nevertheless, their sayings of long ago nagged him when he blogged and their faces lessened his online pleasure. Why did he keep the photo at all? He guessed he still had remnants of family loyalty. But more importantly, the portrait created a more secure environment when students came for advice. They saw the photo, and a greater bond of trust was established. This was good.

But his mother's eyes haunted him. His mother would talk of repentance and Jesus saves and the Ten Commandments. She would open the Bible and point to a verse, in the idiotic belief that the Holy Spirit would speak to her. She never could understand that the book she worshiped was a silly compendium of unreliable sources, and, even so, these simple folk claimed that it was the Word of God! His parents were true BICCs—Biblically Inerrant Conservative Christians—and he was glad he had distanced himself from their fear and prejudice, that he had seen the true light of reason. She and her kind had harmed the world immeasurably, and it was the least he could do to make up for their God footprint. He chuckled with that phrase, making a mental note to use it. How fortunate he was to have their intelligence but not their insanity. The Ten Commandments! *Right!* Those stone tablets given to Moses, the man responsible for the slaughter of millions, the rape of women and children. *Right!* We should follow such a man? Why not follow Jim Jones and drink his Kool-Aid?

He opened Freedom's door. The bird stepped onto his finger, cocking her head. She weighed less than nothing, he thought, as the tiny feet tickled his skin. He slipped her onto his shoulder and lowered himself into the chair. Rolling to the screen he reached for the mouse and arrowed a news source. Freedom nibbled his ear, then ran her beak through his hair, grooming him.

When he noticed another report on *Opus Veritatis*, his blood began to race. His fists tightened and he breathed deeply, hoping to calm himself. Freedom could feel the tension and chirped, swaying from leg to leg. How Lester hated those people! They had defamed his brother, Dalton, a respected academic, and tainted his career. The ensuing controversy resulted in denial of tenure, and Dalton sank into deep depression. They poisoned his parents with their silly lies, promoted in that absurd and pathetic electronic newsletter. His father raged from his pulpit over what he called media distortions about the world against the church, about the apocalypse, about hellfire and brimstone. That one newsletter did more to make his folks paranoid than any other. *Opus Veritatis, the work of truth!* Those delusional crusaders may as well have ordered his parents' early senility, a state requiring appropriate hospitalization, something Lester ensured for their own safety. The leader of this electronic rag, this Keith Gilbert, had done enough damage to Lester's family to stand trial in any just society.

With distaste laced with surging hatred, Lester opened the OV newsletter and scanned the lead: "*Opus Veritatis* Founder Keith Gilbert Dies of Heart Failure, Sunday, May 9." He read the words again, at first not believing them. At last, Keith Gilbert, the old grandmaster, was dead. The priest had destroyed more than his parents and his brother. He had ruined other respected academics, Lester's friends and colleagues, noble scholars of the modern age.

"Well, well, well," he said with a soft chuckle, "and the funeral is today, right here in our beloved Berkeley at his beloved church. How convenient is that? I have a sudden urge to fall on my knees and give thanks."

Lester Sansby studied the article, pondering its implications. Gilbert's long-awaited research on Mary Magdalene had not yet been found. That was good. Rumors of great wealth still circulated. Interesting. Were the rumors true? He checked other online news sources. They said much the same thing. It would be worth his while to see who attended the funeral. The old man must have kept his work somewhere, but where? And, if there was vast wealth, where was it? There appeared to be no living relatives, yet someone must benefit from this sudden death. Besides himself, he smirked.

At that moment, the image of the ascetic ever-virgin Daniel Weaver came to mind. Once his teaching assistant, Weaver had moved quickly up the ranks. There was no denying he was bright, just misguided. Lester was glad to see the last of him, the last of his frown, the last of his implied judgment. Still, he watched as Weaver's name surfaced from time to time in university circles. The fellow was involved with Gilbert's newsletter, or had been—Lester thought he had seen a connection somewhere; the young man had lived for a time in Rome before coming to Berkeley, he recalled.

Lester tried to think back to the shooting—it must have been more than ten years ago—and Gilbert's departure for Rome. He opened his lower desk drawer. The revolver was still there, slipped into a far-back compartment, but fortunately it was never "smoking." Why hadn't he gotten rid of it? It was unregistered, given to him by a friend, and he thought it would be safer in his desk than anywhere else. Lester had been irrational, stupid. He should have stayed away from the seminar.

What had actually happened when Gilbert didn't die? Lester was well-hidden by the trees and the dark of that moonless night, but it had all gone wrong. That eccentric couple, local professors, were with him. What was their name? Robinson? No, shorter. Robson? No. Close. Roberts. Yes, Martin and Katherine Roberts. The ones who got in the way.

Lester leaned in closer to the screen and typed and clicked and arrowed, swirling the mouse with an intensity that made him feel young again, coaxing data from the computer. He recalled the couple had a daughter. Hadn't she been in one of his classes? Who would know more? Nothing was coming up on the screen.

He had expected Keith Gilbert's death, although one never knew when such a thing would occur. But why hadn't he prepared for it? He was losing his touch.

He dialed a friend in Academic Records and soon had the girl's name, an address, and a photo. It was then he noticed that Freedom had flown off his shoulder to the top of her cage. She was working her way down the front to the open door, using her beak and claws to grab the metal bars, probably for a bite to eat. He pocketed the address, for the moment satisfied.

3

Requiem

KELLY PARKED IN THE SHADE OF A MAJESTIC OAK near Saint Mary's. She locked the car, contemplating the church that had been such a part of her growing-up years. A garden courtyard with a tall palm tree and red camellia bushes led to broad stairs and a brick façade. Four glass doors mirrored the courtyard and rose to a steeply pitched roof. The architecture, Kelly had been told, had the Gothic verticality that pointed to heaven, but also the clean modern style popular in the fifties. The church before this one, built in the early twentieth century in a more modest English country style, stood at right angles to the present building and currently housed the Sunday school, library, and offices.

The hundred-year history of Saint Mary's Berkeley settled upon Kelly like mellow sunshine, and with each visit, she felt she was returning to a well-loved place. Her godfather had been her parish priest, her parents had been married there, and it was in this church that Kelly had been baptized and confirmed. In the Christmas Pageant she played a white-robed angel with tag board wings, and later acted the roles of Elizabeth and Mary. She helped decorate the thick white Easter cross with flowers, shoving stems into deep holes drilled into the wood. After the service they posed in front of the colorful cross, which had been carried to the porch, and Kelly thought how those seasonal photos had layered her life in a satisfying, orderly way. Those were happier days. The Sunday school families sailed to Angel Island and hiked in Golden Gate Park. They munched on fried chicken and potato salad, and sipped soft drinks pulled from ice chests. Kelly recalled art contests and writing competitions, food collections and caroling at nursing homes, attendance awards with pins that formed a chain on her Sunday sweater.

After all those years, Father Gilbert was gone. Somehow, she now realized, she had assumed he would one day return to his beloved Saint Mary's. How he would have loved Matt. How Matt would have loved him.

She pulled out her phone, tapping speed-dial. "Andrea, everything okay? Sorry, I forgot to pack his jacket."

"Of course everything's okay, my dear. We're happy as clams at high tide. And no need for a jacket in this lovely weather."

"Good. And you'll remember—no riding trikes in the parking areas? I'm going inside now. I'll call when the service is over."

"Don't you worry about a thing."

Andrea sounded in control, but Kelly worried. There was Matt's asthma. The recent burglaries in the neighborhood. Her son's proclivity to engage in risky behavior—jumping, running, riding in the driveway. Only last month he had found the cotton swabs, which she'd thought were well hidden. He danced toward her on one foot, holding a swab in an ear and giggling. As she reached for him, she could see it all before it happened. He tripped, fell on the swab, and they made another run to the hospital with a perforated eardrum and a frowning doctor challenging her ability to parent.

With determination, Kelly turned off her phone and crossed the garden courtyard. Climbing the front stairs, she entered the large narthex and passed the board crammed with news and photos. An usher handed her a bulletin and pointed to a guestbook. She signed, adding her name to the list of mourners. Entering the hushed space, she deliberated where she should sit, scanning the hundred oak pews. The church was filling up.

A crimson-carpeted central aisle led to a broad, raised sanctuary with a marble altar, one long slab resting on six angled supports. Above the altar, a red-brick wall rose to a cathedral ceiling where sunlight, streaming through skylights, illumined a massive carved wooden crucifix. Stained-glass windows donated by Father Gilbert lined the nave. As Kelly thought with pride how he had built this church, attracted families with children's events, and taught his growing flock about the love of God, her heart ached. The mourning, she recognized, the accepting of his death, was beginning.

Kelly padded up the aisle and slipped into the third row next to Nancy.

The elderly woman took Kelly's hand in her own mottled ones and squeezed it, then gave her a gentle hug, her fine bones delicate under her cashmere sweater. "I can't believe he's gone," Nancy whispered, her face lined with grief, her white hair feathering her mulatto skin.

Kelly nodded. "I know…me too."

She knelt on the padded kneeler, saying her learned prayer of thanksgiving for the people of the parish, the clergy, and the freedom to worship. Then she sat back, her eyes on the altar. The organist played "Jesu, Joy of Man's Desiring," and the notes spilled down from the loft and over the congregation, carrying a sweet poignancy. The Bach piece was one of her father's favorites and, she recalled, loved by Father Gilbert as well. Kelly glanced at the letter in her handbag. Somehow the tangible sheet of paper holding her godfather's words encouraged her.

Her parents' funeral had also been in this church. Kelly had been angry that day, angry at Father Gilbert as he presided and prayed. What he said in the letter was true. If her parents had not been part of his seminar on Mary Magdalene, they would not have died. The gunman was after Keith Gilbert, not Martin and Katherine Roberts, or so the investigation concluded. But it was her parents who were shot as they walked to their car with Father Gilbert. It was her parents who died in the dark.

Kelly had left the campus library and was heading home when she heard the sirens. With time, the wailing had become part of a landscape of horror fixed in her memory: the sirens as she walked up the hill past the stadium; their wail retreating into the distance as she entered her bungalow and stepped out to the deck to view the city lights; the careful, tentative knock on the door; the deepening dread as she listened to the policewoman speak and watched the woman's lips move as though in slow motion, the unbelieving shock, the nausea, the numbness. The tears came later.

Now, as Kelly gazed at the altar, she recalled how pleased she had been when Father Gilbert left Berkeley for Rome, as though his leaving could mute her anger. The last page of the last chapter of her childhood had been turned, and she had faced her future with a new resolve. Her parents had died for the old way, for their faith. Kelly would seek the new way and give her allegiance to nothing and no one.

As a senior, twenty years old, Kelly immersed herself in her last year in school, absorbing the tenets of her professors. Father Gilbert became a person of her past, of her childhood, and she welcomed instead the creeds of modern literature, the distant analysis of plot and form and character, the discussion of style and theme: the stream of consciousness in Joyce and Woolf, the existentialism of Camus and Sartre.

When Father Gilbert left Saint Mary's, Kelly left too, drifting away from belief, insulating herself from its demands. She had told herself that she could manage on her own and without church. She could manage without God who, her professors claimed, was an absurd delusion. Indeed, some of her teachers sneered, some laughed, and most assumed belief to be childish, ridiculous, silly. She'd absorbed their words and, more importantly, their tone, but in moments of honest reflection, she recognized that she often felt out of place, even intellectually handicapped, in this brave new world of academic sophistication.

Upon graduation Kelly had tried to find a job in publishing but settled for clerical work at a bank in the neighboring community of Walnut Creek. She sold the Berkeley cottage to pay outstanding bills and moved to an apartment near her work. The job paid the rent, and she liked working with words, writing reports for the manager.

Kelly's gaze swiveled back to the double doors where the funeral procession would soon appear. The nave was full with the familiar faces of her parish family. When she'd finally returned to Saint Mary's, some knew her from her growing-up years and some didn't, but all cooed over her infant son and asked few questions. Kelly hadn't been sure then what her beliefs were, and she still wasn't sure, yet she liked the artistic and lively liturgy, the sense of belonging and purpose, the ordering of the chaos around her. She liked the tapestry of incense, candles, and chants. She recited the creeds and the prayers mechanically but at least was present, worshiping God in some sort of way. She felt safe, as though sailing in an ark through stormy seas on her own voyage through life. She felt loved and part of a large family, something she'd both coveted as an only child and taken for granted growing up in the Church.

But only ten years after her parents' death, her godfather was gone too. His heart had simply stopped, they said. He was found slumped over his desk, holding his cane. Regret surged. Why hadn't she answered his letters? Why had she kept her distance? When she pictured Father Gilbert, she saw a tall man with a craggy face whose infectious laughter belied a deeply serious temperament. She saw his shock of white hair, merry eyes, lumbering movements around the altar, and flowing white robes.

The organ ended on a sweet lingering note, pulling the melody together, and in the hushed, expectant silence, the doors flung open. Twelve pallbearers, six on each side, rolled the casket of dark gleaming wood up the red carpet. The robed priests followed, these many religious honoring the man of God rumored to be a saint. With them came the crucifer, torchbearers, and acolytes. The casket came to rest in the aisle alongside her pew, between burning candles guarding like sentinels. She could have touched the purple satin draped over the polished lid, it was that close. They had flown her godfather's body from Rome, and here he was.

The Requiem Mass began, and the choir chanted, "Rest eternal grant unto him, O Lord; and may light perpetual shine upon him...."

4
Daniel

IT WAS OVER. At the graveside they had prayed: "We commit his body to the earth, for we are dust and unto dust we shall return. But the Lord Jesus will change our mortal bodies to be like his in glory, for he is risen, the firstborn of the dead." Then they had lowered her godfather's body into the grave.

Full of sadness, Kelly returned to the church for the reception in the parish hall where she was soon shaking hands, kissing cheeks, hugging and smiling and nodding with as much sincerity as possible, wondering if her godfather was watching from somewhere, somewhere with Abraham and his angels, somewhere with her parents.

Slowly, almost imperceptibly, she felt a penetrating gaze and glanced to the far side of the hall. A young man with rimless glasses shifted his attention away. Since she didn't see herself as attractive with her freckles and serious demeanor, his stare caught her off-guard. Her abundant hair, chestnut brown and framing green-gold eyes, she considered her best feature, but this morning she had gathered it into a bun. Her cheeks grew warm with his stare, and she fumbled with her glasses, nervously adjusting the temples. She slipped a stray strand of hair behind her ear.

As the crowd thinned, the young man approached and offered his hand. "Daniel Weaver," he said quickly. "And you, I know, are Kelly Roberts. I'm so very sorry about your godfather, for I held him in high esteem. He was, indeed, my mentor." His brown eyes, set in a darkish complexion, squinted in a friendly way. *Daniel Weaver.* This was her contact, she recalled with both relief and curiosity. They were about the same height, around five-seven. Like so many in the Bay Area, he looked to be of mixed race, with close-cropped dark hair, a trim beard and moustache. He could have been part African, Arabic, Greek, even Indian. She guessed he was in his mid-thirties.

"Thanks," she said. "You're Dr. Weaver? Father Gilbert wanted me to contact you."

He grinned a slightly crooked grin, his straight white teeth accentuated by curved lips and olive skin. "And he said I was to contact *you.* I was hoping you would be here. Is there a quiet place where we could talk?"

*

They sat in one of the children's classrooms in the older building. Kelly pulled out a yellow child-size chair. Daniel sat in a shiny red one. Sunlight splattered onto the low white tables and blue carpet.

"How did you know Father Gilbert?" she asked, a little awkward in the tiny chair and thinking there must have been a better place to meet.

"I spent two years in Rome, taking his classes at the American College," Daniel said seriously. "Father Gilbert was my doctoral advisor. It was a time that changed my life's direction, a true turnaround." He gazed through the tall windows.

Kelly followed his glance to the leaves brushing against the glass. She observed him as he appeared to ponder Father Gilbert's powerful influence.

He took an envelope from the inner pocket of his navy jacket. "Here's the letter your godfather sent me. Do you have yours? We could read one another's and compare…."

Kelly hesitated, considering the personal nature of the letter, but decided to trust the young man. He seemed to know her godfather well and had been recommended by him. That was enough.

They exchanged letters, and Kelly studied Daniel's. "It's much like mine. What does it mean? I can't go to Rome, that's for sure."

"He wants me to help you. I am at your service." He waved an open palm with a flourish, glancing up from the letter expectantly.

She smiled. There was something old-fashioned and charming about him. He seemed to own a quiet strength. "Yes, but how?"

Daniel surveyed the room nervously, touching his tie, as though the low shelves and wicker baskets contained hidden microphones. He lowered his voice. "I don't want to frighten you, but you should know that your godfather's death is being investigated. It's considered suspicious."

"Didn't he die of heart failure, natural causes?" she whispered.

Murder? Someone tried earlier, but failed. My parents died instead. She felt faint as though the floor was collapsing. Was it all happening over again?

"They assumed at first it was a natural death, because of his advanced age. Recently they decided to investigate further. I don't know what the autopsy revealed. He did have a number of enemies in the media." He appeared genuinely concerned. "Have I upset you? I'm truly sorry."

"Dr. Weaver, someone tried to kill Father Gilbert ten years ago. Did you know that?"

"No, to be sure, I did not." He leaned forward, attentive.

"It was kept quiet. But, you see, my parents were with him, heading for their car. They...died instead." She could see the shadows, feel the darkness, hear the shots.

"Instead?" His face paled. "How terrible for you!"

"That's what the investigation concluded."

"Did they find the person who did it?"

Kelly shook her head. "No. It was dark, and he disappeared into the crowd. They thought he acted alone."

"Your parents were helping Father Gilbert with the presentation?"

"They were part of a seminar, a debate sponsored by *Opus Veritatis*. They reported for the newsletter. They left together. It happened in the parking lot."

"I report for the newsletter as well." He paused. "I'm really sorry I've brought back such painful memories."

"I've been reliving it today anyway," she said, wishing she could change the subject.

"Of course." He turned again to the windows as though searching for a way forward. "You said it happened ten years ago? I must have been twenty-five, already in Rome. I wish I had known your parents."

"They think another attempt was made on Father Gilbert's life...this time a successful one?"

"They're investigating." He rubbed his beard thoughtfully. "Certain persons took offense to Father Gilbert's honesty. One could say he was *too* bold in his reporting, and truth can be embarrassing, threatening, even dangerous. He was not, as they like to say in our world today, *politically correct*."

"You're talking about *Opus Veritatis?* But how can a newsletter be a matter of life and death?" Did her parents die for a newsletter?

"Ms. Roberts," Daniel said, unsmiling with a gentle gravity, "in the end, ideas matter. They are vital. It is the intellectual that forms culture, for good or ill. Your parents died for the truth. That is no small thing. It's the stuff saints and martyrs are made of."

Kelly nodded. "I suppose so." *But to have enemies who kill for ideas? Would they be her enemies as well?*

"Father Gilbert spoke the truth, and truth holds power. Much is at stake, and the price for failure in the arena of ideas, the marketplace of debate, is indeed high."

"How so?" *The arena of ideas, the marketplace of debate?*

"Please let me explain. The crisis today is largely about current scholarship. A good deal of biblical history is fraudulent, written by ex-pastors and disgruntled priests wanting to get even with the Church, a Church that demanded their discipline and penance, something they did not want to give. These imposters desire to shape popular opinion and to profit from it."

"What does this have to do with my godfather?"

"When their work was published, he tried to expose them."

"Did he expose them?"

"Oh yes, again and again. Many hated him and wished him dead, thinking the debate would end without him."

"And will it?"

"I think not. There are many brave journalists and scholars who will take up his work. I myself contribute papers to Foundation *Opus Veritatis* for their print quarterly."

Kelly felt a new respect for the young man. "This research he mentions in the letters…would that have been reason to—"

Daniel nodded. "Indeed. Father Gilbert was to present at the annual Rome symposium next month."

"So they—or someone—murdered him, to silence him?" It struck Kelly as too extreme. "Is that what you're saying?"

"Exactly, and given his advanced age, they made his death appear natural, but I fear that we have no proof."

Kelly fought the urge to run. "You think he was presenting the material on Mary Magdalene?"

"I do. He was accumulating further historical validation, documentary evidence that would identify her in history and tradition."

Kelly caught her breath. "My parents were researching Mary Magdalene when they died." Was this a coincidence? She leaned toward him, watching his face with a new interest.

"Did they keep notes?"

She shook her head. "Not any that I found."

As they returned one another's letters, Daniel said, "There is another rumor."

"What rumor is that?" *There was more?*

"It's probably not important."

"It might have a bearing. What rumor?"

"They say that Father Gilbert accumulated a vast treasure of gold from all the donations."

"Donations to Foundation *Opus Veritatis*?"

"Precisely."

"You've got to be kidding." This was sounding more and more like pulp fiction. *Gold?* "If so, what happened to it?"

"We don't know. They say it's hidden, like the Templars' gold. But you know how these stories grow, especially among the greedy." He raised his brows and tilted his head, opening his palms in a denigrating gesture. "There's probably nothing to it."

But what if the stories were true? *Gold. Vast treasure.* "I see. And where do I come in?" Was this her legacy, the legacy her godfather mentioned?

Daniel rubbed his hands. With another man, Kelly would have considered the gesture miserly, but with Daniel, somehow it was simply thoughtful.

He sighed deeply. "A good question. A conundrum, to be sure. Personally, I'm interested in this Magdalene manuscript. The Magdalene generates controversy where none should exist. She's a lodestone. Others will be interested in the gold, certainly."

Kelly reflected on his words. It all sounded risky, but *gold....* "This might be dangerous. I've a little boy, you know."

"You have a child. That's splendid!" He paused, then ventured with a trace of nervous awkwardness, "You're married, then?"

"What I mean is…" She wanted to explain. She had said these words often, and now they tumbled out easily. "The father's not around. He left us." Part of the truth, she thought. Enough of the truth.

"I'm sorry. It must be difficult for you."

"Please don't be sorry." More words she had repeated.

He studied her with sympathy, then spoke slowly, each word weighted. "But that provides even more reason to solve this mystery. The legacy will help with your son's education."

"I could sure use the money," she blurted. If he only knew that not being evicted next month was her primary concern. "Let me think about it." She stood, pulling out her phone, anxious to tap the autodial for Andrea's. Soon, she thought, soon she would see her boy.

As they moved toward the door, Kelly saw a face at the window. Or was it leaves and shadows? Was she growing paranoid? With an effort, she turned and shook Daniel's hand. "Thanks, Dr. Weaver."

Reaching the narthex, they stepped outside to the porch.

"I'm afraid that I haven't told you everything," he said with hesitation.

"What else is there?"

"Your godfather sent me two tickets to Rome, dated June 1, with an open return. That's a week from Tuesday, ten days away. We need to decide soon."

"He sent you airline tickets?"

"Arranged to have them sent. Do you have a current passport?"

Irritated at the assumption she was flying to Rome, Kelly tried to focus on his question. She recalled that her father had always kept her documentation current, although she had never used it. Attention to detail was one of his idiosyncrasies. "Dr. Weaver, I didn't say I was going. This is way too short notice. But I *do* have a passport. Pretty sure, anyway."

"Good. Did you solve the puzzle in the letter?"

"No problem. *Apostles' Creed.*" She had done it in her head right off, wishing life were that simple.

"Appropriate, taking into account his interest in the Early Church."

"He knew I liked puzzles and often gave me crosswords for Christmas. My folks and I did word games when I was little. It was something for us to do together in bad weather, when we couldn't go to the park or hike the trails. That and reading, since the TV never seemed to work."

They had figured out numbers and letters and wordplays, acrostics and crosswords, even coded messages, in front of a burning fire as rain tapped gently on the roof. She recalled oatmeal cookies baking (steel-cut oats, her mother insisted), cookies she helped mix and drop from a tablespoon, arranging lumps in neat rows on broad flat pans, sixteen on one (four rows of four), twelve on another (four rows of three), and nine on the smallest sheet (three rows of three). She scraped the bowl with her spoon, savoring the sweet bits of batter, then lingered close by while the cookies baked, filling the house with their doughy aroma. It seemed like yesterday. Was the past always so simple-seeming, fleeting glimpses through a window, like seeing a framed picture or hearing a few notes of a beloved song?

"I see. I like hiking too," he said, smiling. "That's a good upbringing, with circumscribed media, an excellent way to raise children." He searched his wallet, the leather creased and worn. "Please, here's my card, with my cell phone and office number. Could you call me when you decide?"

She read the small print. *Daniel C. Weaver, Ph.D., Professor of Religious Studies, Berkeley University.* "I'll get back to you."

At the top of the steps he bowed. "And I would be honored if you'd call me Daniel."

"And call me Kelly."

He smiled. "Good-bye, Kelly."

She raised an open palm. "'Bye then, Daniel."

For the moment the aching loss of the morning had receded. Heading to her car, she felt a tentative excitement and wondered if she was at another crossroads in her life. Her parents' death had been one. The pregnancy had been another. Would her godfather's death be one as well? She placed the key in the ignition. For now, she simply wanted to see her son.

She heard a quick honk as a rusty Volkswagen bug sputtered by, Daniel waving through the open window.

*

Lester Sansby liked his coffee black and strong, but he didn't like the prices at this artsy-fartsy coffee house in Walnut Creek. He was in a terrible mood, and it was all the fault of these weirdos. Maybe he should drop the whole thing and hope the Magdalene material would never surface. He was getting too old for this cat-and-mouse game. He cursed, then placed a pill on the back of his tongue and swallowed. He was entitled to a little extra today.

From the back of the church he'd watched the funeral with its Kool-Aid crowd singing songs of mourning to an absent god. He carefully kept an eye on Weaver, whom he recognized a few rows in front of him. The kid gave Lester the creeps. He was clearly a cold fellow, ice running through his veins. Serious and condemning, he reminded Sansby of his father, who must have been a double of Weaver at that age. After the service Lester had waited in his Jaguar for the crowd to return from the cemetery. Then he'd slipped into the parish hall and found a corner where he could discreetly observe Weaver and the girl.

He hadn't recalled the girl from any of his classes although she wasn't unattractive, in a country sort of way, coming across as something from *Little House on the Prairie*. He had tried to imagine her without the thick glasses, and without the severe clothes and with her hair down, but the effort tired him. When he saw the two of them head upstairs, he followed and peered through high windows in the back, glad for the cover of bushes. It was clearly a kids' classroom and they were in deep conversation, but he couldn't ascertain much else. So Lester headed for his car, reaching in his pocket for the address. It had not taken long to find the girl's apartment.

Now, as he sipped his coffee, he checked the bloody scratch on the back of his hand, cursing the cat, and made a mental note to put something on it before it became infected. The place was filling up. It was, after all, Saturday afternoon and every yuppie in suburbia was jogging by, stopping in for their skinny latte. He moved his cup and laptop bag to an outside table to enjoy the sun, so rarely seen in foggy Berkeley.

Settling into his chair, Lester opened his flask and added a shot of whisky.

He was beginning to feel a bit more mellow. Seeing the place had Wi-Fi, he pulled out his computer and logged onto the Internet. He needed to relax. He checked his email. Only two in the last few hours. One from Doris and one from Flasher. He opened Doris's first.

> Haven't seen you lately, Lester. Come visit. Miss you.
> D

Lester felt a twinge of guilt and made a mental note to drop by the rehab center in Oakland. Doris was an old friend, and he would be loyal. They had been in school together, been lovers over the course of two failed marriages, marched for justice and freedom, were colleagues at the university, supported one another's social causes and political campaigns. They had enjoyed the occasional reefer and recreational drug. She had given him a daughter, although he wasn't sure that Deirdre was his. How could he be sure? Nevertheless, Doris hovered in the background of his life, something like faded wallpaper. Now she was drying out. In more ways than one, Lester thought, snickering. When had they last slept together? Women aged faster than men. But he wouldn't forget her. She was a friend, and loyalty was important. He replied that he would swing by Sunday before the faculty volleyball game.

He opened Flasher's.

Always a good source for news, Flasher, he suspected, might be another academic, not sure which school, but they had exchanged some interesting thoughts over the years. This one was short and sweet:

> Check this out for a new approach to our game of truth: San Sylvestro in Wikimedia. I just placed an ad in the sidebar that might be fruitful.
> Yours, F.

Lester followed the link to an article on the Rome church in the popular online encyclopedia, sometimes reliable, sometimes not. He told his students not to use it, but it was good for standard info, weights and measures, basic facts, and it got top listing with Google. One report claimed it was 90 percent more accurate than the major print encyclopedias. Who would have guessed? What a world.

As the page came up on his screen, Lester stared with amazement. Alongside the devout description of the medieval basilica was Flasher's ad: "Visit the doubter's guide to the world: fun, fast, informative. Read the real thing, and get a reality check." The link was to Flasher's website, kind of a skeptics' library with several discussion groups to which Lester had contributed over the years. Not a bad idea, Lester thought, and made a mental note to do the same over the next academic break. He could hit all kinds of religious Wiki sites—saints, churches, the Vatican, the list was endless—and place sidebar ads.

Rome. Gilbert's body was flown home from Rome. Weaver had spent time there too. What was he up to? And with the girl?

Lester closed his laptop and returned to the counter for another tall coffee and a scone. He needed to figure this out. The answer was there, waiting for him. He just needed to see it.

5
Matt

"Oh, Matt," Kelly whispered, relieved. Her boy was in her arms, his dark head nestled in the cleft of her shoulder. Kelly lifted the heavy warm weight a little higher, anchoring his dangling legs around her hips. "Did you have fun, sweetie?"

He leaned back and nodded. "Uh huh." It was his usual reply, two words substituted for precious hours lost.

She set him down, thanked Andrea, and they followed the path home through the juniper and oleander.

She turned the key in the lock and the bolt slid sideways. They entered and Kelly gasped. The room was a shambles. Her books lay scattered about the carpet, the kitchen drawers emptied onto the floor. Her files and papers were everywhere. Someone had been searching for something. Laddie and Lady Jane emerged from the back room, whimpering.

"It's okay, kitties," she said. She stroked them as they brushed against her legs. Kelly felt violated, as though a stranger had rummaged through her soul, had torn her apart. It was an extremely visceral reaction, she thought with some surprise, since they hadn't been physically harmed.

"Mommy, what happened?"

She tried to sound confident, covering her distress. "It's okay, honey." She looked into Matt's room. Toys had been pulled from the shelves, clothing scattered. In her room as well, she saw the same chaos, the disorder drenched with haste and hate.

Kelly sat on her bed and pulled Matt close, rocking him. "Someone was searching for something. We'll straighten it all up like nothing ever happened, and everything will be fine."

Shaking, she dialed the police.

She tapped Daniel's number. "There's no chance I'm going to Rome. I've just been robbed. I'm needed here. Maybe you can get a refund on those tickets."

*

"Milk or sugar?" Kelly asked.

They sat on oak stools at the narrow bar dividing the kitchenette and the living room. The police had left. Daniel had arrived and ordered pizza. He helped her set the place to rights, and now, with Matt in bed, the cats calm and sleeping on the sofa, they studied their decaf. Kelly grew determined, her will crystallizing.

"Black is fine," he said.

"You see why I can't leave."

"I understand your feelings, but—"

"I don't think you do." How could he understand? She was terrified.

"You'll never be totally safe, Kelly."

Kelly gazed into the gentle dark eyes. "Do you think this robbery had something to do with my godfather?"

"I do."

"Nothing seems to be missing."

"They were searching for your letter, for information. It would be better, for your safety, that you give me the letter."

"It's precious to me—his last letter…"

"It's dangerous." He adjusted his glasses with his forefinger.

She found her bag and pulled out the envelope. He placed the two letters in the sink, lit a match, and watched the papers flame to ash. *Another loss.* "Now it's settled," she said, thinking at least she wouldn't have to go to Rome.

"You needn't worry as to the letters' contents. I've memorized them." He touched his temple. "It's a gift and a curse to have a photographic memory."

"Oh." She wasn't sure whether to be relieved or concerned.

He leaned toward her. "Kelly, these people are serious. They'll return to find what they seek, for they've much to lose and even more to gain. They're not only after treasure, but needing to guard their prestige and power." He looked into the distance. "Sometimes I think that at the end of the day, the esteem of one's colleagues, at least in the academic world, is worth far more than any financial gain."

Kelly considered his words. Her parents had been academics. Her mother had taught Classics and her father History. Overly bookish and withdrawn, they seemed to see teaching as a means of support so they could do what they loved: research and writing. She recalled her own professors. Some clearly wanted to share their enthusiasm for their subject. Some merely passed the time until the next paycheck. Others were inflated with their own self-worth, enjoying a captive audience of malleable minds who stoked and stroked their egos. She nodded. "I think I know what you mean."

"Come to Rome, Kelly. You really have no choice, for it's the best solution, the best way to solve this puzzle, the best way to ensure your future safety and that of your son. And don't forget…this was Father Gilbert's last wish for you."

His argument made sense, Kelly slowly acknowledged, but could she trust this Dr. Weaver? "Why are you so keen on going? Couldn't someone in Rome handle this?"

Daniel blanched. "Father Gilbert's last wish was directed to me as well."

"True, but wouldn't he understand if you delegated this?"

He hesitated, then said, "I owe him."

Should she pry? "How?" She studied his expression, one of deep reflection.

"He saved my life."

"I see." Kelly could see that the link between her godfather and Daniel was strong. For now, she would trust him. After all, he appeared to be on the faculty at Berkeley U.

"Good. Then we go to Rome."

"What about Matt?" How could she leave him? But…how could she take him with her?

"You mentioned you have a reliable neighbor?"

"Andrea's going to Lake Tahoe for the summer."

"It would probably be good for Matt to leave the Bay Area, so that is even better. Can Andrea take him with her, for, say, two weeks? The *Opus Veritatis* Symposium is June 12. I'd like to find your godfather's research well before then. I'm sure he would agree."

"Why would it be good for Matt to leave the Bay Area?" Kelly challenged.

Daniel frowned. "It's better to err on the side of safety, wouldn't you say? We don't know how far these people will go. We know they killed once. They may see kidnapping as a means to an end, and with these folks, ends justify means."

Kelly felt sick. "I see."

"I don't want to worry you, but we need to face the truth of the situation. We need to face reality."

This was all happening way too fast. How could she be separated from her son, especially at a time like this? They had never been apart for more than a few hours.

Daniel finished his coffee and reached for his jacket. "I'll confirm the flight and call you tomorrow."

"But..." She hadn't said *yes* yet. "There's something else."

He waited, looking at her with curiosity and concern.

"I've...never been on a plane. I'm not too...sure...about that." Was she stuttering?

"You've never been on a plane?" He sounded incredulous, this man who had all the answers.

Lots of people haven't been on planes, she thought. "I was twenty when my parents died. We pinched pennies for as long as I can remember. Vacations were nearby, usually camping in the Sierras. Some summers we drove to Oregon for the Shakespeare Festival. I couldn't afford to fly once I was on my own, that's for sure."

"Are you *afraid* of flying?"

"I like to think I have a healthy fear of flying."

He shook his head. "It's nothing, trust me. It's actually a lot of fun."

He didn't sound too convincing. She glanced at him with suspicion. "Right. I've seen the airport scanners on the news. They x-ray your whole body. No thank you very much."

"But you must see what is at stake here!"

She stood and washed the cups out in the sink. "No flying to Rome. No flying anywhere." She fought to control her quivering lip. Why wouldn't everyone leave her alone?

He set down his jacket, found a towel, and dried the cups. "Where should I put these?"

She pointed to a caddie in the corner under the cupboard.

He slipped each handle carefully over a hook, speaking quietly. "Kelly, you need to get this whole thing behind you. I don't think you can, unless you follow your godfather's plan."

"You don't understand; this sounds so dangerous. I still have nightmares about my parents' death, my trying to stop the shooter, my trying to warn Mom and Dad, screaming..."

Yet, she thought, as her dawn dream surfaced, she'd had a wonderful dream last night. She was high on a mountaintop, a gentle breeze in her face, the sky a dome of blue, and there was singing, a lovely melody at once so foreign and so familiar. She wanted to hold it, keep it, but it faded into the early morning light....

He held her shoulders gently. "Kelly, we need to do this, and do it *now*. I didn't want to frighten you, but you and Matt are in danger, *right here*."

She hoped she didn't look too helpless, too lost, too scared. She summoned from somewhere a spark of courage. "Okay," she said as they walked to the door. "I'll talk to Andrea. Call me tomorrow." She shivered. "What about my cats?"

Daniel checked his watch. "That reminds me. I've got to get back to Berkeley and walk the dogs, before it's totally dark."

Kelly checked her watch. 7:30. It was still light, but the day was ending. "You have dogs?"

Daniel smiled. "Not mine. Daisy and Major belong to my landlords, the Kennedys, an elderly couple. I walk them in exchange for a lower rent on my apartment. We head into the hills and hike one of the fire trails. It gets me away from my books, and I love dogs and the fresh air." He watched Lady and Laddie curl up on the sofa together. "I love cats too," he added quickly. "I love all animals." Then added, "Well, most animals."

Kelly imagined him loping with the dogs. "What kind of dogs?"

"German short-haired pointers. They call them GSPs. So cute. Midsize I suppose. I grew up with brown labs and assorted cats, but I love these guys."

"I used to hike the fire trails with my dad." She paused, then pulled herself into the present. "I'll find a cat sitter. Maybe Andrea knows someone to come in and feed Laddie and Lady Jane. And Lady Jane needs to be brushed or she gets hairballs."

"I'll call you with details," he said, grabbing his jacket and moving toward the door, "but I've got to run—the Kennedys depend on me. It won't be the fire trails tonight, too late for that, but I'd better take them out for a bit and find someone to walk them for me when I'm away."

"Right," she said, smiling, feeling more at ease, "we'll be in touch."

*

Lester Sansby tallied his options as he stirred his coffee.

The girl's apartment had revealed nothing and was a classic bourgeois nest. The cats had been an issue, but he silenced them with a few kicks. He even checked out the bedroom and fantasized whether the ever-virgin Weaver would fumble for more than a desperate grab. The image was depressing.

Lester nibbled a scone, wondering why they couldn't have real sandwiches at these places, and tried to focus on the problem at hand. He needed to find out more. It would be helpful to know if the rumors of wealth were true, but the manuscript was crucial. Gilbert's research could threaten his own stuff on Mary Magdalene. Did Gilbert's even exist? Could it be found, manipulated, destroyed? He had to decide and soon. *Settle down,* he told himself, his blood racing again, *think this through.* He stared at his pouch of pills and decided to hold off. One way or another he needed a clear head. He needed to protect himself from these crazies.

Lester's own studies, published in academic quarterlies, on the sinner-saint had stopped much of the inane guesswork out there. A New Testament group, the Galilee Seminar, was eager to publish his updated analysis. Colleagues in this culture war, they agreed with his thesis about the Magdalene and her romance with Jesus the Galilean, agreed even with Lester's conclusions that the Holy Grail was Mary Magdalene's bloodline. Lester's work had become the substance of a popular novel and even a movie, although he had been entitled to a bigger cut of the proceeds from both. He had a respected reputation, which he was entitled to protect. He wasn't going to lose it now.

The old wizard Gilbert might have been a foolish man of faith, but he was thorough in his foolishness. If there *was* a manuscript out there, it must not remain for long. Lester and his friends had caused other "discoveries" to disappear and their authors to seek new lines of work. It wasn't difficult, planting seeds in the fertile soil of the blogging garden. The media was always hungry for fresh blood, particularly religious blood. One merely needed the network and, of course, the disciples.

Should he call on his disciples? His sweet Treats? He mulled the idea over. How many *Treats*, as he called them, had he enlisted? He thought he was probably beyond his original goal, the excellent number twelve. Who knew how many others were out there, undeclared, doing his bidding, unawares? Spreading the anti-gospel, the true gospel, the *really* good news? There was corker, tease2, meddle, killerbee, kickass, giantbro, Fab, wizard, tetra6, cocobean, frizzle, and snake. Where did these kids get these names? They were even sending in reports, god bless those sorry little fingers tapping those shiny little keys.

Lester opened his laptop. Which site should he try? His followers were all out there, sprinkled through the blogs and discussion groups. They tweeted and retweeted and hacked on command. They posted and trolled and flamed. But, best of all, they were remarkably amenable to his suggestions. Had they contributed in some way to the old man's death? Lester had hinted often enough. Fab, his most recent online associate, came to mind. Fab's profile photo revealed a young man, extremely handsome in a boyish way, with thick dark hair, large eyes, and a bit of a baby face, a fellow clearly impressed with himself. For some reason that Lester had not discovered, Fab hated Gilbert. That was fine. It qualified him for service.

Lester logged on to *FaithFacts,* a group he'd recently joined. He had been moving in slowly, testing the moderator for weak spots. The crowd was pretty straightforward and young, the perfect takeover. Several of his Treats worked the group with him, some newbies coming on board when they caught on to the game.

He had visited the kids on *SmartReads* earlier this morning. Gave them the usual material on the discrepancies of the Gospel accounts, then segued into the ridiculous statements in Leviticus about an eye for an eye, etc. The literalists always balked at those bits of evidence—they had no answers. They spoke in syllogisms, circles, self-supporting statements, totally biased. Today's post was a good answer to their silly comments about the Bible as the Word of God. If the Bible was the Word of God, he pointed out, the Word of God certainly changed often enough, doing 180s on a regular basis. These BICCs, just like his folks, drove him to distraction, and it was satisfying indeed to set them straight, to remove these deranged crazies in the cyber-world ready to string up anyone who didn't follow their ways.

He found several of his Treats working the groups. He needed to know what Weaver and the girl were up to. His gut instinct told him they could be the link, possibly the only link, to Gilbert's work. He typed quickly, suggesting obliquely, using a simple code, that there might be some benefit to following the movements of the goddaughter and her new friend, the meek and mild Daniel Weaver. He reminded his friends of the recent events, the death of the grandmaster, and also of the great wealth of Foundation *Opus Veritatis.* He threw out the net. Now he would see what he caught.

An attractive blond in a tight halter top and running shorts took a seat nearby and stared at him, sipping something. He stared back. She ran her tongue over her lips, and Lester could see moisture condensing in her cleavage. She wasn't as young as he liked, but young enough. After all, he reminded himself, he was nearing sixty. But he still had good hair and great bones and, as the ladies soon discovered, talented hands.

He wiped his forehead and returned to the screen, thinking about shutting down for the day. Surely he was entitled to a little fun. Tonight he would visit the sites with the pretty ones, both boys and girls, usually amusing and satisfying. They would be his reward for crusading in the name of American culture. But in the meantime?

He gazed at the blond and raised his brows, tilting his head. He ran his hand through his thick graying hair and eyed her provocatively with just the right touch of admiration. She picked up her drink and swayed over to his table.

6

Rome

MIDDAY ON WEDNESDAY, JUNE 2, Kelly Roberts and Daniel Weaver landed in Rome's Fiumicino Airport and took the train to the central Termini Station. From there they wheeled their bags two blocks to a modest hotel recommended by one of Daniel's school friends.

"We need to try and stay awake the rest of the day." Daniel paused at the door to Kelly's room. "I know we've been up all night and it's three in the morning at home, but let's try. It's 12:30 in the afternoon now. Why don't you unpack while I do some online work in the lobby? Let's meet in an hour for lunch and then take the city bus tour. It will orient you and re-orient me."

"Sure, but I may just take a short nap," Kelly said groggily.

Her room was small but clean. The owners had tried to brighten the place with yellow muslin curtains tied with green grosgrain ribbon. A worn quilt of faded colors covered a narrow bed. A wash basin stood next to a small chest of drawers. She walked to the narrow window.

The hotel was on the rise of a hill, and they were fortunate to be on the top floor, in the attic, she guessed, considering the pitched ceiling. Through the window she could see beyond a hodgepodge of red tiled roofs and chimneypots, generators and vents, penthouses and rooftop gardens, out to a hazy, smudged horizon. Numerous domes rose from the cityscape, and she realized that Rome was indeed a city of churches.

The window jamb was stuck, but Kelly shoved and pushed until it jerked open with a screech. She peered out. The midday light filtered through the smog and a touch of humidity moistened her skin. Traffic bellowed, echoing from road canyons. An office building, tall and steely, stood nearby, soon to block the sun. She pulled the window down, shutting it tightly, seized once again with the sensation that this trip would change her life.

"Better unpack," she said to herself as she tugged open a dresser drawer. "Then a wee little nap. I'll call Matt later, since it's the middle of the night back home. No wonder I'm so sleepy."

As she placed tees in a drawer and hung skirts in a closet, she recalled the long flight. The trip had felt like they would be flying forever, and she had dozed on and off. They had watched movies on small screens and chatted a bit and read their books. Daniel was deep into something by Alexander Schmemann about the Eucharist. The book was worn, with pages turned down at the corners. He read quickly, holding a pencil and jotting notes in the margin. She recalled the author's name because it was so foreign sounding. Daniel said that Father Schmemann was a Russian who grew up in Paris and had been head of an Orthodox seminary in New York. He was brilliant but accessible, Daniel said, his eyes alight.

Kelly had brought a comforting novel she'd wanted to reread for a long time—*Watership Down*, about a society of rabbits and their quest for a safe home. Richard Adams told the tale with simplicity and sincerity, and Kelly was once again in the burrows with Hazel and Bigwig, once more silflaying (feeding) in the green grass. For the most part, Kelly wasn't a fan of animal stories, but this one had been dear to her for many years. On her tenth birthday her parents had given her this book, and they had begun a ritual of reading a chapter together each evening after dinner. Too old for bedtime stories, this half hour—sometimes before a roaring fire in the grate—was precious. Sometimes her mother read, sometimes her father, and sometimes Kelly herself. The words read aloud, the rhythm of the language heard and felt, the quiet camaraderie that grew as the story knitted them together, would always be a part of her. Now, here in Rome, she set the novel on the nightstand. It was a consoling piece of her parents.

She had learned a bit about Daniel's life; he was an only child too. He clearly didn't want to talk about his family, so she changed the direction of their conversation. But he loved teaching and his face beamed when he spoke of his students at Berkeley. They compared years at Berkeley U and figured there had been an overlap, as he worked on his Masters before going to Rome for his Doctorate, then returning to teach. He had put himself through school since he didn't believe in loans, so he worked hard day and night, mostly waiting tables and washing dishes, and never had a social life.

She had laughed with appreciation. Her loans had been small and paid off when she sold the house, but even their short, nagging presence had made her nervous. They had both lived at home so that had helped with room and board. She learned that he was a coffee addict, and that Rome had the best coffee in the world, so Kelly hoped she might try the little shots of espresso they served in the corner bars and bistros. They shared a hobby, browsing used-book shops for bargains, but here in Rome, Kelly guessed, everything would be in Italian. She was glad she had brought a small guidebook in English and a street map, both foraged from a secondhand shop in Berkeley.

She liked knowing where she was and where she was going, and with some anxiety realized, as they made their way from the airport to the hotel, that she was surrounded by melodic but rapid Italian words and phrases completely foreign, unintelligible and sealing her off from her surroundings. Rome would pose definite challenges.

After unpacking and closing the yellow curtains, she thought about these things, lying on the bed and slipping into a deep sleep....

*

The phone jangled. It was Daniel, sounding far away, urging wakefulness. She mumbled something into the receiver, moved toward the shower, and soon met him in the lobby.

Over pasta and salad and the long-awaited espresso at a corner café she listened to Daniel's online adventures, sorting out half-truths and correcting lies. In his work for *Opus Veritatis* he patrolled discussion groups to check on fair play. He spoke of trolls and flaming and moderators. Today he had found a new "bandit" recruiting young innocents, and she wondered what he meant but couldn't quite follow it all. Her head seemed so foggy, but the espresso, strong and rich and sweet with the sugar cube melting at the bottom of the demitasse, helped a bit, and they headed for a city bus tour.

The afternoon sun seeped through the humid haze, and a welcome cool breeze fluttered her hair, falling loose, as she traded her regular glasses for sunglasses. They boarded the bus at a nearby stop and she tried to concentrate, to stay awake. Here she was, after all, in Rome!

She settled into the roof-deck seat and watched cafés, newsstands, shops, and churches slip by. A guide chatted in English through minute earphones, and Kelly strained to take it all in. The winding streets, narrow and congested, loud and smelling of exhaust, were nearly overwhelming. She stared and listened and struggled to focus her camera before the site disappeared as the bus maneuvered between cars battling for inches of asphalt. Horns blared and drivers swore from windows, raising fists. She attempted to trace the bus route on her map, but soon found she was lost, realizing with some panic that she'd missed several sites by examining the map. Daniel pointed out churches with colorful names.

But in spite of the commotion of sight and sound, a soft beauty lay beneath the surface, and the city beckoned her. There was a rhythm to Rome, like a poem in a certain pentameter, a ballad moving through time, a great aria sung by a host of divas in harmony.

Finally, Kelly sat back and enjoyed the ride, tying her hair up in a band, and allowing the strangely foreign yet hauntingly familiar images to wash over her. Their bus rumbled through the centuries, jumping from the nineteenth to the fourth with the twentieth and twenty-first in between. The massive white monument to King Vittorio Emanuele II in the Piazza Venezia rose in startling contrast to the gray ruins of the adjoining ancient Forum. Soon they circled the Coliseum with its three tiers of skeletal stone and arched tiered openings, and briefly Kelly envisioned the screaming crowd and the roaring beasts. She recalled seeing on television the Pope walk and pray the Stations of the Cross on Good Friday as a crowd of pilgrims held flaming candles in the dark.

When they crossed the Tiber, the vista opened and Kelly breathed the cleaner air of the moving waters, the river in its June fullness tumbling between shorelines of leafy shade. Then she saw Saint Peter's in the distance, at the end of a long straight avenue, the basilica's colonnades on either side embracing a massive piazza. Michelangelo's smooth dome rose against the sky, and statues of Peter and Paul both guarded and welcomed. Kelly knew this church was the heart of Christian Rome, perhaps even the heart of the Christian world. She wanted to pinch herself. It seemed so unreal to see Saint Peter's with her own eyes—something so famous, something she had only seen on television and in the large book with its shiny pages on her nightstand as a child.

The nightstand, with its pink lampshade gently filtering the light, was home to the books read each evening at bedtime. In her early childhood, picture books filled the lower shelf of the stand. By grade school, chapter books took their place, some read to her by her mother, sometimes her father, and sometimes she would try reading on her own. In time, the pictures became smaller as the words multiplied and sentences grew into longer paragraphs, and soon she relied on her imagination to create the pictures from the words read.

But prayers came first, kneeling on the multi-colored braided rug, her hands folded on the cool white sheet of her bed. Her father led her in their memorized prayers—the Our Father, the Hail Mary, the Creed. Next Kelly asked God to bless their family and friends. Finally she gave thanks for the day given, now past, and asked for a good night's sleep, that if "I should die before I wake, I pray the Lord my soul to take." As though working in tandem, her mother then read the story or chapter for the night, and it was rare that Kelly remained awake for long, nestled as she was in this loving and poetic cocoon. The stories were steadying, ordering her world. They told of knights and princesses and magical charms. Good triumphed, evil was vanquished; the poor found riches and the rich found love; the proud fell and the humble rose.

When Kelly thought of those evenings, she often recalled her mother's whisper in the hall, "I think she's asleep, Martin," and her father's low reply, "Good. Did you get the light, Katherine?" Then the soft, reassuring click of the wall switch by the door.

Now, as the bus circled the Vatican and turned back across the Tiber, she saw again in her mind Saint Peter's Basilica on the shiny page of *Shrines and Saints for Children*. She smiled with the memory, then wanted to cry with the loss. All the while the grogginess of jet lag surged, as though an undertow pulled to drown her. She was grateful when they disembarked near the Borghese Gardens and headed up the street to their hotel.

*

Before bed, Kelly called home. She missed her cell phone but couldn't afford a phone in Rome. Instead, she would settle for landline connections wherever she could. She noticed Daniel didn't have a phone either, but relied on email through his laptop connection when he could find Wi-Fi signals. Not having a cell phone—or mobile phone as they called them here—was going to be a challenge, but maybe a good challenge.

She reached for the old-fashioned black handset and dialed the front desk clerk, who connected her to the States. Soon Andrea was on the line, assuring her that all was well. Then Matt came on, and Kelly winced when she heard his high, thin voice.

"Mommy, come home."

"I'll be home soon," she said, trying to convince them both. "I'm glad you found someone to take care of Laddie and Lady Jane."

"Yeah. Todd."

"Andrea's son?" Kelly recalled his occasional visits next door.

"He likes Laddie and Lady Jane."

"Good." She would ask Andrea about Todd. "And you're packing for Tahoe? How exciting! It's a big lake, and you can go swimming!"

"Yeah, I guess I'll go swimming." Kelly could hear the note of anticipation. "That's pretty cool," he added.

"And don't forget your trucks. Lots of sand at Tahoe. Lots of construction projects required."

"Yeah!" With that final burst of pleasure, Kelly could hear Andrea in the background, and Matt added, "I love you. 'Bye, Mommy."

"I love you too, honey." When Andrea returned, Kelly asked, "Todd is taking care of the cats?"

"He sure is, the good lad. A sweet boy but can't seem to settle down. He showed up and wanted to stay with me. I said he could stay if he fed the cats while we were in Tahoe. I thought he would try and come to Tahoe and forget the cats, but he didn't and said that was fine, he was filling out applications. I'm sure he'll have interviews to go to and such."

"Does Todd like cats?"

"He loves animals. He was going to be a vet at one point. Then he switched to architect, and then to art history. Or was it art history and then architect? Don't know what he's applying for at the moment. Just hope it isn't another degree. It's time the boy went to work—he's turning thirty-seven next month. The loans are piling up. He keeps coming home, and all I have is a two-bedroom here. But Kelly, how's Rome?"

"Fine. Crowded. We took a bus tour today, and I saw Saint Peter's! It looks just like it does on TV." *And in the picture book,* she thought. "Andrea, I've got to get off the line."

"Right you are. But, Kelly, you're being careful, aren't you? You took off so suddenly, and with someone we don't know."

Kelly smiled at her concern and appreciated the friendly *we*. "Yes, Andrea. I trust Daniel completely. He was a friend of my godfather, Father Gilbert."

"The priest who moved to Rome?"

"That's the one."

"The fellow who just died?"

"That's right."

"But I thought you blamed him for your parents' death?"

Kelly hesitated, recalling that one afternoon when she had unloaded her grief and anger. "I did blame him at one time, but I came to realize that he wasn't responsible. It wasn't his fault. I needed someone to blame."

"Well, don't you go worrying about what doesn't concern you."

"But it does concern me, Andrea. I'm in Rome because of the letter I received from Father Gilbert. Remember?" *Where was Andrea going with this?*

"I remember you showing me the letter. We all have our own ways of thinking, our own beliefs, now don't we? Those folks at Saint Mary's are pretty conservative, as I recall. Maybe you should stay out of the conflict that seems to be brewing."

"Andrea, has someone been talking to you?"

"No one in particular…say, I nearly forgot! There was a nice fellow who came by yesterday, quite handsome if you like silver-haired and distinguished, which I've always found attractive. He was asking about you and that priest who died. He was sorry to miss you. He was quite important, a Berkeley professor! Quite the gentleman, with such a lovely smile and tan—to my mind rather like Sean Connery. Charming, really. He said he wanted to offer his condolences. Said he was an old friend of the family. I told him I was more than pleased to make his acquaintance."

Kelly swallowed hard. "What was his name? A friend of whose family?" She had no family left that she knew of. Maybe some distant cousins on the East Coast.

"Let me see now, his name's right there in my head. It was a smooth name but old-fashioned, if you know what I mean. Let me see…Dr. Swift…no that's not right…hmm…I'll see if I can remember and let you know. I'm sorry, Kelly. My memory just does this at times. Is it important? He was so polite, but I didn't say where you were since I didn't know exactly, except Rome of course. Now I have your number with this Caller ID thing."

Kelly's pulse raced. "Andrea, don't let anyone know where I am, and don't give out my number. And don't let anyone know where you are going…Tahoe, I mean. And keep a close watch on Matt."

"Righto, ma'am! Is there something I should know? What's so top secret?"

"I don't want to worry you, but just do as I say, okay?"

"Well, sure, I'll do that, my dear. Not to worry about a thing. Mum's the word. But it all sounds pretty fishy to me."

"How's the packing going?"

"Nearly done, although we heard there was a fire over the mountain near Reno last night, which should cloud things up a bit with the ash and so forth. But it's so beautiful there anyway. Wish you could come with us."

"Maybe next year, Andrea." After thanking her, Kelly hung up, more than a little rattled. What had the man said to Andrea? And who was he?

When she finally went to bed, her last thought was, *Daniel's across the hall and that's good.* She would ask him tomorrow. Her eyes closed like doors slamming shut, and she fell instantly into a deep, dreamless sleep.

*

Lester Sansby settled into his seat as the midday flight leveled and the *Fasten seat belts* sign blinked off overhead. It was Wednesday, June 2, and the flight from San Francisco was packed. He had enjoyed the view from the window as the plane departed, banking in an arc and heading east. Now he regarded the stewardess, or *flight attendant,* as they liked to be called. He smiled and ordered a double whiskey. *A sweet girl,* he thought. And *this* was sweet, flying. He should fly more often. "Staying on in Rome?" he asked her.

"Not this time." She winked. "Are you traveling for business or pleasure, Dr. Sansby?"

"A little of both."

"Been to Rome before?"

"Can't say I have. But there's a first for everything, right?"

"It's colorful. And holy."

"I prefer the colorful part. Not too interested in the holy. Any good restaurants that won't mortgage my home?"

"Sure—I'll give you a list."

"Where's the night life?"

"Try the Trastevere area. You might like it there—lots of action, if you know what I mean."

"I think I do."

She grinned, tossed her head, and moved on. Lester reclined his seat and stretched his long legs.

Searching the girl's apartment turned up nothing, but the neighbor lady was helpful. She was attractive in a classic sort of way, and most hospitable. Lester thought he played his cards well. He'd have liked more detail about where they were staying in Rome, etc., but didn't want to push it. Knowing their destination was good enough for now. He had guessed as much anyway.

His daughter, Deirdre, had agreed reluctantly to take Freedom home to her studio, and to look in on her mother. She wasn't happy about it—somehow she didn't trust him—but she said she would do it, just this one time. That was Deirdre's famous phrase, *just this one time*, and it was evident she said it often with regards to food consumption, for she was grossly overweight. She couldn't land a job—no surprise there, Lester judged—and she was glad for the hundred dollars he paid her up front.

As for travel arrangements, he had called in a few favors from his disciples. One found him this seat in Business Class, although he had to race to make the flight. Another gave him the name of a friend who would give him a room in Rome at a good rate. Another gave him the names of media folks who might be sympathetic to his cause, although he didn't want too much attention yet. Most other information he could Google online himself. It was all a question of timing and a little luck. One thing for sure—this was a game he intended to win, one way or another.

7

Father Francis

THURSDAY AFTERNOON KELLY AND DANIEL STOOD ON THE CORNER of Via 20 Settembre and Largo Santa Susanna, facing two churches with similar facades. A brisk breeze had cleared the air, turning the sky a brilliant blue.

"I should have woken up earlier." Kelly squinted at the sky. "It's nearly four in the afternoon."

Daniel shifted his backpack and straightened his yellow tie. He wore jeans and a blue blazer, and Kelly thought him quite handsome.

"It's okay," he said. "I wanted to let you sleep since yesterday was so long and tiring. And I needed to file a report, catch up with the newsletter. I even made some notes for my summer class coming up. Anyway, our appointment with Father Fitzroy wasn't until four, when the church re-opens." He glanced at his watch, a black face on a worn leather band. "We still have a few minutes to spare."

"I suppose I *was* tired." Her brain still felt foggy, as though weighted by heavy blankets. She wondered how long it would take to get over jet lag. She had awakened in the middle of the night to airbrakes whistling and tires screeching in the alley below, a loud metallic bang as the garbage bin slammed shut, echoing, and the rumble of the truck as it roared into the night. Awake for hours, she finally disappeared into deep sleep. Then the phone jangled and Daniel's tentative voice told her it was time to get up. They met for a light breakfast at three in the afternoon and headed to Santa Susanna and Father Fitzroy.

Now Daniel pointed to the church on the right. "That's Santa Maria della Vittoria. The other one is our Santa Susanna." He sighed happily, rubbing his hands together. "I can't believe I've returned to this incredible city."

"I can't believe I'm here either. And Rome's so big! And not as warm as I'd thought it would be." Andrea's news about the stranger nagged her, but she wouldn't spoil this first day. Soon she would tell Daniel, but not yet. What difference could it make when they were so far from California?

She slipped on her beige cable sweater, pulling the lower band over her skirt. The brown crinkly fabric had packed well and fell nearly to her calves, giving her some warmth, but with today's chill, she wondered about the sandals. Perhaps slacks, socks, and lace-up walkers would have been better. She tightened the black band on her ponytail and reached into her bag.

Andrea had loaned her a small digital camera, and Kelly now focused on the two churches, trying to squeeze the button in the split second when traffic cleared. The façades, she guessed, were Baroque, recalling the drawings in her guidebook: symmetrical with two tiers and inset columns. She checked the results in the camera's minute screen. Not too bad, she decided, and carefully returned the camera to her bag, pulling out a blue knit scarf and wrapping it around her neck.

"It should warm up soon," Daniel replied, smiling. "It's early June and the weather is still changeable." He pointed to Santa Maria della Vittoria. "That's the church in the notorious novel and movie."

"Which novel? Which movie?"

"*Angels and Demons.* In fact, I understand that Father Francis gives tours of the scenes filmed in the area. I hope he corrects the author's blatant errors. Santa Maria della Vittoria has the Bernini sculpture—in the transept, as I recall—*Saint Theresa in Ecstasy.* The book claims that it's a portrayal of sexual ecstasy, implying that religious ecstasy is sexual."

"I've heard that said before. In a class, I think." Or at least hinted, often with a snicker.

"I find these claims unbelievably arrogant, not to say untrue. There are many forms of ecstasy, and all find their source in God." Daniel straightened his tie. "With the decline of faith—as early as the Renaissance—man found substitutes for divine love. At first the substitute was nature—hence Romanticism. When science explained nature—in other words, sunsets were atmospheric phenomena—the substitute became art itself."

"The sweet landscapes with the ruins? An interesting progression— religion to nature to art. What about romantic love?"

"Another substitution for divine love. Romantic love thus demanded perfection, unreasonable expectations that some say raised the divorce rate over time. One could even say romantic love began much earlier, with the Cult of the Virgin in the Middle Ages, and the idealization of courtly love." He took a cloth from his pocket, removed his glasses, and gently wiped the lenses.

Kelly recalled her art history class: the medieval Madonnas, the many women painted by men, idealized visions of the female. She could see how it all developed and was interconnected—the role of art and love and ideals, the conflation of ecstasy and sexual passion. Did she have ideals like that? Did she demand that if and when a man entered her life, that he be perfect?

"I suppose our romantic ideals *are* influenced by the arts—movies, books, and so forth." She thought of Mr. Darcy and Mr. Knightly in Jane Austen's novels, men of integrity and sense who championed right and condemned wrong. They were chivalric, like the knights of old.

Daniel turned his gaze from the church to Kelly. "Indeed. But today's art has become a religion, a cult, with its own rituals of angst, chaos, and isolation, not to say aesthetic of ugliness."

"No place for love?"

"Love of self perhaps."

"No wonder there's so much angst." She smiled at his enthusiasm. He really worried about these things.

"I'm sorry," he said, his face genuinely apologetic. "I've digressed. It's a subject that truly troubles me, the abuse of art, art turned into self-therapy. So many artists and critics twist truth, appealing to our animal instincts. Misunderstanding Bernini is a classic example." He checked his watch. "It's four. We can ring the bell."

Twist truth. Was she twisting truth now? She touched his shoulder. "Daniel, before we go in, I need to tell you something."

He glanced at her with concern. "Sounds serious."

"I called Andrea last night," she said.

"That's good. Is everything okay?" He searched her eyes.

"Not exactly," she said, wondering how best to phrase the news.

"What is it?"

"Matt's fine. But someone visited Andrea, asking about me."

"Who?"

"She couldn't recall his name. She said that he was an academic, a professor who claimed to be a friend of the family."

"Did she say what he looked like?"

"She thought him attractive, hair slightly graying, and he reminded her of Sean Connery."

Daniel frowned. "Did she let on where you were going?"

"She said Rome, but Rome's a big place."

Daniel grew silent, then said, "Of course, it's a big place." He glanced at Santa Susanna, then his watch again. "But we're late, and we'd better find Father Fitzroy."

They crossed the street and ascended the church steps. A scripted sign over a door to the right of the entrance read *Parish Library*. "He said to meet him here, his temporary office. Hopefully we can see the church afterwards." He touched the buzzer.

A voice came through the intercom. "Signore Weaver and Signorina Roberts? Might I trouble you for the password?"

Daniel grinned.

Together, they replied into the speaker, "Apostles' Creed."

*

"Let me say, Kelly," Father Fitzroy began earnestly, "but do you mind me calling you that? Your godfather called you Kelly." Father Fitzroy had an elfin quality about him, as though life held magic wherever he turned, surprising him, even in his middle age. His silvery hair was combed back from his temples and his square ruddy face, lined at the eyes and mouth, turned to the two of them with serious purpose. "Please call me Father Francis. We like first names here."

Kelly nodded, at once feeling at ease. "Of course I don't mind, I mean, yes, please do call me Kelly…Father Francis." She smiled.

They sat at a table in a small room crammed with books on shelves, the spines neatly numbered and lettered. As the American church in Rome, Santa Susanna loaned books in English, and near the doorway Kelly had seen ads tacked to a large corkboard, layered slips of paper announcing housing, transportation, events, local restaurants, papal audience tickets. The church was clearly a gathering place, and Kelly felt at home in the room of books. It was cozy.

The priest touched his white collar, then felt for a small crucifix on a cord. "Jolly good then. I do apologize for meeting here. My office is a bit of a mess, I'm afraid." His ruddy complexion seemed to pale. "Someone broke in yesterday and ransacked it, and I'm still setting the place to rights. Very upsetting, as you can well imagine!" He rubbed his temples. "But nothing seems to be missing. Crime increases daily, doesn't it? I should be more careful about locking my door."

Kelly started. "That happened to me. It's a horrible experience."

"We aren't sure the reason," Daniel said, "but someone broke into Kelly's apartment during Father Gilbert's funeral."

"Oh my!" Francis shook his head. "This is bad news indeed. Alas! Do you think they're connected?"

"It's a strange coincidence." Kelly tried to stifle her alarm.

Daniel glanced at Father Francis, then turned to Kelly. "It seems likely they would be connected, with the rumors of wealth surrounding Foundation *Opus Veritatis*, and with the unsettling question of Father Gilbert's death."

Father Francis nodded. "There is that, to be sure. The investigation is ongoing."

"But what would they be searching for in your office?" Daniel asked.

"Clues. Let's proceed, and you'll see what I mean." Father Francis composed himself, breathing in deeply. "Let me first welcome you both to Rome. Daniel, it's a blessing to see you here with Kelly. We shared a few excellent meals with Father Gilbert, didn't we? Some good wine too."

The change of mood and subject was welcome, but Kelly waited tensely for the first clue. She adjusted her glasses with her index finger and thumb.

Daniel nodded. "They are dinners I shall never forget. He was quite an expert on wine, although I'm afraid I wasn't as appreciative as I should have been."

Father Francis nodded. "Indeed! A fine palate or *nose,* as they say. I probably didn't do the wines justice, either. I do like my beer." He paused, as though gathering his thoughts. "Now, Kelly. Your godfather was a good man. A godly man. Like a real father to me. I was his assistant at *Opus Veritatis.* And I still work for the newsletter, filing reports. We try to set the media straight when they go a bit crooked." He beamed, his blue eyes sparkling. "He loved you, Kelly, and he entrusted to my care something precious, something to give you." Just as quickly, he grew serious again.

"Something precious?" Kelly thought Father Francis's face held some powerful emotion, grief perhaps, but something else, as though the grief was laced with love, devotion, amazement. There was also mystery, as if he was groping, finding his way in the dark, choosing his words carefully, listening to an inner voice.

The priest folded his hands. "He was engaged on a great work of scholarship, hoping once again, with this research, to put false rumors to rest. Research about the first Christians."

"I greatly admired Father Gilbert," Daniel said in a subdued voice. "I took his classes here at the university and found them challenging indeed." He turned to Kelly. "They covered the Early Church through the sixth century."

The priest brightened. "Excellent, to be sure. Took his classes myself and learned a good deal."

"You were saying, Father?" Kelly asked, wanting to stay on track. The robbery and Matt's asthma competed for her concern, and the question returned, cluttering her mind with a nervous panic: what *was* she doing here, in Rome of all places, *so far away?* Perhaps Father Francis had her legacy. She could collect it and return home tomorrow or the day after, certainly by early next week.

"I believe," the priest said to Kelly, eyes shimmering, "your godfather made new discoveries. He instructed me to give you his papers. But I didn't expect this conundrum." He wrung his hands. "Why couldn't he simply have left you the manuscript in his will?"

"He wants to educate me," Kelly said nervously, shame touching her. "He tried to teach me the Faith, and I didn't pay much attention. This was his last chance, I guess."

Daniel contemplated Father Francis. "Father Gilbert lived as though he had no enemies. I don't believe he thought the manuscript valuable."

Father Francis nodded in agreement. "So true, my son. He was an innocent in these matters. But now here we are with puzzles and not much time."

"Not much time?"

The priest turned to Kelly. "Father Gilbert was scheduled to speak at the symposium on June 12, here at Santa Susanna. He was to reveal his recent findings on Mary Magdalene. It's been widely advertised. We don't want to cancel the meetings."

"That's the one you mentioned?" Kelly asked Daniel.

"Right," Daniel said. "But now with Father Gilbert's death, we have issues with time. We need to find the material before others do."

"Others? What others?" Kelly immediately thought of Andrea's strange visitor.

"Like all of us at *Opus Veritatis*," Father Francis explained to Kelly, "your godfather had enemies, for there are those who seek to change one thing or another from what it is to what it isn't. Father Gilbert had enemies in academia, and the media didn't like him much either. He nipped at their heels, like a collie with the sheep, calling for footnotes in scholarly papers, source citations, quotation references. He pushed to the edge of libel, then backed off." Father Francis waved his fingers in the air as if swatting flies. "He was troublesome as a hornets' nest. Truth can be a tiresome thing. And dangerous. So each hour counts."

Kelly made an effort to ignore the mention of danger. "Then how do we find the papers? You mentioned clues?"

The priest raised bristly brows. "I'll get to that. Here's the message I promised to give you. First, Father Gilbert instructed me to tell you not to write anything down. You must keep these words in your head and heart."

"Okay." Kelly glanced at Daniel, recalling his keen memory and seeing again her godfather's letters turn to ash in her kitchen sink.

"Agreed." Daniel leaned forward, his hands on the table.

"Your quest is to find his research. When you do, you will receive your legacy."

"But how?" Kelly asked.

Father Francis raised his hand to reassure her. "Patience. All in good time. I must do as instructed." He steepled his fingers on his chest. "In the process of this seeking, you will find God." He seemed to be reciting. "You may know God now, for you have been baptized in the Faith, but God wants you to know him better. He wants all of you."

The priest grew quiet and gazed at the books lining the wall beyond them, his face transfixed. Kelly followed his gaze to the shelves where a gilded icon rested against the volumes. It was the same image, only larger, that her godfather had given her—the "Trinity" icon.

Father Francis continued. "You proclaim the Creed in Church, but do you know what you say? The Creed is the story of God and man, the story of the Trinity. You must enter the story, as God entered our world in the Incarnation. You must live your belief, understand your reasonable faith. Only then will you find the treasure you seek. Enter the mystery at the heart of the world, so you witness it and can witness to it."

"Father, that's Rublev's 'Trinity,' isn't it?" Daniel whispered, pointing.

"I have one like it," Kelly said.

"Indeed it is Andrei Rublev's," the priest replied, "a copy of course. He painted the original in 1410. The three angels are God the Father, God the Son, and God the Holy Spirit. The middle angel, God the Son, points to the lamb in the dish, revealing that He will be the sacrifice for man, the Lamb of God. God acted sacramentally. Do you know what that means?" he asked Kelly.

"Like Baptism and the Eucharist?" Kelly recalled her confirmation instruction, sitting at the round oak table in the sacristy, the air sweetly musty from vestments perfumed with incense. She could smell the same scent now, emanating from Father Francis.

Daniel nodded. "He worked through matter and still does, proclaiming the ultimate mystery. The waters of Baptism and the bread and wine of the Blessed Sacrament are our prime examples."

"Exactly," Father Francis said, exultant, palms raised. "A more miraculous and spectacular mystery than any publisher could hope for. Here in Rome the signs of God's presence, in the past *and* the present, are everywhere." His voice shifted in tone, and he seemed to be returning to his memorized passage. "You must enter the story of God and Man and find answers in the churches here, for through art and word, God will speak to you. You must solve the mystery, and as your eyes open, you will be drawn further into the Church's sacramental life and into the life of the first Christians. Today's church will lead to the next, the next to the next, and so on, just as the apostles passed down their authority from bishop to bishop through the centuries. The last church will point to the manuscript that Father Gilbert guards so carefully, even in death."

"Do you know, Father? Do you know where it is?" Kelly watched his ingenuous face, now so earnest with the desire to explain, to share his joy.

The priest appeared conflicted, as though arguing with himself, almost as though he was playing a part and could not deviate from the script. "Alas, I do not. But it's just as well, as…I would be tempted to tell you. I am guessing that my recent intruder thought I knew, or even that I kept Father Gilbert's research here."

"Father," Daniel asked, "why *is* he being so careful? Shouldn't he have given this research to you or someone else in the Foundation?" His voice rose with doubt.

"Yes, Father, why?" Kelly agreed. It seemed a great risk, to trust her to find it.

The priest took Kelly's hands, locking his eyes on hers. "My child, don't you see? Your godfather loved you, and this was all he had to give. He felt horribly responsible for the death of your parents—he often spoke to me of his grief—and the guilt he felt, however false, tore at him constantly. He wanted you to be firm in your faith. He saw a great battle raging, one between truth and lies, freedom and tyranny. And his vision was clear. It was, and is, correct."

"Freedom and tyranny?" Daniel smoothed his beard. "If I didn't know Father Gilbert better, I'd say he was exaggerating. But he didn't exaggerate, nor did he understate."

Father Francis walked to the icon and gazed upon it as though seeking both rest and guidance. "The State is slowly taking away freedoms of the individual, the family, and the Church. Lines are being drawn, and we must fight this tyranny at every step."

Daniel moved to his side. "Do you remember my series on Canadian pastors who were jailed for speaking their beliefs from the pulpit?"

"Is that true?" Kelly eyed Daniel, then Father Francis. It sounded so extreme.

The priest nodded. "Too true. We like to ignore these things, to keep the peace, and pretend it isn't happening. But we mustn't be blind; we mustn't turn away. Father Gilbert was right. And Kelly, he wants to make sure you are on the correct side of the battle—the good side, the true side."

Kelly thought about his words with growing unease. "Battle?"

"Yes, battle." Father Francis withdrew an envelope from an inner pocket. "Find the research quickly and return to me. Only then can I release your legacy."

"I guess I have no choice. What is the first church?" She stared at the envelope in his hand.

Father Francis beamed. "It is this church, my church, my Santa Susanna." He gave her the envelope. "Are you going inside now? May I join you?" he asked, his blue eyes wide with hope and curiosity. "You might have some questions about the marvelous frescoes." He clapped his hands.

Kelly studied the sealed envelope. "Shall we open it in the church?"

"That would be appropriate," Daniel said. "And, Father, we would be most happy to have your company."

Kelly smiled. "Of course."

8

Susanna

When they entered the Church of Santa Susanna and Father Francis turned on the lights, Kelly gasped at the beauty, nearly forgetting the envelope she clutched in her fingers.

Frescoes covered the walls leading to a domed apse and transept. It was a golden space awash with color, and Kelly thought this must be what heaven was like. The church danced with light.

"Let's sit in a pew," Daniel said. "I'd forgotten how beautiful this church is. I visited once with a friend."

Kelly sat between Daniel and Father Francis, the envelope in her hands. She slipped her thumb under the seal, a dove above a heart, and opened it, then pulled out the tri-folded letter. She considered whether she should read it aloud, hesitated, then glanced at Daniel. His eyes told her he wished she would, and she trusted him and the priest. "I'll read it aloud," she barely whispered.

She began to read, haltingly at first, then picking up stride and falling into an easy pace, keeping her voice low and glancing up occasionally at the walls of color:

Dear Kelly,
If you are reading this you have found Father Francis and are now in the glorious Church of Santa Susanna.

Father Francis laughed and slapped his knee. "Indeed. Glorious, indeed!"
Kelly smiled, thinking suddenly how Matt would love Father Francis. She continued:

> Consider the sacred space around you and thank God for His presence here, the freedom to worship, and the people and clergy of the parish, mostly Americans just like you.
> This parish, like all churches in Christ's Body, proclaims the astounding truths of God and man: Birth, Death, and Resurrection. I have long loved this church, because the stories of the two Susannas, so

beautifully rendered on these walls, are stories of truth, and truth is the overarching theme of your quest, as it has been mine.

The Old Testament tells of Susanna, a beautiful and wealthy young mother. Two powerful men try to seduce her. When she rebuffs them, she is sentenced to death. She prays for deliverance, the prophet Daniel witnesses to her innocence, and she is spared.

In the first centuries of the Early Church, this story was told on catacomb walls and sarcophagi panels as a story of salvation and encouragement. The scenes you see here reflect the importance of community and justice in an ordered society.

The second Susanna's story ended quite differently. This Susanna lived in third-century Rome, was unmarried, beautiful, and wealthy. She was a niece of Pope Caius. She was a Christian and lived in a house on this site with her father and her Uncle Caius. But the family was related to Emperor Diocletian, who persecuted Christians.

From 280 to 293 AD, Susanna's house was a *domus ecclesia*, a house church where Christians worshiped illegally. When Diocletian ordered Susanna to deny her belief in Christ and marry his stepson, Susanna refused. Soldiers stormed the house, beheaded her, and arrested her father, who died in prison. Pope Caius survived.

In 330, fifteen years after Christianity became legal, a basilica was built over Susanna's house, and the relics of Susanna and her father were transferred from the catacombs. Pilgrims prayed before the graves, and many were healed.

The frescoes in the apse tell Susanna's story so we do not forget. And you, Kelly, must not forget. Susanna's house has been found beneath this hallowed church. It is a sanctuary of time, a place of truth, as far as man can witness to truth, for we are fragile, imperfect creatures.

Here, too, consider history and how we know the past. How do we decide that these stories of the first Christians are true? We cannot know for certain. But we can guess with a good degree of accuracy. We study the texts, examine the witnesses, and allow for human error. Through two thousand years the Church has labored to find and to witness to the truth of God and his great acts among men. The Church listens for the hymn of history, the song sung through the years. There are notes and words to the hymn. There is a melody.

In your journey I pray you will come to understand your faith. We live in an age of doubt, and you must find answers to the questions that will challenge you.

To continue your quest, solve the following riddle:

> *Four names this church does own,*
> *As spirit transforms flesh,*
> *God leaves his home, his heavenly throne,*
> *Born a babe in a wooden crèche.*
>
> With love and blessings,
> Your Godfather Gilbert

Kelly studied Daniel for signs that he knew the answer to the riddle. He appeared to recognize the description. "What do you think?" she asked.

"I have an idea, but first I'd like to see these frescoes closer up. They are so luminous! They carry the church into the heavens."

"Sure, but I've no idea what the next church is. Do you? Four names?"

His eyes teased. "I believe I do know."

Summoning patience, Kelly turned to the glowing walls and stepped up the aisle with her two companions. They entered the story of the first Susanna's trial, this public test of communal truth.

"Community is so important," Daniel said. "Each of us is afraid of being alone—we need each other, we are meant to be together, to love. The Church shows us how to do this. An ordered society shows us how to do this."

"Right," Father Francis said thoughtfully. "Consider the Trinity. Saint Augustine talks about the love between the Father and the Son and the Holy Ghost. We are created to love. A loving, ordered community cancels chaos. Sin separates us from God and from one another. Christ redeems us from sin and restores community."

Kelly listened to Daniel and the enthusiastic priest, trying to understand and absorb their words. She would have to agree that when she had done wrong, her sense of isolation from others was real. Her conscience nagged her to be sorry, to make amends, so she could be restored to community. She felt *shame*. Father Gilbert had often said sin was simply selfishness, so she could see where being self-centered would be the opposite of community. Sin would isolate you from love by isolating you from God. The largeness of the ideas touched her unexpectedly, but she remained silent, appreciating the moment. It was like the satisfaction she felt when she completed a crossword.

Daniel nodded. "Our own society is reverting to chaos, some say *jungle*, because of the lack of moral authority. You're saying that we isolate ourselves when we sin."

Kelly had been thinking much the same thing. *Success.*

"Righto, my boy, righto. We are commanded to love one another. Now, see this frescoed apse. Amazing, it is, don't you think, simply amazing."

They gazed at the colorful apse and followed the story of the Roman Susanna to her death. Kelly shuddered. The girl's martyrdom had happened here, under this church, in her own home. "Can we see Susanna's house, Father?" she asked.

Daniel added, "I read that recent excavations have uncovered it."

The priest shook his head. "I'm afraid the excavations aren't open. But you can see a bit of the earlier church through a window. Follow me."

Father Francis led them into the sacristy off the narthex where, through a glass panel in the floor, partial walls could be seen. Kelly peered, seeing little, wondering, was this all true?

"The house itself," Father Francis explained, "is on the convent side of our property—and the nuns don't give tours. We love having the sisters here, so we respect their wishes." He eyed Kelly. "Oh, you can be sure it's all true, my dear. We're standing on history."

They returned to the narthex, and as they opened the front doors, bells rang in the distance, muted by thick stone. Kelly glanced back at the stunning apse, wanting to memorize it.

"Well, my son," Father Francis said to Daniel, "have you guessed the next church?"

"I believe I have, Father."

"I believe I have, too," Father Francis replied, chuckling. "But, Kelly, I'm afraid I have to ask you for the letter. Father Gilbert told me to burn it for safety's sake. You do understand?"

Kelly pulled the letter from her bag. As she did, she touched the camera. "I understand, Father. Then let's take a photo of the letter. That would be okay, right?" She gazed imploringly at Father Francis.

"Great idea," Daniel said. "Less strain on my memory, that is if the image is readable. And we can check it in the viewfinder, even zoom if we need to."

Father Francis nodded. "I suppose no one would think to find a letter in a camera."

"We can download the image into my laptop," Daniel added, "and erase the one on the camera."

Kelly laid out the letter on a small table near the entrance. She turned on her flash, focused, and clicked. "Done." With a twinge of loss, she handed the letter to Father Francis but kept the envelope. Still holding the camera, she photographed the nave and apse, hoping to capture the color and light. "So beautiful."

"And here is a token remembrance from Santa Susanna." The priest handed her a pale green brochure describing the church.

"Thank you." She opened the glossy trifold. She could see it provided a short summary of the history and art. Her first souvenir. What other mementos would she add on this trip? Icons? Saints statues? Menus? She placed it alongside the camera in her bag and stepped outside, onto the porch.

Kelly looked at Daniel, then Father Francis. "Can we walk to the next church, or do we need to find a bus?"

"I'd like to get an espresso first," Daniel said, smiling enigmatically with his crooked smile. "A double, at the very least."

They said their good-byes and descended the steps of Santa Susanna. Kelly turned to look back. Father Francis waved, his thick open palm raised in blessing.

*

Lester Sansby surveyed the small room, dragging deeply on his cigarette. The place was a dump, located at the end of a narrow alley defaced with graffiti, but would do for a day or two until he could find something better. At least he had the hole to himself—its owner was away—and he could work unobserved. He unzipped a side compartment in his duffle and pulled out his pills. He set a tablet on the back of his tongue and swallowed.

It was midday, Thursday, June 3. He wondered where the little couple was right now. He searched the Internet for events in Rome. It wasn't long before he found what he wanted, a major religious procession. He arrowed the link, double-clicked, and soon had the details required. It seemed likely Weaver and the girl would be there.

Thinking of Weaver, he studied a draft email, a note to Dr. Weaver, checking for any hint of threat that could be construed as illegal.

> Dear Dr. Weaver,
> I understand you are searching for a valuable manuscript. Please do not trouble yourself with it. It will be found and used by far more capable folks than you, and Rome is a dangerous place. Not only that, but there are fellow academics who are most interested in your activities, how you spend inter-session break, playing around in Rome. I believe your tenure ranking is coming up soon.
> Ciao,
> Dr. L. Sansby

Lester smiled. *Perfect.* He was *so* good. He arrowed *Send* and clicked.

Next, he visited his discussion groups. He scrutinized a new posting from someone called *FlowerGirl*. She was making the usual statements about believing in Jesus as her Lord and Savior. She seemed to be in Rome. He checked her profile. Interesting. He might just lure her in slowly. She was in her twenties, so of the happy and fortuitous age of consent, a college student, someone who could be useful in many ways. And she even posted a few fuzzy photos—dark and tempting, perhaps Italian or Hispanic, perhaps part of the evangelical Catholic crowd, always an extra challenge, for their authorities were older and harder to break down, but just as crazy. And he liked the dark ones, having grown up in Texas and living for a while in New Mexico. She was exotic and hauntingly familiar.

Lester eyed his duffle and for a moment regretted not bringing the gun. He had vowed he would never again carry it in public, and airport security would have been tough, if not impossible. He took a sip from his flask, pulled a last drag from his cigarette, and stubbed it out.

Ah well, he had other ways to get what he wanted.

9

Maria Maggiore

IT WAS SHORTLY AFTER FIVE when they left Father Francis and found an Internet café to get a bite and check on Daniel's bandit. They decided to have supper later, so ordered espressos and bruschetta. Daniel opened his laptop and went online. Kelly observed him read a blog entry on a common networking site, this one a book discussion group. She leaned in to read the text.

Hank, as Daniel called his phantom bandit, was discoursing at great length on why Christianity was a fool's errand. The tone was nasty and mean. But his argument was loaded with detail, so much detail that it was difficult to follow. It reminded Kelly of what they called a "snow job" in school, when students stuffed their term papers with minutiae in hopes that the teacher would be impressed or not see the lack of coherency. The short responses to Hank's diatribe-post were from younger sounding voices with few words in their arsenal. Daniel jumped in, defending the innocents who had become a target of a particularly vile attack. In a way, Kelly observed, Daniel had become a bandit too, only one of the good guys.

"Truth is so important," he said as he closed his laptop. "My father…was hurt by this kind of thing once."

"An online discussion group like this one?"

Daniel shook his head with such genuine sorrow that Kelly regretted her light tone. "No," he replied, "it was a much more direct attack." He motioned to the server for the check.

A gray shadow seemed to cloud his eyes, but Kelly guessed she couldn't reach him, or perhaps this wasn't the right moment to try. He would have to deal with his own ghosts. If his father had been a victim of fraud or slander of some kind, it would explain Daniel's passion to set records straight. It was a piece, however small, of Daniel's puzzle.

"It was fascinating, seeing the Internet book groups," she said, angling away from his unease. "I don't have a computer, so I only go online at the library." She had shared her parents' home computer, one long ago outdated. Now that Matt was nearing school age, she would have to consider another one, when she could pay the rent, that is.

He grinned. "Well then, welcome to my world. I'll tutor you."

She laughed, glad to see his equanimity return. "Offer accepted. I was just thinking I need to learn more about the Internet for Matt's sake."

"Is he going into Kindergarten? You said he was five?"

"He starts in September." How good it felt to be talking about her son.

"Did he go to preschool? It seems to be the thing these days."

"No, I'm afraid not a real preschool, rather a daycare when I was working at the bank." The early mornings, the late evenings, the little time with her son had haunted her. But still, she needed an income. What other choice did she have?

"He seems like a pretty normal boy." Daniel shut down his laptop, pointing and clicking, and they watched the screen go dark. "Maybe he'd like to walk the dogs with me some time." He glanced at her. "Or catch a ballgame."

"He'd like that." The thought of a trusted man in her son's life was pleasing. Would the offer come to anything? Time would tell. She knew better than to count on anyone for very much.

She pulled out a rumpled photo of her son, worn and fingered, loved. He needed a haircut, but Andrea had taken the picture in a thoughtful moment. Matt looked as if he was seriously solving the world's problems, when suddenly asked to face Andrea and her camera. In that sense it was a good shot—it captured a boy deeply involved with his world and poised to return. Kelly recalled the few times Daniel had seen Matt—the day of the robbery, the day he picked her up for the airport and they were saying their good-byes, once at church when Matt nearly ran into him in the hall downstairs, chasing one of his friends. "He's pretty normal, I guess. Right now he's obsessed with construction vehicles."

Daniel smiled, examining the photo. "I was more into trucks and race cars…those little die-cast ones. I liked building—mostly with Legos." He studied the check. "Let me get this," he said, raising his hand. "And I had an old set of Lincoln Logs that my grandmother gave me that I loved."

"You said you were an only child as well?" She recalled he mentioned it on the plane.

"Indeed. And no preschool. No daycare. Pretty sheltered until Kindergarten."

"Me too. I was homeschooled." She would have liked to shelter Matt the same way. "You went to public?"

"Yes," he replied guardedly. "My mother would not have felt qualified to teach me. She only had a high school education. She was a good woman, a wonderful mother, and she trusted the public school system. She had no choice—they couldn't afford private. My education wasn't great. I sailed through everything, the standards were so low. But I tried to make up for it with extra reading, and my mother took me to the library in hopes she could help. My books became my friends, since it was unpopular to be a serious reader, or a serious student." He sounded cynical, as though he had been cheated of childhood friendships by social bullies.

Kelly felt sad that such a thing could be true. Should she send Matt to private school? It was unpopular to read? How could a child possibly learn anything without reading book after book? "That's terrible," she said.

"I did have one good friend, Max. But he moved away when I started high school."

"I had a few friends from church and from social gatherings with other homeschoolers. We had sports events, soccer teams, that sort of thing. Not too bad." But she hadn't kept in touch with any of those friends.

He appeared happy with a sudden memory. "Max and I played tennis. I used his brother's racket, and we went to the public park. We'd scrounge for balls in the bushes. He always beat me, but it was fun anyway." He seemed distant for a moment, then said, "Sometimes I wonder what became of him."

Daniel positioned his laptop in his backpack, then had second thoughts and pulled it out again. "Let's download that photo of the letter."

"Do you remember the contents?" She found the camera and removed the memory chip.

He inserted it into the port and nodded. "I think I have the main parts of the letter down—community, love, trinity, truth, justice, perhaps even art itself. And the poem was the easy part:

Four names this church does own,
As spirit transforms flesh,
God leaves his home, his heavenly throne,
Born a babe in a wooden crèche.

"Perfect," Kelly said, checking the text as it appeared on the screen.

"But I'm glad to have this backup."

"Me too." And it would be part of her memory album, she thought gratefully. It would be another part of Father Gilbert.

*

They stepped into the early evening. The espresso and the snack had been welcome and seemed to slightly counteract the grogginess. Kelly's body clock was severely off, she realized. How could she be so sleepy having slept half the day?

"It's just after six. The next church is a major basilica, so it should still be open. We have a few more hours of daylight. I think the church has to do with birth, the birth of Christ."

"Which church is it? How many churches in Rome have four names?" She unfolded her map. She was ready for a good walk.

"Which church?" he repeated, and his crooked grin caught Kelly off-guard, intriguing her again. "Romans love names, and many churches have several names, often reflecting different parts of the church's history." He shifted his pack to the other shoulder. "And every church is, in some way, about the Incarnation, wouldn't you agree? But the *wooden crèche* was the defining clue. We seem to be beginning at the beginning, the birth of Christ, with Santa Susanna a sort of prologue that set the tone." He gazed up the long straight street. "Let's head this way, up the Via Torino. But first let's pick up some gelato across the street. I've been in Rome twenty-four hours and haven't had my gelato fix yet."

Kelly had heard of gelato, the Italian ice cream. *Her first gelato.* They came to a shop with many colorful choices, temptingly displayed behind a glass freezer case fronting the sidewalk. They left with small cups of dark chocolate, their mutual flavor of choice. Kelly spooned the rich ice cream and decided it tasted more intense than American ice cream, rather a cross between sorbet and ice cream. She savored each bite as they headed up the Via Torino.

Dodging serious walkers maneuvering around them, they walked single file. As they passed various small shops, Kelly noticed a large bookstore selling titles in English. She pointed.

"That's a major Italian chain," Daniel said, his voice slightly hoarse, "and all the books are new. I'll take you to a good used-book store in Trastevere when we have a chance. The books are a fraction of the cost, and a good number of them are in English."

Kelly could see now at the far end of the street a white dome intersecting the paling blue sky, as the sun moved lower toward the earth, or as she often reminded herself, the earth turned in its orbit.

Daniel spoke from behind her, sounding short of breath. "We're heading for the Esquilino, or Esquiline Hill…one of the Seven Hills…of Rome."

"I read about the Seven Hills in my guidebook," she said, trying to speak over her shoulder, "but it doesn't feel as though we are going uphill at all."

"The hills have settled a great deal. Some are steeper than others, but this one always surprises me…with its gentle slope, especially approaching from the Viminale…another of the Seven Hills."

They paused to toss their ice cream cups into a trash receptacle, and Kelly pulled out her map and folded it to the appropriate section showing Maria Maggiore. They continued in a comfortable silence along the shady Via Torino, Kelly glancing at her map, and emerged onto a busy square surrounding the basilica.

"This is actually the back of the church, the chevet or apse, behind the high altar." His voice was hoarse now, and he coughed a bit, covering his mouth with his hand. "I apologize for the cough. It's my asthma. Probably the car fumes." He took out a small inhaler from his pocket and pumped it twice into his mouth.

"You have asthma? Matt does too." She felt a surge of sympathy.

"I'm sorry to hear it, but then you must understand. I only have occasional spells now. Matt will probably outgrow his as well." His voice was returning, and his brown eyes held relief. He breathed normally and touched his chest.

"I hope so," she said.

They walked around the piazza's perimeter to the front of the basilica where a broad paved terrace led to a massive façade and side buildings.

Daniel rested his backpack on the ground and lifted his open palms, gesturing to the entrance. "I give to you the Patriarchal Basilica of Santa Maria Maggiore." He half-smiled as though gathering his memories.

As Kelly studied the church, she wondered if they were nearing the end of their quest. She was close to something, she was sure. "Maria Maggiore?" She slipped her map into her bag and pulled out her camera. She focused, soon realizing she couldn't fit the basilica into the viewfinder. Settling on the central portion, she turned the camera vertically, wanting to include the bell tower. The church façade, to her taste, seemed severe with all that stone, and there wasn't a tree in sight.

"The Basilica of Mary Major," Daniel said thoughtfully, "is the largest and the leading Marian church in the world. More to the point, it has three other names: *Santa Maria ad Nives, Basilica Liberiana,* and *Santa Maria del Presepio,* so it meets our requirements."

"It must be old."

"Fifth-century, although the original church was fourth-century. But this façade is only eighteenth-century, both Classical and Baroque—you see the orderly double levels, the sculptures, porticoes, arcades. And it was built on a hill that was once a cemetery for the poor."

"But what about the names?"

"The names reflect the church's history," Daniel continued. "*Santa Maria ad Nives* translates to *Saint Mary of the Snows.*"

"Snow? Here in Rome?"

"Indeed, it does snow on occasion, but not at the height of summer. This snow fell on August 5, 350. The Virgin Mary appeared to Ionnes Patricius—John the Patrician—in a dream. She said she would show him the place where she wanted him to build a basilica." Daniel watched Kelly's face for signs of interest, and she nodded encouragement. "Pope Liberius had the same dream, so when snow fell on the Esquiline Hill in the heat of August, they believed the visions were real. The Pope marked out a church in the snowfall."

"That's interesting history." She was beginning to be intrigued by the stories of Rome. This would be one to add to Santa Susanna's.

Daniel smiled as he continued. "Every August 5, the church celebrates the founding of the basilica by dropping white petals from one of the vaults, to imitate snowfall."

"That's lovely," Kelly said. "Is the story true, do you think?"

"We can only date the legend to the seventh century. Archaeologists think the church we see today was built in 432, after the Council of Ephesus declared Mary the *Theotokos,* the Mother of God. It is probable that the legend is true, although the first church may have been built in another location on this hill. At any rate, that is why this church is called *Saint Mary of the Snows* as well as *Basilica Liberiana.*"

"After Pope Liberius. And what about the other name—*Presepio?*" The church was a puzzle all on its own, she thought, a colorful word puzzle.

"You'll see." He raised his brows, clearly enjoying the suspense. "We need to be watchful, at this point, as we enter the church, to recognize the next clue, or at least the source for the next clue."

They stepped into the giant nave as bells rang seven.

10

Incarnation

KELLY ESTIMATED THAT THE GOLDEN SPACE was easily twice the size of Santa Susanna. Green and pink marble tiles covered the floors. White columns lined the nave, leading to a golden altar, and she could see that the ceiling was golden as well. Above the columns, mosaics told stories, and above the mosaics, light streamed through high windows. The musty air felt cooler than outside, sheltered by the stone. Traces of incense lingered, mingling with the scent of burning candles.

"Beautiful," Kelly said, unable to think of something more descriptive. "Stunning," she added, recalling it was a favorite word of her mother's.

"The thirty-six columns, the mosaics running above the columns, and the mosaics on the apsidal arch are all fifth-century."

"That's pretty old."

Kelly heard singing, and she followed the music, stepping up the central aisle. The marble slid smoothly under her feet, and soon she saw that the song came from a side chapel near the high altar. They weren't a professional choir, she guessed, as inharmonious voices wove together, echoing. They sounded like ordinary folks, gathering and singing their praises. They sang in French, and she recognized a few words from one of her home-school courses. Maybe they were pilgrims.

"They are probably part of a parish pilgrimage," Daniel said. "I went on one once from Saint Mary's."

"I remember reading the announcements. Always sounded adventurous. It never seemed to be an option for us."

"I got to go as part of Saint Mary's Singers."

"Nice. You must have a good voice. I mostly follow along." Kelly was envious.

"Tenor. Used to be boy soprano." He appeared wistful. "Someday, I'd like to join a choir again—it's a wonderful experience."

Reaching the high altar, they looked up to a golden canopy under the glimmering mosaic arch and descended stairs to an area about eight by ten. An oversize sculpture of a pope knelt in prayer.

"This space beneath the high altar is the *confessio*," Daniel explained. "Relics are traditionally kept here to sanctify the altar for the celebration of the Eucharist."

It was as though she had entered a marble tomb. About a dozen seats faced a glass window, and through the window she could see a reliquary in the shape of an ark. Tourists and pilgrims knelt, and visitors stood in the back, full of awe and possibly curiosity. Some walked up to the glass to see the relic. Kelly and Daniel peered inside, studying the wood that could be seen in its golden house.

Daniel lowered his voice. "According to tradition, this relic is a piece of wood from Jesus' cradle, brought from Bethlehem by pilgrims."

"From the first crèche, Christ's manger?"

"I find it profound—a bit of humble wood in such an ornate church."

"But how do you know this is real?" She scrutinized the relic as though the answer might come to her miraculously.

"We don't *know*, at least not for certain. What we do know from historic documents is that chapels have housed this wood since the seventh century, and oral tradition has dated it earlier to Saint Jerome, fourth century. We speak of probabilities, not facts, but then we do that with many things in life, and many aspects of such history we accept as fact."

She thought about his words, and as they ascended into the nave, asked, "Do *you* believe this wood is from the stable at Bethlehem?"

"I do," Daniel said. "And even if I didn't, it could still be a focus of my prayers, a way to recall the story of the Incarnation. It's one of the things I love about Catholicism, the sacramental objects that bring our faith to life, into the present moment—the poetry, the image, all speaking of a great truth." Daniel pointed to the walls along the sides of the immense nave. "The frieze mosaics tell Old Testament stories prefiguring Christ's birth. The apsidal mosaics tell of the life of Mary, his mother. And here, we have the cradle itself."

"Deep under the high altar." Kelly thought it fit together like a great poem or painting, with such intensity of color and meaning. It was satisfying in a way she couldn't fully express. Maybe that was what art and image did—express the inexpressible.

He gazed into her eyes. "Exactly. The child and the man. The baby and the crucified one, the bread and wine transformed into the Body and Blood of the Eucharist. It's all so wonderful!"

A quiet glow settled over his features, and she was almost embarrassed to glimpse this intimate place. She glanced away.

"Where to now?" she asked hesitantly.

He gazed down the nave to the front doors, up to the ceiling of gold, and to the chapel on their right. "I'm not sure. Let's make one more stop and then see where we are...in reference to what we know and what we need to know. When I visit Maria Maggiore I like to visit Our Lady."

*

They found the singers in the ornate chapel in the northern transept. Pilgrims sang the *Ave Maria,* the hymn telling of Angel Gabriel's announcement to Mary that she would give birth to the Son of God. The sanctuary gleamed with gilt and bronze, but the image of the Madonna and Child, high above the altar, was an earthy one of dark browns and deep reds. Kelly and Daniel listened and watched from the back, absorbing the beauty.

"The Madonna," Daniel whispered, "is the *Salus Populi Romani,* meaning 'Salvation of the Roman People.'"

Kelly squinted to see the image better, for it was high above the altar. Even so, it was mysteriously poignant.

"Oral tradition from the seventh century says it was painted by Saint Luke."

"Really?"

"It's been carbon-dated to the first century, so it's possible."

Kelly moved to the side to lessen the glare of the light glancing off the protective glass. The date would explain its primitive quality.

"In 594," Daniel said, "the *Salus Populi Romani* was paraded through Rome by Gregory the Great to pray for the end of a plague."

"And the plague ended?"

He nodded. "Exactly right. I love icons. I have a few at home, a small collection from my time living here. Copies, of course. But they help me to focus my prayer. Maybe we should ask for Mary's help just like the Romans did."

"Good idea," she said. Any help was welcome.

They found a place in the back pew, set their bags down, and knelt on the hard wooden kneelers. From the little French she knew, she could tell the chanting had moved from the "Ave Maria" to the opening prayers of a Mass. She bowed her head and prayed for guidance, for they had come a long way and seemed to be at a dead end. She contemplated the icon. Mary must know where they should go next. Would she show them?

Kelly wasn't sure how long they knelt, but soon she sat back in the pew and allowed the singing of the Mass to wash over her, giving her a kind of peace. Daniel remained kneeling, his rosary in his left hand. He seemed so devout, she wondered why he hadn't become a priest.

She sensed someone's eyes upon her and abruptly turned. In the doorway a tall man with an arrogant bearing stood with his legs straight and set apart, his hands on his hips. He wore a hat, which Kelly knew was a sign of disrespect in a church, and the wide brim eclipsed his features. His dark glasses struck an odd note in this dim space. He sauntered away.

Kelly shivered. "Let's go," she said, touching Daniel's arm.

"Sure." He made the Sign of the Cross and reached for his backpack.

As they left the chapel and re-entered the nave, Kelly explained quietly but with some urgency, "There was a strange man staring at me."

"What did he look like?"

She described the hat, the jeans, the dark glasses, his proud manner. "He was pretty tall." Somehow he was familiar.

"I believe he may be Dr. Sansby," Daniel said. "I was afraid this might happen."

"You know him?"

"Let's sit in the back of the nave where we can talk."

As they found seats near the entrance doors, Daniel scanned the meandering groups of pilgrims and tourists. "Dr. Lester Sansby teaches at Berkeley University. Humanities."

Kelly suddenly recalled where she had seen him. "I took a class from him once, or rather began a class, then dropped it."

"Did you? I'm glad you dropped it. He hates *Opus Veritatis*. He claims we destroyed his brother and probably worries we will expose him as well."

"He was kind of creepy, and my father disapproved of him. Is he dangerous?"

"I don't think so, but who knows for sure? He has a vicious pen, that's for sure, or perhaps vicious blog would be more accurate. He's been blogging against the Foundation since its first successes. In that regard he's dangerous."

"You said he hates you."

"He's an atheist, with few moral restraints. Of course, many atheists and agnostics are respectful of other points of view. My colleague Bruce Harrington is an agnostic. We often agree to disagree and are still friends. In fact he debates so well, that engaging him in discussion sharpens my own argument. But Sansby thinks we are simpletons and wants to set the record straight. He ridicules rather than reasons. Respect is not part of his vocabulary, and neither is honesty. Ironically, he sees himself as the savior of mankind."

"You said he is afraid of being exposed?"

"He's done some spurious first-century scholarship, the kind your godfather loved to turn upside down with a few simple facts."

"Why is he here? Is he following us?"

"I'm not sure." He hesitated. "Kelly, I don't want to worry you."

"I'd rather know."

"I received a nasty email from Lester Sansby."

"What did it say?"

"Essentially to give up the search for the manuscript, or my tenure might be in jeopardy. He's a powerful man at the university, and not a man I want as an enemy, although he's no longer my department chair since I moved into Religious Studies. Even so, he has connections. I was hoping to keep a low profile, but I'm afraid that's not possible any longer. I'm not sure how far he would go to secure these papers."

"But in what way does my godfather's research on Mary Magdalene threaten him?"

"I've heard that Sansby has also done work on Mary Magdalene. He could have known about your godfather's research—it wasn't secret. Put that together with a nasty grudge and the hope of treasure, who knows?"

Kelly's alarm was rising in light fluttery waves and she breathed deeply, hoping to loosen the panic. She needed to escape, to get away. She needed to call Matt. She needed to go home. *Now.* She forced herself to ask the most difficult question of all. "I think I mentioned that my parents were researching Mary Magdalene when they died. Do you think…Sansby was in any way involved in that attack on Father Gilbert? Involved in their death?"

Daniel heaved a huge sigh and rubbed his hands. Clearly wanting to reassure her, he replied, "We don't know, but I can't believe he's capable of murder. Yet he certainly has the motivation. He's a man with a past to save and a future to protect. I thought he was simply a braggart, but students admire him and pack his lectures, so he's a bit of a star as well. It's also true he isn't exactly known for marital fidelity and is often seen with students young enough to be his granddaughters—he's probably close to sixty now."

"Was he the one who broke into my place?"

"Again, I can't believe he would break and enter. That's a risky thing to do, and he's highly respected."

"Maybe he was the man who visited Andrea?"

"That could very well be." Daniel grew thoughtful. "Let's focus on our own search, find the papers and go home, the sooner the better. I may be able to slip from his sights after all. We must be missing something obvious, some clue to the next church. I thought we would have come across it by now."

"Well, Maria Maggiore is about the Incarnation, right? About birth? Maybe the next one is about the Crucifixion? About death?"

Daniel smoothed his beard. "But every church is about Christ's death in some sense. There's a crucifix over every altar."

"Maybe we should watch out for a person, someone to give us another letter."

Daniel pointed to the gift shop off the narthex. "Someone in the shop should know where we can find the priest-in-charge. He might know something."

*

Lester Sansby watched them from a dark corner as they entered the shop, then left. They crossed the nave and stepped into a side chapel as bells rang eight.

He would stay close, very close.

11

Father Timothy

"SO YOU FOUND ME." Father Timothy sat in a wheelchair in the sacristy, an ornate room that housed the vestments and chalices used for the liturgies. Gilded cabinets lined the walls and a long mahogany table, polished to a high gloss, occupied the center of the room. "When I learned of Father Gilbert's death, I knew you would arrive sooner or later." He spoke with an American accent.

The priest's thick black hair waved behind his ears, combed to the side and trimmed neatly above his collar, and his robe draped loosely about his malformed body. He gave the appearance of a man once ruggedly handsome who, through sickness and suffering, had lost his attractiveness but had long ago accepted the change. His small gray eyes were friendly, his demeanor inviting. Kelly had the feeling that as he uttered his enigmatic words of greeting, he desired to enter their lives, to warm and to be warmed by them.

Kelly had purchased a small icon of the *Salus Populi Romani* in the gift shop. The rustic browns and reds of the image touched her, the gaze of Mary both poignant and demanding, sweet and knowing, and the colorful Madonna lingered in her mind as they followed a young volunteer to the sacristy. It would be good to be like her—full of feeling, but also full of the knowledge of right and wrong. One attribute did not necessarily preclude the other.

Now she turned her gaze from Father Timothy to the icon in her bag, wrapped in cellophane. *Yes,* she thought. *Poignant, yet demanding...sweet, yet knowing.* The priest before her appeared to have those qualities, and Kelly studied him with both wonder and respect, for she had not expected the wheelchair, the twisted limbs. What terrible illness was ravaging him?

Father Timothy could see the question on Kelly's face. "I have ALS, Amyotrophic Lateral Sclerosis, also known as Lou Gehrig's Disease, named after the ball player. It is a steady paralysis of the body caused by the degeneration of spinal nerves."

"We're so sorry," Daniel said.

"The disease is progressing rapidly, thanks be to God." His voice was high-pitched, but oddly happy, as his limp fingers, splayed at odd angles, struggled toward a pocket. "You have the password?" His eyes rested on Kelly.

"*Apostles' Creed*," they said together. Kelly glanced back toward the door nervously, expecting Dr. Sansby to appear at any moment.

"Indeed, you are correct." His face grew flushed. "I knew your godfather, Ms. Roberts. A fine man and a fine priest. A brave man, to be sure, and a loving, sacrificial priest. He cared for me when other folks were too busy." He gazed beyond them, as though remembering, then pulled himself together. "I have something for you. From him."

They waited in hopeful silence as he struggled to remove an envelope from his pocket.

"I've been carrying this around with me since his passing. Read it now. I must burn it afterwards." He handed it to Kelly, observing her with curiosity. "Dramatic, wouldn't you say? But an honor to execute these wishes for an old friend."

It did strike Kelly as dramatic, as though she were in an Agatha Christie or P. D. James mystery. Was there more at stake than she knew? Than Daniel guessed?

"Thank you," she said, sliding her finger under the dove-and-heart seal and carefully pulling out the thin paper. Unlike the Santa Susanna letter, this one was short.

> My dear Kelly,
> You have found Father Timothy at Santa Maria Maggiore. He is an old friend, and a great help to us.
>
> You have experienced Love and Community, Truth and Art, in the exquisite church of Santa Susanna. In this glorious basilica of Santa Maria Maggiore you see Birth and Incarnation, as you enter the sacramental world in which God works through matter. Here you see the wood of the crèche and the Madonna of the Snows. Our Lady will watch over you on your journey.
>
> Solve this riddle, and you will know the name of the next historic church and experience the next chapter of your quest into the mysteries of God:
>
> *An empress traveled far from home*
> *To find what had been lost,*
> *And bring the sacred back to Rome,*
> *The wood of the true cross.*
>
> Your loving Godfather Gilbert

Kelly handed the letter to Daniel, who read it quickly. "You know, don't you?" she asked as she photographed the letter.

"I have a good guess, but we should visit in the morning when it's light." He handed the letter to Father Timothy.

The priest rang a small bell tied to his chair arm, and soon a young woman arrived, dressed in a flowered skirt, white tee, and blue shawl. Her silver bracelets and hoop earrings glimmered, her dark hair falling in thick curls over her shoulders. She was attractive in an exotic way, with olive skin and large brown eyes. She possessed a calm confidence.

Father Timothy pointed to a lower cabinet. "The bowl and matches please, my dear."

She removed a metal basin and a box of matches. Daniel placed the letter in the bowl.

"Are you ready, Father?" The woman gazed at the priest expectantly.

He nodded, and she lit a match. They watched the paper burn to ash.

Father Timothy turned to Kelly and Daniel. "May I introduce my niece, Teresa Morales. She helps with my care."

Teresa offered them her beringed hand, cool from the metal bowl, and they exchanged greetings.

"You're Americans?" the girl asked.

Kelly nodded, feeling a connection. "We're from California. How about you?"

"New Mexico. Santa Fe. A long ways away, it seems now. I came here on a university program and stayed. I love Rome. And Uncle Tim was here too." She glanced at him with affection.

Kelly could see they were close, perhaps bonded by gratitude.

Bells rang in the distance and Daniel said, "Is there a service this late? It's nearly eight."

Father Timothy beamed. "Don't you know?"

"What's today?" Kelly asked Daniel.

"June third," Daniel said. "Must be a saint's day?" he asked Father Timothy.

At that moment Kelly heard chanting in the distance. There were thousands, she guessed, as the gentle singing swelled and receded, like waves in the night. She turned, drawn by the rushing loveliness of the song.

Daniel raised his hands in recollection. "It's Corpus Christi! Today is the Thursday after Trinity Sunday, the Feast of Corpus Christi, when the Pope processes with the Blessed Sacrament from the Lateran Basilica."

"The Lateran?" Kelly asked. Rome had so many secrets, so many names, so many churches.

"Saint John Lateran," Daniel explained, "the papal basilica and cathedral of Rome."

Father Timothy gestured weakly toward the doors. "Please, go outside and watch them arrive. It's splendid! I must prepare for Benediction. My dears, may Our Lord be with you." He made the Sign of the Cross in blessing above their heads. Teresa nodded good-bye and wheeled her uncle through a side door, her bracelets jangling.

Daniel shook his head as they left the sacristy. "How could I have forgotten? This is an event not to be missed."

As they headed toward the main entrance opening onto the porch, Kelly glanced back at the golden nave of Maria Maggiore. She sighed deeply.

*

A large crowd waited quietly in the piazza as the twilight deepened. The side streets were packed as well, the streets roped off to traffic. But one street had also been cleared of pedestrians, and as Kelly scrutinized the dark passage, a procession came into view.

Groups of nuns and monks in full habit walked solemnly, carrying flaming lanterns and singing. The procession moved up the stairs to the basilica. Kelly sensed she was riding a tide of joy, immersed in the song, the gathering dusk, the lanterns bright in the encroaching darkness.

Soon in the distance she saw an open van with a canopy. "What's that?" she asked, pointing.

"The Holy Father kneeling before the Blessed Sacrament, the Body of Christ."

"The Pope?"

"Indeed." Daniel stared as though memorizing the moment. "I saw him in a general audience at Saint Peter's years ago, but this is special indeed."

Incense billowed, and through the sweet-smelling smoke, Kelly could see the elderly pontiff in his white robes kneeling before a golden-rayed monstrance.

"Do you truly believe the bread becomes—is—Christ's body?" Kelly said suddenly and immediately regretted her terse tone. While she knew Catholic teaching affirmed that Christ was present in the Host, was it really true? The doctrine, to her, seemed so fantastic, so unreal. Over the years she had avoided the belief, as though it would unfairly test her faith, flimsy as that faith was.

But now, in this dim light in this mysterious city, she was curiously bold and feeling surprisingly comfortable with the young man at her side. And she had always loved processions, as though they acted out life's journey.

Daniel searched her eyes. "I do believe it. We call it the *Real Presence*, meaning Christ is present as both God and Man." He gazed at the canopied altar, and Kelly could see the large white Host in the center of the golden rays.

The van halted. The Pope stepped to the piazza and followed the Blessed Sacrament, raised high, up the steps and into Mary's church.

*

They dined in a small trattoria near their hotel. Photographs of famous patrons covered the walls, and bouquets of flowers in ceramic vases rested on dark sideboards, under artistic lamps, upon pedestals in corners. They ordered the day's special—salami and cheese slices, cappellini with tomato, white fish with pesto—and sipped a house Chianti. Kelly, still groggy with jet lag, listened to her companion, now her guide, absorbing the warm ambiance of the cluttered dining room, her mind full of the day's rich colors and soaring songs.

"To faith," Daniel toasted, swirling his wine as though it was a priceless vintage. "I like these ordinary wines."

"To faith," she said, wondering again about his strong belief. "Tell me about it, about the procession."

He regarded her with satisfaction. "Corpus Christi? All of the religious orders in Rome take part. They begin with Mass at Saint John Lateran, up the street, since the Lateran basilica is the Pope's cathedral as Bishop of Rome."

"I thought Saint Peter's was the Pope's church."

"That's the papal basilica."

"Oh. That makes sense, I guess." Two titles, two churches.

"So they process with the Blessed Sacrament to the Basilica of Maria Maggiore, appropriately, for Mary was the first true tabernacle of Our Lord and, as they say here, 'She will teach us how to make a fitting place for the Eucharistic Lord in our souls.' " Daniel smiled with satisfaction. "A friend of mine liked that line, and quoted it often."

Kelly nodded. "Nice." It was a phrase of flourishes, she thought, as she surveyed the room, the flowers, the linens, the servers weaving between tables, carrying their trays high. Italy seemed a place of decorated motifs, spandrels, curls, and gilt. The simple things of the earth—bread, wine, flowers, music—were celebrated in song, art, and manners. They were given flourishes. *"She will teach us how to make a fitting place for the Eucharistic*

Lord in our souls." The words were tendrils growing from one another, like an ornamental border on a frame. "What do they mean by 'Eucharistic Lord'?"

"Christ truly, actually present under the signs of bread and wine." Daniel gestured with his hands, his voice eager. "The procession begins in the daylight, but ends in the dark, yet with the sky still holding some afterglow of the day. The only light comes from the altar itself and from the lanterns."

"It *was* dramatic. And beautiful." The singing wove through her memory like fragrant incense swirling through the air.

Daniel set down his fork, as though his mind had moved into another sphere. "I've never seen the Corpus Christi procession before. It's wonderful the way the personal pilgrimage unites with the public witness. That struck me as I watched the faces in the crowd. It's like the Eucharist is food for the journey of life, privately for each person and also publicly for the whole Church."

Kelly used her fork to twirl some cappellini into the bowl of her spoon. As she tasted sweet tomato, pungent green olive oil, and savory basil, she thought, *Food for the journey.* She had been in Rome for less than two days and already she was in a poem. But she still wasn't certain about the content of the poem. "I'm not sure I believe all of this," she said as she sipped her wine.

Daniel regarded her with understanding. "I appreciate your honesty and respect your feelings, but your belief will grow if you want it to. Sometimes simply the desire makes all the difference. In the meantime, read the sixth chapter of John, an excellent passage to recall in moments of doubt. 'Except ye eat the flesh of the Son of man, and drink his blood, ye have no life in you. He that eateth my flesh, and drinketh my blood, dwelleth in me, and I in him.' Those are the actual words of Christ."

"But you don't take everything literally in the Bible."

"No, I don't, and that brings us to the question of authorities, choosing interpretations."

"Father Gilbert said something like that." Was it in a letter? A suddenly recalled sermon?

"He was right. Choosing authorities was a major theme in his classes. We need to choose whom to trust. Unless, of course, one is an expert in the field, and even the experts have their experts." He grinned, studied his wine, then sipped slowly.

"In this case the authority is the Church?"

"It's the best we have. We interpret Scripture according to the words and intent of the author and the living tradition of the Church. The Church represents two thousand years of expertise, scholarship, assent and dissent, inspiration by the Holy Spirit. I'll trust that authority over any individual in any particular time. I'll trust many experts over a few. We do this in other areas of our lives without a second thought."

Daniel's words rang true, but even so, as Kelly relived the procession in her mind, she still harbored doubt that the Host was Christ, even in a mystical sense. "I don't know. It seems strange."

"I know. I find the debate both fascinating and frustrating. Unfortunately, our Dr. Sansby and his ilk use the confusion, the debate itself, to attack Christianity."

"How so? You said he was a blogger?"

"He blogs, steals his way into Christian online forums, seeking to tear apart believers, like a beast in the Coliseum. Most of the folks in these groups are young and ill equipped to answer him. He may well be the bandit I'm currently tracking. Online, he goes by many names of course, but the verbosity of Dr. Sansby tallies well with the wordiness of my current fellow, Hank."

"Give me an example. I saw Hank online earlier." Her Internet experience was growing. Would she one day surf the Net, engage in chat rooms, join Facebook and Twitter? Would Matt? The new frontier was both exciting and scary.

"Once I came across Hank in a Christian discussion group. The particular discussion was titled 'I believe in Jesus,' so you would think the members had that quality in common. Becoming a member is easy, but somehow he was able to become one of the moderators, which gave him power to delete posts he didn't like, which he often did. When members protested, he said he deleted them because they were 'stupid.'"

"That's disrespectful, awful. Like a breach of trust."

"A breach of trust." He leaned toward her earnestly. "That's exactly right. Trust is so precious, and when people betray one another it's hard to bear. My father...trusted people too much, I think. He trusted and was terribly hurt."

Kelly listened, waiting for more, but after an awkward pause, he returned to his explanation of Hank's activities.

"I inquired," Daniel continued, "with the site administration as to how this was possible, and they replied that if a member didn't like the group, they could leave."

Kelly shook her head. "There's no courtesy police, I guess."

"Right. Anyway, one of this fellow's arguments against Christianity was that the Gospels couldn't be true because they didn't agree on important details, such as the date of the birth of Christ."

"But shouldn't they agree on such an important fact?"

Daniel sipped his wine. "It's more complicated than that, for dating was different then, not uniform. For example, Jewish calendars differed from Roman. In addition, history was written with different purposes than today. Roman historians at the time of Christ wrote to morally edify, rather than to record. Therefore all their accounts, in this sense, were biased, coming from this narrow purpose."

"So what do we have to go on?" The subject was becoming more and more intriguing, like solving a puzzle all on its own: How do we know what truly happened?

"We have manuscripts dating to the second century, which are clearly copies of the original Gospels. We have the accounts written by early Christians, stating what they believed. We have, in the end, what historians generally accept as history, that is, probability, not strict proof." Daniel grew silent, and Kelly sensed he was close to brooding.

"And our bandit?"

"He troubles me. These so-called scholars show little respect for others. Such arrogance threatens not only our freedom of speech, but our freedom of religion. It threatens Western culture."

He appeared to be talking to himself, and Kelly was suddenly sleepy again, as though a great weight held her to the earth. She yawned, reaching too late to cover her mouth.

He caught the yawn. "I'm sorry. I've kept you too long. It's late. Let's order some dessert and head back. The profiteroles are good here."

"No, thank you, Daniel. I need to get some sleep." And she needed to call Matt. "I was awake for hours in the middle of the night, then slept all day."

"That's normal, the first week in Europe." He reached into his pocket and pulled out a small enamel tin. A tabby cat had been painted on the lid. "I found this in a shop in Trastevere. The cat is like a cat I had as a boy. Herbie." He opened it and handed her several small tablets. "Melatonin. A natural enzyme that helps you go back to sleep once you wake up. One should be enough each night."

"Thanks." She slipped the pills into a side pocket in her bag.

He signalled the server. "Let's get the check."

They stepped into the cool of the evening and made their way back to the hotel. Waiting for a pedestrian light to change to *Avante,* Daniel said, "Tomorrow will be another day in our search. I think this idea of authorities may be a clue."

"How so?"

"The Apostles' Creed was the product of generations of oral phrases finally written down, the faith of the apostles. The Creed became an authority in the Church, stating what we believe." He opened the door to their hotel and they climbed upstairs to their rooms.

"Interesting." Kelly paused at her door, the weariness overwhelming. She understood fully the saying, "Feet like lead." How about, "Body like lead." Trite but so true.

"Take a pill and get some sleep. In the morning we'll visit Father Gilbert's next church. We'll sort out the mystery soon enough and you'll be home before you know it." His voice held kindness and concern, but also doubt. She ignored the doubt.

"You get some sleep too." She tried to look hopeful.

"And don't be concerned about not believing enough. Keep an open mind and leave it up to God." He gazed at her. "Did you know that you have beautiful eyes?"

She removed her glasses, holding them thoughtfully. "That's kind of you to say," she replied, her cheeks warm.

"*Buona notte*, Kelly." Daniel waved casually with an open palm.

"*Buona notte*, Daniel."

Was there some hesitation in his leave-taking? He was an attractive man, she thought groggily. Did she feel relief as she watched him saunter down the hall, glance back and grin, his hand raised one more time? Was his comment a flirtation or merely an observation? Should she have been more encouraging, or less? She would worry about it in the morning.

*

Kelly called home but soon realized that Andrea and the boys were probably on their way to Tahoe. She left a message.

That night she dreamed....

The singing pulled her higher and the valley below grew distant. It was a joyous dream, and she climbed farther and farther, happy, so happy, nearing the top of the rocky pinnacle. The song swelled into a chorus, the harmonies weaving, the melody intensely sweet. Soon, soon, she would find what she was seeking. Soon, soon, she would see the singers. Then abruptly the blue dome of sky turned black, and no stars lit the impenetrable dark....

She awoke, startled, her heart pounding. Sitting up, she gripped the sheets. Had she called out? The clock read 3:18. She threw off the blankets, stepped to the window, and raised the sash. A cold breeze slapped her cheeks.

That's better, she thought as her mind cleared. What had she dreamed? The images were fading fast, lost in realms she could not reach. She tried to glimpse those other worlds but couldn't as a profound loss, edged with dread, engulfed her.

Kelly turned from the window and took a second sleeping tablet, hoping that the mild enzyme would redeem the remaining hours of the night.

*

Somewhere between the café and their hotel Lester lost them. He was still cursing when he climbed the stairs to his place in Trastevere.

He checked his Internet groups and was pleased to see something from Frizzle, something about relics and the next basilica. He retrieved a pill from his bag and swilled it down with whisky. He promised Frizzle a reward.

The others didn't have much, but Fab was bragging that the deed was done. What deed, exactly, was done?

12

Brother Sebastian

FRIDAY MORNING WAS FAIR BUT STILL NIPPY, a day of wispy clouds slipping over Rome, diminishing the June light. As bells rang eleven, Kelly and Daniel paused before a majestic white church. In the slight chill, Kelly buttoned her cardigan, feeling more prepared for cooler weather with slacks and her sturdy walking shoes. Daniel wore his jeans and blazer, but today no tie. Perhaps, she thought, this was his casual look.

The Basilica of Santa Croce in Gerusalemme rose beyond a lawn bordered by a cobblestone drive and towering shade trees. The church had a feminine façade, Kelly decided, prettier than Maria Maggiore's. This façade, with its straight pillars and gently rounded portico, its bell tower tucked behind, was sweet and simple, with flourishes, statues, and a charming balustrade crowning the vertical movement of stone.

As she listened to Daniel's quiet recitation she moved a stray strand of hair from her eyes and checked the poem on her camera's display panel.

An empress traveled far from home
To find what had been lost,
And bring the sacred back to Rome,
The wood of the true cross.

"Perfect," she said and focused the camera on the basilica.

The white façade contrasted with the dark city walls, and Kelly thought she was beginning to recognize a pattern in Rome, one of historical layers. The walls encircling classical Rome witnessed the first churches being built in the fourth to fifth centuries. In time those churches were rebuilt, some in the ninth century, some again in the sixteenth to seventeenth centuries. Today the tourist could often see, however partially, all these restorations, representing all these eras.

"So, here you have what is, I believe," Daniel was saying, "the answer to your godfather's riddle: the Basilica of the Holy Cross in Jerusalem, Santa Croce in Gerusalemme."

"I understand *Holy Cross*," Kelly said. "But *empress*?"

"This church was once a palace belonging to Empress Helena, a British princess who married the emperor Constantius. When her son Constantine became emperor, he gave her the Sessorian Palace near the old Roman wall that Emperor Aurelius built in the third century." Daniel reached for Kelly's hand, surprising her. "Come, I'll show you."

His hand was cool and delicate, his grip firm. She told herself she was growing fond of him in a sisterly sort of way. He was like an older brother, the sibling she never had. Both strange and familiar in his bookish ways and confident beliefs, he was becoming her guard, mentor, and friend. The gesture, Kelly presumed, was one of camaraderie in this adventure of discovery, and at this moment she felt safe with him. She hoped that one day she might trust him in a way she had not trusted anyone since her parents died. She had few close friends; her life hadn't given her the time or opportunities to find and nourish friendship.

"This," he said, eagerly pulling her across the grass, "is the perfect church to illustrate how we know history, how we recognize truth. And this may be part of your godfather's plan, even part of his work on Mary Magdalene. Let's see what we know about Helena, mother of Constantine."

"But who will give us the next letter? Is this a monastery church?" Kelly glanced at the side buildings. "We need to find the third letter."

"Cistercians from Saint Saba are in residence. Perhaps one of them is waiting." His tone was both hopeful and teasing.

He led her in the morning light through the oval portico and into the church. They paused at the foot of the nave. Rows of empty chairs covered the circular-tiled floor of the long narrow nave, and beyond, a cobalt blue apse rose over the high altar. Daniel released her hand, dipped a finger in the holy water font, and made the Sign of the Cross.

"It's beautiful," Kelly whispered, staring at the apse. Realizing that she was holding her breath, she exhaled slowly into the cool air. "What a lovely blue." The color drew her in, like a deep ocean of sky.

"The apsidal fresco is fifteenth-century." Daniel led her up the aisle for a closer view. "We aren't sure who painted it—some say Antoniazzo Romano, but it's one of the loveliest frescoes in Rome." Daniel pointed to a large medallion in the center. "That's Christ blessing his followers as he holds the Book of the Gospels with the Latin, *Ego sum via et veritas et vita:* I am the Way, the Truth, and the Life."

"The truth," Kelly repeated. "It's the theme you were talking about."

"Yes, I think we're on the right track." Daniel studied the frescoes. "The figures along the base tell the story of Helena finding the cross of Christ's crucifixion."

Kelly searched the nave for someone who might help them. A few tourists wandered the aisles.

Daniel glanced at her, his eyes bright with discovery. "I think I might guess as to the next church on Father Gilbert's list."

"But we haven't found the letter—"

"I may be wrong, but the first church was Maria Maggiore—*birth*. And this one is Santa Croce, which would be *death*. In the eighteenth century, the area between the basilicas of Santa Croce, San Giovanni Laterano, and Santa Maria Maggiore was leveled to create straight avenues connecting them. The resulting triangle told the story of Christ and created a processional route. Remember the Corpus Christi procession last night? That was one side of the triangle—from San Giovanni Laterano to Maria Maggiore."

"Aren't you jumping ahead?"

"It's a possibility." He scratched his beard.

"Finish the story of Helena. The clue should be in her story." *Not in the triangle,* Kelly thought.

They sat in the first row of chairs and gazed at the blue dome soaring over the ornate canopied altar.

Daniel said quietly, "Okay, here's Helena's story. She was Empress of the Roman Empire, and later Dowager Empress. Toward the end of her life she made a pilgrimage to Jerusalem, where she found Christ's cross. At the time, basilicas were being constructed over sacred sites in the Jerusalem area, by order of her son Constantine. The basilica over the site of Christ's crucifixion was called the Martyrion and the one over the site of Christ's tomb was called the Holy Sepulchre. In the process she found the cross of his crucifixion."

"That's remarkable." As she listened to Daniel, Kelly saw Helena. She saw the digs. "I wonder how old she was."

"Quite elderly, probably in her eighties. Writers at the time, including Ambrose of Milan, report that she left a third of the cross in Jerusalem, sent a third to her son in Constantinople, and brought a third back to Rome with other relics. She also brought soil from Mount Calvary and spread it over the floor of her private chapel, where she kept the relics."

"She spread the soil over the floor? Is her chapel still here?" Kelly kept her eye on the massive nave, still hoping to see someone who might help them.

"It's in the back, behind the sanctuary. So when Helena died, Constantine converted the atrium of her palace into this basilica, incorporating her bedroom and chapel into the back wall. As early as the fourth century this basilica was known as the Jerusalem Church and associated with the relics of the True Cross."

"Big atrium," Kelly said, thinking over what he said. "So we know she lived and died, we know she traveled to Jerusalem, and we know a church was built to house relics of the cross. We can say that much is true."

"But we do not know for sure," Daniel added, "that Helena was the one who brought back the wood of the Cross. It is *probable* that this was the case. So we have a somewhat different type of truth, parallel but most likely converging."

They stepped to the south aisle, where wide shallow steps descended through a tunnel-like passage, and Kelly sensed she was once again traveling into the past, to an age different, yet similar to her own. She wanted to know the empress, to speak with her. Would she meet her one day in heaven? She thought of her mother, who had lived in these other worlds of research and teaching, and Kelly glimpsed the allure of history. Her mother had often seemed distant, her love partially hidden by other thoughts and feelings, as though a gauzy drape separated her from the present. Now gripped by yearning, Kelly longed to turn the clock back, to be her mother's little girl again, and she faced Daniel with renewed attention, partly to escape the pull and partly to allow it, feeling oddly ambivalent.

"These rooms are not actually the crypt," he was saying, "that is, not a traditional crypt beneath the basilica, as one finds in many churches. This chapel is a bit lower than the main church, only because they raised the basilica flooring in the twelfth century. The fact that they didn't touch the flooring of Helena's chapel is further evidence they believed something special was there—in this case, the soil."

"More conjecture," Kelly said, "but pretty convincing." They entered the first room, which opened onto a second room. "Look at the mosaics!" She pointed to the ceiling. "They're beautiful. Another medallion of Christ holding a book. What does the book say?" She squinted at the Latin.

" '*Ego sum lux mundi,*' meaning, 'I am the Light of the World.' "

"There's definitely a theme of seeing, of vision. True Cross. Truth. Light. Was this the floor where Helena spread the soil?"

Daniel nodded. "It was. This room was her chapel, called *Cubiculum Sanctae Helenae.*" He pointed to the right wall. "At some point the relics were walled in a niche in the apsidal arch and not discovered until a fifteenth-century restoration. Inscriptions claimed they were fragments of the True Cross."

"That's pretty good evidence."

"For most of us. But historians distrust what we call *interested* accounts, that is, records or evidence given by those who have something to gain by their being true."

"Like prejudiced? But everyone has their own set of prejudices." She thought of Dr. Sansby, who saw truth a little differently than her godfather did, or than Daniel did. She shivered. One could say he was prejudiced in a false direction, with false intentions.

"That's exactly the point. Honesty is the key to a reliable authority. Every historian has a prejudicial viewpoint, for that's human nature. The question we ask is whether the person's intentions are honest and of course whether or not he or she is qualified."

"But where does all this leave us? And what is in the second room? There seems to be an altar."

"That was Helena's bedroom, but today it's used as a chapel for the monks."

A wrought-iron grill separated the sanctuary from a small choir, the pews running along the sides. Behind the grill, Kelly could see a red candle flaming on the altar. Daniel genuflected, and they returned to the main basilica.

"The Jerusalem relics aren't in the chapel anymore. They've been moved upstairs. Would you like to see them?"

"Sure." Sensing that Helena's chapel was more important than the relics, she was reluctant to leave.

They crossed to the northern aisle and passed through a doorway to a wide stairwell lined with Stations of the Cross. At the top of the stairs they passed under a wooden beam mounted over the landing that read *The Cross of the Good Thief.* Beyond, behind glass, smaller relics were displayed: fragments of the cross, the title on the cross, a nail, two thorns, the finger of Saint Thomas, bits of the scourging column.

"The relics of death," Daniel said quietly, "kept here for a good reason."

"And what would that be?" Kelly whispered.

"Relics remind us of our own death, that suffering is a part of life. These relics recall Good Friday and God's immense love for us." He turned to her, observing her reaction.

"Today is Friday," she said.

"So it is." His dark eyes squinted as he nodded with appreciation.

They descended the stairs and returned to the nave. As they gazed at the blue apse once again, Kelly heard chanting, faint and faraway. As though in counterpoint, bells rang noon from the distant tower.

Daniel contemplated the high altar and tabernacle beneath the golden canopy. "This church unites the mystical Body of Christ in the tabernacle with the wood of the cross that made it all possible, uniting the Eucharist with the crucifixion."

Kelly considered the connection, and although she appreciated the powerful association, felt a mounting impatience. "But where does that leave us? What's the clue? Where should we inquire? The monastery next door?"

"And ask if there's a secret letter addressed to one Kelly Roberts?"

"There might be. We could ask."

"Let's return to Helena's Chapel where the monks must be singing the noon office. I love to hear them sing." He looked wistful, and Kelly wondered if he would indeed join an order.

*

They paused in the chapel doorway. In the far room, a dozen white-robed monks chanted in Latin, the song floating through the mosaic vaults. One of the men raised his eyes from his missal and gazed at them briefly. He closed his book, set it down carefully, and, leaning on a wooden cane, joined them. He beckoned them into the main church.

"Welcome," he said quietly with a heavy Italian accent, his haggard face expectant. "We sing the Psalms in praise to God." He was tall, with gray ethereal eyes. A tonsure of silver hair circled his head and the pale skin of his face was mapped with red spider veins.

"What about the *Apostles' Creed*," Daniel said hopefully. "Do you sing that too?"

The old monk's face lit up. "Ah, Santa Maria! At last, you have come. I watch for you, always watching. I am Brother Sebastian. I am pleased to make your acquaintance." He bowed from the waist and pulled a letter from his robe, his eyes roving from Daniel to Kelly. He touched his finger to his lips, then whispered, "You are Signore Weaver and Signorina Roberts, am I correct?"

"We are," they said.

Kelly studied his face, mystical in the half light as though a halo had settled over his features, giving him a soft glow.

He bent toward them earnestly. "A big man with a large hat visited this morning, asking about a letter he was to receive. He wore dark glasses, and I could not see his eyes. I do not like it when I cannot see the eyes. And hats are not good in church. And he did not say the right words." He shook his head with worry and wrinkled his brow, the skin tight over his forehead. "He said he came from Maria Maggiore. Do you know him?" He handed the letter to Kelly with fingers that were red and swollen at the joints.

Kelly felt faint as she took the letter. "The man with the hat in Maria Maggiore." She tried to concentrate and with shaking fingers slipped her thumbnail under the now-familiar seal and pulled out the delicate paper.

Daniel glanced at the monk. "You did the right thing. Someone seems to be following us." He turned to Kelly, and they read the words silently.

My dear Kelly,
Sebastian is a good man, a brother in Christ. If you are reading this, you have met this saint of Santa Croce.

In this church of the Holy Cross you see Saint Helena. Here you travel into the early days of our Church, the beginnings.

In the passion of Christ we face death. Because of our sin, our selfishness, we deserve death. But Our Lord heals the great rift between the Creator and the Creation by his own death and resurrection. Sin is literally of *deadly* consequence. Like a parasite, it feeds off the good of creation. Sin negates the order, the making sense of life, taking us back to chaos. The sacraments return us to union with God, to the good, to life. They are Christ; they are the Way, the Truth, and the Life.

The Apostles' Creed is the clue to the universe.

You saw in Santa Susanna the nature of truth and lies. You have seen birth and death. And now you must experience the third great event in man's history. Solve this clue in order to understand the mysterious Magdalene:

Life and death and life again
In canopy, tomb, and gold:
Peter, Paul, Martin, Magdalene,
The ancient story told.

Daniel appeared confused. Kelly asked him, "Does this fit in with your idea of the next church?" She took out her camera.

"Yes and no. Let's talk about it over lunch."

Kelly photographed the letter and checked her display panel.

"Please," said Sebastian, "I need to destroy this. I promised."

Kelly kept the letter for another moment, feeling its fragility. Her godfather had written these words. She recognized the script. He had written the words of the letter at Santa Susanna and the words of the letter at Maria

Maggiore. The one that had come in the mail had been typed, as though either his scrawl was illegible, or he had needed help at the last minute. How she longed to keep these relics of him. She handed the letter to Brother Sebastian but kept the envelope.

The monk turned to a burning candle on a low chest and lit the corner of the paper. The flames leapt into the dim light, and he dropped the letter onto a pewter plate. Soon the ash sent a wisp of smoke and smell of char into the air.

With apparent relief, Brother Sebastian glanced up to the mosaic Christ in the vaulted ceiling and nodded. He gazed upon Kelly and Daniel with affection, as though they were beloved reminders of his good friend Keith Gilbert. He withdrew from his pocket a wooden crucifix on a long brown cord and handed it to Kelly. "Keep this to remember," he said, "to remember Santa Croce and to keep us in your prayers. It once belonged to your godfather. It now belongs to you. It is carved from the cedars of Lebanon."

Kelly studied the small crucifix, about one by two inches. She closed her fingers upon it, feeling its lightness and somehow its strength. She looked into Sebastian's eyes with gratitude. "Thank you. This means a lot to me." What else could she say, here in this mystical space at this moment in her life? Too little, she knew, but she kissed the old man on the cheek and giddily put her godfather's crucifix into a safe pocket in her bag. She would not forget Santa Croce, and she would keep the monks in her all-too-infrequent prayers. Perhaps she would learn to pray.

Brother Sebastian smiled. "*Grazie,* my child." He blessed them, making the Sign of the Cross over their heads. "Go in peace." His voice was thin and reedy, but his eyes burned warm with encouragement. He laced his long fingers together and bowed again from the waist.

"Thank you, Brother," they said.

They returned to the nave and, after a fleeting glance back to Helena's chapel, walked down the south aisle to the front doors. The chapel and the monk, the letters from her godfather, the delicate crucifix on the leather thong, all lingered in Kelly's mind as they stepped through the vaulted oval porch and crossed the green lawn, blinded by the sudden light.

13

Hank

IT WAS NEARLY ONE when they bought *panini* and sodas at a roadside stand and headed up the Via Carlo Felice. A wide, straight sidewalk lined by leafy plane trees ran between the road and a park where children played. They entered the park, found a bench, and unwrapped mozzarella and tomato sandwiches. Kelly popped open her can of soda, thinking with some nervousness of the stalker.

"The man Brother Sebastian saw," Kelly said, "must be this Dr. Sansby, the same man as in Maria Maggiore."

"Let's not jump to conclusions too quickly." Daniel's manner was reserved, but he turned to her with honest eyes. "Still it sounds like he could be Sansby. On the other hand, neither of us has seen him up close."

"Are you sure he's not dangerous? That is, other than his blogs? Is he physically dangerous?"

Pain flashed across his features. "He could be. And there are many ways of destroying people that don't involve bloodletting."

Kelly started to ask what he meant, but stopped, concerned that she was intruding. "But what about my apartment? And Father Francis's office? What about Father Gilbert's suspicious death?" What about her parents? As she made the list, her fear grew, and her chest tightened. "We should give this thing up and go home. It's not worth it, Daniel."

"Let's address these issues one by one."

His calm tone steadied her. If logic prevailed, Kelly held on as though it offered safety, sanity. Or was it all an illusion? The working of their minds? The comfort of reason?

"First your apartment," Daniel began. "I've been thinking that one of his followers, or possibly Sansby himself, broke into your apartment, but of course we have no proof, other than his interest in the manuscript, his note to me, and his general character. The same would go for Father Francis's office. Your description of the man in Maria Maggiore sounds like him, but it sounds like a lot of people."

"True," Kelly said, realizing she was jumping to conclusions.

"As for Father Gilbert's death being connected to Sansby—we have no idea, and we don't even know for sure that there was foul play."

Kelly sipped her cola. "That's true. We shouldn't rush to judgment."

In spite of his words, Daniel looked uncertain. It was as though his mind was trying to govern his heart, his reason trying to rule his feelings. "But then, on the other hand, we should face the fact that Internet trolls can urge folks who might be slightly unstable into actions they may later regret. Recent studies show a link between incendiary bloggers and violence." He took small bites, chewing thoughtfully, then removed his laptop from his backpack. "Here, let's see what our bandit is up to at the moment, and if I need to rescue anyone. That is, if I can get a signal and log on."

He was able to tap into a signal, and Kelly watched him find the *SmartReads* site, then click to a discussion group.

"Let's check the group I mentioned at dinner last night."

"The 'We believe in Jesus' site?"

"Right. What Hank did here is pretty dishonest. As I said, he took over the group's moderator position. He joined and participated, bringing in his friends, until he could be voted in and then changed the character of the group, keeping the title and the description. So now it is the atheists and agnostics who are moderating, and trying to convert, or de-convert if you will, the Christians who walk into what they think is a friendly group, a self-described Christian group."

"But they're doing the same thing the Christians were doing."

"That's okay. But I do mind that the group keeps the Christian name and description, which is fraudulent and confusing. It's below-the-belt and dirty pool, as my father used to say."

Kelly adjusted her glasses, squinting to see some of the text. "It's like an ambush."

"Precisely." Daniel pointed to a passage and zoomed in on it. "Here is one of his shorter replies, around two thousand words."

Kelly began to read and soon grew discouraged. "This is a very long answer to a very short comment."

"Let's check out the original discussion question: 'Why do you believe in Jesus?' This Christian, whose screen name is Sophie, posted a particularly well-known defense, the 'Liar, Lunatic, Lord' argument. Simply put, the argument states that Christ would have to be either a liar or a lunatic or who he claimed to be, that is, the Son of God."

"And the reply? Look at this! He goes on and on."

"The point here isn't actually the argument, but the tone and the bullying. Clearly Sophie is young. In fact I've read her profile on *SmartReads,* and she states she's seventeen. Our professor here is much older and used to manipulating words. This is hardly a fair match. But in his treatise he brings in all sorts of prophecies and Gospel inconsistencies which may or may not bear weight. The danger is the tone. He calls her arguments silly, stupid, asinine, tired. If she reads the entire thing, I believe she will feel pretty beaten down, and will begin to question her faith for the wrong reasons. For she hasn't heard the Christian scholar's answer to this atheist scholar. The playing field is grossly unfair."

As Kelly listened to Daniel, her admiration grew. He really cared about these kids. "So, as their knight in shining armor, what do you do?" She recalled his father and guessed he was Daniel's knight in shining armor.

"Watch and learn." Daniel began to type a few words into the dialogue box, replying positively to Sophie's comments and briefly answering Hank's arguments. He was respectful of both, while supporting Sophie. "I can't enter her heart and mind. But I can support her right to respect and dignity in the debate." He clicked *publish* and his comment flashed onto the screen. "One more hostage released." He signed off.

"That's good of you to do that."

"Perhaps, but it's a drop in a sea of malice that is swamping young believers. Anyway, my real work is with the newsletter. The twisting of the truth seems to be everywhere, not just with the kids online."

"Give me an example from your work with *Opus Veritatis.*"

He considered for a moment. "Here's an ongoing issue. A recurring and dangerous theme circulated by the media is the idea that we are overpopulating the earth. While it's true there is a rise in worldwide population, the West is actually shrinking. In my articles I quote the statistics, give the facts. Paul Ehrlich's book *The Population Bomb* back in 1968 started it all. He warned there would be mass starvation and other dire consequences in the seventies. His theories have been discredited again and again, but they resurface regularly. So I set folks straight with a few simple facts."

"Does it make a big difference? It sounds like bad science."

Daniel grew troubled. "Indeed, it makes a huge difference what folks believe about this issue. A crowded world invites population control, abortion, euthanasia. The trends are already here—assisted suicide, the right to die, other movements that turn people into objects, embryos into scientific experiments, the elderly no longer revered but unwanted. To say we have too many people is to dehumanize every one of us." He raised his hands as though imploring heaven to help. "What these doomsayers don't take into account is the human spirit and the remarkable ability of man to solve problems. As numbers rose in Asia and Africa in the last fifty years, more efficient means of food production were developed. Folks actually live better worldwide than ever before."

"I see what you mean. *Dehumanize* is a good word."

"It's scary sometimes—the consequences of half-truths."

"I agree, Daniel, but you tell the truth—to the kids online and to the world. That's so noble."

"Maybe noble, but so necessary! I get so angry at the lies out there. My father…" Daniel wrung his hands, as though gripped by a tension that was nearly crippling. He was controlling his anger and paying the price somewhere deep.

Kelly ventured, "Was your father a victim of lies as well?"

Daniel blanched. "He was indeed. But I'd rather not talk about it. It devastated our family."

"I'm sorry. I shouldn't have asked. I understand." Then, with a lighter tone, she said, "We need to find Father Gilbert's research."

"I think we're close." He was gazing out to the horizon now, seeming to pull himself together. He closed his laptop, stretched, and massaged the back of his neck with his fingertips.

She smiled hopefully. "Where to now?"

He pointed up the walkway. "I think the next church is Saint John Lateran, but I'm not positive."

"The church where the Corpus Christi procession began?"

"The same. The three churches form a triangle, as I said. It was a triangle of faith, a triangle of the creed: birth, death, resurrection."

"The Creed! So it would fit into the pattern of belief. *Apostles' Creed* isn't just a password. It's more of a code."

"Exactly. Let's review the Creed. 'I believe in God, the Father Almighty, Creator of heaven and earth; and in Jesus Christ, His only Son, our Lord: Who was conceived by the Holy Spirit, born of the Virgin Mary.' "

"So that was Maria Maggiore."

"Right. And then it goes on to say, 'suffered under Pontius Pilate, was crucified, died and was buried.' "

"And that was Santa Croce."

"So the next church, I thought, must reflect the Creed as well: 'He descended into hell; the third day He rose again from the dead; He ascended into heaven, is seated at the right hand of God the Father Almighty; from thence He shall come to judge the living and the dead. I believe in the Holy

Spirit, the Holy Catholic Church, the communion of saints, the forgiveness of sins, the resurrection of the body, and life everlasting.'"

"So you think the next church is John Lateran?"

"The pattern is clearly birth, death, resurrection. All of Rome's churches celebrate the Resurrection, but the Lateran has traditionally been associated with the resurrection portion of the triangle. Now, the riddle:

Life and death and life again
In canopy, tomb, and gold:
Peter, Paul, Martin, Magdalene,
The ancient story told.

Kelly was confused. "Peter, Paul, Martin, Magdalene. The church is dedicated to John, right? And aren't there two Johns? The Baptist and the Evangelist? But John isn't even mentioned in the poem."

"The church is dedicated to both Johns, as co-patrons, but the original dedication was to Christ the Savior. The heads of Peter and Paul are in the reliquary above the altar. Pope Martin V is buried in the *confessio*."

It was coming together. "So that's it! Let's go!" She smoothed out her map and examined the fine print, the lines intersecting. She figured out where they were and where they wanted to go. *San Giovanni Laterano.*

Daniel shook his head. "I'm not sure, and I hate to waste precious time on a wild goose chase. It's a giant basilica—it could take days to find what we are searching for. And we don't know where our friend with the hat is."

"What's the problem?"

"I'm not sure about the poem's reference to Mary Magdalene. I've never heard that she or her relics have any association with this basilica. I do recall one legend that claimed she was in Rome and preached to the Emperor Tiberius. But she is mainly associated with Ephesus and Provence."

"Ephesus? As in Paul's letter to the Ephesians?"

"The same—it was a Greek city, then a Roman city, in what is today Turkey."

"Still, there must be some connection with Rome. Maybe we'll find out at the Lateran church."

"Maybe, and maybe not."

"When did you say the Magdalene symposium is?"

"A week from tomorrow."

"Maybe Santa Susanna has something to do with all of this."

"I don't think so. Santa Susanna was the Prologue—remember? And had its own themes of art and community and truth."

"Now I'm totally confused. Isn't there a church in Rome that is dedicated to Mary Magdalene? There must be. All the other saints seem to have churches."

"There is, and that's a possibility. La Maddalena is certainly golden, Rococo Baroque, charming. It's not far from the Pantheon. But there's no Peter or Paul or Martin. There's a Saint Camillus and a haunting Madonna and Child. Then again, I believe the Camillians once helped Father Gilbert's family, so that would be a connection."

"Father Gilbert was connected to the Magdalene church?" Kelly's heart skipped a beat. "That must be it!"

"Let's go to the Laterano first. The riddle and the Apostles' Creed triangle both point to the basilica."

They tossed the wrappings and cans into a trash bin and headed up the walkway.

Daniel squinted toward her. "And keep your eye out for the saintly beggar from Assisi, Francis Bernadone."

Kelly laughed. Drawn into these colorful churches with their colorful saints, along with the challenging mystery and veiled threats, she had nearly forgotten home. She had nearly, but not quite, forgotten to worry about Matt.

*

From his corner table, Lester Sansby surveyed the bistro bar as it filled up with lunch customers. Even with the packed tables, the mood was quiet this time of day, the way he liked it, and the server, a college student with gorgeous breasts that nearly bounced out of her low-cut tee, was most attentive. She wore a leather mini-skirt that he appreciated as well, particularly when she bent over to pull glassware from a lower cabinet.

"Can I get you anything else, handsome?" She spoke English, American English, as she polished the countertop, her long burgundy-black nails caressing the terry cloth. She leaned forward, smiling, as her precious puppies jiggled.

"Hit me once more, sweetie," Lester said, drowning in her cleavage.

She brought him another shot of whiskey, and he laid the cash on the table, a little extra with a wink and a nod.

He had grown so tired of waiting for Weaver and the girl to show up at Santa Croce, watching from behind a massive shade tree, he feared that he had lost his intuition and timing. Earlier, Frizzle had said that the Santa Croce basilica, like Maria Maggiore, housed famous relics. It stood to reason that relics might be a pattern, a clue, in the movement of the odd couple, and when Lester spoke to the giant monk in Santa Croce, he thought he was on the right track. The old man clearly had been watching for someone, no doubt about it. Lester owed Frizzle for that one.

But he grew tired of waiting outside and had finally settled into this bistro bar across the street. They had Wi-Fi so he could get some online work done. Drinking one espresso after another, he watched the church through the window, occasionally checking his sites and posting. When Weaver and the girl showed up, he congratulated himself, deciding to wait for their exit. At noon he ordered lunch. The lunch had been welcome—the cannelloni and mushroom sauce not bad, and the bottle of house red nearly adequate.

When the cute little couple left the church he watched them stop at a food stand, then settle on a park bench under a flowering elm. *How precious, a picnic.*

But why couldn't his Treats come up with something better than minor facts about relics? One of his disciples took credit for a search at the Santa Susanna church but found nothing. Fab kept hinting involvement in Gilbert's death but wouldn't elaborate. How had Gilbert died? Was it more than heart failure?

Lester *had* suggested that Gilbert would be happier if he went to his just reward in heaven than he could ever be on earth. Several disciples claimed credit for the collapse, using codes, but Fab's claim sounded eerily authentic. Earlier, there had been a note of cold desperation in his online comments that was downright chilling. Had the young man gone that far? Was he, Lester Sansby, that powerful? His Treats frustrated him—it was difficult to know what was true. He had offered an enticing reward, a cut of the treasure, and you would think these young folks might at least get off their butts and scratch the surface. They seemed to have no ambition these days, no stamina. They lost interest way too quickly with their cartoon attention spans. They diddled and they dawdled.

But where were Weaver and friend going next? He could see they were still on the park bench and probably would be for a while. He groaned. This was way too tedious. But he would persist; he would conquer. There was so much to gain and so much to lose, he repeated to himself.

Soon the wine and the whiskey restored Lester's sense of control. He swallowed a pill. He lit a cigarette. He went so far as to state to himself that he was quite optimistic as to the outcome of this adventure. He decided he would move to the counter and enjoy a little conversation with the beguiling breasts.

They seemed sort of lonely. They needed cheering up. He could glance back from time to time through the window and up the street. He deserved a little break. He was entitled.

He slid out of the booth and onto the chrome stool. He sipped his whiskey slowly, savoring the warmth, eyeing the breasts, taking an occasional puff of his cigarette. Rome wasn't half bad, he thought, not half bad at all.

14

Resurrection

THE HUGE STATUE OF FRANCIS OF ASSISI rose above the traffic, swallows resting on his outstretched arms. Kelly wondered if this depicted the moment Francis received the stigmata. She recalled the story but not the details—Francis desiring the pain of Christ's crucifixion. She focused her camera on the sculpted image, dark against the bright sky, hoping the sensitive eye of the camera saw what she could not. At least it was a reminder of the moment, their standing in the busy intersection in Rome, waiting for the pedestrian light to change and anticipating their visit to San Giovanni in Laterano.

The light turned green, and they crossed to a wide drive that led to the basilica. The drive parted a broad swath of weedy grass, but Kelly thought the church looked like an elegant palace with double-tiered porticoes and columns and an impressive entrance. A reddish three-storied building stood to the right, a contrast to the white basilica.

"In 1209," Daniel said, "Francis came here—a poor, young beggar—to ask the Pope for approval of his new order, the Friars Minor, but was denied. That night the Pope dreamed Francis was supporting the Church with his hands, preventing it from falling down. He called Francis back and approved the order."

"So they met here?" Kelly focused on the façade and clicked, then showed the image to Daniel.

"You have a good eye. They met in the palace next door." He gestured to the ocher building. "This was the Pope's residence. Francis lived in the early thirteenth century, and Rome looked quite different then, before the Renaissance works of Borromini, Bernini, and Michelangelo, before the modern city crowded the churches. Before the present Saint Peter's Basilica was built."

Kelly tried to imagine the times. Today's traffic noise and fumes, the tour buses, the souvenir vendors, all made it difficult.

Daniel pointed to the white façade. "Eighteenth-century. Much of the interior is seventeenth. But the first church and palace were built by Constantine in the fourth century."

"Why is it called Lateran?" Kelly hoped some piece of information might lead them to the next clue.

Daniel smiled. "One of those flukes of history. Constantine defeated Maxentius, his rival. You may remember the story. In a dream Constantine saw the *Chi-Rho*, the sign of Christ. Constantine made the letters his standard, his banner, and his troops were victorious."

"I do remember something like that."

"Maxentius was part of the Lateran family, so this property—his old barracks—was owned by his family, hence *in Laterano*."

"A location name."

"Right."

"Look at the sculptures on the roof…" She pointed to the parapet where the white figures intersected the sky. "That must be Christ holding the cross—it *is* a resurrection basilica like you said."

"Constantine's dedication, vanquishing the pagan gods."

"Dedicated to Christ Our Savior." She climbed the steps to the porch, Daniel alongside.

"Popes lived here for the next thousand years. In the late fourteenth century they returned from France—having lived in Avignon for seventy years—and found it crumbling, destroyed by fires, so they moved to Vatican Hill."

"Where Saint Peter was buried."

"And where the fourth-century church remained. From there Martin V began restorations on this one."

"So if the papacy hadn't moved to Avignon, the Pope would still be living here?"

Daniel nodded. "But I think that the importance of Peter's grave and martyrdom site eventually would have lured them to Vatican Hill."

They passed through the massive portico and entered the church, pausing at the foot of the nave. Kelly's first impression was one of light, light pouring from clerestory windows high above, light splashing on the marble floor. White oversized statues seemed to leap from side aisles, and she judged they must be the twelve apostles. Far up the nave, at the transept crossing, a tall steeple-like structure crowned the high altar. It was golden and intricate with frescoes and gilded screens.

Daniel followed her eye. "Behind the uppermost screen, near the top, reliquaries contain the heads of Peter and Paul."

"Their heads?" Kelly strained to see, but the silver busts were too high and far up. She focused her camera, zooming in, but guessed the image would be blurred. Maybe there would be a book with pictures. The church was fascinating, with these details, like an intricate historic puzzle.

"Indeed! The relics in Rome are astounding, some more believable than others."

"I'll bet the history—the provenance as they say in art—of *these* relics is trustworthy. They would be more important, so folks would document them."

"That's right." They walked slowly up the central aisle between the giant apostles, toward the transept. "This high altar contains the old wooden altar of the first popes going back to Peter. Today, only the Pope or his nominated representative is allowed to celebrate Mass at this altar."

"The basilica is a historic treasure house, like a living museum. So that would be the early, early, early Church?"

"The Church of the first-to-fourth centuries. It was once believed that Pope Sylvester baptized Constantine in the fourth century…in the baptistery next door."

Kelly absorbed the facts, fitting the pieces of history together, annoyed at the gaps in her education. Midway up the aisle, she paused to survey the vast nave behind and before her, the gleaming marbles, the intricate inlays of gold and blue. It was a giant jewel box. As Daniel spoke, she slipped into this dream of beauty, born of visual richness and texture but also born of the many faith-stories. "So, clearly Peter and Paul are here. Where's Martin? Martin, by the way, was my father's name."

"A good name." He smiled. "Now follow me." They reached the high altar with its canopied tower and peered down into the half circle ringing the *confessio*. "Pope Martin V is buried here, under the altar, since he built much of this church."

Once again things were falling into place in Kelly's mind. "But where's the fourth name? Where's Mary Magdalene?" *And she would be the most important in this quest.*

"That's the problem, but I think we're on the right track." He turned left toward a gleaming chapel in the north transept.

"Magnificent." Kelly stared at the giant gilded columns behind the altar rail, and the smaller green marble columns framing the altar itself. A red candle burned alongside a glittering bronze tabernacle that resembled a miniature domed church. High above the altar Kelly could see a golden Last Supper scene hammered in brass. Light poured from clerestory windows. The chapel glimmered.

Daniel rubbed his beard. "It is said that the cedar of the table of the Last Supper is enshrined in the altar, but I'm not so sure."

Kelly strained to study the Last Supper scene, even at the high distance. It reminded her of Leonardo da Vinci's more famous one. "You aren't sure?" She studied the altar, which seemed plain compared with its bronze tabernacle.

"From what I've read, tables weren't used for meals in the days of Christ. Diners reclined on cushions. But who's to say for sure? Wisdom is knowing what you do not know, the knowledge of not-knowing."

"So some relics are in doubt?"

"Many have some degree of doubt, so we speak of degrees of probability. The Church has long fought superstition and is careful to use the right words when dealing with authenticity. Some relics aren't mentioned at all in guidebooks, which is going too far, to my way of thinking. Guides like to talk about the provenance of pillars and such." He shook his head. "But it all helps reconstruct the scene, I suppose." He studied the massive bronze pillars. "Those are said to come from the fourth-century church, and before that, from a Roman temple."

Kelly photographed the altar and tabernacle, then the Last Supper frieze high above. "So beautiful." Daniel now seemed to be praying, making the Sign of the Cross, and genuflecting. She genuflected as well, and they turned toward the giant apsidal bay directly behind the high altar.

"The mosaic shows Christ the Savior reigning from heaven," he explained as he pointed to the papal chair in the center. "On Maundy Thursday, this is where the Pope washes the feet of his cardinals, just as Christ washed the feet of his disciples at the Last Supper, in an act of sacrificial love, as their servant."

"This church emphasizes the Last Supper? As well as the Resurrection?"

"Yes, which means emphasizing the Eucharist. Let me think this through…. The Eucharist—the liturgy—is thought to be a journey of the Church into the Kingdom of God. Alexander Schmemann wrote that it is 'our sacramental entrance into the risen life of Christ.' "

"Risen life! So that ties in the Resurrection, doesn't it?"

Daniel laughed. "It does, of course! And I didn't see it right in front of me. This is a Eucharistic church—the cedar from the Last Supper table, the wood from Saint Peter's altar, the washing of the feet at the Last Supper. They all point to the new life given through the sacrifice and resurrection of Christ, and through the Eucharistic action of the Mass, effected by the Church through the years. So the Eucharist becomes a conduit of Christ's love for us." He glanced back to the great nave with the giant apostles. "The Eucharist brings Christ among us, merging past, present, and future. The apostles of that Last Supper lining the nave all point to the altar where the eternal supper is offered."

Kelly worked to follow the reasoning, the images, one upon another. She was beginning to understand. But clearly there were many resurrections in this church, or perhaps facets of resurrections, like great art, a fugue, a symphony. "It's a true resurrection church, even our own resurrections."

"Exactly right. It fits in with the theme of the triangle, and the Apostle's Creed: birth, death, resurrection. We must be close. There must be some connection with all of this to Mary Magdalene."

"She was the one who witnessed the resurrected Christ, wasn't she?" The image came to her unbidden, as though she recalled a painting or a fresco from long ago. The young woman reaching to touch her risen Lord, and his words to her, "Mary…*Noli me tangere.* Do not hinder me."

"True, she was the first witness, but there must be more than that. There must be something of hers, here in this church."

"What about the Baptism angle? You said there's a baptistery here? That would be a kind of resurrection too, wouldn't it?" Maybe they would find the next person with the next clue in the baptistery. She scanned the nave. No one waiting for them here. "Or we could try the gift shop if there's a gift shop and inquire like we did in Maria Maggiore."

"There is a gift shop, but let's visit the baptistery first," Daniel said. "Baptism is our first resurrection, and in the basilica the Eucharist is our second, and one could say, ongoing resurrection."

They exited through the south transept. Outside, a domed octagon stood between the basilica and the road. The brick baptistery was brown with age, a heavy contrast to the light marble of the basilica.

"This was built in 315," Daniel explained, "so was probably the model for the first baptisteries. These are actually the original Constantinian walls."

Kelly touched the gritty brick, and they entered through a low door. A large octagonal basin, about eight feet in diameter, was encircled by a wide aisle and thick columns. The basin was dry but contained a small altar and a few chairs. "There was once water in here? Was this where Pope Sylvester baptized Constantine?"

"Tradition says so, but the legend has recently been disputed. The age of the baptistery and its importance are unquestioned, and this would have been the only place to be baptized in Rome in the fourth century."

"The only place? What about the other churches?"

"In those first decades after Christianity was legalized, this was the only place, the central place. As the faith grew, more conversions meant more Baptisms, and churches built their own fonts close by, finally moving them into the church. But at first, cathedrals were the centers of Baptisms, and baptisteries were separate buildings."

"That makes sense." Kelly imagined the trip to the Lateran font for the great event. It must have been like a pilgrimage, walking out to the city walls.

Daniel nodded. "Converts became *catechumens* and received instruction during Lent. On Easter Eve, they recited a creed similar to the Apostles' Creed. In fact, our creed evolved from those early phrases linked together. Next the catechumens were immersed in the pool of water. When they emerged they put on white robes. They were washed of their sins and made one with the Body of Christ, the Church."

They paused before a Madonna and Child, where a bank of votives burned in an iron stand, then explored two chapels. Daniel showed her the original entrance that would have connected the baptistery to the basilica. But there was no letter, no clue.

She followed Daniel outside into the hazily bright morning. "What's that across the street?" She pointed to people climbing stairs on their knees. The stairs led to a landing and open doors.

"Those are the *Scala Sancta*, the Sacred Stairs, leading to several chapels. The staircase is older than the basilica, part of the original palace. But that's not why the stairs are considered sacred."

"Why are they sacred?"

"Legend claims that Saint Helena brought them from Jerusalem. They are said to be from Pilate's palace, the stairs that Christ climbed at his trial."

"Do you think the stairs are actually Pilate's?"

"They could be. But how were they transported? But then again, who would think to make up such a thing?" He grew pensive, as though working through one of the more shadowy areas of belief. "Pilgrims climb and pray. The ascent is a way of touching God. I have no problem with that; indeed, that is the mission of the Church, to give people ways to touch God."

Kelly judged that many would question this practice. "Why isn't this considered a superstition?"

"Because there's enough evidence to make it possible, unlike real superstitions."

"And becoming physically involved helps one spiritually." The day was heating up, and as they stood in the bright haze, Kelly exchanged her glasses for dark ones.

"It's the catholic way, the sacramental way."

"So where does all of this leave us?"

"Let's go over what we've learned," Daniel said, facing the basilica. "In Maria Maggiore we found Father Timothy in the sacristy. In Santa Croce we found Brother Sebastian in the chapel. *We* found *them*. Let's go back to the main church."

"And ask at the gift shop."

15

Sister Gabriella

THE GIFT SHOP OFF THE SOUTHERN TRANSEPT was long and narrow, probably a former side chapel, and crowded with tourists and pilgrims buying souvenirs. Several nuns in forest-green habits stood behind a counter displaying icons, rosaries, books, and medals. Kelly found a glossy book in English with colorful photos of the basilica. She approached the counter.

Daniel spoke a few words in Italian to one of the sisters. She nodded, disappeared through a side door, and soon returned with a bright-eyed nun in the same green habit.

"How can I help you?" the nun asked with an Irish lilt.

Kelly thought they were about the same age and was relieved to hear English spoken. The sister was attractive in a country manner, with a fresh, ingenuous face, strong brows, and regular features. She carried a sense of controlled energy, but most importantly, she invited trust.

"We are interested in the *Apostles' Creed*," Kelly said with more confidence than she had felt in some time.

"Aye, the *Apostles' Creed!* Welcome. I have been expecting you! God be praised, to be sure. You are from our dear Father Gilbert? Oh, my, that is lovely, lovely." She clapped her hands together and shifted her weight from side to side, regarding Kelly and Daniel with shining eyes. "Just like he said, to be sure! Just like he said! But forgive me, I have forgotten my manners, that I have. I am Sister Gabriella." She offered her hand.

Daniel and Kelly introduced themselves, and Daniel searched Gabriella's face as he asked, "Do you have a letter for us, Sister?"

"A letter? No, I do not have a letter, but I have something else. Come with me, if you will be so kind." Gabriella spoke a few quick words in Italian to a sister at the counter, and led them into the transept, her long skirts dusting the marble floors.

Kelly tried to hide her disappointment that there was no letter and followed Gabriella across the nave, through a door off the north aisle, and out to the cloisters. The pleasing corridors framed a square garden, creating a balanced space, and, Kelly thought, combined aesthetic appreciation with otherworldly peace. Lining the corridors, marble columns spiraled to scrolled capitals, and they reminded her of tree trunks growing together reaching for the light, like decorative ficus winding to a leafy crown. A mosaic frieze ran above the columns. In the center of the manicured green lawn, stood an ancient well of white stone, surrounded by pine, palm, and olive trees.

"When was this built?" Kelly asked, increasingly aware of the importance of history in their search.

"These cloisters are thirteenth century. They are all that remain of the Benedictine monastery that stood between the basilica and the city walls. Except for what I am going to show you." Sister Gabriella winked, tantalizing them, clearly enjoying her role as keeper of secrets.

They followed her along the colonnade of spiraling stone and stopped before a collection of sculpted fragments embedded in the interior wall. One grouping was labeled *MARIA MADDALENA*. Sun cascaded onto the pale terracotta.

"Mary Magdalene!" Kelly cried, glancing at Daniel.

Daniel stepped closer to inspect the fragments. "This must have been the tabernacle. It's a shame there are only pieces, but you can see how it could have been put together. This tabernacle and columns—they're spiraled too—must have been on the actual altar, which we don't seem to have."

"No, sadly," Gabriella said, "but here is a description that might help you picture it." She pointed to another plaque, this one in both English and Italian.

> In February of 1297 Cardinal Gerardo Bianchi from Parma consecrated the new Altar of Mary Magdalene, which had been erected in the Lateran basilica at the command of Pope Boniface VIII by the Roman sculptor Deodato di Cosma. The altar was situated at the center of the Canons' choir which is the space reserved for their prayer in the central nave. It was a complex and imposing structure on two levels placed on a podium of six steps. The lower part was the proper altar and had at the center a tabernacle containing other important relics exposed for the veneration of the faithful on particular feast days.
>
> During the reworking of the naves by Francesco Borromini the Altar of Mary Magdalene was dismantled, with many of its parts disappearing and those surviving eventually finding their final collocation in the cloister.

Kelly absorbed the information, searching for the next clue.

Daniel's eyes were wide. "Six steps led to the altar! And it was situated in the center of the choir. They clearly believed the altar contained Mary Magdalene's relics, or it wouldn't be in such an honored position." He sighed, his shoulders relaxing. "This explains the riddle."

Kelly caught his eye and nodded, feeling this was an important step forward, but, then again, where was the clue? Where to next? And with no letter…

"The riddle?" The nun raised her brows in curiosity. "I was told to bring you here, don't you know, and I am happy you are pleased, but—"

"Oh we are, Sister," Kelly said quickly, with appreciation, "very pleased."

"But there is a riddle?" Sister Gabriella cocked her head to the side and slipped her hands in her side pockets. "I was told to give you a message, but I am not sure the why or the wherefore, if you don't mind my saying. Nevertheless I am pleased to be doing the good Father's bidding, for I am greatly indebted to him, to be sure."

Kelly had the sense that she had entered a song, for the nun's Irish accent seemed to carry its own melody, and as she listened, she was entranced, watching Gabriella's lips forming her words, her dark eyes crinkling in good humor.

"Here is the riddle," Daniel said.

Life and death and life again
In canopy, tomb, and gold:
Peter, Paul, Martin, Magdalene,
The ancient story told.

Gabriella grinned, moving her head knowingly up and down. "Aye, Mary Magdalene's relics were here once, I do believe! And I must say, don't you know, there are written accounts of medieval pilgrimages to this church to venerate those relics. But some of the best evidence we have is from a biography of the Magdalene written by Henry Lacordaire in 1859."

"The French historian?" Daniel leaned toward her, intent on each word. "A Dominican, if I recall correctly."

Sister Gabriella raised her finger as though, Kelly thought, she was teaching a class of slow learners, or perhaps to structure her own memory. "Lacordaire wrote that Mary Magdalene died in southern France, and that when the Saracens invaded in 710, some of her bones were sent north to Vézelay and some east to Rome for safekeeping, and her body was buried deeper underground. Then, in 1279, her remains, hidden in a plain sarcophagus, were discovered by Charles of Anjou at Saint-Maximin in

Provence. But it wasn't until 1294, when Boniface VIII became Pope, that the find was taken seriously. Charles traveled to Rome and showed the skull to the Pope. When it was clear that the lower jaw was missing, Boniface called for the relics from this church, the Lateran—those sent to Rome for safekeeping—to be brought to him. Sure enough, one of the relics fit the upper jaw perfectly! He declared the remains discovered by Charles to be Santa Maria Maddalena herself, indeed!" Gabriella touched the top of her head as if to say it was merely a matter of common sense. "So he built this new shrine for the Magdalene's remaining relics in his Lateran basilica."

Gabriella paused to give them a moment to realize the implications of her words, then continued, motioning to the wall of fragments. "So these are parts of the altar of the late medieval shrine, when they knew for sure they were Mary Magdalene's relics."

Daniel ran his hands along the rough stone. "I've heard of the Provençal tradition but not this evidence in Rome. It's remarkable." He seemed to be tallying up the data, methodically evaluating. "Of course it's not proof, but it adds weight to the legend that she spent her last years in Provence. Clearly those who reburied the body in the early eighth century believed it was the Magdalene. That much is for certain, added to the fact of the previous centuries of veneration in that location."

They returned to the massive marble nave and, pausing in the north aisle, Kelly worried they were forgetting the importance of the next clue. After all, her godfather's papers would logically be here in Rome, not in France. She turned to the nun. "Sister, you said you have a message from Father Gilbert?"

Gabriella nodded calmly, as though she wanted to fully enjoy the moment. She clasped her hands together. "Yes, yes, Father Gilbert was a mighty fine priest and maybe even a saint. Did you know he helped to found our order? We are the Sisters of Divine Truth. We are responsible for educating visitors to Rome. We are called to explain the wondrous mysteries of this holy city and her sacred churches. We are enjoined to be missionaries of the Gospel! Right here in Rome!" Her arms flew up, hands open to the heavens, and she laughed a hefty, contagious laugh. "But we do go on missions to other places," she added quickly, examining the marble floor with attempted humility. "On occasion, we do that certainly, if required, and our Mother Superior desires it."

Kelly laughed, drawn into Gabriella's happiness. "The Divine Gospel?"

Gabriella studied her, her features holding a mysterious joy. "Oh yes, we tell the story over and again, over and again, the story of God's love for us. In all the art of this Eternal City, in all the churches, in all the stories of the saints. And most of all in the Eucharist, to which the art, the churches, the saints all point. They do that, you know, they truly do."

"That is a fine work you do," Daniel said. Then, hesitating, he added, "But there is no letter? You said you have a message?"

"No letter, but I've a poem, a sort of message, and one I can see may be added to yours. Father said to learn it and repeat it. He said that would be enough. You expected a letter? Now it's come to me that he said he would be writing one, but I never received it."

Kelly started. A letter gone missing? Did he not write it? Or forget to post it? Or had it been intercepted?

Daniel looked worried as well. "We've had letters leading us to the next church and its meaning, relating to the Apostles' Creed, the triangle of birth, death, and resurrection."

"I see," Sister Gabriella said, nodding. "Father Gilbert has been giving you a run for your money, hasn't he now! He always liked a good mystery. We shared a love of mystery novels. I lent him mine, and he lent me his, our little secret." She clapped her hands and slipped them into her pockets. She winked.

"I like mystery novels too," Kelly said, "but you said you have a poem?"

"Aye, I've a poem, just like the rhymes from the old country! So here goes." She squinted in concentration, holding the sides of her head, and Kelly listened breathlessly, like a child at bedtime who hopes that one more chapter will be read.

Truth and art do take their part
In wondrous tales and telling,
But holy healing was not the start
Of Magdalene's love indwelling.

From the Cross Christ speaks to men,
Though statues silent be,
She knows his love, this Magdalene,
And answers with a key.

Kelly studied Daniel's reaction, and as his face showed some understanding, she told herself to be patient. But this poem seemed the most difficult of all, and one she couldn't photograph.

"Does it help you?" The nun tilted her head hopefully.

"I have an idea as to the meaning, Sister, and thank you," Daniel replied. "But it would be best if you could forget that poem—for your own safety."

Clearly surprised, Gabriella nodded her assent. "Aye, what poem?" She winked conspiratorially, opening her palms in innocence.

Daniel gazed down the marble nave with its leaping apostles. He bowed to the nun, gently grasping her hands in his own. "Thank you, Sister."

"I'll walk you to the doors," she said, grinning with delight.

"Could I ask you a question, Sister?" Daniel ventured as they moved down the side aisle, past several chapels Kelly had not noticed, one with a haunting Madonna icon.

"But of course, ask away!" she said.

"How did you come to be a nun?"

Kelly listened closely, curious as well, but even so wished they could move on to the next church, slightly annoyed at the delay.

"My story is a good one, I think, and one I love to tell, so I'm so very glad you have asked, Daniel. Come, let's pause in the back here, near the front doors, where we can see the entire nave and sanctuary. It is so inspiring to me, a simple country girl from Lancashire in the north of England...."

Kelly watched the nun gather herself together, relishing the moment.

"I was mighty successful, you know. I went to Oxford and landed an excellent management job in the medical field. I was fast-tracked and rose quickly. By twenty-seven I had reached the top of my profession, in charge of hundreds of employees."

Kelly was impressed that she was so young to have accomplished so much.

"I'm thirty-four now, and I have to tell you that the last seven years were most astonishing! You might say they were God's years. He totally worked me over! First you must realize that I thought myself a good person. I contributed to charities, looked after my aging parents, helped out my sister with her kids. I thought that was enough, since I didn't go to church. I'm not sure what I believed. I think now, looking back, that I was a member of what you might call the 'Church of Christian Works.' In fact, I would have said I was a Christian person, if not devout. I was proud."

Daniel smiled ruefully. It was a half-smile of recognition, and Kelly studied his face as he said, "I know exactly what you mean. I know colleagues who are professed agnostics, some even atheists, who are real do-gooders. They look out for the downtrodden, as they see it. They're kind to animals. Yet their only authority is themselves. They are their own gods."

"That was me, to be sure! That was me!" Gabriella chuckled, shaking her head. "But on a holiday in Rome, I visited a friend who was a nun here. The visit changed my life."

"How so?" Kelly asked quietly.

Gabriella laid her hand on Kelly's shoulder and looked into her eyes. "They truly believed in Jesus, these nuns, in His great acts, His life, death, and resurrection, His divinity. They believed in His mother, who appeared to their founder many years ago. I believed *them*, they were so convincing."

"Mary appeared to them?" Daniel said, attentive. "I hadn't heard of that apparition."

"Aye, in the late forties, she did, in a grotto outside the city walls. She told them to tell everyone about her son, about God's love, and how He saves them from death. She said to tell everyone about these divine truths, this good news."

"So," Kelly said, smiling, "they called themselves the Sisters of Divine Truth. And you became one of them, a nun?"

"Ah, there's the rub! No, I didn't, not yet. I went back to London and my fancy job. I worked hard and played hard, but all the while I had this pull, this urge to join the order. My parents said I was crazy. My sister wondered how I could give up all that I had worked for. My friends wouldn't even listen to me. They just laughed."

Kelly was intrigued. "How long did it take for God to pull on the thread?" She remembered that phrase from a Chesterton novel, God pulling you back to him like a fisherman twitching the line.

Gabriella laughed knowingly. "I know that one, and a good one it is. It was in *Father Brown;* then Evelyn Waugh used it in *Brideshead Revisited*, it was so good. But it took God four years to reel *me* in. And I've never been happier."

"So you have a teaching charism?" Daniel asked.

"Aye, we catechize in churches and schools and guide visitors through all the churches of Rome, all the sacred and holy manifestations of God's love for us. Such a joy it is, I can tell you, such a joy!" She raised her palms heavenward in thanksgiving.

"Thank you, Sister," Kelly said gratefully, her heart full. "That's a wonderful story." She rested for the moment in Sister Gabriella's joy.

Daniel was quiet as well, as though doing the same.

"God be with you, then," Gabriella said, nodding to them both, breaking the spell. "I must be going. Blessings, blessings! And I shall keep you in my prayer intentions at Holy Mass."

"Thank you, Sister," Kelly said, "and I hope we meet again."

"And I too, my dear," Gabriella said, beaming. "Trust me; you are part of a great plan, a great drama. You may not know the act that came before, and you may not know the act that will follow. Just do your part in the act you are given! Trust God that this is so, for it is, and one day we shall see how it all comes together. Now go and solve the real mystery, God's great love!"

Gabriella kissed them on each cheek and headed up the aisle to the shop. As Kelly turned to the front doors, she glanced at the basilica guidebook, now tucked in her bag, and tried to recall some of the poem. There was healing and a cross that spoke to men. There was something about silent statues and a key. She hoped these images might help trigger Daniel's memory.

She glanced back to the green-robed young woman, amazed at the path she chose and how she became a nun with the Sisters of Divine Truth. She took a last photograph of the bright nave with the twelve apostles leaping from the sides. She hoped she could one day return.

*

Lester Sansby turned from the bar and the server with the incredible breasts. He looked out the window and down the street and cursed. They were gone. Weaver and the girl, so securely settled on the park bench, had disappeared, *poof!* Lester paid his bill, slipped the server's number into his pocket, and dashed outside.

They were gone. Into thin air.

16

La Maddalena

"You were right about La Maddalena," Daniel said. "And it's late. We'd better take a taxi." They found a taxi stand nearby and slipped inside, onto the worn backseat. Daniel told the driver, "*Chiesa Maria Maddalena.*"

Kelly now focused on their quest, regretting the time lost in the basilica. "Are we finally going to the Magdalene church?" Would they ever find her godfather's manuscript? Should she head out on her own? Not a good idea, she decided—not here, not in Rome, in Italy, where she knew no one, couldn't speak the language, and where there seemed to be a stalker on their trail.

Daniel studied her with concern as though he could read her mind. "You must be impatient to go home."

She only slightly regretted her outburst, but after all, there had been one diversion after another. Her impatience continued to surge.

He stared out the window at the passing sites, ruins, and the huge white palazzo she had seen from the tour bus. "The Forum," he said coolly, pointing. "The Capitolino." He was silent for a moment. "I'm sorry, I've been lecturing again."

"No, go ahead, I need to know as much as possible. You'd better tell me about this church we're going to. Tell me about Santa Maddalena." She breathed deeply and struggled to be patient, to control the rising irritation, all the time hating the sound of her voice. Her heartbeat slowed, and she stopped clenching her bag.

He turned toward her, and she felt a warmth he'd only allowed on occasional, surprising moments. Like over coffee in her apartment at home. Like saying good night at her door in the hotel. Like taking her hand and crossing the lawn to Santa Croce. "Okay then. The riddle referred to healing," he said in a gentler voice. "The church of the Magdalene has been run by a nursing order called the Camillians since the sixteenth century."

The fleeting memories of those moments were sweet, she reflected, and now his voice, deep and softly coaxing, was sweet. As she gazed out the window, she asked, "The Camillians?" Another strange name. Perhaps she was a sponge too full, unable to absorb one more drop. Even so, this new mystery beckoned. Matt seemed far away as she watched Rome speed by, and she missed him more with the passing of time. Not hearing his voice the night before added to her sense of loss, as though the deep hollow in her chest got deeper and more hollow. Tonight she would call.

The driver, a swarthy fellow with shiny black hair, tapped the dashboard with a thick finger, drumming to the beat of an American pop song and leaning on his horn every few blocks as he edged another car out of his lane. A rabbit's foot dangled from the rearview mirror.

Daniel was silent, perhaps hesitant. "Yes," he replied slowly in answer to her question, "the Camillians, a religious order. There is evidence of a small oratory on the site of the present church as early as 1320 that was dedicated to Mary Magdalene and connected to a hospital near the Pantheon. A confraternity was in charge of the charity."

"A confraternity?" Another new word.

"Confraternities were guilds of lay religious who dedicated themselves to helping others. Usually they were devoted to a particular saint or relic. When a priest named Camillus founded the order toward the end of the sixteenth century, the Pope gave him this church as his base. Groups like this are often given churches to look after. In exchange they hold services and live in residence."

"Camillus?" She was enjoying his careful voice, his attention. Perhaps that was enough. It might be a good thing for her to slow down a bit. He might be good for her. She could learn to be patient.

"His full name was Camillus Lellis. He was a crippled soldier, converted by Philip Neri in Rome. After being ordained, he devoted his life to the needy, forming the Order of the Ministers of the Sick. The Camillians wore a red-cross emblem centuries before today's Red Cross Society. They visited hospitals and homes, caring for the dying and nursing the sick, particularly plague victims. They distributed food and clothing from Santa Maddalena."

"Didn't you say that Father Gilbert was connected in some way?"

"One of the Camillians reports for *Opus Veritatis*. But, more importantly, the Camillians cared for Father Gilbert's sister in her last months. He told me the story, and he kept in touch with the monks over the years. She had leukemia, and she was only a child."

"How awful! I didn't know he had a sister."

"Her name was Nora. She was young, probably no more than twelve when the family lived in Rome. The Camillians visited often. It was a terrible loss for everyone when she died. I've often thought Nora's death might have encouraged him to become a priest. Death has a way of doing that."

"I'd never heard the story." She watched Daniel's face, which had turned pale.

He stared into the distance. "Sometimes family tragedies are difficult to talk about. Sometimes one never really gets over them, and talking about them makes it worse…sort of keeps the memories alive when they are better left buried."

Kelly studied his profile. He sounded as though he had known such tragedy, and now steeled himself to again forget. She wanted to ask what he meant but dared not open the wound.

She thought of her mother and father and their tragic death. It was true she often chose to avoid thinking about it, the wailing sirens, the mourners at the funeral, the awful silence in the house as she packed a bag. Nancy from church taking her home with her for a few days, the social workers interviewing her. Father Gilbert and his words at the graveside. His words to her in his office, tender, consoling, encouraging. His grief and guilt ravaging him and seeping through the edges of his speech, and her measured coolness toward him, so heartless, so cruel. Forcing herself through her last semesters at school as though nothing had happened.

How did one cope with such loss year after year? It seemed to Kelly that the pain never went away, but rather, the pain was slowly accepted as a part of her life. She thought too of Sally Hamilton, a friend from school, who brought her home to Boston for spring break that year. Where was Sally now? She must have lost touch when Matt was born, or even earlier when she worked at the bank and Sally married and settled on the East Coast.

The taxi, wedged in traffic on a major thoroughfare, came to a stop as horns blared and scooters darted between cars. Finally the driver lifted open palms, swore, and asked if they wanted to walk.

"It's not far," Daniel said to Kelly, "let's walk. The Corso is always jammed like this."

They crossed a busy piazza, passed a monumental carved column, and entered a dark alley. Soon they found themselves in a warren of shady winding lanes.

Kelly was enchanted by the unexpected sudden silence, broken only by feet tapping the cobblestones, and the startling vistas of quaint piazzas and alleys. She glimpsed classical ruins, pillars and porch scaffolded, and thought she saw the Pantheon down a narrow passage. Shops sold leather goods and souvenirs, and quaint cafés spilled onto the walkway.

Daniel explained the church didn't open until four, so they stopped for double espressos, standing at a bar, and nibbled on squares of bittersweet chocolate. Kelly's impatience had been soothed with the leisurely afternoon pace of Rome.

Revived, they continued to a small piazza that appeared around a corner. Bells chimed four, and Daniel pointed to a modest church that reigned over the square like an elegant queen mother. "Santa Maria Maddalena," he announced, grinning, his face full of affection as though seeing an old friend.

*

Three half-circle steps led to doors in an ocher façade.

"When Camillus was canonized in 1746," Daniel explained, "the church was renovated in the Baroque style." He glanced at her. "Let me know if I'm lecturing."

"Of course not," she said quickly. "I'm so sorry for my bad mood. I'm tired, I suppose. And I do tend to get impatient."

"It's okay—we've had an intense few days with poor sleep."

They stepped inside the church and Kelly focused on the gilded space. The nave was not large, so the feeling was more intimate than the Lateran basilica, Santa Croce, or Maria Maggiore. Three aisles, running under gold-and-white vaults, led to an airy apse and frescoed dome. Light shafted on marble columns from high windows. The church seemed to float.

"The gilt and marble," Daniel said, "are effective in such a small nave. This is one of my favorite churches. It's not far from my old school, and I often came here to think and pray." They walked halfway up the central aisle. "Now, turn around and look back to see the organ loft."

A golden garden of leaves, florets, cherubs, acanthus, and tendrils swirled around marble figures and the pipes themselves, as though dancing to the music that was to come. "Classic Baroque Rococo," Daniel said. "Either you like it or not. I like it, but then I love flourishes, always more interesting, to my way of thinking, than straight lines."

"I like it too."

They continued up the aisle toward the high altar. Daniel genuflected before the tabernacle, then turned toward the south transept. In a tucked-away chapel with three wooden pews, a wrought-iron grill protected an altar with a life-size crucifix above. To the right of the altar stood a primitive wooden sculpture, also life-size, of a woman holding a jar, and Kelly thought it must be Mary Magdalene.

Daniel spoke quietly, as though on holy ground, but his eyes were fixed upon the crucifix, not Mary Magdalene. "The Camillians believe the crucifix is miraculous. Legend claims that Christ spoke to Camillus, through the crucifix, saying, 'Take courage, faint-hearted one, continue the work you have begun. I will be with you, because it is my work.'"

"Remarkable."

"That's how the story goes. But whether an exterior or interior voice spoke to him, there's no question that Camillus was inspired to spread the love of Christ. He was transformed, given the strength to do God's will."

"And the statue? That's Mary Magdalene, right?"

Daniel nodded, and his eyes softened. "Sweet, isn't she? Very simple, very medieval, although she dates to the fifteenth century, actually Renaissance."

"So where does this leave us? How did the last poem go?"

Daniel gazed at the Magdalene and recited:

Truth and art do take their part
In wondrous tales and telling,
But holy healing was not the start
Of Magdalene's love indwelling.

He paused, searching for the words, then resumed,

From the Cross Christ speaks to men,
Though statues silent be,
She knows his love, this Magdalene,
And answers with a key.

"And that must be the cross." Kelly glanced at the crucifix. "Although I suppose it's meant metaphorically as well. And the statue of Mary is *silent be*."

"That's what I'm thinking. But the *key*?" Daniel studied the chapel. "See—there, opposite the sculpture, is a keyhole...in an ambry."

"An ambry?" Kelly could see the outline of a door in the wall to the left of the altar, about two feet high, one foot wide.

"An ambry is a small storage cabinet. In churches they are often part of the wall, like in a niche or recess, and were once used to store chalices. Anglicans often use them to reserve the Blessed Sacrament. Today Roman Catholics sometimes use them for holy oils."

Kelly peered through the wrought-iron grill. The ambry door had been painted like the space around it, but yes, there was a keyhole barely visible.

"But where's the key?" The voice came from behind them, and they turned to see Teresa, Father Timothy's niece from Santa Maria Maggiore.

Kelly recalled how composed Teresa had been when she burned Father Gilbert's letter. She now stood calmly before them, her hands folded, a black-and-white flowered skirt falling in tiers to her calves. She wore a red shawl.

17

Teresa

"What are you doing here?" Daniel demanded, his tone close to threatening. "Have you been eavesdropping?"

"I'm sorry," Teresa said quickly, stepping back. "I didn't mean to startle you."

"Have you been following us?" Kelly asked.

"Yes and no. Let me explain." She regarded them earnestly, raising her hand in peace, her bracelets falling together. "Uncle Timothy asked me to watch out for you. I thought from the clue at Maria Maggiore that the next church would be Santa Croce. I saw you there this morning. But then I lost the trail after that. I guessed you might end up here, so I've been checking with the sacristan occasionally. I know him from school."

She waved a young man over, and they spoke quickly in Italian. His dark hair was pulled into a ponytail. He regarded Teresa with hesitant admiration.

"Perhaps he can help you," Teresa said.

Kelly searched Teresa's eyes. "Do you know anything about the key? Does your friend know anything?" The young woman seemed sincere. She seemed honest.

"This ambry," Daniel interjected, "is that what we've been searching for? What's inside? Is it still used?"

Teresa translated to the sacristan, and he shook his head with regret, waving his arms as he spoke in a softly melodic Italian. "He says," Teresa translated, "that he doesn't know where the key is. He's never seen it. He thinks that the ambry has not been used for many years. Masses are at the high altar, over Saint Camillus's relics, and they use a different ambry. He says to ask his older brother, a postulant with the Camillians."

They followed the young man to the northern transept and into the sacristy. A monk in a black cassock rose from behind a table of postcards, booklets, medals, prints, and figurines for sale.

"May I help you?" he asked with a heavy accent. "Ah, Daniel!" His face lit up. "It is good to see you again!" His hair was dark like his brother's but trimmed short. Heavy brows framed unusually pale blue eyes. He seemed to bustle with nervous energy, as if carving the space around him into orderly units. He nodded to Teresa in recognition.

"Alessandro? How are you?" Daniel shook his hand. "Allow me to introduce Kelly Roberts. Father Gilbert is her godfather." He turned to Kelly. "Alessandro is the friend I mentioned. He reports for *Opus Veritatis*—Father Gilbert and I had dinner with him many years ago. And, Alessandro, you know Teresa, it seems."

Alessandro clasped his hands together, bowing from the waist. "A pleasure to make your acquaintance, Ms. Roberts, and it is always good to see you, Teresa. And Daniel, I am ever vigilant, ever vigilant! I post many reports these dark days."

Daniel nodded. "Excellent. My friend, we need your help. We are searching for the key to the ambry in the Crucifix Chapel. Or even better, do you have anything, perhaps a message, for Kelly from Father Gilbert?"

"Ah, Father Gilbert, *si, si*. I had nearly forgotten, and here you are. But of course you have the words? One cannot be too careful, and I do apologize, but I made my promise to ask."

Daniel glanced at Teresa, who had moved aside, chatting with the sacristan. "*Apostles' Creed*," he said under his breath.

Alessandro nodded and opened a drawer in the table. He reached to the far back and extracted a sealed envelope. "*Bene*. I give this to you." He looked relieved, as if a burden had been lifted.

The young sacristan left to greet visitors entering the church, and Kelly and Daniel stepped away from Alessandro and Teresa. Slipping her thumb under the seal, Kelly unfolded the letter at an angle so Daniel could read it too.

> My dear Kelly,
> You have seen the triangle of birth, death, and resurrection, all witnessed in the Apostles' Creed. You have come to the Magdalene's church. Now you must visit Mary Magdalene's resting place in order to fully know not only this wondrous saint but the foundations of your beliefs.
>   You must fly to Marseilles. From the airport, call my good friend, Brigitte Durieux, who will direct you to her home. Her number is listed. Stay with her in her manor house hotel. You will find the key in La Sainte Baume.
>   May God and all his saints be with you,
>   Be ever vigilant,
>   Your Godfather Gilbert

"Marseilles!" Kelly could not keep the worry and disappointment from her voice. "And what did he mean, 'be ever vigilant'?"

"There's a new tone here. Something must have happened to worry him."

"La Sainte Baume?" *France!*

"We have no choice but to go there and at once," Daniel said. "He must be referring to the grotto legend. It's the story Sister Gabriella mentioned, how Mary Magdalene spent her last days in a cave in Provence. I'm not too familiar with the details."

"A cave in Provence." Kelly groaned. "But why couldn't we just force the door to the ambry?"

Daniel flinched. "Force? Force an ambry door? In a sacred place? Not a good plan. No, we must do as Father Gilbert asks, Kelly. Trust me on this."

Kelly could see his point. It was holy ground, she supposed, and they shouldn't be forcing anything. But her worry and distress were mounting, and she tried to pull herself together as she peered into the envelope, hoping for more information. Instead she found cash, wrapped in tissue. "Three thousand Euros. Is that enough for the flight?"

"More than enough. But we'll need a car when we get there."

Kelly gazed at the vaulted apse, turned, and glanced back to the Baroque organ loft. She was so weary. "But I thought I'd be home this weekend. I'd planned on it. Matt expects me. Andrea expects me. Laddie and Lady Jane expect me…" Kelly could feel her lower lip quiver as she dropped her voice and said thinly, in barely a whisper, "Daniel, I want to go home." She fell into a pew, limp. She hated her high childish whine but couldn't control it.

"I know," Daniel said, sitting next to her. "I thought you would be home this weekend too. Still, we'd better finish this, or you'll never have peace. I'll see if I can book flights to Marseilles for tomorrow morning. Call Andrea, and let her know and say we'll contact them soon. I'll call Brigitte Durieux. I met her and Alain, her husband, at a conference a few years ago."

Teresa and Alessandro joined them. "You are going to France?" Teresa asked. "I couldn't help but overhear."

"Teresa," Daniel said, "what do you know about Mary Magdalene in Provence?"

"As a matter of fact, the legend was the subject of my thesis." She smiled broadly, her teeth white against her olive skin, and her eyes grew wide with sincerity. "Father Gilbert was helpful in that regard, as well as my uncle. Could I come along? I speak fluent French, and I know the area. I can help you. I'll pay my way."

"She is very smart," Alessandro acknowledged. "She can help. But now I have something for Signorina Roberts as a memento." He opened his hand and revealed a three-inch clay figurine, a replica of the carved wooden Magdalene in the Crucifix Chapel.

"So sweet," Kelly said, examining it. Mysterious, from another world, she thought. The little saint would be a treasured souvenir. *"Grazie,* Alessandro. *Molto grazie."*

As they said their farewells, Kelly sensed someone watching, as though a feather brushed the back of her neck. She shivered and turned. A tall figure slipped out through the narthex doors. "I think that man just left," she said to Daniel. "I can't be sure. Just guessing. A feeling I have. He was tall with the same hat."

"What man?" Teresa asked, brows knit. She lifted her shawl over her head, and Kelly saw fear in her eyes.

"Sansby?" Daniele strode down the central aisle, nearly breaking into a run.

The women followed him to the church porch and scanned the square. In the far corner a crowd gathered around an accordion player. Nearby, a woman spoke to a tour group. A taxi maneuvered between pedestrians into a narrow lane. There was no sign of a tall man with a broad-brimmed hat.

"Maybe I'm a little jumpy," Kelly admitted.

"What man?" Teresa repeated, face ashen. She slipped on large dark glasses.

"Someone might be following us," Kelly explained. "We're pretty sure he's from Berkeley, a Dr. Sansby. Daniel thought he recognized him. He knows him from his school."

Teresa's face twitched, and she glanced away.

"Let's head back." Daniel led them up the lane.

As they reached the Corso, Teresa said with a shaky voice, "I must return to Trastevere. Call when you have the reservations?" She wrote her number on the back of a card and handed it to Daniel. "We'll find the answers in Provence, I'm sure." She hesitated, then added, "There's something else you should know."

Kelly waited with expectation and dread.

"The police say Father Gilbert was poisoned. They now have a suspect."

"Murder? A suspect?"

"They've been questioning a young man who was a postulant at the monastery. Evidently Father Gilbert told him not to return after the summer break."

"Why?" Kelly asked.

"Father Timothy said his name is Fabio, and that he was a poor student, didn't apply himself, and that he had threatened some of the other postulants." She pulled her shawl around her face. "Please, call me with the reservations? I can help with expenses. *Ciao.*"

She swiveled on her heel, her long skirt swaying.

"At least there's a suspect," Kelly said as they maneuvered along the crowded Corso. Once again she felt sick with the thought of her godfather being murdered. "To think someone hated him enough to do something like that."

"The suspect sounds like a young man with a grudge."

They walked through a neighborhood of lanes and piazzas, passed the Trevi Fountain, and followed the winding Via Veneto to their small hotel. At Kelly's door, they agreed to meet for dinner and compare notes.

"I'm not sure about Teresa," Daniel said. "If she should call, don't give her any information unless you need to. Why didn't she tell us about Father Timothy's news immediately?"

"We were pretty busy with other things. She seems trustworthy to me," Kelly said, glad to have the female companionship.

"I have a bad feeling about this."

"What do you mean?"

"There's more to Teresa than she's letting on."

"Like what?"

"I'm not sure. But until we know more, let's be careful."

"I get those feelings too," Kelly admitted, "but I feel good about Teresa."

"Perhaps we shouldn't let our feelings control things one way or another. Let's gather facts instead, and until then, use common sense."

"Agreed."

"I'll work on the flights and give Father Francis our new number."

"And I'll call Andrea."

*

With her heart skipping a beat, Kelly dialed the front desk, and the manager put her call through. She waited for the familiar voices, the link with her son, the audible touch.

"Andrea? How's everything?"

"Oh, we're just as cozy as four peas in a pod."

"Good. How's Matt?"

"He's fine, but he misses you."

"Be sure and read him a bedtime story. And prayers. That always settles him for the night."

"Sure. Any particular prayer?"

"The Our Father, then God bless…family and friends, you know how it goes."

"I'll do my best. How's the trip going? Not a wild goose chase, is it?"

Kelly decided to choose her words carefully. "No, of course not. We're right on track. But we're flying to France tomorrow. You can reach us through Father Francis Fitzroy." She gave Andrea the number. "I'll call you when we get in."

"France! Kelly, you aren't getting yourself involved with some kind of cult, are you?"

"Why would you say that?"

"Oh, something Todd said on the phone about *Opus Veritatis*."

"Andrea, my parents worked for *Opus Veritatis*. It's not a cult."

"Some think it's a hate group, even a little crazy, fanatical."

"Not true."

"Truth, I guess, is relative."

Kelly started. It was a phrase she had heard often in school, a phrase often corrected by her parents. "Truth is truth," her mother would say. "It's never relative. It's our job to find it, search for it. Either something is true, or it isn't. That's what the word means. Beware of changing language like that."

Now Kelly replied, "It will all work out. Just put Matt on the line, okay?"

Soon she heard her boy's voice. "What are you doing now, Matt?"

"Talking to you."

"Right. What are you doing later?"

"Going swimming!"

She recalled it was morning at Lake Tahoe. "That's cool."

"When are you coming home?"

His voice sounded so young, much younger than she remembered. Had it only been three days? "Soon."

"We're going on a boat tomorrow."

"That's cool too. Wish I was there!"

"Andrea says I gotta go, Mommy. I love you."

"I love you too, honey."

Click. Heartbreak. Emptiness.

*

From a café's dark doorway, Lester Sansby watched them leave the little church of La Maddalena. He then settled into a sidewalk table in front of the nearby Pantheon for supper *al fresco*, ordering the daily special—pasta with mixed shellfish—and a local wine.

A band played in the piazza, and he eyed with admiration the high school coeds as they blew into their flutes and tapped their clarinets. *So innocent. So fresh. So young.* Their shirts and hats said *Louisville High.*

He opened his laptop and checked his Treats. Nothing new there. The information they fed him he could have found just as easily on his own. Useless. All except for Fab, who sounded terrified.

Lester read the words again. "Arrested for the old man's murder. Questioned. Help me."

He typed back immediately. "Don't know what you mean."

"Help me or else."

"Or else?" Lester typed, his blood racing. "Are you threatening me?"

"I'll talk, Dr. Sansby, don't think I won't. You're involved too."

"What do you want?"

"Get me out of Rome, and with enough to start over."

Would he talk? Lester didn't trust him. It wouldn't take much to cast suspicion in Lester's direction. He didn't need the publicity. Not this kind of publicity. "Meet me tonight," he said.

"Where?"

"Someplace quiet. Deserted."

"The river."

"Ponte Fabricio. Seems appropriate." Lester had seen the ancient footbridge on a travel poster. It came to mind immediately.

"Midnight," Fabio replied.

Lester frowned, his temper flaring. The kid would squeal, he knew it. Could the boy be bought? Lester felt in his pocket for his knife, a collapsible gadget he had purchased in Trastevere and came in handy to open things. He signaled for the check and reached for his pills. This would take some thought, but he had all evening. How should he proceed? He would go back to his room and retrieve some cash. The boy sounded crazed. But perhaps he could be paid off.

Lester needed to take control.

18

Mary Magdalene

KELLY'S DREAM RETURNED UNBIDDEN AND SOON FORGOTTEN, with a tone both warm and commanding, as though she had entered the heart of a rose to be bathed in the colors of a rainbow....

The melody of the singers ebbed and flowed, but her desire to draw near was greater than before. She climbed lightly, with no pull of the earth, and soon broke away from the pinnacle of smooth stone. To her sweet surprise she flew, soaring over a green valley to the sea, but turned as the sapphire waters receded from sight...turned back toward the crystal mountain. Now, arms outspread and palming the warm air, she glided low over forested hills, the leaves beckoning, the boughs bending. She moved her arms as a bird with wings, pushing the air down and away as though swimming, and rose higher, catching the soft current...then saw the stone chapel on the top of the mountain. She found herself inside the sacred space. There was a tabernacle and a door and a key with a green tassel. A woman called her name: "Kelly Ann Roberts..."

*

The Monday morning light pulled Kelly from her dream, and she lingered in the shadow-land, aching as though mourning a lost love. She recalled a woman's face coming near and disappearing, a face from another time and world, brown eyes and thick wavy hair falling over a homespun gown....

Kelly shook her head, the loss of the image wrenching. She sat up, wondering where she was. Footsteps crunched the gravel in the courtyard below her window.

Now she remembered. She was in Provence, at a country hotel near Marseilles. She slipped out of bed, crossed the room to the open window, and peered between green gingham panels falling to the floor from brass rings high on a rod. She inhaled sharp pine and pungent lavender. Below in the courtyard guests mingled around a breakfast buffet set in the shade. She searched, but couldn't see Daniel. She recalled that Teresa was staying at a Dominican hostelry up the road. Soon Teresa would pick them up in the car.

Soon she would drive them to Mary Magdalene's grotto in the Massif de La Sainte Baume.

*

Early Saturday evening their plane had touched down in Marseilles under steel-gray skies. Teresa drove their small rental car, Kelly in the passenger seat and Daniel in the back. Kelly could see that Daniel didn't completely trust Teresa, but for her part Kelly had been glad to have the young woman along. Her fluency had maneuvered them through the airport to Baggage Claim and Car Rental. She knew her way out of Marseilles, a larger port city than Kelly had imagined, and soon they were on the auto-route, heading east in the growing darkness toward the Durieux' manor house hotel.

They had driven through rolling hills striped with vines, following narrow roads through villages with saints' names. As they approached the old château set back from the road at the end of a long straight drive, the rain hit, slashing in large drops, furiously swept off by the windshield wipers. They pulled into a graveled yard and ran for cover into the small foyer.

Soon Brigitte Durieux was greeting them warmly, kissing them on each cheek and lamenting the downpour. "*Quel dommage! Il fait très ...Mes chers, allons-y...*"

Kelly had been struck by her ingenuous charm, which seemed to banish the dark and the rain. She was slim, tall, and athletic, with short blond hair framing a heart-shaped face, and she led them upstairs to single rooms, explaining in a husky voice that her husband had already gone to bed, for he rose early. He was, after all, *le chef,* and duty called, but he sent his most warm greetings.

Porters followed with their bags, bumping the wooden stairs. Kelly entered her peaceful corner room and hadn't unpacked but merely changed into pajamas and slipped between the cool sheets, exhausted from a long day in lines and airports and security checks.

The rain had continued into Sunday. At breakfast their hostess insisted the hike to the grotto was not a good plan. "*Trop dangéreux,*" she said, shaking a long tanned finger toward the grotto. They learned from Brigitte that no, she had no letter from Father Gilbert. Kelly asked how she knew him.

"From our time in Rome. It is so sad to lose such a fine priest. He has helped my family again and again. I am greatly in…how do you say…greatly in his *debt,* I think, is the word. I miss him. I…mourn. And you?"

Daniel shot Kelly a warning glance, and Kelly let him do the talking.

"Father Gilbert was Kelly's godfather," Daniel said. "He recommended visiting the grotto."

"Ah *oui,*" Brigitte said, nodding. "He sends many travelers this way, many pilgrims! But I must go and attend to others…"

Daniel and Kelly had used the day to rest and regroup. Teresa didn't mind the delay, wanting to post an *Opus Veritatis* article and check in with her Uncle Timothy. They read and researched online and caught up with email. Daniel checked his blogs and bloggers.

Kelly had phoned home and spoken to an excited Matt, who had ridden his first pony.

"Mommy, I did it!"

"What did you do?"

"I climbed on the pony and rode all around."

"That's great! How brave you are!"

"Yeah, pretty brave."

Andrea came on the line. "Did you see the news?"

"What news?"

"The story of Gilbert's death made the ten o'clock broadcast last night. They did a special report."

Kelly started. "What did they say?"

"They think it was murder."

"I'm aware that's a possibility."

"You be careful, you hear? Those fanatics can steer you down the wrong path."

"They aren't fanatics, Andrea."

"The news said this Opus group is a cult and has enemies because of their hate speech."

Kelly didn't reply and let the silence speak. She didn't think her parents, or Daniel for that matter, were involved in hate speech. How could the news so miss-state? "The reporters must be wrong, Andrea," she said firmly. "You can't believe everything in the news."

"Well, you just come home ASAP, you hear? You seem to be in the middle of a hornets' nest. Think of your boy."

That hurt. "I think of him all the time, Andrea. I'll be home probably next week. I'll keep you posted."

Daniel had reached Father Francis, and Kelly had picked up another line to hear his report.

"It's true, my dears," Father Francis said. "It's been on the news. I didn't want to worry you and slow you down. The inspector has been all over us, interviewing everyone who knew Father Gilbert, which, as you can well imagine, was quite a number of folks here in Rome. I said you would be back in a few days, in time surely for Saturday's symposium."

"We should be," Daniel said. Then, his voice subdued, he asked, "Do they know the cause of death?"

"An extra dose of meds. The stuff is called digoxin, sometimes digitalis. Slows the heart rate, but in this case too much. Someone must have given him an extra dose. It had to be an inside job, they say, for Father Gilbert rarely left his rooms. They think it was someone close by."

Kelly thought of Teresa's information. "We heard there was a suspect, but couldn't it have been an accident?"

"They've ruled out accidental death, not sure why. And they've been questioning a lad with a grudge. But I can't say more at this time. It's all rather hush-hush."

"We understand," Daniel said.

"How's the search going?" Father Francis probed tentatively, clearly concerned.

"Slow," Daniel said. "It's been pouring rain. Hopefully tomorrow we can visit Mary Magdalene's grotto. We should find something there."

"Alas, we have only a few days left until the symposium on Saturday. I shall keep you in my prayers, and consider a substitute speaker. You know how I hate to give speeches. My stutter tends to come back."

"We'll find the key and the manuscript soon, I'm sure," Kelly said, wanting to comfort him.

"Aye, my dear, to be sure. Pray for discernment as you walk the trail to the grotto. It's been many years since I made the pilgrimage through that lovely forest."

"We will, Father," Daniel replied. "And thank you."

"Yes, Father," Kelly added, "thank you."

*

Now, Monday morning, Kelly gazed up through green leaves to a blue sky, and her excitement grew. Today they would visit Mary Magdalene's grotto. Today they would find the mysterious key. Then to Rome and the Magdalene church and the papers and her legacy. And home. She knew at last she was close. She turned to her closet and pulled out her jeans, a tee, and her cable sweater. She laced her thick-soled trainers. She found a pink hair band and wrapped it around her ponytail. La Sainte Baume!

*

"Sorry to be late," Teresa said as she placed the key in the ignition, her silver bracelets rustling. "The sisters and I wanted to catch up, and I lost track of the time. It was so good to see them again, my sweet Sœurs de Nazareth." She beamed. "And I wanted to help clean up the breakfast things."

They left the hotel by way of the same long straight drive, bordered by majestic beeches. Soon, once again, they were winding through vineyards.

"You stayed with the sisters before?" Kelly asked from the passenger seat. She studied the silver charms that dangled from Teresa's wrist as she rested her fingers lightly on the steering wheel: a cross, a fish, a miniature church, several saints' medals, silver and gold. A delicate silver chain with a medal hung in the vee of her white cotton blouse. She wore a tiered multi-blue Provençal skirt.

Teresa tapped the wheel, punctuating her reply. "I was researching my thesis. The Dominican brothers care for the grotto up the mountain, and the sisters help them with the pilgrims in the valley. Anyway, the nuns reminded me that I should tell you the story of the Magdalene's time in France."

"Indeed, Teresa, please do," Daniel said from the back seat.

Kelly glanced at him as he touched his shirt pocket, pulling out a small pump spray. "Is that your asthma inhaler?" she asked, thinking of Matt.

Daniel nodded. "I might need it on the hike, and I like to be prepared."

"Good idea," Kelly agreed. "Please, Teresa, go on, tell us the story."

"Legend claims," she began, her voice falling into a rhythm, "that Mary Magdalene spent her last thirty years in the cave after preaching in the valley."

Daniel interrupted. "Didn't they arrive by boat along the coast? Was it Marseilles?" His hand was on Kelly's seatback, and he leaned forward with interest, his eyes moving from Teresa to the vineyards. The stalks were neatly trained onto posts and in full leaf, although the grapes were tucked away unseen.

"They arrived at Saintes-Maries-de-la-Mer, west of Marseilles. They say Mary Magdalene sailed from Jerusalem with Martha, Lazarus, Maximin, Zaccheus, and others. Mary Magdalene, Lazarus, and Maximin went east to Marseilles, a Greek port at the time. Mary Magdalene and Maximin continued north to Aix-en-Provence, where Maximin became bishop. He was one of the seventy-two apostles sent out by Christ."

As they drove through the hills Kelly gazed beyond to a broad stone massif that stood like a silvery altar against the cobalt blue sky. A dark green forest skirted the white rock. The air was clear from the rain, and the blues seemed bluer, the greens greener, the colors more vibrant with the overhead journey of the sun, and Kelly felt the thrill of a traveler in a foreign land, an explorer searching the unknown, not knowing what to expect.

Teresa removed one hand from the wheel and pulled her long fingers through her thick, dark curls, raising her hair and letting it cascade over her blouse. She appeared tense, troubled, and Kelly sensed that something ached in a place deep and faraway.

"Why did Mary Magdalene live in the cave?" Kelly asked, uneasy with Teresa's sudden disquiet.

"*If* she lived in the cave, one of many caves in the limestone massif. It's a disputed claim. The legend places her there, saying she worked out her penance as a hermit. She prayed and fasted. The medieval chroniclers emphasized her sinner side, the penitential prostitute side. Modern historians often try to change that image."

"Why would they do that?" Kelly considered penitence a major part of Christianity, even if the most difficult part. Father Gilbert used to say, *"All doubt is moral."*

"They want her to be a feminist icon. No regrets, total self-appreciation, healthy self-esteem, as folks like to say today."

"What do *you* think?" Watching Teresa, Kelly felt a twinge of envy in spite of the woman's underlying sadness. She was beautiful. Her skin was smooth and tawny, her cheekbones high and classic, her figure full yet slim. She exuded a simple sensuality, accentuated today by her hair falling free over her shoulders, and for a fleeting moment Kelly wished she could be like that. She gazed at her own sensible clothes, her jeans and sweater. Her glasses felt heavy and her ponytail boyish. Daniel, she thought, must think Teresa attractive. But then, why should she, Kelly, care?

Teresa glanced at Kelly, as though reading her thoughts, and refocused on the road. "The Church for centuries claimed Mary Magdalene was the woman who washed Christ's feet with her hair. She was the sister of Lazarus and Martha. There is no conclusive evidence that they are the same Mary. In the twentieth century the Church said she could only be the Mary from Magdala and the Mary of the seven demons and the Mary who saw the resurrected Christ."

Daniel appeared to be listening to Teresa with open admiration and, while Kelly was glad he was beginning to trust their new companion, Kelly knew her envy was coming way too close to jealousy.

"The seven demons expelled by Christ," Daniel said, nodding. "They could represent many or major sins, or indeed a multitude of demons—seven was meant to mean many, a figurative number. If the demons meant sins, she would still be a penitent."

Teresa flashed Daniel a broad white smile. "Exactly right. What does it matter what the sins were? She should still be deemed a penitent. She is one who repents and changes. Today the Church is reconsidering the other roles. Some scholars are arguing they are all the same Mary."

"And you mentioned there was a question about her living in the grotto?" Daniel asked, gazing out the window. "This countryside is so charming," he added, almost to himself.

"It *is* charming," Kelly said, wishing she could think of something more descriptive to add. Teresa would have.

The road narrowed. Teresa swerved to dodge cyclists in racing gear, appearing suddenly in their lane. She pounded the horn, muttering under her breath, pointing to them in frustration. "*Merde!*" she swore. "One day I'm going to hit one of these fools. They ride like they own the road."

As she passed the last of them, she replied to Daniel's question. "Historians dispute the grotto part. Some think Mary preached only in the valley. Some think she never came to Provence at all, but spent her last days in Ephesus along the coast of Asia Minor with the Virgin Mary and Saint John."

"And what do *you* think?" Daniel asked. Once again he gripped Kelly's seatback and leaned forward.

"I *like* to think she retired in the cave as a hermitess. I presented my arguments in my paper. I was hoping Father Gilbert might have found something conclusive. Isn't his research about the Magdalene? She's quite popular these days, as a goddess figure, especially with Gnostics. Some of those groups have some pretty spooky Internet sites. Have you seen them?"

"I've come across a few," Daniel said, then added in a different tone, "You said you worked with Father Gilbert? Is that how you knew about his research?"

Kelly could hear suspicion creep into his voice.

"He helped me with my paper, pointed me to sources. But his work was no secret. What we *don't* know is what he found."

They wound up the road, Teresa slowing on the blind curves, and often pulling to the side to let faster cars pass. Finally, they edged into a graveled lot and parked amid scrub oaks. "*Nous voici!*" Teresa said, beaming. "We are here, the grotto known as La Sainte Baume."

*

Monday afternoon Lester Sansby settled himself on a chaise lounge and gazed across the swimming pool to three sexy ladies gently massaging lotion onto their shapely legs and flat tummies. Beyond the girls, immense beech trees with mottled trunks bordered a long straight drive that led to the green-shuttered château. Lester inhaled the fresh scent of towering pines and newly mowed grass. He appreciated the place. Provence was indeed picturesque and peaceful, he thought, a far cry from Berkeley with the ranting students and highly charged politics, a far cry from a moonless midnight on a Roman bridge.

He ran his fingers over his early beard, the rough dark stubble slowly taking shape and changing his appearance satisfactorily, but the image of Fabio was an intrusion into his present state of well-being—the handsome face, the beautiful mouth and cold eyes, those long lashes and thick wavy hair, his startled look as he tumbled backwards into the rushing Tiber. Lester stared at his hands, the hands that held the knife. The young man had been demanding, way too demanding. And Fabio had been a killer at loose. Lester had simply helped out the *polizia,* safeguarded the good citizens of Rome. Today, here in this sensual countryside, he would forget about the incident on the bridge. He would erase Fabio's image from his memory. He would move forward and not look back. He wiped his palms on the towel and refocused on the girls on the other side of the pool.

They were young, slim, and tan. How young? Were they of an age of consent? Consent was important. After all, he was no beast, but were they jailbait? They could be. Even so, such scruples had not troubled him in the past. Why should they now?

As he watched, he counted his blessings. Gilbert was gone. Gilbert's killer was gone. Lester was close to Weaver and the girl, no thanks to his Treats who had come up with *nada*, except more reports of Gilbert's wealth. Still, he had recruited *FlowerGirl*, and she had fed him timely information. He wondered how she obtained it, but rarely did he question his sources. She had alerted him to Weaver's flight to Marseilles, and even mentioned this lovely château. Lester had arrived that morning, found a room far from the center of things, and kept a low profile. He put away his signature hat and donned a golf cap purchased in the hotel. He was no longer clean-shaven. He would work on simple disguises to use in the public areas, just in case they should see him, but his plan was to avoid them entirely. The property was large and with a little luck he could stay out of their way. And Lady Luck liked him.

Best of all, FlowerGirl had told him about the key, although not what it was for. She teased him. She tantalized. He liked that. FlowerGirl was certainly an excellent addition to his tribe. In fact, if he truly counted his blessings, he would say the gods were smiling upon him.

Lester Sansby grew sleepy with the heat of the day and the soft breeze and allowed himself to doze. Leaves rustled and somewhere a fountain splashed. He began to snore, waking himself abruptly and then nodding off again, his head jerking sporadically.

19

John Cassian

ANTICIPATING WITH PLEASURE A HIKE IN THE WOODS, Kelly photographed the trailhead sign as Teresa translated. "Welcome to this protected national forest…hikers walk these paths and enjoy the natural beauty and vistas… respect the land…don't take anything away and don't leave anything behind." Teresa regarded the wide path leading into the trees. "They say it's about a forty-minute walk to the grotto."

As a child Kelly had hiked with her parents and sometimes with other homeschoolers, and it was this moment that she particularly remembered, this moment of starting, not knowing where the trail would lead, or what would show up around the next corner. She recalled the sun slanting through the giant sequoias of Muir Woods and the moist smell of damp redwood bark, and she often thought that the light filtering through mist was not unlike the rays filtering through incense in a church. Then there were the Eucalyptus groves of Tilden Park, the sharp penetrating scent of long leaves and mottled bark. Whatever the path, it took her away from ordinary life and led her into another world of sight and smell and always hushed silence. Kelly recalled there was an unquestioned assumption of silence, of few words so that the woods could be heard, and perhaps God as well.

Here, in southern France, the ancient Provencal trail had its own character. The trail was dry and dusty in summer and breezes rustled the leafy trees. The path ran between and under them, beckoning through the moving shadows. Kelly checked the images in her camera and wished photos could preserve the entire experience.

Teresa resumed reading the board as she scanned the fine print. "The area is a unique microclimate of yews, oaks, and beeches, covering one hundred and thirty hectares, the remains of the primeval forest of Provence from the Tertiary Era."

"Is this the famous Chemin des Rois?" Daniel asked. "I've heard it was a wide pilgrimage route in the Middle Ages."

Teresa nodded, shifting her pack. "Many walked this path to her cave—kings, princes, ordinary pilgrims. They came up the Huveaune River valley from Marseilles, much as we did Saturday, and followed this trail. The Saint Victor Abbey, founded by John Cassian in 415, sent monks into this region. You can still see the ruins of their hermitages."

"John Cassian, John Chrysostom's deacon," Daniel said quickly. "I've read quite a bit about him."

Teresa nodded. "When Chrysostom was exiled from Constantinople, Cassian was exiled too. Eventually he came to Provence, which some believe was his home."

Kelly tried to follow their conversation but felt left out and a bit jealous, something she had difficulty admitting. She had, of course, heard of John Chrysostom, but would not have been able to place him. She recalled Ephesus, and the book in the Bible called Ephesians, Saint Paul's letter to the church in Ephesus, and earlier Daniel had mentioned that there was an Ephesus tradition relating to Mary Magdalene, the Virgin Mary, and Saint John. But that was pretty much it.

"The Ephesus shrine," Daniel explained to Kelly, "was to Diana, the Roman goddess, the same as Artemis, the Greek goddess. In the years after Christ's resurrection, Saint Paul preached in the Ephesus amphitheater and many were converted. He also preached against idolatry, which angered the silversmiths who made a living off goddess images. They rioted because Paul's success hurt their trade."

"That would make sense," Kelly said.

Daniel continued. "Later, when pagan shrines became illegal, John Chrysostom tore down the shrine to Diana."

Teresa checked her watch as they headed into the forest. "Some think this grotto was a shrine to Artemis, since Marseilles was a Greek community, with an Artemis temple. Some say Mary Magdalene could have preached here just as Paul preached in Ephesus."

"Then Cassian could have done the same," Kelly said tentatively. "He could have closed down a shrine here, in the same way Chrysostom closed the shrine in Ephesus."

They passed signs requesting silence and Teresa lowered her voice as she replied, "It's possible. As deacon, Cassian could have been with John Chrysostom in 401 when he demolished the Ephesus shrine."

"So," Daniel said, "we know he was in Marseilles, and we know the Cassianites were associated with this grotto."

"But there's no mention of Mary Magdalene in Cassian's letters," Teresa added.

"Or at least in the letters we have," Daniel said.

"True." Teresa appeared thoughtful, considering his point.

They stepped silently up the wide path, moving deeper into the ancient forest. The morning sun danced through broad leaves, lightening the shades of green and landing on lichen, moss, and wild mushrooms, and through the trees Kelly glimpsed patches of blue sky. They passed more signs along the way, requesting silence, and soon, in her own silence Kelly could hear other sounds: birds chattering, breezes rustling, the soft pad, pad of her feet on the trail, the beat of her own heart. She fell into a rhythm and, like those hikes of her childhood, became part of the forest. The path was well-worn but well-kept with benches for rest and small stone oratories with etched scenes from Mary's life that marked the way. After a time the fine gravel turned to boulders and sharp shards. Finally, they arrived at the base of a cliff. At the top of a sheer rock wall Kelly could see buildings that appeared to be carved out of the mountainside.

Stairs switchbacked and large crosses and carved plaques marked the way. Kelly read the etched stone.

Heureux les artisans de paix
Car ils seront appelés fils de Dieu.
Heureux les persécutés pour la justice
Car le royaume des cieux est à eux.

Teresa's whisper was nearly inaudible as she translated, and Kelly and Daniel drew close, watching her lips move. "Blessed are the peacemakers, for they shall be called sons of God. Blessed are those who are persecuted for righteousness' sake, for theirs is the kingdom of heaven."

"The Beatitudes," Kelly said.

They ascended into the limestone massif, leaving the forest far below. At a wooden gateway, a blue sign read:

MONASTÈRE
CASSIANITES 415-1079
BENEDICTINS 1075-1295

DOMINICAINS
(frères prècheurs)
1295-1793
1840-

"Cassianites are recorded as being here from the days of the founding of the Marseilles abbey." Daniel scratched his beard. "But why here? They must have believed Mary Magdalene was associated with the spot."

"That's pretty good evidence, isn't it?" Kelly whispered. In this grotto, she was certain, she would find the mysterious key, or even the manuscript itself.

Daniel nodded seriously. "It proves a strong tradition, but not the fact."

Kelly eyed him closely. *The tradition and not the fact.* "Still, it adds to the probability."

"Indeed, it does."

They passed through the gateway and ascended more stairs to a life-size crucifixion scene in a hollowed-out portion of the rock face. Kelly studied the crucified Christ. His head tilted to the side, and blood-red lash marks covered his body. His mother Mary and the apostle John stood on either side, and Mary Magdalene knelt at the base, her arms raised in prayer and petition, nearly touching Christ's feet. Her russet hair fell loose and long in curls over a green robe and red shawl. Real crimson roses bloomed, a living part of the tableau, nearly touching Mary Magdalene's figure. Kelly tried to imagine Mary's grief, knowing Jesus as a man on earth and losing him in this horrible way. Her sorrow must have been great. Kelly reflected that Mary Magdalene knew the grief of all ordinary women who have lost those they loved—*she represents me*, Kelly said to herself.

She caught up with Daniel and Teresa, who were nearing the top of the stairs. She paused to catch her breath and saw that she stood on a deep-set terrace overlooking the valley floor, far below. On the opposite side of the terrace was the grotto, a natural rock cavern formed in the mountain itself. Ten wide but shallow stairs led to its brick façade, gabled entrance doors, and curved stained-glass windows. Nearby, fronting the terrace, stood two buildings, built into the cliff-face, and Kelly judged these to be the monastery. Entranced with this world of mountain and sky, she inhaled the sweet, fresh air. She was on the edge of the world. She stepped past a life-size bronze Pietà commanding the center of the promontory and out to a low stone balustrade, where she gazed out to the broad sweep of forested plain.

"You can see Mont Sainte-Victoire today," Teresa whispered, pointing. "We're over three thousand feet above sea level. And there's my little hostelry in the valley where the sisters live and work."

"What a view!" Kelly whispered. To the north rolling green hills merged into the misty horizon where, she guessed, she saw the craggy Mont Sainte-Victoire, a familiar subject of Cézanne's paintings. Far below, at the bottom of the cliff, tiny buildings clustered on the valley floor near a parking lot with cars, buses, and vans, minute dark smudges.

They crossed the terrace to Mary Magdalene's grotto. Lingering in the doorway, their eyes adjusting to the dark, Kelly could see the chapel was large and semi-circular with high natural rock ceilings. She could hear the echo of water dripping into pools on the cavern floor, but the small marble chancel and nave, to the left of the doorway, was dry. From the nave, steps ascended to an altar supported by pedestals. A sculpted reredos with columns and gable depicted Mary Magdalene kneeling before the crucified Christ. Stairs curved up behind the sanctuary, and seven tapers burned on the right. Wooden pews with kneelers, divided by an aisle, faced the altar. Two smaller altars nested in the craggy rock face to the left. One altar reserved the Blessed Sacrament and one honored the Virgin Mary, a bank of burning votives flaming before her.

In the back, along the cavern wall, another white image was lit by more candles burning in the dark. The entire chapel was unlike anything Kelly could recall. The careful creation of man, carved in white marble, had been embedded in the natural creation of God. It was, she thought, at once rustic and polished, somehow uniting God and man, bound in time.

Teresa led them to Mary Magdalene's sculpted image in the back. "We're early for the Mass so I can show you around a bit," she whispered.

Daniel slipped a coin into a slotted metal box and removed a taper from a tray. Angling it, he held the wick close to one already lit, and in the cold damp the wick burned and died, then burned again. He handed the flaming candle to Kelly, who placed it in an iron stand with others aflame.

Kelly had lit candles with her mother at Saint Mary's in the Lady Chapel, a small bay to the left of the sanctuary. As she had watched the flame rise, they had prayed together, "Hail Mary...," and somehow the flame helped her to see the prayer rising too. The memory brought her mother close, brought her here into the dark cave, to be with her, in this moment in time. How many others had lit candles before this image? How many would light them after she left? Kelly gazed upon the Magdalene. The white marble flowed and swirled as though dancing. Angels on either side lifted the saint whose robes, like the angels, spun upwards.

"It's the story of Mont Saint Pilon," Daniel said. "Legend claims angels carried Mary Magdalene to the top of the mountain to hear heaven sing."

Teresa nodded. "It's a metaphor for the song of prayer, of meeting God, of knowing joy. Of course it could be true."

"That's lovely." Kelly absorbed the image and the story, which somehow felt familiar. Had she read about it, or was it one of the stories in the thick book of saints her father used to read to her at bedtime? There had been hundreds of one-page accounts with colorful pictures. She turned to Daniel. "But even if the angel part wasn't true, she probably heard singing in a sense, being so close to Christ in her earthly life."

Daniel regarded her with a new appreciation, Kelly thought. "Exactly," he said. "That's the real point, isn't it?"

Teresa seemed to be praying. Kelly prayed too, asking Mary Magdalene to aid them in their search. Daniel was kneeling on the cold cavern floor. He made the Sign of the Cross and stood.

Teresa led them to a glass case. "A few of her relics are here, her femur and some hair." Kelly peered inside, doubtful. Could they be real? She noticed that Daniel was fascinated. A woman knelt nearby. "Above the shrine, where you see the lit candles," Teresa continued, "is where she slept and prayed."

They turned toward the entrance. A luminous light spilled through the doorway, and as they approached the stained-glass windows, Kelly recognized scenes from Mary Magdalene's life: Christ forgiving her, Christ with her at her home in Bethany, Christ appearing to her in the garden. They were all glimmering images of the simple woman from Magdala, colored glass decorating her humble cavern.

Bells rang for it was nearing eleven. Visitors, young and old, were taking seats, and Kelly and Daniel followed Teresa to a pew in the back. They watched and waited in the cold and damp, and Kelly tugged her sweater closer about her. The wooden pew was hard, the back straight, and she shifted to find a comfortable position, all the while trying to imagine Mary Magdalene living in the grotto, praying and fasting. Was it all real? Any of it?

Was this grotto the subject of her godfather's research? Was it also the work of her parents when they died? Was this the reason they died? She recalled her mother's home office with its disorder, the stacks of papers and books with clips marking pages, the soft smell of accumulated dust. Bach and Mozart played as her mother bent over her work with an intensity that was nearly fierce. When Kelly approached, her mother would glance up with otherworldly eyes, then slowly focus on her, finally pulled into the here and now. Her father worked at his campus office, demanding and meticulous, escaping the cluttered environment at home. He wore the same brown corduroy jacket for years, always over a white cotton shirt. He carried a canvas backpack, and in spite of his need for order, always appeared rumpled. They both spent long hours in the university library and at times took her with them. The halls were a second home, a place to wander. She did her homework on shiny wooden desks with quaint lamps. The librarians didn't mind, and Kelly anticipated with pleasure those times, sitting in the great hall of wood and books and subdued light, the smell of old leather and dusty paper and lemon oil, the hard surface of the tables and their patterned grain.

Now Father Gilbert had sent her to Provence, with the mission of finding the key to the little ambry in Rome. Where was the key? How were they to find it? Kelly studied the sanctuary, her eye moving to the Madonna and Child, to the side altar and tabernacle, to the luminous Magdalene and angels in the dark. No key in sight. Was it hidden somewhere? Should they inquire at the monastery?

A bell rang and two Dominicans processed in, robed in white—one young, one middle-aged. The older one stepped to the high altar. He sang the Mass, his voice echoing in the damp air, and, in spite of the French, Kelly recognized the order of the service, the lessons, the prayers, the sermon. Next, she knew, the priest would consecrate the bread and wine, and as she watched his movements, she saw him approach the tabernacle on the side altar in the rough rock wall. From a pocket in his robe he pulled out a key with a green tassel. Kelly stared, stunned, and in that fleeting moment recalled her dream of last night. She had seen in her dream an old stone tabernacle with a key and a green tassel. She nudged Daniel. He nodded.

Now, impatient, Kelly thought the Mass interminable, but even so she knelt on the hard wooden slat in the glowing candlelight and prayed for trust. She prayed for wisdom. She prayed for Matt and Andrea, and her parents and Father Gilbert in heaven. She tried to confess her sins—she knew she had been envious of Teresa, jealous as well, angry with the delays, too worried over safety, not trusting Andrea. Perhaps pride? Perhaps they were all parts of pride? It came to her gradually that to know what was true and what was not, she would have to search for the lies in her own heart. Only in a place of humility with a heart washed clean, only there could God write the truth, only then could she discern what was real and unreal. Soon she joined the others to receive Holy Communion, forgetting for the moment her worries.

As she returned to her pew, Kelly glanced beyond the high altar to the white swirling Magdalene in the back. Mary Magdalene saw the resurrected Christ. She ran to tell the others. At least that much was true. At least according to the Bible. What had her godfather written about this woman? What had he learned?

20

Father Bidwell

AT A CAFÉ ADJACENT TO THE PILGRIMS' HOSTEL, they found tables under broad umbrellas, shading them from the noonday's harsh sun. Father Bidwell, the celebrant of the Mass, joined them, and they were soon reading plasticized menus *en français* with English translations. An attractive young woman served them, jauntily setting down a carafe of water and arranging glasses on paper mats. She gave the impression she enjoyed her job, Kelly thought, moving from table to table, checking on everyone with a big smile.

The friar leaned toward them doubtfully. "You want this key? I cannot imagine why," he said with a faint British accent. He handed Daniel the tabernacle key. The shiny brass caught the light, and the green tassel seemed new.

Father Bidwell now wore a black cassock. He had a rugged face, Kelly thought, darkened by the Provençal sun, with strong facial bones, a prominent nose, and gray-blue eyes. His fair hair, thinning at the top, was cut short, with early streaks of gray. She guessed he was in his late forties. His face and figure were both athletic and ascetic, a curious combination, but perhaps appropriate for a monastery set in this landscape of mountain and forest.

"We don't know for sure if this is the right one," Daniel said doubtfully, studying the key in his palm. "We're searching for a key to an ambry in Rome."

The priest eyed them curiously. "But this is a new key. We only recently had it cut. The old one needed replacement. It was rusty and sticking in the lock, so we had the lock refitted to match."

Kelly's disappointment hit her hard. She glanced at Daniel and could see he too was taken aback. Teresa's face, on the other hand, was unreadable, a mask. But her jaw muscle twitched and she gripped her fork.

"What happened to the old key?" Kelly asked.

"Please, Father," Daniel said, "can you recall what you did with it?" He returned the new one to the priest.

Father Bidwell assessed his attentive audience with increased interest. "Is it valuable? How could such a thing be valuable? It's just a key."

"It could be," Kelly said, not sure how much to say.

Daniel nodded. "You must trust us that it's valuable in many ways. Can you tell us what happened to it?"

"Well, it was around Easter—Holy Week, I believe. We had been meaning to refit the key and the lock for months and had postponed the work until after the winter season, which is far slower than the summer, with few communicants. Let me think." He ran his hand over his balding crown. "I do recall now. The sacristan kept the old one on a chain around his neck. He said it was a reminder of the sacredness of things. But he's no longer with us."

"Where is he?" Daniel asked. "Was he one of your Dominicans?"

Bidwell paused. "No, he was, is, a lay brother. His name is Pierre Durand. sweet simple soul, rather like those Down syndrome children. But he isn't Downs, normal as far as I know, just not very bright. He followed instructions well, as long as you didn't make too many changes. He liked repetition. A large young man, and strong, and he took good care of our shrine. He actually had a…well I'd say…a *glow* about him. I miss him."

"Where is he now, Father?" Kelly asked, dreading the answer.

The priest gazed across the forested plateau to the limestone massif. The grotto could barely be seen, the windowed façades merging into the cliff face. "A good lad, to be sure. He loved God, and he loved the Eucharist." Bidwell turned to Kelly. "I'm not at all sure where he is now. The last I heard he was sacristan at Saint Victor's in Marseilles. I'll see if I can find his mobile number." He pulled out his phone and tapped the screen. "Sorry, it's been delisted."

"Saint Victor's? The Cassianite Abbey?" Daniel asked.

"Exactly so. Although it's not an abbey anymore, but a parish church. Now please tell me, what is behind all this interest in a tabernacle key, and an unusable one at that?"

As their meals arrived, Daniel explained briefly the reason for their visit.

"*Opus Veritatis?* Father Gilbert?" The friar bit into his sandwich and ate rapidly, dabbing his mouth with a napkin. "I heard of his passing, may his soul rest in peace," he said soberly as he made the Sign of the Cross. "And I subscribe to the newsletter—excellent work. But you speak of gold? And valuable research? Here at the grotto? I haven't heard of this. But he could have been here before my time."

"My godfather wanted to educate me." Kelly tasted a bite of warm goat cheese nesting in a bed of greens and tomatoes. The tart richness jolted her senses. "This is a wonderful salad."

Daniel glanced at her with tenderness, she thought. "Upon his death,"

Daniel explained, "he left letters for Kelly and me, creating an elaborate path to Kelly's inheritance."

"Daniel has been my guide," Kelly added. "He took classes from Father Gilbert in Rome."

"And I joined them to help out," Teresa said. "I speak French, and I'm familiar with the Magdalene histories." She touched the priest's sleeve. "Do you recall me, Father?"

Bidwell studied the young woman, then grinned with recognition, showing long teeth faintly yellowing. "But of course! You studied the documents in our archives in Nans-les-Pins. How did the research go?"

"Good enough for my Master's in History," she said with pride. "My advisor was impressed with the use of primary sources. My subject was Mary Magdalene's last years. And the Lacordaire material was superb."

"Ah yes! Henri Lacordaire changed everything, did he not?"

"He certainly brought things to light."

Kelly recalled Sister Gabriella mentioning Henri Lacordaire. She listened carefully, interested in this part of Teresa's story.

"Then your paper is about real history. That's good," Bidwell said.

"What do you mean, Father?" Daniel asked.

Bidwell tapped his fingers together thoughtfully. "I took my vows three years ago. Until then I was an academic, dean of a college in England, a quite prestigious one actually. I was Dr. Bidwell then." He laughed with the memory, and his face relaxed. "It seems like another life now, but I have no regrets. You asked what I meant by *real history*, and I will give you the short answer, for the long one is, well, too long." He glanced at his watch.

"Yes, please," Daniel urged, glancing at Kelly, "please go on."

"Real history is just that," Father Bidwell continued, "the true study of the past. We are in a postmodern age in which most fields have been over-researched, literally saturated, but there is tremendous pressure on historians and students to produce new material. Thus the researchers find a new angle, a narrow aspect which is either completely unimportant or outright invention. They *overcomplicate* history, something encouraged by technology. "

"That happened to me when I chose my thesis," Daniel said. "I had to narrow the subject in order to make it original."

"And what did you title your paper?" Father Bidwell asked, clearly intrigued.

"*Copied Ninth-Century Codices and Their Effect on Historical Accuracy.*"

Kelly wondered why she had never asked him about his thesis, but then, she had only known him a few weeks. It seemed much longer.

Bidwell nodded. "A good example, although yours sounds worthy of the effort, a valuable contribution. So, you have the need to publish something new and thus you narrow the topic. Secondly you have the subjective attitude of the historian. I'm not sure which came first, the subjective view or the need to publish. They probably fed one another, the attitude and the need. It is this subjectivity, which denies the fixity of the past and embraces the opinion of the present, that defines Postmodernism."

"That's so true," Daniel said. "I teach at the university level, and many of my colleagues see the past as solely defined by the individual historian, as though objective truth doesn't exist. I agree that we see history from our own viewpoint, prejudiced to a degree. Still this attitude has gone too far. That is, *in my opinion*," he added, laughing.

Father Bidwell nodded with appreciation. "It is fair to state that, Daniel. I sympathize with the intention to truly *do* history, to find out what actually happened in the past. But Postmodernist history recognizes *no* reality principle, only the pleasure principle—history at the pleasure of the historian. But it sounds as if Teresa was doing real research, real history, rather than reporting on the use of teaspoons in the year 1830 in Dorset in the lower middle class."

"Thank you," she said.

"What are you doing now?" the friar asked.

"I'm working in Rome for my uncle, a priest at Maria Maggiore. He reports for *Opus Veritatis,* as well as being on staff at the basilica. I'm twenty-six, so I need to decide what to do next, but I'm not sure. I love Rome and don't want to leave. I need to clear up a few odds and ends in my life before deciding." She once again looked troubled, her voice weighted with sadness and, Kelly thought, some fear. Twenty-six was so young to be afraid, but then Kelly had been only twenty when she lost her parents and had been plunged into her own world of uncertainty and, to a very real degree, fear.

"You don't have to decide right away. You're still young," the priest said, as though concerned with Teresa's unexpected change of mood. "You've done well. Ever think about teaching real history? You'd need a doctorate, of course."

"With due respect, Father, I've heard the world of academia is a jungle."

"That's for sure," Daniel said. "I just finished a book surveying academia, and I think the author's right. Most professors do little teaching, so that they can research. Seventy percent of the teaching is done by part-timers, temps, and grad students! *Seventy percent!* And colleges hire more administrators, doubling the administrator-student ratio in the last thirty years."

Kelly jumped in. "All because of pressure to write about nineteenth-century teaspoons."

Teresa clapped her hands. "And the effect of daffodils on feline sinuses in the subtropical Sahara."

"You would be a true missionary," Bidwell challenged.

Teresa shook her head. "More likely fodder for the mills."

Bidwell sat back, locking his fingers. "You may be right, but someone has to straighten things out, now that I've escaped." He checked his watch.

Daniel said seriously, "Father, I for one will try. And thank you. You've been most gracious with your time."

Bidwell nodded. "My pleasure. Indeed, I must go. But I almost forgot." He rummaged in his pocket, pulled out a small silver medal, and handed it to Kelly. "I believe Teresa has one already. Please keep this as a souvenir. The Magdalene will guard you."

Kelly examined the finely wrought image. Mary Magdalene's hair was long, flowing over her shoulders. She held a long narrow-necked jar in her arms. Did it contain oil for anointing Christ's body in the tomb?

"Thank you so much," she said, earnestly gazing into the friar's eyes. "It's lovely."

"You're most welcome! And now I must go. We are on a strict schedule, and there will be another service soon." They exchanged farewells.

"Do you have a chain?" Teresa asked, watching the friar head up the trail to the grotto.

Kelly shook her head. "I'm afraid I don't."

"Then take this one." She unclasped her own and slipped her own medal in a pocket. "I have others," she said, handing the silver necklace to Kelly. "This will help you on your quest." She smiled, as though hoping for friendship.

Kelly was touched. "Thank you, Teresa." At first she was going to refuse, but Teresa's expression made it impossible. Rejecting the chain could have been rejecting Teresa.

"It is my pleasure," Teresa replied, clearly satisfied.

Kelly slipped the medal onto the chain, then around her neck. It felt feather light against her tee. She turned to Daniel. "When do we go to Saint Victor's?"

"Tomorrow."

*

Kelly dialed from her room. It was five p.m., eight in the morning, California time. She needed to reach them before they went out for the day.

"Andrea?"

"Kelly, so glad you called again. We were just on our way out, getting an early start, taking a ferry boat ride with Todd."

"Is Todd with you? What about the cats?"

"He's only here for two days. He left plenty of food and water."

"But…" Kelly's heart clutched with the thought of her kitties unattended for two days, but asked, "How's Matt? How's his asthma? You have his inhaler and medication?"

Andrea laughed lightly. "Sure do. And he's just fine—he scraped his knee yesterday, but it's healing up okay. Todd checked it. He was a nurse's aide for a time, you know."

Kelly had lost count of Todd's jobs. "Can I talk to Matt?"

"He's already in the car with the boys."

"Then could you get him, please?"

"Sure can. Just a sec."

The line went quiet; then she heard, "Hi, Kelly."

Kelly recognized Todd's voice, deep and masculine, so self-assured. She had seen him come and go from time to time next door. She'd also seen a parade of young ladies come and go with him. She never asked Andrea about Todd. He was too good-looking in a high school athletic sort of way, the kind of guy who was captain of the football team, who sailed through life with numerous doors opening and he unable to choose which ones to go through. Blond, blue-eyed, tall, muscular, strong-jawed. But he must now be in his late thirties, she guessed. She wondered if he ever questioned his life choices. His lack of direction.

"Hi, Todd. Thanks for feeding the cats. And checking on Matt's knee."

"No problemo. Always glad to be of service. How's Rome? Or is it France?"

For some reason he sounded interested in her. She had been below his radar until now. Was it Rome, and now France that caught his attention? That she was in Europe, a world traveler?

"Fine."

"Been watchin' the news—lots of things on TV and the Internet about this group you're involved with."

"I know."

"A murder investigation!"

"Yes."

"You believe this stuff that *Opus Veritatis* writes? I've been reading their online newsletter."

"Of course. I trust them."

"They're pretty harsh and judgmental, to my way of thinking. I say live and let live. Be happy. They say we are all selfish…what do you say, Kelly?"

"Where's Matt?"

"Ah, here comes the little lad now."

"Hi, Mommy." Matt sounded so far away, so vulnerable, so young.

"Hi, sweetie."

"I'm going on a big boat."

"That's great. How's your knee?"

"It hurts, but Todd says it's better."

"Good."

"When are you coming home?"

"Soon."

*

Lester Sansby woke with a jerk. He had slipped down the chaise and into a cramped position. Now he was ravenous. How long had he been dozing? His watch said five-thirty.

He closed his laptop and scanned the patio. The girls were gone. A shame. An elderly couple had settled nearby.

He decided to head back to the room and order room service. He needed to recharge his laptop. He needed to make plans.

21

The Cassianites

TUESDAY MORNING DANIEL DROVE. They followed the curve of the road through more vine-covered hills, along the River Huveaune, toward the village of Saint-Zacharie. In the bright light of the cloudless morning Kelly recognized little of the Saturday drive from Marseilles to the château in the then dimming dusk.

Her call to Matt the previous evening had flooded her with homesickness. She reassured Andrea it wouldn't be long now, but as she hung up she knew she had no idea how long it would be. When *would* she return? Should she give up? Each time she asked herself the question, she saw not only her godfather's encouraging eyes, but her father as well, pointing his finger to unfinished homework. She saw her mother watching with a loving trust. How could she let them down? Then there was Mary Magdalene, who hovered on the edges of her consciousness, a white sculpted image, more real each day.

She gazed out the open window of the car to the sunlit fields, enjoying the fresh air. The day was warming, and she glanced at her skirt and sandals, then checked her sweater, folded in her tote, alongside Daniel's Oakland A's cap on the backseat. Her Magdalene medal lay against her heart, and she touched it lightly with her fingertips. Should she have bought a sun hat in the hotel shop? She smoothed her hair behind her ears and checked the wide pink elastic that bound her ponytail. "Teresa works hard," she said. "She spent Sunday working and now today."

Daniel, in short sleeves and khakis, seemed at home behind the wheel of the Renault. "We don't know for certain what she does, do we? She's online a great deal. We only have her word that she's filing reports for *Opus Veritatis*. But I trust her uncle, and he clearly knew Father Gilbert. So that's something."

"She's mysterious, that's for sure. And troubled, I think."

"I had the same impression. She's very secretive." Daniel glanced at Kelly, then fell silent.

Kelly thought the description applied to Daniel as well, but then she herself had secrets too, she supposed. When did reserved become withholding? When did withholding become secretive? It was a continuum.

They curved south through forested hills, then followed signs to the auto-route, stopped at a pay station for a ticket, and merged into speeding traffic. Kelly raised her window, feeling the steady drum of the wheels on the asphalt, safe within the now-sealed vehicle. She examined her roadmap, searching for the Aubagne interchange, where they would head west to Marseilles.

"Daniel…do you think we'll ever find this key?" Kelly watched the fast-moving cars, vans, and produce haulers. Signs announcing off-ramps and routes to villages flashed by.

"I hope so."

"That stranger in the back of Santa Maddalena—do you think he was Sansby? Do you think he knows about the key?"

"He could be Sansby, but we don't know. I don't see how he could know about the key, even if he was Sansby. And we haven't seen anyone like him in these parts. Maybe we lost him. Sansby has been particularly active online, but I'm not sure what that means. There's some kind of code he's using I haven't been able to figure out."

He sounded discouraged. Kelly wished she could lift his spirits, somehow reach him. At times he retreated behind a protective shell, thin but durable. "I don't see how this Dr. Sansby could know we're in France, let alone Marseilles. Rome must have been just a good guess."

Daniel nodded. "I hope you're right." He tapped the turn signal and, glancing back, cautiously changed lanes, the clicking like a metronome pacing their journey.

"Tell me again about Saint Victor's Abbey," she said, hoping to raise his spirits.

A half smile appeared. "It's one of the earliest sites of French Christianity."

Kelly could see he was more at ease now, talking about what he loved. "Earliest, because of the Cassianites?" she asked. "And all the hermitages they founded in the valley below the cave?" Kelly pictured the monks going into the countryside, building huts that would become chapels that would become villages.

Daniel glanced at her briefly, and Kelly thought that for the moment she had drawn him away from his worry over Lester Sansby. "Exactly," he said. "The hermitages prove there was a monastic interest in the region. And this morning—because of recent excavations—we should be able to see the remains of the first abbey."

"And hopefully we will find this Pierre Durand."

"Yes, Durand and the key."

"But the abbey sounds fascinating."

"Indeed. I often imagine what it was like to be a Christian in the first century. And this particular region near a major Greek-Roman port would have been bustling. Pilgrims would be journeying from the Temple of Artemis in Marseilles to the Grotto of Artemis in the Sainte-Baume Massif, although the Romans must have changed the name to Diana at some point."

"Do you think Mary Magdalene preached in Marseilles like Saint Paul did in Ephesus?"

"It's possible, maybe even probable. There is a strong tradition in Marseilles that she preached from the temple square, where an audience would already be gathered."

"And it would make sense that she would have followed them to the grotto shrine as well."

"Precisely."

They again fell into silence, as Daniel maneuvered away from lorries, passing slower traffic only to see faster cars appear abruptly behind them, horns blaring.

"I'm beginning to believe," Daniel said, "that 391 AD must have been a watershed year. In some ways it was more important than Constantine's conversion in 312 and the Council of Nicaea in 325. In 391, Emperor Theodosius outlawed pagan cults and closed their shrines. As Teresa said, the Patriarch of Constantinople, John Chrysostom, probably with his deacon Cassian, destroyed the Ephesus temple in 401. There must have been a church building boom in that first decade of the fifth century, as these properties became available. The Marseilles Temple to Diana would have been closed by edict. The grotto as well."

"Do you think Cassian rebuilt them as Christian churches?"

"We don't know. We know that two monasteries were founded, perhaps simply groups bound by a rule of life, one for men and one for women. The women's was located near the Greco-Roman market. The men's was across the harbor, built over a third-century quarry and cemetery. It's probable Saint Victor was buried there, and the men's monastery and abbey built over his grave."

"And Victor—?"

"Victor was a Christian soldier martyred in Marseilles in 290."

"So how much of this would you say is possible, probable, or true?"

"It's the usual problem of proof." He squinted as though organizing his argument. "Some histories say they can't associate Cassian with this monastic foundation because the oldest parts of the earlier church only date to the *late* fifth century, not the *early*. But documents found by Chanoine Albanès in the nineteenth century state that Cassian founded the abbey and sent his monks into the hills. So it is highly probable, nearing fact. You cannot prove a negative any more than you can a positive."

"In other words, you evaluate the entire picture."

They approached the Aubagne interchange and turned onto the highway to Marseilles.

"Precisely, we evaluate it all. *In fact*, always an interesting phrase," he said with an ironic smile, "this must have been one of the earliest Christian monastic foundations. Saint Benedict, early sixth century, recognized as the Founder of Western Monasticism because of the widespread adoption of his rule, actually didn't establish the first monastery. Before Benedict, there were monasteries in Ligugé, Tours, and Lérins, as well as Cassian's Saint Victor's. John Cassian's writings influenced the later foundations."

"Did any of these Saint Victor monks live as hermits?"

"Probably at some point. For a time Cassian lived among the Eastern desert fathers who were hermits in Palestine and Egypt. And this is where the term *monk* comes from, from the Greek meaning 'single, solitary, alone.' By the way, desert doesn't necessarily mean 'sand,' but merely 'wild and isolated, deserted.' "

"So the Saint Victor monks naturally would have lived in the wilds as well."

"And perhaps the area had become more deserted as pagan cults lost their popularity. These men came to Marseilles to learn and live Cassian's rule of life. The monastery would have educated and trained them, then sent them out. Numerous churches in the Provençal area were begun by Cassianites. Open my laptop. There should be a John Cassian file in Documents."

Kelly reached for his laptop in the backseat, opened it, and found the file with its list of local hermitage sites. "There's one near here that still has monks—Montrieux—associated with Petrarch's brother." She recalled Petrarch had been known for his love sonnets and letters. "Did Petrarch live around here?"

"He was associated with the Avignon papacy in the fourteenth century, so he would have been north of here. He writes in his letters about his brother being in Montrieux. Today the monastery is Carthusian, so it's enclosed and private, but it was founded by Cassianites. Their website showed a chapel open to the public, but the rest is walled off. If I ever come back to this area, it would be interesting to see the chapel. It appears to be in the mountains north of Toulon."

Kelly smiled with recognition. "Here's one name that's on my map: La Celle, early fifth century, near Brignoles. And here's Saint-Jean-du-Puy, west of Saint-Maximin near Trets. You say that Saint Ser was trained there in the fifth century, that he had heard of Cassian, and that he had come from the north to study with him."

"And Saint Ser set up his hermitage on Mont Sainte-Victoire."

"The mountain Cézanne painted—we could see it from the terrace of La Sainte Baume." Kelly was growing excited by the facts forming a pattern, and she saw again how historical research could be fascinating. She continued, surprised by her own breathlessness, "And then there are the villages: Saint-Zacharie, Saint-Clair, Saint-Quinis, whose hermitage was near Besse-sur-Issole. Is that how you say it?"

"Good accent, Kelly." His appreciation warmed her cheeks. "They think Saint Victor's sent out five thousand monks at its peak."

"Five thousand! So there are hundreds more undiscovered sites, ruins." Kelly gazed out the window, a bit flustered by the intensity of Daniel's glance. "And the nuns?"

"They would have been cloistered for safety in their own convent, Saint-Sauveur, on the other side of the harbor. These were dangerous times for women. The Saracens destroyed both of the monasteries in the seventh and eighth centuries, murdered abbesses and nuns. In the tenth century the men's Saint Victor's was rebuilt, but not the women's Saint-Sauveur. The church we'll see today is a real medieval fortress, according to the photos, with massive towers and turrets, and with its history I understand why."

Kelly sensed that they were nearing Marseilles. The traffic had increased, yet slowed down, the exit signs more frequent. She studied the map. "Watch for a tunnel to *Le Vieux Port*," she said, scrutinizing the fine print.

Soon they descended beneath the city's surface, into a dark, lamp-lit tunnel, giving Kelly the sense of burrowing deeper and deeper underground, mole-like. But within minutes they surfaced to the bright light of day. The roadway clover-leafed, and they navigated up a hill to a promontory overlooking a harbor and quay. Behind them rose the towers of Saint Victor's. Below them spread the Mediterranean and the old port of Marseilles.

22

The Creed of the Apostles

WHILE DANIEL PURCHASED A PARKING TICKET FROM A NEARBY KIOSK, Kelly studied the abbey's rosy blocks of stone jutting into the sky. Here on this hill high above the sea, the medieval abbey guarded the white city from all invasion. It stood strong, timeless, permanent.

She followed Daniel to the edge of a viewing terrace. Gulls cried, swooping and diving, and a light breeze rippled the warm summer air. White sails and straight masts, row after row, waited in the bay below, as though for the next stage of history. On the opposite shore, stone spires and domes competed with cement high-rises that silhouetted against the big sky.

Daniel pointed across the harbor. "That's the historic Greco-Roman district where Saint-Sauveur would have been. Further north would have been the Temple of Diana. In the sixth century the temple was sanctified as a Christian baptistery, and in the nineteenth century the present cathedral was built over it. According to recent excavations, the temple was octagonal and richly decorated."

"So that would have been where Mary Magdalene preached."

Daniel adjusted his glasses. "Right. She would have been reporting the good news, the *gospel*, from the eastern borders of the empire."

"Christianity was illegal, but still she preached."

"Actually it wasn't illegal until Nero came to power, about thirty years after Christ died. But once illegal, Christians worshiped in secret, sharing these good-news stories, accounts that became oral histories. Eventually they recorded the histories on scrolls or codices, writing the repeated phrases of the first witnesses, such as Mary Magdalene."

"Codices?"

"The codex, or the early book form, uses pages that turn, unlike the scroll that unrolls. Some scholars speculate that Christians originated, invented, the codex to distinguish their writings from the scrolls of the Jews and the Romans."

"Makes sense. So Mary Magdalene and the apostles began the oral telling."

"Exactly, and the tellings became the writings. The writings reflected what these early Christians believed to be true accounts of enormous significance, both personally and publicly. Over time the accounts crystallized into creedal phrases: First, there was the Creation and God's journey with His chosen People of Israel; then the Son's birth, suffering, death, resurrection, ascension, judgment; finally, the coming of the Holy Spirit, the founding of the Church, the Communion of Saints, the forgiveness of sins, and our own bodily resurrections."

Kelly observed his profile. Beads of perspiration had formed on his forehead, and he swept his hand over the area in an easy gesture. His blue cotton shirt was open at the neck, exposing olive skin and black curly hair. As though catching herself spying, she turned back to the harbor and those earlier days. "The Creed," she said quickly, "was what Father Gilbert was stressing in the Rome churches. The *Apostles' Creed.* How the catechumens recited the phrases in the baptisteries." Rome now seemed like a collection of distant images.

"That's right. The Creed brings each believer inside the Christian story. Father Gilbert was trying to make the story real for you with this journey, even having us memorize phrases in the letters and poems. We are brought inside the story in Baptism and the promise of eternal life. We are brought inside the story again in this journey."

"You make it sound cosmic, on a grand scale."

"When you stand back, it is cosmic." He opened his palms in awe, facing her. "Because the story is about God, it is truly mythic, which is not to say untrue, but rather of huge consequence for mankind, for you and me. Christians live inside this God-story."

Inside this God-story. "I like that." It made sense of her world, her life.

Daniel leaned back on the low wall and looked up to the towers. His face glowed. Kelly too felt exhilaration, as though she owned both the past and the future, yet stood outside of time, stepping into eternity. Here, on this ridge over this historic city, she felt like one of the gulls, soaring between heaven and earth. She had forgotten for the moment her life in California. She had tucked Matt into a corner of her mind, safe with Andrea. She had traveled far on this journey of hers, of theirs, and now for the first time she longed to learn where it would lead her.

She studied Daniel's face, so full of joy. Was she falling in love? She shook herself. How could she think such a thing? Allow such a thing?

"The Christian claims," Daniel said, turning to her, "that there is more to life than the material world, that there is mystery and miracle." He rubbed his hands. "We say this mystery cannot always be measured or manipulated. We say it is found in matter as well as spirit, in sensory things, in bodily things. So the world becomes precious, full of meaning, a gift we celebrate." He opened his hands to the abbey's towers, then out to the sea.

Kelly pulled out her camera, then focused on the harbor, the white masts, the spires, the domes. She turned and focused on his profile and clicked. "Is that what people mean when they call themselves *spiritual* rather than *religious?*"

"Partly…"

Kelly felt his gaze as she focused her camera on the abbey's towers. It was agreeable, pleasant, to own his attention and hear his voice.

"Although," he continued, "those who say they are spiritual, while they say they are seeking God, are not too happy when they find him."

She refocused on a particularly old vessel in the port, somewhat like a clipper ship, and said, "Why is that?" *He's talking about me.*

"I think they enjoy the process of seeking, dabbling, never truly knowing. So they say they are not *religious* because that means being committed to a church that offers answers, that tells them who God is, and most importantly, tells them what he commands."

Kelly slipped her camera into her bag, considering his words. Before the last few weeks, she would have described herself as *spiritual, not religious,* as though the phrase distanced her from precisely such commitments. *Spiritual* meant she was superior, free of restraints imposed by a church. Now that she was finding answers, through her own seeking, did she accept them? Or did she want to keep on seeking and never finding? Was she a dabbler? She didn't want to be. "I called myself that once," she admitted, facing him.

"Somehow I thought so."

His smile held no trace of judgment. It was such a smooth smile, Kelly thought, such a comfortable easy smile with the curious uplift on one side, and now his features relaxed as though released by the smile itself. His eyes crinkled. He lightly traced her cheek with his finger as he said, "You are beautiful, Miss Kelly Ann Roberts. Do you know that?"

She wanted to kiss him, to feel his lips, but shyness mingled with apprehension pulled her away. She replied, "Thank you, but we'd better find Pierre Durand and see the church." She turned away quickly, heading toward the basilica. She didn't need to get involved like that. She didn't need complications. But she hoped he was following. She didn't look back, but paused at the doors at the base of one of the towers.

He stepped in front of her. "I'm so sorry. I was too forward."

"It's okay." Unable to look him in the eye, she stared beyond him to the open doors.

"But you were so pretty back there, the freckles running over your nose, the sun turning your hair all golden brown, taking those photos, so intent. The words just burst out. Now I'm miserable, for you are upset."

She forced herself to face him. His dark eyes were clouded over. "It's okay, Daniel. I'm the one who's sorry. Once hurt, twice shy, as they say. I'm still a little scared of male attention. But I like you, Daniel, so I have to be extra careful." She was startled by her own honesty and astonished when she kissed him lightly on the lips, feeling the brush of his beard. "Let's go in," she said, feeling more in control.

*

Late Tuesday morning, Lester Sansby peered through the open window of his attic room. Situated in an outlying building of Domaine Châteauneuf, probably once the stables, his room was perfect. He didn't have to enter through the lobby of the main house and risk Weaver recognizing him. But from his window, in spite of the leafy chestnut trees, he could monitor the château's entrance and watch guests coming and going. Slipping a hefty tip to a housemaid had loosened her tongue, and he was able to supplement FlowerGirl's cryptic clues with these gleanings.

Lester had seen Weaver and the girl leave earlier, and he cursed himself for not being prepared to follow at once. He hoped FlowerGirl would shed some light on their movements. Today he would enjoy the sun and keep up-to-date with his online groups. He deserved a little relaxation.

Lester placed his laptop in his satchel and headed for the pool, wearing a hotel robe over his red Lycra Speedo. He could monitor his mail and his sites here as well as in his room, with the modern miracle of Wi-Fi. He entered through a wrought-iron gate, grabbed two towels, and laid his things on a chaise. For the time being he had the pool to himself. He slipped out of his robe and paused at the foot of the rectangle of turquoise water, his feet balanced on the tiled rim. The sun beat hard on his back and he rotated his shoulders to loosen up, twisting his neck and shaking his hands to loosen his fingers. He readied himself, his eye on the glassy surface. He dove, arms straight, hoping to slice at a shallow angle.

The cold sent ripples through his skin and he caught his breath with a brief gasp, then settled into a rhythmic crawl, his arms rising and sliding into the water, pushing down and away. He felt in control when he swam laps, his muscles working to propel his body forward like a sleek craft. As he swam, his mind drifted to the evening before. He had enjoyed himself. These resorts did have their benefits.

He had hooked up with a pretty co-ed from Nice in the bar and the evening had progressed satisfactorily, at least he thought she was pleased, but he also sensed she was ready to move on. After all, he knew he wasn't in as good shape as he once was, and a fifty-nine-year-old man was never as supple as a younger one, even if he *was* blessed with excellent genes and the discipline to diet and exercise. Lester prided himself on his physique, robust but not threatening. His hair was thick and wavy, his face tough yet sensitive, rather like Harrison Ford or George Clooney, he often speculated. He had a strong jaw line and didn't need this silly beard with its unwelcome silver flecking the dark, but even so a beard might not be a bad idea in terms of image, and he was giving his new look serious consideration. He knew he was sexy, and over the years his workouts, swimming and weight training, had kept him in good stead, but he had to say that the girls were easy marks in Berkeley.

But if and when he was totally honest with himself, he realized he had let himself go just a tad. His stomach sagged (almost imperceptibly) even when he focused on tightening his abs, and his arms had lost some of their muscle tone. Recently he had noticed the beginnings of a double chin, so he tried not to linger in front of the mirror too often, a difficult habit to break.

Still, he had his hair, graying nicely, his good bones, and his natural chemistry with women. He knew how to laugh with appreciation, color his conversation with subtle innuendoes, and compliment while flirting. Then there was his experience. He was gifted with sensing where to touch, how to touch, and how long to linger. Women appreciated that. They liked *slow*. Most men were brutes and didn't appreciate *slow*. He was sensitive to the ladies' needs.

Lester pulled himself from the pool and dried off. He made himself comfortable and opened his laptop. He needed to review this tedious Gilbert business. His busy little Treats were certain it was indeed a lucrative venture. He was actually beginning to believe the rumors of wealth that circulated around *Opus Veritatis* Foundation, or OVF as they called it.

Lester tipped the laptop screen for better viewing and checked his Inbox, delighted to see a message from FlowerGirl.

No key at cave. Today S. Victor, Marseilles. More soon.
FG

He arrowed and clicked *Reply*.

Many thanks. No reward too great for such excellent service, my dear. Urgent need to find this material. I will not forget!

He clicked *Send*. Weaver and his girlfriend could do the legwork, and then, *voilà*, they might be encouraged, required, if you will, to share their finds.

He signaled to an attractive pool server to bring him lunch. He had heard that a new group was checking in that night, students from Toulon. He patted his soft stomach and decided to have a green salad, dressing on the side, and a double vodka. Then perhaps a nap.

23

The Crypt

THE GUIDEBOOK DESCRIBED THE FOURTEENTH-CENTURY TRIPLE NAVE and soaring ribbed vaults as Provençal Romanesque, but Kelly would have added *ethereal*. She could picture long processions in the dark with incense and candles, even in today's parish church. The chanting would rise with the smoke, higher and higher, just as the people's hearts and souls would rise, reaching upwards and also in some mysterious counterpoint, inwards.

With some difficulty she pulled herself into the present and said, "Let's ask someone about Pierre Durand."

They found a vendor selling souvenirs at the foot of the central aisle. He ran his hands down a creased apron. "Pierre Durand? Ah, no, he is gone, to another basilica, near his home." He raised mottled fingers and fluttered them upwards as though the young man had flown through the thick walls.

Daniel frowned. "His home? Where? *Où se trouve-t-il maintenant? Cette église, comment s'appelle-t-elle?*"

The man was elderly and weary-looking, with deep lines in a dark face. He put his hands on his hips and glanced beyond Kelly and Daniel to tourists entering through the tower doors. "Saint-Maximin. Here. I give you." He opened a small notepad, copied the address, tore the page off with a flourish, and handed it to Daniel. "*Sa famille...sa sœur.*"

Kelly touched Daniel's arm as he thanked the clerk. "What about the crypt?" she asked. "We've come all this way, we may as well see it."

"Are you sure? We still might make it to Saint-Maximin before dark."

"We'd better see the crypt. It might make a difference in the long run. This whole search has been one long mystery, and I'm beginning to follow my nose, as it were."

"And as I said, a most pretty nose it is, freckles and all." He grinned.

Kelly tried to accept the compliment with grace but couldn't escape the slight rush of embarrassment. "Thanks." She slipped a strand of hair behind her ear nervously.

They bought tickets to the crypt, pulled open a heavy door, and descended stone stairs into the earlier church.

At the foot of the stairs they paused, surveying a foyer that opened onto several rooms. Columns ran under arches and vaults; spotlights shone from craggy ceilings. Kelly studied the information panels in English and French and wondered at the sarcophagi, partial frescoes, statuary. Centuries collided and telescoped into the present. She had but to see to understand.

"Fifth century," Daniel said as they stepped into one of the rooms, still used as a chapel. "This is the original nave, chancel, altar." He pointed to a stone slab on top of an intricately carved sarcophagus. A candle burned to the side.

The cool and damp space was surprisingly bright and Kelly read a plaque stating that the sarcophagus supporting the altar contained the remains of John Cassian.

Daniel drew in his breath. "Here he is." He stared as though in a trance. "I didn't expect this."

"You okay?"

"I need to sit down for a moment."

They found a bench, and Kelly studied his face. His moist eyes remained fixed on the altar. He wiped one eye with his forefinger and Kelly wondered if his careful control was ready to break. He began to shake, his hands tightly folded, his fingers interlocked tightly. He bowed his head and moaned.

Kelly touched his shoulder gently. "What is it, Daniel? What's wrong?"

"It's so overwhelming." The words barely escaped. He turned to her, his face wet, and let out a sob, wrapping his arms around her, trembling. "Oh God," he gasped. "The despair will never leave. I'm cursed."

Kelly stroked the back of his head as she would have done with Matt. She held him firmly, hoping to quiet the shaking. "Hey…it's okay. It's going to be okay." For the moment, he *was* Matt, and she was consoling him after a fall. But this was Daniel, and he wasn't okay.

Slowly, the shaking subsided. He pulled away and covered his face with his hands. "I'm so sorry…"

"Daniel, what are you talking about? Why are you cursed?"

"It's a terrible story. I don't want to burden you. And you don't want to hear it."

"Tell me."

He took the tissue she handed him. He spoke in a low voice, deliberately as though forcing the words from somewhere deep. "My father's name was John Cassian Weaver."

"Really?"

"John Cassian has been a name in our family for centuries. Usually one or the other cropped up in each generation, but my father had both and was so proud. He said it stood for truth, for telling the truth no matter what." He shook his head and studied the floor.

"Like Cassian did when he stood for truth and sent out his monks?"

"Yes, and the way he educated them so they were prepared, so they knew what they were talking about. Cassian was known for the training of monks. He was even connected to Lérins, another great learning center."

"Lérins?" Kelly tried to follow where all this was leading.

"In fact, my middle name is Cassian."

His middle name. Daniel C. Weaver. "Why didn't you tell me?"

"I don't use it often. Too painful."

"Why?" Was she probing too deep? "You don't have to say."

"Let's go back outside, shall we? I need some air."

*

They returned to the terrace above the Old Port and bought sandwiches from a vendor. Sitting on a bench facing the bay, their lunch untouched and set to the side, they gazed over the water and the city, out to the far horizon. The afternoon sun was moving slowly over the Mediterranean in its broad June arc and somewhere bells rang three, muffled by stone.

Daniel whispered, his eyes focused on the far distance, "My father committed suicide."

The words fell on her ears like bricks, and she flinched. "That's terrible. I'm so sorry." He appeared calm, even relieved. "How? Why?" she ventured quietly. What could she say? What should she say?

"He was a proud man, an upright man. He worked hard to support us— my mother and me. My mother was a simple woman, enthusiastic, ingenuous. I never understood how they fell in love, for they were so different, but in love they were. He left every morning, taking the bus, carrying the bag lunch my mother had made. He worked in San Francisco for Hamilton Enterprises in the Human Resources Department. Every evening he returned home at six, kissed my mother, and made a double Scotch. After dinner they would watch their favorite shows and go to bed by nine, be up again at five so he could make it to the office by eight. We lived in Oakland, so it was a bit of a commute."

Kelly studied his face. Clearly there was more, and his voice grew darker and more tense as he continued.

"I loved him, loved his regular ways. I loved playing ball with him on the weekends. We went to A's games. He was a good man, often silent, often distant, but a good man. Dependable. I could trust him. He was a good father." Kelly held on to each word as Daniel continued.

"His job involved investigating the backgrounds of applicants and answering queries about former personnel. Evidently, one of those former employees came by his office and asked him to leave out a few negative parts of her report, why she left Hamilton, that sort of thing." Daniel began wringing his hands again.

"She wanted him to lie," Kelly said softly.

"Yes, she wanted him to lie and he refused."

"He was an honest man."

"I was so proud of him, although I didn't understand all of the particulars. I was only fourteen. I knew that he had been asked to lie and he had refused. He and my mother had discussed it often, my mother always concerned that they were raising their voices too high, that I might overhear."

Kelly guessed what he was going to say next.

"When this woman, whom I won't dignify with a name, didn't get what she wanted, she filed a sexual harassment suit against my father. She accused him of demanding she sleep with him in exchange for a promotion."

"But how could anyone believe her?"

"Some did and some didn't. She didn't win the case, but the publicity mortified my father."

"I can imagine it would, since he was innocent."

"The company put him on leave with half pay. They wanted to distance themselves from the whole thing."

"So he was punished for something he didn't do."

"And that was just the beginning. The local paper ran a story on the hearing, and it generated TV coverage."

"It became public. His good name had been slighted and he couldn't right the wrong."

Daniel nodded. "He began receiving threatening letters, anonymous. And it was difficult for me at school—the kids teased me. There were a few bullies…. He saw himself to blame even though he wasn't guilty of anything. He couldn't cope. Seven months and four days after it made the news, he sealed the garage door and turned on the engine. He left a note."

Kelly could feel his anguish. She could touch it. "Oh, Daniel. And your mother?"

"She kept up a brave front for me. She knew what he had been going through. But it devastated her that he would leave her, leave us, like that.

Then we learned that he hadn't been at work for months. The office thought he was on leave. My mother thought he was at work. He was in a park feeding the birds and falling deeper and deeper into despair. After his death she became a ghost. She was barely hanging on, for me." He ran his finger along the frayed band of his wristwatch. "She wore his watch, his company thirty-year award. Now I wear it for both of them. I treasure it." He glanced up at her. "It still keeps time. He was proud of his Omega *with a crocodile band*. The band's wearing a bit now."

"That's good that you wear it." Kelly examined the watch. The large black face had gold markings, and the band was reddish brown, stitched in gold. The gold and the black and the brown gave the watch a feeling of rich permanence. "And your mother?"

"The year I finished my Masters, she died in her sleep. That's when I decided to get away—and went to Rome for my Doctorate."

"Oh, Daniel. How did you ever survive?"

"If it wasn't for Father Gilbert, I don't know if I would have."

"Is that what you meant when you said he saved your life?"

"He pulled me out of my depression. I was fine if I focused on my studies, but I became a workaholic, running away from life. In my time in Rome, he slowly brought me back, included me in his social circle. He weaned me off antidepressants and suicidal thoughts. He introduced me to Christ as healer, not Christ as an academic subject from the past."

"Now I understand. He converted you."

"Re-converted, I suppose. Our Lord became an intimate focus of my daily prayers. I knew he would always be with me, close. I wish my father had known him, truly known him."

"Was he religious? Did he go to church?"

"No…special occasions—Easter, Christmas, Baptisms, that sort of thing. Congregational, sometimes Lutheran, sometimes Episcopal. Today we would call him a grazer. He liked to say he was spiritual and could worship any way he wished as long as he was a good person. Goodness was what counted. Goodness made him a Christian. He had all the discipline of being a Christian, without the joy of belief, without the healing side, the experience of Christ."

They walked to the stone parapet, gazing in silence, unseeing, at the harbor. At the same moment they turned and faced one another, and Kelly slipped into his arms, pulling him close again. "Such a tragedy."

He pushed away gently. "There is something else you should know, Kelly, since I've told you this much." His eyes held concern as though preparing himself for a great disappointment.

Kelly feared his next words would be more difficult, if that was possible, for her to bear than the earlier ones.

"Kelly, I like you a lot. Probably more than a lot." His hands touched her shoulders lightly; then he backed away. "Some years ago, I...took...vows of celibacy."

"What?" She hadn't expected these words. She wasn't sure what she had expected, but this statement had not entered her mind, not today, not in the twenty-first century. "Are you becoming a priest? Joining an order?" *Let him finish in his own time,* she thought. *He's been through a lot.*

"I'm not sure." He swept his gaze over the bay and the historic quarter, the cubical high-rises crowding the domes. He turned toward her, but he seemed to be searching his own heart, struggling with the mystery of his possible vocation.

With the thought of his becoming a priest, Kelly realized that she had hoped for more from Daniel than she realized. She breathed deeply. What exactly had she hoped for?

"A group of us took vows of celibacy several years ago. The vow was a simple one: celibacy until marriage. Of course if I became a priest, the vow would be renewed, rephrased. In other words, we're trying to follow God's law."

"I've heard of groups like that for women."

"Men do it too. It's a natural extension of belief. The logical consequence of loving God is to obey his laws, and the vows help us keep this discipline of love."

"I'm impressed," Kelly said, "and somewhat relieved, I have to say." Should she explain her own misgivings about men—and relationships? Or had he already guessed?

"It's all part of NFP."

"Natural Family Planning?"

"Right. Theology of the body, if you will. The right use of the body, the right use of...the gift of sex."

"I can see that."

"It takes a lot of pressure off a relationship."

"Gives the couple a chance to get to know one another."

"They used to call it courting."

Kelly liked the old-fashioned term. "Yes, courting. That's sweet."

Daniel sighed and kissed her on the forehead. "*You* are sweet. I'm so relieved you understand. I suppose my father's experience made me rethink some modern assumptions. Truth and lies seemed awfully important, and how we use our bodies seemed awfully important. The definition of love seemed awfully important. I want to live a true life, with true love, free of lies. So I'm glad, or maybe hope, you understand."

"I do understand. A friendly kiss is okay?"

He laughed, throwing his head back. "Indeed. Kisses are good, in moderation." He touched her hair. "We'd better head back if we want to avoid the afternoon commute traffic." He gathered the sandwiches and sodas. "Let's eat while we drive."

Then he kissed her, ever so lightly, on the lips.

*

Before dinner that evening, Kelly called home. Andrea picked up.

"Everything okay?" Kelly asked.

"Well, yes and no. My Todd is leaving this afternoon for Walnut Creek."

"Good. Don't forget that Lady needs brushing, or she gets hairballs."

"I told him. He has a couple of interviews in Walnut Creek, so I think he'll stay at the apartment for a little longer. He also has some volunteer hours scheduled for the homeless shelter he helps out with."

Kelly had forgotten how perfect Todd was. "How's Matt?"

"He's just fine, Kelly. Not to worry. We're snug as a bug in a rug."

"Are you alone with the boys now?"

"Well, Josie's visiting tomorrow. She's an old friend who lives in Reno. She's staying for a few days."

"Good." Kelly recalled Josie, a big-hearted woman who worked in one of the clubs. "Is Matt there?"

"He's in the bath, Kelly. Can we call back later?"

"No, that's okay." Better not trouble him. "I'll call tomorrow, then."

"Fine. Have you made any progress with those extremists?"

Kelly's temper flared. Why did she have to use phrases like that? "We're following the trail, Andrea. I should be home soon."

"Todd says that no one believes that stuff anymore."

"Some of us do." Kelly was struck by her own words, her tone of certainty.

"He says that Jesus is a myth made up by the first Christians."

Kelly swallowed hard. "Is that so?"

"He says that miracles are impossible, just wishful thinking."

"Does he believe in God, Andrea? Do you?"

"Todd says that God is whatever we want him or her to be. I think that makes sense. A projection, he says. The important thing is to be centered, to think good thoughts, and to have good self-esteem."

"Self-esteem?"

"Todd says these conservative cults make everyone feel terrible about themselves, and that's not right. I'm just worried about you, Kelly. Just worried, that's all."

Kelly inhaled deeply, steadying herself. She peeked through the gingham panels to the leaves brushing the window. "I have to go, Andrea."

24

Antoinette

WEDNESDAY MORNING TERESA WAS HAPPY TO TAKE THE BACK SEAT, and she spent most of the drive to Saint Maximin texting on her phone. Kelly navigated, examining her map, and Daniel drove. She wondered what a Provençal home would be like, the home of Pierre Durand.

Their hotel was two hundred years old, La Sainte Baume Grotto and Saint Victor Abbey far older. They had driven under the surface of Marseilles, but she guessed that above ground the city had slums and mansions like any other. The quaint, historic villages, overrun by traffic and congestion, with buildings fronting narrow roads and delivery trucks blocking intersections, were another aspect of rural Provence, but what about ordinary folks who lived in the area? Their quest had been colored by the journey, and she was beginning to appreciate the world around her.

Feeling closer to Daniel and wondering where their friendship might lead, Kelly had taken extra care with her appearance. She wore a cotton paisley skirt she bought on impulse in the hotel shop and a scoop-neck tee. She found lavender oil in the bath and dabbed her wrist. She slipped on her Magdalene medal. Her feelings were a jumble. She was nervous, yet anticipating what might happen next. She lectured herself not to expect too much, or anything, or perhaps, not to expect too little. One way or another, such feelings must take a back seat to their search for the manuscript. And they had to be close to finding it. She told herself she needed to stay focused.

Daniel drove with his own intensity, watching for road signs, and Kelly pointed and directed, her fingers occasionally touching the figure on her medal. She glanced back at Teresa, who held her phone at an angle to get reception, tapping the screen furiously, her face tense. "That should do it," she muttered under her breath.

About thirty minutes north of their hotel, they turned off the highway and meandered through a new section of housing on the outskirts of the village. The townhouses were similar to one another, two-storied indiscriminate architecture and small unplanted yards edged with newly paved driveways. Daniel pulled up to a freshly painted curb.

A tall, thin woman, in her mid-twenties, Kelly guessed, met them at the door. She held a baby in one arm and a phone in the other. A toddler peered from behind her jeans, grasping her legs with pudgy fingers dabbed red and green, probably from children's markers. The woman's face was lined with worry and confusion. "Monsieur phoned from Saint Victor's," she said, her voice shrill. "You want Pierre? What has he done?"

"Nothing, Madame," Kelly said quickly, hoping to reassure her. "We only want to speak with him. Is he home?"

The woman's eye moved from Kelly to Daniel to Teresa. "Forgive me. I am Antoinette Santerre, Pierre's sister. Please come in."

"*Merci, Madame,*" Teresa said, smiling broadly. "*Je suis Thérèse et je voudrais vous présenter mes amis, Daniel Weaver et Kelly Roberts.*"

"*Ah! Vous parlez français!*" Antoinette launched into a torrent of French as Kelly and Daniel followed the two women inside, into the front room.

The beige-carpeted area looked to be both nursery and family room, not unlike her own apartment, Kelly thought. Stairs ascended to the left. Beyond the stairs, an oval oak table and four chairs occupied a small nook opening to a narrow kitchen. The furnishings were spare and modern, in light hues.

Antoinette laid the baby on her back in a white canvas bassinet that hung from a frame and handed her a bottle. The child, about six months, held the bottle firmly with chubby fingers and sucked with relish, her eyes moving without focusing, as though wholly absorbed in the feeding. Her mother cleared a space on a sage green sofa, moving coloring books and handing a toy truck to her toddler. She offered the armchair as well and pulled a dining chair into the room. "I do not keep house well, or speak English well. I am sorry."

"*Pas de problème, Madame,*" Teresa said, taking a seat in the armchair.

Daniel sat in the dining chair. Kelly took the cleared space on the sofa, her eyes on the baby. The smell of talcum and milk reminded her of Matt, those first weeks with her newborn, the feedings, the changings, the exhaustion, her complete devotion. When his small warm body merged into her own, as he nestled into the cleft of her arm and his eyes sought hers, or when she propped him over her shoulder for his burp and his wet face smeared her neck—these were moments of sheer happiness. The pregnancy center sent a volunteer every now and then to check on her, but Kelly's greatest support came from the women she had come to know in Oakview Gardens, single mothers like herself as well as Andrea, a widowed grandmother. When Matt was three months she returned to Saint Mary's for his Baptism, and all the elderly ladies gathered around, waiting for a turn to hold little Mathew.

"Pierre is not here." Antoinette shook her head, watching her son fill the dump truck with bright plastic shapes. "Why you wish to see him?" she asked nervously.

Daniel pulled out his room key from the hotel. "Madame, it is okay. Pierre is okay. We ask about his…*clés.*" He held up the key and pointed to his chest.

Teresa spoke quickly in French and Antoinette's face relaxed. Seeing the baby nodding asleep, she removed the bottle and raised the child over her shoulder, patting and rubbing her back, releasing the bubble of gas. Kelly watched, feeling as though she had picked up the child herself. They remained silent as Antoinette soothed and rubbed, patted and cooed, until a gentle burp escaped, and the mother settled her baby in the bassinet to sleep. "*C'est bon. Je comprends.*"

Kelly watched Antoinette gently rock the cradle with her long fingers, her eye on her son who rolled his truck back and forth, making motor noises, just like Matt. Kelly smiled, feeling more comfortable in this foreign land. In some ways mothers and children were the same everywhere.

Antoinette resumed her light swift French and Teresa translated. "She says it is true," Teresa said, "that Pierre wears his keys. They are important to him. To him they are holy, for they come from tabernacle doors."

Kelly and Daniel exchanged glances as Antoinette spoke even more earnestly to Teresa.

Teresa translated. "Pierre is what they call *simple*, but he is very loving, and he means well. He often speaks too openly about his beliefs. He is staying with them for now, but she does not know for how long, and whether or not the police will press charges for what they say are hate crimes. He offends people without meaning to. She says he doesn't know any better. He states the truth as he sees it. She is afraid the authorities will send him away."

Antoinette's voice rose and fell, and Kelly, while concerned about Pierre, was entranced with the softly lilting language. Blue eyes wide, Antoinette ended with, "*C'est formidable!*"

Daniel nodded with understanding, and Kelly asked, "What did she say?"

Teresa glanced at Daniel.

"If I have it right," Daniel began, "she's saying that most often Pierre is correct, and that everything today is a hate crime, that her uncle, a pastor, was fined for something he said in a sermon."

Kelly regarded Antoinette with sympathy. "I've heard of that happening."

Antoinette continued. Teresa explained that Pierre worked as sacristan at the cathedral in Saint-Maximin, that he watched over the holy shrine of Mary

Magdalene in the crypt, and that he was a good boy no matter what they said. The toddler carried the truck to Kelly and placed it in her lap. She tousled his thick yellow curls, the hair silky smooth, and studied his freckled face. His eyes were the blue of his mother's and set wide apart, his nose flat, his mouth bud-shaped. "Hi," she said, smiling.

Antoinette tapped her phone and spoke quickly, then looked as if she was offering them refreshment, and as Daniel rose, Kelly and Teresa stood as well. Soon they were saying good-bye and heading toward the car.

"She called her brother," Teresa said to Kelly. "He will meet us during his lunch break at 12:15 in front of the main entrance to the basilica. He is wearing a red shirt; he's quite tall and blond. They're fraternal twins."

Teresa noticed Kelly's Magdalene medal and smiled. Their eyes locked, and at that moment Kelly was close to certain that they would be friends, that a bond of trust had been forged. Teresa's frenetic work online must be part of her job, and if she showed occasional anxiety or even fear, there must be a good reason. Everyone had secrets.

Kelly smiled back, fingering her medal. "I love this, Teresa," she said. "Thank you so much."

Teresa grinned. "I'm glad."

*

Bells tolled noon as the sun beat upon the market square in front of the Basilique Sainte Marie-Madeleine. Kelly took photos of the colorful stands of petunias, chrysanthemums, and daisies, displayed under blue-and-white umbrellas. Shoppers meandered, carrying straw satchels, and aromas of cheese and lavender added to the festive feeling. One vendor sold shawls and Provençal skirts, another offered spices in angled canisters, another fresh bread, and it was with regret that Kelly turned toward the heavy cathedral façade. Teresa and Daniel were approaching the doors to inspect a plaque, and Kelly moved quickly to join them.

"Mainly fifteenth century," Teresa was saying, "begun in 1295 and completed in 1535."

"There's no bell tower," Daniel said, glancing up.

"Unfinished," she explained. "Much of it was unfinished, it appears, with these rough bricks and heavy buttresses along the sides. The whole effect is rather primitive, which, considering it was built upon a sixth-century Merovingian church, is appropriate."

"The first centuries of Christianity," Daniel said thoughtfully.

"Certainly we could call the five-hundreds—the sixth century—part of the first centuries of *legalized* Christianity."

Kelly studied the rustic wall of stone, now dim in its own shadow. "So this is a fifteenth-century basilica, built over the sixth-century church, built over Mary Magdalene's grave?" She gazed at the carved wooden doors and the gracefully arched frieze.

"Right," Daniel said, "although the sixth-century church probably stood over an earlier oratory, maybe hermitage, that honored the grave." Daniel scanned the square. "I don't see Pierre Durand anywhere."

"We're early," Kelly said, watching Teresa as she studied the façade. "May I ask you a question, Teresa?"

"Of course," she replied, her eyes large with curiosity.

"How did you become interested in Mary Magdalene?"

She laughed. "I'm afraid not for a very academic reason. I simply reacted to a popular novel that disturbed me. Did you ever read the one that claimed Mary Magdalene was married to Jesus? And *she*—that is, her bloodline—was the Holy Grail?"

Kelly nodded. "*The Da Vinci Code*? I remember it. I told myself that, after all, it was just fiction. But even so, something about it troubled me too. It seemed such a direct attack on traditional Christianity."

"That novel was the reason I became interested in the Magdalene. And the more I learned, the angrier I became. That's what I remember most about last summer, how angry I was! And over a silly novel," Teresa said, shaking her head, as though both embarrassed and triumphant. "I suppose I'm still upset over it. I should thank the author for causing me to enroll in the Masters' program in Rome. I may never have considered it."

"I remember the book," Daniel said. "It was based on the spurious claims, long since debunked, of two so-called historians in the 1980s."

"That's the one. It wouldn't matter to me," Teresa added, "but friends of mine believed the lies. It amazed me, the power of fiction, and how readers could be so gullible."

"Fiction reaches people on a different level," Kelly said, thinking how a well-told story pulled her into another world, sometimes good, sometimes not so good. "And fiction often reaches a different group of people. I'm sure there's a market overlap but even so there's a wide gulf as well." Kelly reflected on her own reading, for the most part fiction, but lately she had been intrigued with some of the books that Father Gilbert had sent her, histories by Paul Johnson, Barbara Tuchman, Gertrude Himmelfarb, Thomas E. Woods, Thomas Cahill. They held her attention with historic ironies and the power of the individual to change events. The books demanded more, but at the same time gave her more, a better grounding, a clearer vision of the world. Or did they? Perhaps fiction was just as powerful, but more subtle. And maybe subtlety added to its power, this power of art.

"The novel also lied about the Early Church," Teresa continued, eyeing Daniel.

"How so?" Daniel asked, watching for Pierre.

"The author stated, through his professorial character, and thus the one carrying the most weight in terms of authority, that early Christians saw Jesus as a mortal teacher and that it wasn't until the Council of Nicaea in 325 that Jesus was deemed to be divine."

"But that's a clear falsehood," Daniel said quickly. "We have the Gospels and letters of Paul, ample documents from other sources in the first two centuries, attesting to Christian belief that Jesus was the Son of God. The Christian community clearly worshiped Christ from the earliest days. You can argue about evidence that he *was* the Son of God, but you can't say the early Christians had any doubts about his divinity."

"I once doubted," Kelly admitted. "So many people encouraged questioning the Church's dogma, and I wanted to be part of the majority." She wanted to be accepted by her fellow students in college, she thought. She didn't want them laughing at her.

Daniel looked sympathetic. "Most of us want that. Most folks accept what they are told, wanting to go with the flow, be part of the culture. And they are often good people, even good Christian people."

Teresa waved an open hand through the air as though clearing away cobwebs, and her bracelets jangled lightly. "But it's muddy logic. I hate muddy logic. They are simply replacing the authority of the church with the authority of the media. There is always an authority."

Kelly studied her face, so animated. "I suppose everyone is influenced by others and accept false authorities without thinking." She considered her own habits of watching TV newscasts, reading newspapers, all with an assumption that they were true.

Teresa was now on a mission. "Exactly. How crazy is that? Just thinking about those lies makes me furious all over again. The author even claims that the New Testament is unreliable because thousands of accounts were circulated in the first centuries and then burned by Constantine. In other words, the collection of documents found in today's Scriptures is the result of a power play, one's man's selection, a conspiracy to hide the truth."

Daniel stared at her. "You've got to be kidding! I confess that I never read the novel—it sounded so silly and I do prefer nonfiction. But that is a preposterous claim. Indeed, there *were* later texts not included in the canon—including the Gospel of Mary—but few have links to the first century and early second century, the period we call *apostolic*, when the first apostles lived, the closest witnesses. By mid-second century, *after* the time of the apostles, writers cited the Gospels of Matthew, Mark, Luke, and John, as well as Paul's letters, clearly judging them to be the most reliable."

Teresa folded her arms. "Yes, the Gospel of Mary, that is, Mary Magdalene, is a good example. The fragments we have today were clearly not circulated by the first Christians. They were written many generations after the Gospels, a late development."

Daniel added, "It was one of the Gnostic texts purported to be heretical."

"And," continued Teresa, "the final choice for the canon had nothing to do with Constantine. The final choice was made decades later by entire councils, not just one man."

Daniel nodded. "And those accounts and letters chosen had to meet four criteria: did they have apostolic roots, that is, a lineage to the apostles; were they catholic, that is, widely known and valued; were they orthodox, that is, in keeping with the Apostles Creed; were they used in liturgical worship. All other candidates were suspect."

"It's so unfair," Kelly said, watching the two of them, a SWAT team of reason out to slay dragons, "that an author like this gets away with it, that so many people believe him. What about the marriage claim? That Mary Magdalene and Jesus were married? Couldn't that have been at least possible?"

Teresa and Daniel exchanged glances. Daniel gallantly waved his arm, making dramatic loops in the air, in deference to Teresa. She smiled with appreciation, then explained, "The novel claims that marriage was the norm of the time, and Jesus wouldn't have been taken seriously if he wasn't married. Let's see if I can simplify this answer without laughing. The Gospels, which are among our earliest documents, say nothing about Jesus being married but they describe his parents, other family members, the women followers, and the disciples. There would have been no reason to omit his married status if he was married, for family was important. Family identified you. And being unmarried would not in any way have lessened his authority. There's Jeremiah, John the Baptist, Paul, the Essenes of the first century—all unmarried and revered."

"And what about Mary Magdalene herself?" Kelly glanced at the church doors, curious about the crypt, curious to see the relics which, as she recalled with a slight shudder, included her skull.

"The book," Teresa said, "makes three hugely fraudulent claims about Mary. The first is that she was married to Jesus, clearly absurd for the reasons I stated. The second is that she bore his child, for which there is absolutely no evidence. The third claim is that Jesus designated Mary to be head of his church, but Peter displaced her, demonizing her. The truth is that there has never been a conspiracy to demonize Mary Magdalene. For two thousand years she has been honored and loved as a saint for her faithfulness and her witness to the Resurrection. She is called *Apostle-to-the-Apostles* because of this witness."

"And," added Daniel, "the Gospel testimony about Mary Magdalene is particularly believable. In those days women were not allowed to follow a Rabbi, but she does, as does wealthy Joanna. A false writing would not choose a woman to be the first witness to the Resurrection, to be the first to see the resurrected Christ. For that matter, no one actually *sees* the actual Resurrection. If the Resurrection had been made up, such a witness would have been provided."

"Indeed," Teresa said. "Mary Magdalene preaches the Resurrection immediately, something today's Christians are afraid to do. Today, we are warned to keep silent." Teresa's eyes were now on fire, and Kelly caught the warmth, the glint. Belief was contagious when shared.

Daniel clapped. "Well said, to be sure. Have you considered a career in television?"

"No chance."

Daniel checked his watch. "Just about time." He turned to Kelly. "I don't think any historian takes those claims in the novel seriously. Scholars generally agree that these later texts, most from the late second through fifth centuries, tell us nothing of value about Jesus or the first Christians."

"But who reads those scholars?" Kelly asked, wishing someone would, besides other scholars. "History can be difficult, not so much fun, not so much of an escape."

"And then the movie followed the book," Teresa said. "*So* popular. My Uncle Tim says the whole thesis—the attack on the Church especially, but the attack on any kind of authority requiring behavioral discipline—tapped into American Gnostic culture. Hence the success."

Daniel nodded. "We want our individual freedom, our autonomy. Modern Gnosticism says we can know all things and be saved by knowledge, that we need no outside authority, that we search individually by how we feel, by our instincts, and that source identification and consensus do not matter."

Kelly spotted a tall, fair-haired young man coming toward them, holding a bag lunch in his hand. "I think that must be Pierre."

His red shirt hung loosely over khaki trousers, and he lumbered with a measured step. His looked about, then saw them. He wasn't albino, but close, very fair, like his sister. As he drew near, large blue eyes blinked in a moon face. He grinned ingenuously and bowed from the waist, offering a thick hand to each of them. His grip was calloused and faintly moist, lingering.

"It is good. I meet you," he said hoarsely. Half a dozen keys hung from a brown leather cord around his thick neck. He touched his heart. "I am Pierre. Pierre Durand."

*

Wednesday morning Lester Sansby stood at his window. As he watched Weaver and the girl leave the hotel, he wondered if they were sleeping together yet. The young man's hand was under her elbow as though he were some *gallant* from the nineteenth century. They crossed the gravel yard, passed through the wrought-iron gates and were heading, Lester assumed, to their car in the parking lot.

What had they found yesterday? FlowerGirl was curiously silent.

He checked his email. *Finally.*

Sorry, no key. But they have a name. More later. FlowerGirl.

Where are you?

Not as far and not as close as you think.

Lester paused for a moment.

Send me a photo, you sound so lovely.

What makes you think I'm a girl?

The name? Did I say you were? Send me a photo, my dear. Maybe I'll be surprised. I like surprises.

Sure. Pleased to hear you like surprises.

She sent a photo. She was familiar, but he couldn't place her. Her oversize dark glasses covered her eyes, and her face was deep in shadow. But the tilt of her head was uncannily reminiscent of some encounter in his past, a pleasurable one, he thought, probably a former student.

Who are you? Why are you being so helpful?

That's for me to know and you to find out. I've got my reasons. I've got a few scores to settle.

And they are?

Wouldn't you like to know. Will you help me settle the scores?

Lester caught a whiff of being led, being pursued. Vaguely wary of a trap, he confessed he was titillated.

Send me another photo, a real photo.

Maybe later. Be in touch!

Lester wiped his brow. He moved to the bed and got comfortable. He checked *SmartReads*. Another simpleton Christian had signed up and was taking the bait. This could be fun. He was entitled to a little fun.

25

Relics

THEY FOLLOWED PIERRE INTO THE CHURCH and stood at the foot of the Gothic nave.

"Pierre," Daniel said slowly, "do you have the key to the tabernacle of La Sainte Baume?"

Teresa repeated the question in French, and the young man's face lit up. "*Ah, oui!*" he replied, touching the keys around his neck, "I do not wear it now. *Je vais le chercher!* I go and return."

"He's going to find it for us," Teresa said, watching Pierre lumber toward a side aisle.

Kelly didn't mind the slight delay if they could pause here in this soaring space. Luminous light poured through the tall windows in the apse, and she felt she was flying up and off to the shimmering air, as though pulled by the white stone columns rising from the pews. An oriental carpet ran up the central aisle, a gratifying path with its orderly pattern of reds and golds, and led to a dark wood choir. Kelly's eye returned to the columns and the ribbed vaults with their symmetrical crossings. She drew a deep breath. True, it was unpolished, but the space soared. And, in the end, wasn't that what a church was intended to do?

Daniel also looked entranced. "So this was the basilica built by Charles of Anjou in 1295. Remarkable."

Kelly recalled Mary Magdalene's altar in the cloister at the Lateran Basilica in Rome. "Weren't her relics discovered earlier than that?"

Daniel nodded. "When was the archeological work done, Teresa?"

"1279, sixteen years before the building of this church. But since you seem to know a bit of the story, you might remember that it took a few years for Charles to visit Pope Boniface to show him the relics. Only after the Pope declared their authenticity could Charles build this church to honor the Magdalene."

Daniel nodded. "Wasn't Saint Louis related to Charles in some way?"

Teresa nodded. "Louis IX, King of France, who became as you say, Saint Louis, was Charles' uncle. In 1254, on the king's return from the seventh crusade, he visited Saint-Maximin and La Sainte Baume. He found only a few monks and a poorly kept oratory and an empty alabaster sarcophagus. Nevertheless, his visit showed that the shrine was clearly recognized to be Mary Magdalene's."

"Where does this information come from?" Daniel asked, his eyes on the north aisle's side door, watching for Pierre. "Is there a primary source?"

"J.H. Albanès, nineteenth-century, in *Le Couvent Royal de Saint-Maximin*. His history is based on thirteenth-century accounts, judged to be contemporary. Albanès suggests that King Louis spoke with his brother, the Count of Provence, in Aix. His brother's son, Charles—later King Charles II—was intrigued and decided to excavate around the oratory."

Kelly was fascinated with the progression of events. She listened, absorbing every word.

"Tell us about the digs," Daniel said, regarding Teresa with increased interest.

"Charles discovered a marble sarcophagus near the empty alabaster sarcophagus that was Mary Magdalene's original coffin. When they pried the marble one open, there was a pleasing aroma coming from the coffin, and Charles closed and sealed it immediately, guessing it might be hers, for he wanted official witnesses to legitimize the discovery."

Daniel rubbed his beard. "A pleasing aroma—the classic sign of sanctity. There have been many cases where a saint's remains smell of roses or perfume, rather than the usual putrefaction."

"Right," Teresa said, eyeing them both. "Charles could see he might have made an important discovery. So he assembled the Bishops of Provence and numerous secular officials. He broke the seal and found a complete skeleton, minus the lower jawbone. Long hair was attached to the skull, and, oddly, a piece of skin was attached to the forehead."

"How strange," Kelly said. "A piece of skin on the forehead. What would that be?"

Daniel nodded. "It's the *Noli me tangere*, isn't it?"

"Exactly. It's only conjecture, but it's possible it's the place where Christ touched her in the garden when he said, 'Do not touch me, do not hinder me.' It remained attached to the skull until the late eighteenth century, when the piece became loose and was preserved in liquid."

"You are saying, if I understand you," Daniel said, "that they have a piece of flesh that Jesus Christ touched!"

"Again, conjecture, but I think highly possible. I'm not sure if I would say *probable*. But they found more evidence, a wax-coated tablet with the words,

177

Hic requiescit corpus Mariae Magdalenae."

"*Here lies the body of Mary Magdalene,*" Daniel translated.

"Charles took the bones," Teresa continued, "and placed them in a silver reliquary. He enclosed the skull with its flowing hair in a special case for display."

Kelly gazed at the high altar and luminous apse. "And once Pope Boniface decreed the relics to be Mary Magdalene's, Charles built this basilica to honor her." She turned to Teresa.

Teresa smiled in assent. "So now Charles needed the authority of the Pope to install Dominicans as guardians of the shrine."

Daniel looked into the distance as though seeing the scene, then asked Teresa, "You said Albanès based his account on the historians of those times? What about eyewitnesses to the discovery of the tomb? Charles made such a point of forming that group of witnesses. Don't we have anything from them?"

Teresa frowned. "I'm afraid not. We only have *copies* of the transcript written by Bernard Gui, a Dominican, in 1320. But he was known to be a shrewd, tough historian and claims he saw the original documents found in the coffin. We have a second account from Philippe de Cabassole, Bishop of Cavaillon. He was a close friend of Charles' son, Robert, who told Philippe stories of the excavations, stories from his father."

"That would be colorful," Kelly mused. "I wonder what he said." To have an eyewitness description of the digs would be better than a good novel, she thought. The suspense must have been incredible.

"As a matter of fact," Teresa said, "we have Philippe's document, full of detail: Charles' search in the Aix library for any mention of Mary Magdalene; Charles' interviews with local elders about oral traditions; the day when Charles joined the search, shoveling in every corner."

Kelly could see it all, feel the excitement. "That's amazing."

"Enough talk," Teresa said. "What's taking Pierre so long? You should see the relics. I'll keep an eye out for him while you go down to the crypt. Her grave is in the center, so that the whole church becomes her tomb."

Kelly and Daniel followed Teresa up the north aisle to a short flight of stairs.

"I'll keep watch for Pierre," Teresa said, remaining above.

As they descended, the dim light grew dimmer, the dark lit by a small wall lantern. They entered the low-ceilinged underground chamber and Kelly's eyes were immediately drawn to the far end where sculpted bronze hair ran in waves down the sides of the skull. She stepped closer and peered through a latticed iron grate. The brownish skull had large eye sockets above small nasal cavities and angled cheek indentations. The mouth bones gave the impression of puckering. Yet somehow she was regal, framed by the waves of hair. Along one side were fragments preserved in liquid, in a phial in a bronze reliquary carved with swirls, mini-columns, and rosettes. This was the *Noli me tangere*, she guessed. This skin had adhered to her skull for all those years—nearly eighteen hundred—and remained preserved today.

Kelly made the Sign of the Cross and whispered, "Pray for us, Saint Mary Magdalene." She thought of her godfather and her parents and their research. She thought of her own waywardness, her lack of direction, her confusion. She thought of Daniel's desire to lead a "true life." She desired to lead a true life too.

"*Priez pour nous*," Daniel said, his eyes resting on the relics.

Kelly noticed sarcophagi against the side walls. "Who are the others?"

Daniel examined the inscriptions. "Saint Maximin, Saint Sidonius, and the Holy Innocents, identified by some as Marcella and Susan. Mary Magdalene's tomb is under her reliquary."

They returned to the nave, where Teresa was slipping her phone into her pocket. "Here's Pierre," she said pointing to the side aisle.

The young man stepped toward them, his face serious. "You must come with me."

*

Pierre opened a door off the north aisle, and they entered the cathedral's cloisters. Kelly squinted in the bright light. Vaulted porticoes lined the garden and the midday sun shafted through leafy trees, dappling a stone well. As their footsteps crunched the gravel path crossing the garden, Kelly wondered where they were going. Teresa had left, perhaps to visit the relics in the crypt.

"Where's Teresa?" she asked Daniel.

"She'll catch up with us, I'm sure." Daniel studied Pierre's broad face. "Where are we going? *Où allons-nous?*"

"To Father Paul."

"Father Paul has the key?"

"*Oui.* In his tabernacle. Very old."

Abruptly, Teresa appeared alongside. She glanced at Kelly, her face drained of color. "What's happening?"

"The key is with a Father Paul." Kelly tried to hear what the men were saying as she explained quickly, wondering what had frightened her. Was it a phone message?

"Good." Teresa glanced back to the doors leading to the basilica. Her hands shook as she adjusted her quilted tote nervously over her shoulder. "I'm glad," she added. "Father Paul is a good man, a Dominican here. He was my confessor last summer. He began as a monk, and became a priest as well so that he could celebrate the Mass."

They entered a room off the cloister where Pierre spoke to a young nun behind a desk. She nodded and motioned to a door nearby.

"His chapel," Pierre whispered, opening the door.

They entered the hushed silence and stood for a moment in the back. Benches lined unadorned walls, and a monk, his shoulders bent and his hair white, knelt on a single prie-dieu before a tabernacle on a stone altar. A red candle burned and light streamed from two windows high in the rounded apse. A crucifix of pale wood, perhaps pine, Kelly supposed, hung suspended over the altar in the still air.

The old man's black robe fell to the hard floor like a tent. He mumbled his prayers, beating his chest with his fist. The four watchers remained motionless, silent. The heartrending scene reminded Kelly of Father Gilbert many years ago at Saint Mary's. She had chanced upon him in his office, had entered without knocking, a bumbling and enthusiastic child. He too had knelt in much the same way before the red-robed Christ the King, kneeling on a velvet cushion in his black clericals. She had the remarkable sense then, as she had now, that time and space had fallen into this central fixed point, somewhere between the monk and the tabernacle, between the priest and the crucifix, so that they became one, as though dwelling inside the prayer itself.

Now she watched the old monk, his back bent, his legs hanging from the lower slat. He wore sandals and Kelly could see a hole in the heel of one of the socks. His hands had become still, no longer beating his chest but clasped as though pointing to the tabernacle, and she had the feeling he was listening with every fiber of his being, as though experiencing the transcendent. He was experiencing God, the vision of God.

She stared at the tabernacle. A key was in the lock. A green tassel, slightly frayed, hung from it.

It was the key in her dream.

26

Father Paul

THEY SAT IN THE CLOISTER. The air was poignant with jasmine and musty stone, and patterns of light and dark danced with the sun falling through the leaves. Pierre had returned to the basilica, and Kelly and Teresa had taken seats on either side of Father Paul on a low stone bench, as Daniel stood nearby. Teresa looked as though she were about to faint. She touched her forehead, shivering.

Father Paul, hunched with bone loss, his fingers swollen at the joints, emanated a gentle peacefulness. His thin face glowed, as though the years, while making their inevitable mark upon his skin and bones, had sanctified his spirit, making it beautiful. Kelly waited for the old priest to speak, the key and her dream hovering in her mind like a sweet cloud of expectation.

"You desire the key," Father Paul asked Kelly.

"Yes, Father, it's my godfather's wish," Kelly said quietly.

"Why?"

"It's a long story. But you must trust me that the key belonged to my godfather, Father Keith Gilbert, now passed on. He wished me to have it."

"Did you say Keith Gilbert? He has passed away, then?"

"Yes, Father. Last month. Do you know him?"

Father Paul made the Sign of the Cross. "A dear man. I shall see him again soon then." He examined the rusty metal in his hand and chuckled quietly. "So it has come to this. God does indeed have a sense of humor."

"What do you mean, Father?" Kelly asked, although slightly concerned she had intruded.

The old man grinned and laughed heartily, throwing his head back with delight and clapping his hands. "We were in school together in Rome, two Americans searching for ourselves. We competed for everything. We desired God so much, we competed even for him. We didn't realize we already had him! This key was precious to Keith and to me, for it came to represent our friendship. But that is another story. How odd it is that I have it now." He glanced upwards and smiled, waving his hand, then turned to Kelly. "I will give you what you desire, what my dear brother-in-God desires." He offered Kelly the key. "But you must promise to keep it safe. It has guarded many tabernacles, many Blessed Sacraments." He coughed a dry cough and nodded.

Kelly showed the key to Daniel. "See, MM is engraved on the top." She turned it over. "And an ointment jar on the other side." She showed it to Teresa who smiled faintly, as though staring without seeing.

"A symbol of the Magdalene," Daniel said.

Rust had darkened the metal. Was this actually the key they were searching for? Kelly judged it must be, with those etchings and with Father Paul's words. But they couldn't be sure until they returned to Rome. How did it come here, or even to the Sainte Baume grotto? Each answer led to more questions. She tucked it carefully into an inner pocket of her bag.

"And, my dear," Father Paul said to Teresa, his voice hoarse, "I will hear your confession now. I know it will be the same as always, but I will hear it again. And again. And again. Perhaps finally you will listen to your old Father Paul. For he speaks with God's authority. You must not forget this. You have been forgiven! And your imaginary sins do not need forgiveness."

The words were for Teresa, but Kelly overheard, and was more concerned than ever. She watched the priest slip a green stole around his neck and lead Teresa to a corner of the garden. Teresa began to speak quietly, her eyes fixed on Father Paul's, running her hands up and down her shirt as though drying them, or maybe cleaning them, in great agitation, Kelly thought.

"She's really upset," Kelly said to Daniel.

"I'm afraid she bears a great burden."

"Do you suppose there was something in her text messages that frightened her?"

"Maybe so. She's online quite a lot, but I know she needs to keep up with her assigned news sites, just as I do."

Kelly watched the young woman and the old priest, as she checked her bag for the key to make sure it was still there, safe. At first envious of Teresa's beauty, she had increasingly become aware of her delicacy and sadness, and over the last few days had grown protective, as though she were Teresa's older sister. Only four years her senior, Kelly felt much older, and she wondered if motherhood made a difference.

Now she observed Teresa and Father Paul, the penitent and the confessor, in the corner of the garden. After a few minutes of intense conversation, Father Paul turned to Teresa and took her hands in his own. Then he made the sign of the cross over her head in blessing. Teresa nodded and crossed the courtyard to Kelly, glancing at Daniel. She smiled as tears ran down her cheeks.

"I'm sorry," she said. "I'm okay now. Something frightened me earlier."

"Is there anything we can do?" Kelly asked.

Daniel stepped away as though respecting Teresa's privacy.

Father Paul said his good-byes, then lifted his hand in blessing, "God be with you, my children, until we meet again." He headed toward the chapel, glancing to the sky with a curious smile, then bowing his head.

"I'm going back into the main church," Daniel said. "I'll meet you in the narthex." He crossed through the garden and paused, looking back at them before going inside.

"Let's walk," Teresa said. "I need to explain something to you." The two women stepped through the vaulted corridors, glimpsing the garden through the stone arches. "The monks and nuns say their prayers in these halls of light and dark. Someday I may do the same."

"Are you joining an order?"

"I'm considering it. One of those working orders, like the Sisters of Jerusalem, where they take vows but work secular jobs, then sing the offices together, share their meals. I think I might like that."

"Yes." Kelly felt relieved, but soon recognized the cause of her relief, that Teresa's plans didn't include Daniel. Shame brushed her lightly.

"But that's not what I wanted to tell you. I sense you have suffered. You are a woman. You may understand."

"Please don't feel you have to explain—"

"I want to." Teresa's voice had fallen into a deeper register, more serious, more commanding, more terrifying. Kelly watched the ashen face, so determined. "I have to. You need to know."

Teresa stepped slowly, her eyes on the flagstones as she spoke in measured bursts. "I was...," she began, "abused by my stepfather. Sexually." She hesitated. "My mother died when we were young. When I turned sixteen, I ran away to Rome to Uncle Tim, my mother's brother. Melanie, my sister, was...already gone." A tear slid from one eye and lingered on her cheek.

Kelly caught her breath. She touched Teresa on the arm, nervous, unsure what to do or say. "That's terrible. That's just terrible." The words sounded flippant, thin, like the flat raspy sound of their sandals as they brushed the stones.

"Uncle Tim cared for me, hid me from my stepfather, who...searched for me for many years."

"Teresa, why are you telling me this?"

"You need to know, but I cannot share this with Daniel. It's too personal. But...you need to know...it affects your search for this key." She paused, as though to marshal her courage.

Kelly pulled the key from the pocket in her bag and held it in her palm. It felt warm and consoling as though her godfather's touch was still upon it, as though Father Paul's touch was there too, and even Pierre's. "But now we've found it."

Teresa shook her head and raised a finger to let her finish. "As I helped my uncle and Father Gilbert with their news service, I learned of my stepfather's activities online, and I've been waiting for the right moment, my chance for revenge." She grew silent, then added abruptly, "For what he did to me. And I'm close, very close." Her last words, spoken swiftly, carried a warm hatred, like lava boiling, her eyes fixed on the key in Kelly's palm.

Kelly thought of Teresa's ongoing texting and checking for messages. "Is that what the calls have been about?"

Teresa nodded. "I do have news sites I'm assigned to watch. But my stepfather's activities have become my major focus recently."

"Your focus?" Kelly felt a tension in the air as though a net closed around them, tightening.

"You won't like what I have to tell you, but I must. I feel guilty. And after talking with Father Paul, I want to be honest with you…and Daniel."

"Go on." Kelly searched Teresa's face.

"I've been feeding my stepfather clues about our whereabouts, pulling him in. He doesn't know who I am." Her eyes glittered. "My moniker is FlowerGirl, and I've been using the *SmartReads* forum. He's so gullible, the fool. He's desperate for the key. He's a respected professor and scholar, a supposed expert in New Testament manuscripts. His latest work has been on Mary Magdalene. And he wants the key enough to steal it, enough to risk jail."

Kelly shivered and her grip on the key tightened. He sounded like Daniel's old enemy, the Berkeley professor, their suspected stalker. "Are you saying your stepfather is the one who was following us in Rome?" Her throat was tight and her heart pounded. "Lester Sansby?"

"Yes, Lester Sansby."

"Daniel knows him. They teach at the same school!"

"I know. Berkeley." They were nearing the door to the basilica. "The man is a filthy beast. He is corrupt. He thinks he can create his own morality, that he is the only authority. He has no regrets for his actions. He is responsible to no one. He would say I had consented, that I wanted it…or even that I was making it all up…like Melanie…" Teresa shivered and held her head between her hands as though trying to erase her memories.

"You can have him prosecuted!"

Teresa gazed at Kelly through veiled lids. "I'm too ashamed to testify. Too public. And probably too late—it was over ten years ago, now."

Kelly wrapped her arms about Teresa, holding her close. "I understand. You poor girl."

A sob caught in Teresa's throat and she rasped, "He hurt Melanie, too." She pulled away, wiping her eyes with the back of her hand. "I'm sorry." She found a tissue in her tote and dabbed her nose. "You won't tell Daniel, will you? I just want you to be careful is all, just be careful. He's dangerous, and I'm so sorry I let things go this far."

"It's okay." Kelly said, while knowing it wasn't okay, that she didn't want to keep a secret like this from Daniel, that she was growing terrified of this Lester Sansby. "He isn't here, is he? In Provence?"

Teresa ignored the question. "I often think," she said, glancing furtively around the empty cloister, "that he had Melanie committed to a psychiatric hospital because she tried to talk, to tell tales and lies, as he put it. He claimed she was delusionary, needed medication. He would do that to me, too. He could. But I'm prepared. I have this." She opened her tote and Kelly could see in the corner of the bag a small pearl-handled revolver. It caught the light, gleaming.

"You have a gun?" Kelly said quietly, not wanting to further upset her. Kelly was trying to absorb the information, incredible information coming too quickly. Somehow the gun seemed appropriate, taking into account the threat. Even so, the situation was so highly charged, Kelly let out a short gasp, then covered her mouth.

"And trust me, it's loaded. I keep it with me always. And I know how to use it. Otherwise, why bother?" Teresa looked back to Father Paul's chapel. "The priests of the Church are good men, at least those *I've* known. Father Paul is a good man. He cleanses me of all of this." She rubbed her arms and then the sides of her torso as she had done earlier. "When things get bad, I talk to them, and they cleanse me. But the nightmares always return. Again and again. Then I confess, again and again. And I'm cleansed, again and again."

"But it's not your fault!"

"Are you two okay?" Daniel approached them cautiously, his brows raised in gentle concern.

"Oh, Daniel," Kelly said, feeling way out of her depth. This, she thought, must be what despair felt like, or at least depression, as though the world were tilting out of control, as though the suffering would go on forever, that evil would always pinch and prod, cut and maim and kill. Suddenly she recalled Father Gilbert, how he would say in the midst of tragedy, *"Then there's God.*

God wins in the end. That's the great Christian hope and the great Christian truth." How she longed for Father Gilbert to make good of this evil. Why wasn't he here to help? But then, maybe he was. And where was God, to make good of this evil? Was he with them too? The answer came from somewhere deep inside her memory, *"And lo, I am with you always, even unto the ends of the earth."*

Teresa shook her head. "I can't go into it. It's enough that Kelly knows."

"I'm sorry," he said quietly. "I didn't mean to—"

"It's okay. Let's forget about it. Let's go."

They followed Teresa back into the church, down the north aisle and to the main entrance, the doors open wide to the bustling square. Light streamed over the threshold onto the oriental carpet and Kelly's eyes moved from the faded pattern to the luminous soaring space, memorizing it.

Daniel asked Teresa, "Are you all right?"

"Sure." She forced a half smile. "It helps to talk over things." She glanced at Kelly, then Daniel. "By the way, they think Father Paul is hallucinating."

"Is that right? How so?" Daniel asked. "Who's *they*?"

"I wanted to see him one more time. He fears they will put him in an institution. He claims that the Virgin Mary has spoken to him, as well as Mary Magdalene and her brother Lazarus. I believe him. His cousins see this as an opportunity to take his vineyard outside of Nans-les-Pins."

"It's like the hate speech, isn't it," Kelly replied, "this war against belief? Can't the Church protect him?"

"They'll try to," Teresa said. "But even so, he's too old to bear this persecution. But he was happy about giving you the key. Very pleased."

Kelly pulled the key from her bag. "We need a safe place for this tonight. Then tomorrow we can go to Rome, then home." *Home. Matt.* "But what about Lester Sansby?" She glanced at Teresa, hoping she would at least tell Daniel that she knew Sansby, that she had been leading him on. But then, what difference would it make? They were so close now to finding the manuscript, and it was Teresa's story to tell, not hers. They should forget Lester Sansby. But there was the gun. Should she worry about the gun?

"He'll get what he deserves in the end," Teresa said and Kelly shuddered. "These folks always do. And we finally have the key. Why don't I keep it with the sisters? It will be safe there."

"Good idea," Kelly said, seeing her need for it and placing it in her palm.

As Teresa held the key, something close to pleasure flickered over her face. Her fingers closed over it, the frayed green tassel dangling from her hand.

Daniel appeared confused. "I think we should put it in the hotel safety deposit."

"If you wish," Teresa said but made no move to give it to them. She eyed Kelly, beseeching.

Kelly turned to Daniel. "What could possibly happen to the key in one night?" While Kelly saw this key as the end of her journey, she also felt Teresa's great desire to be trusted. "We know you will keep it safe," she said to Teresa.

Daniel frowned. "Take good care of it. I'll try and get a flight out tomorrow or Friday. We may have to go stand-by."

Pierre approached and bowed gallantly. He turned to Teresa. "You have the key. Keep it safe. I give you my cord of leather…for the key."

"I promise," Teresa said, making the Sign of the Cross. She took the cord and slipped it through the link holding the tassel. "Thank you. It's safe with me." She placed it in her tote.

He nodded and touched his heart with his fist.

They said good-bye and walked through the open doors into the bright square.

*

That evening Kelly dialed Andrea's Tahoe number.

"Matt?" Silence.

Kelly guessed that Matt was on the other end of the line. He was still learning the nature of telephones, that when one answered, one said "hello." He hadn't learned that yet. "Matt? Are you there? Say something, honey."

"Mommy?" he ventured.

"How are you, sweetheart? Did you go on the boat?"

"Yeah. It was fun. We saw stuff."

"Great. Are you saying your prayers?"

"Yeah."

"What are you doing today?"

"Going for a hike."

"That sounds like fun. Wear your sunscreen and take your inhaler."

"Okay. Mommy?"

"Yes?"

"When are you coming home?"

"Soon. Real soon."

Andrea came on the line. "He got here before I did. Getting old, I guess, old and slower than molasses. Sorry about that, Kelly!"

"Everything okay? Did Todd go back to Walnut Creek? Is he taking care of the kitties?"

"He called when he arrived at the apartment and all is right as rain."

Relieved, Kelly realized that Todd was dependable for day-to-day things. It was the bigger picture he found difficult, like what to do with his life. She guessed he was what they call a boomerang child, the ones who keep coming home. Andrea seemed to both worry about it and encourage it.

"Are Matt and the boys doing all right?"

"Well, Ethan got a touch of poison ivy, but a little calamine lotion cleared it up just fine. You staying out of trouble? I'm worried about you, Kelly. Todd says the murder suspect has disappeared, and there's a manhunt out for him."

"Oh dear." What did that mean? Probably nothing. "We'll be heading back to Rome tomorrow. I'll call you when I have a new number. You have Father Francis's number? You can reach me through him."

"Sure do. You just play it real cool now, cool as a cucumber. Don't get too involved with these people. Keep your distance."

"Right."

*

The same evening Lester Sansby read the message with more interest than he wanted to admit, his heart oddly tight. FlowerGirl! The girl tantalized him, the way she kept him dangling, and she had been useful as well. Very useful. But enough was enough. He needed to reel her in.

Key found. Secreted away for the night in a high and lofty place. Green fringe, leather cord.

Where?

What's it worth to you, Lester?

What's it worth to you, my little FlowerGirl?

That depends.

On what?

Check out SmartReads.

Lester's patience was thinning but he found the page, arrowed, clicked, and scrolled down for her comment. He could see that she liked puzzles, but now others viewing this page would see the clues as well. Still, they had no idea as to the key's value, no idea at all. He read her post:

I cannot tell
If there's a bell
Above a cave
Meant to save.
She lived alone
But now is gone
Meet me there
If you really care,
Close to ten
Day breaks again.

Bingo! The only appropriate cave in the area was the Grotto de La Sainte Baume. Ten o'clock in the morning. Finally, he would unmask her. Finally he would take possession of the key. The chase excited him, and he turned to his screen and found some of his favorite photo galleries, just for a little relief.

He swallowed a pill and downed a shot. He deserved it all.

27

The Grotto

THURSDAY MORNING KELLY LINGERED IN THE BREAKFAST ROOM, sipping a double espresso. She had pulled her hair high, fastened it with a barrette, and allowed it to fall loose onto her shoulders. Not sure what the day would bring, she wore jeans, tee, and cable sweater, but found a pink neck scarf for color, one that framed the silver chain holding her Magdalene medal. She wondered if Teresa had influenced her a bit, and if so, she was glad. She was grieved by the young woman's tragic history but admired her ability to survive.

Their return flight, Marseilles to Rome, had been confirmed for Friday morning. Was this journey finally coming to an end? She thought back to her moments with Daniel, those times she had felt close to him, and she played with the memory for a minute, then shoved it to a corner of her mind. How could she even think of getting involved again?

The breakfast room was all white linens and pale walls, with tall arched windows opening to chestnut trees shading the château. A brilliant blue sky could be seen through the leaves and Kelly felt unexpected twinges of regret that things were ending. In spite of the vague danger that hovered, there had been moments of color and loveliness, as though she had stepped into a past that impacted the present in powerful ways. She sighed, stirring her coffee, and nibbled a large buttery croissant as she watched Daniel approach, carrying a loaded plate from the buffet.

A dark cloud had settled over his face. "I can't reach Teresa. I wanted to let her know about our flights and check on the key. The sister I spoke with said she'd left suddenly—some emergency—but didn't know anything more."

"An emergency? I'm sure we'll find out." Kelly digested the news.

"I don't know about that. She's been secretive, you've got to admit. And it seems she took the key with her." He grew quiet, appearing to be working through the possibilities.

Disturbed, Kelly sipped her coffee, ambivalent as to what to reveal. "Have you noticed any new postings from someone called FlowerGirl?"

"FlowerGirl? Why?"

"Just wondering."

"As a matter of fact, I have. A cryptic poem showed up. Reminded me of the grotto."

Kelly groaned. "I'd better come clean. I just found out...Teresa is FlowerGirl."

Daniel raised his brows. "Teresa is FlowerGirl," he repeated, processing the implications, probably thinking over the latest postings. "You're kidding. But how do you know?"

"She mentioned it yesterday."

"I see." He paused. "She's only recently shown up as far as I can tell. She often writes in puzzles and poems, which was curious but not that unusual. Maybe it's part of her work for Father Tim."

Kelly felt weak. Had it been a mistake to let her have the key? Was Teresa using it as bait? If so, how? And would they lose it in the process?

"I'm sorry," she said. "I'd better tell you more of Teresa's story. I should have told you yesterday but couldn't see the point. I felt I would be betraying her trust. She confessed something to me." Kelly's heart pounded as she tried to fathom what it all meant.

Daniel's eyes narrowed. "What are you saying? There's something I don't know? Something I need to know?" His voice rose, then leveled off as he fought for control.

"There's no easy way of saying this. Lester Sansby is...her stepfather."

Daniel gripped the table edge with one hand and leaned toward her. "Is that true? What, then, has been going on?" He rubbed his temples. "Are they in this together?"

Kelly could see his mind explore the possibilities, adding up the evidence. Why would Father Tim's niece, who was also a friend of Father Gilbert, be involved with them at this moment? What was the connection? It couldn't be good.

Carefully and with some nervousness, Kelly selected the important facts. "She's been feeding him clues." She hesitated, searching for a narrative. "Let me put it this way. She has a score to settle with him—which has nothing to do with us—and she's trying to trap him into doing something stupid. Something illegal. Something that would put him in jail."

"But why?"

"I can't tell you that. *She* needs to tell you, if anyone. I can only say that he has harmed her in a serious way. She wants revenge, and I understand why, although I can't explain it. You have to trust me that it's justified. She's not on his side, if that's what you're thinking." Should she tell him about the gun?

"So where does that leave us?" Daniel stroked his beard. "No key, and Teresa out for revenge." He hesitated, then said, "Although Sansby is clearly corrupt. He should be removed from social interaction of any kind, especially teaching impressionable students. Jail is way too good for this man."

Kelly could see Daniel's equanimity dissolve. In another century he would have been a knight doing battle. In a way, she thought, he *was* a knight, and doing battle.

"FlowerGirl!" Daniel repeated. "Now that I think of it, she could have been feeding Sansby clues in those puzzles and poems."

"Or emails. Where's your laptop?"

"Here in my bag." He pulled it out and soon found the *SmartReads* site. "Here's the poem."

I cannot tell
If there's a bell
Above a cave
Meant to save.
She lived alone
But now is gone
Meet me there
If you really care,
Close to ten
Day breaks again.

"Sainte Baume!" Kelly cried. "Mary Magdalene's grotto at ten o'clock. It's nine now. Do you think she's meeting him there? Why? Does she think she can trap him?"

Daniel shook his head. "She's playing a dangerous game. Sansby has few scruples. We'd better follow, do what we can." He shut down his laptop and slipped it in his bag.

"Shouldn't we call the police?"

"What can we tell them? We have nothing to tell them."

Kelly recalled the hatred in Teresa's voice. Did she have more serious plans than to have Sansby arrested? And what was her intention when she met him? How did the key fit in? And what about the gun?

"Teresa has the car," Kelly said.

"We'll order a taxi. *And now.* We need to hurry. I'm worried about Teresa, even if she did set us up. She doesn't know with whom she's dealing. And then there's the key, once again disappearing." He gulped his coffee. "I'll see about the taxi and meet you in front." He shoved back his chair and headed for the lobby, his backpack slung over his shoulder.

Kelly slipped into her sweater and reached for her bag. Daniel was wrong. Teresa knew full well with whom she was dealing.

*

The taxi arrived within the half hour and they wound through the vineyards, following the narrow road toward the forest and the limestone massif. They were silent, in their own thoughts, and Kelly mulled over these new developments. There were so many threads woven into the fabric of this mystery: in a sense, so many locks with so many keys. She recalled their ascent three days earlier, with the air so clear and sparkling, the sun so warm. But today storm clouds gathered in the distance. The morning sun, rising in the east, could be seen only as a steely brightness pushing through banks of charcoal grays.

The taxi pulled to a stop at the base of Mary Magdalene's trail, and Daniel paid the driver. They headed up the wide path through the foliage of silvery green. Kelly walked quickly in the delicate silence. To ease her panic, she visualized Mary Magdalene walking to the sepulcher that dawn so long ago, the first Easter. This woman disciple from the town of Magdala, healed by Christ, had come to anoint her Lord's body. Kelly was soon lost in the scene as she walked beside Daniel, also quiet. Reaching the staircase that switchbacked the cliff face, she paid increased attention to her surroundings. They passed the Stations of the Cross and the etched Beatitudes and rested at the Dominican gate to catch their breath. Bells tolled ten. She turned to Daniel, and he raised a finger to his lips. *Silence.*

They began the final ascent to the grotto. As Kelly climbed, she saw again the Magdalene arriving at the sepulcher so long ago. Was it true? The Gospel accounts agreed on the main details. On Friday Mary Magdalene witnessed the crucifixion. She saw the body taken to Joseph of Arimathea's tomb. On Sunday morning she arrived at the tomb, where the stone covering the entry had been shoved aside. Two angels announced that Jesus had risen from the dead, just as he had said he would. She ran to tell the other disciples and returned with Peter and John. After they left, Mary stayed on, weeping, and someone whom she thought was the gardener, called her by her name, *Mary.* She recognized him and knelt at his feet.

Mary. The story touched Kelly with a sweet joy, the fact that hearing her name caused her to recognize, to see, to know. In the end, Kelly glimpsed, that personal relationship was the heart of Christianity, the God-Man relationship, the relationship of love, of naming, of seeing and of knowing.

They climbed the last stairs to the broad terrace, now deserted. "Wait here," Daniel said, "in case she shows up." Breathing heavily, he strode to the chapel.

Where was Teresa? Had they misread the riddle? Kelly turned and gazed out to the broad valley as though she could find the answer. The silence hovered in the moist air, and a breeze rustled the shade tree sheltering the sculpted Pietà behind her. The weak sun remained hidden behind the mountain, the terrace in its dim light, and it seemed to Kelly that the world waited for the next minute, for the next hour, as though poised on the edge of time.

Daniel emerged from the chapel, shaking his head, his arms outstretched. "A few pilgrims, tourists, but no sign of Teresa or Sansby."

Kelly heard a loud wail from high above. "What was that?"

"Could have been a hawk, but I haven't seen any here." Daniel studied the solid rock face of the mountain, then regarded the chapel doorway where a man leaned on a walking stick.

The man approached, carrying a canvas rucksack. In spite of his advanced age, he looked like a seasoned hiker. He wore shorts, heavy boots, and a Bavarian cap, his hair pulled into a ponytail. His graying beard, falling in wiry waves, dusted a denim jacket. He had numerous travel badges decorating his sack, and he reminded Kelly of an old hippie. "Are you going on up?" he asked, glancing up the cliff face. His accent was American.

"Up?" Daniel repeated. "You mean to Mont Saint Pilon?"

"*Oui*, Mont Saint Pilon. There's a chapel at the top and a marvelous view all around. You can see the Mediterranean from there."

"Maybe not with this sky," Kelly said, trying to be polite. She wished he would move on. They needed to decide what to do next. It was after ten, the hour when Sansby and Teresa were to meet. Where was Teresa? Where was Sansby? What was that scream?

"But one must seize the day, such as it is! *Carpe diem!*"

"May we join you?" Daniel asked. He turned to Kelly. "What do you think?"

Kelly didn't know what else to do. She nodded, puzzled by the turn of events.

*

Lester Sansby washed down a pill with a swig from his flask and paused on the precipice. Quite a view, higher than the grotto. He turned and strode into the chapel. A key with green fringe on a leather thong was protruding from the door of the altar tabernacle. *The key. Thank you, FlowerGirl!*

The hike through the forest to the Magdalene cave had been simple enough, urged on as he was by an adrenaline rush he found familiar and intoxicating, the sexual allure of a quasi-stranger, the centuries-old and genetically wired thrill of the chase. But when he entered the dark grotto at the appointed time, he saw no one who could possibly be FlowerGirl. Old women and pale priests, but no one nearly young enough.

He had fled the dripping cavern of mumbo jumbo and paused on the outside terrace. He reexamined the poem jotted on a scrap of paper. Where had he gone wrong?

I cannot tell
If there's a bell
Above a cave
Meant to save.
She lived alone
But now is gone
Meet me there
If you really care,
Close to ten
Day breaks again.

Then he had seen a young woman moving up a rocky path ascending the mountain. She wore a shawl over her head and large dark glasses. Her hips swayed provocatively. He thought he recognized the glasses and even the sway. He followed her, smiling, enticed, teased.

But he couldn't keep up with her swift pace. He cursed his way up the steep trail, and when he reached the top, wincing with the pain in his legs, perspiring heavily, and having difficulty breathing, she was nowhere to be seen. He saw a chapel farther up the path and headed for it.

Now, pausing in the back, he was victorious. The dark space was empty of pews or chairs. Only the stone altar remained as though it had erupted from the earth. And the key! He strode to the tabernacle. With an angry, impatient gesture he yanked it from the lock and slipped it around his neck. He peered inside the tabernacle. Empty, dusty, dirty. FlowerGirl would tell him what the key unlocked. He sniggered. The gods were smiling indeed.

Suddenly a shadow blocked the pallid light coming through the doorway and he turned. The young woman in the shawl stood silhouetted against the white glare. Lester peered toward her. She had removed her glasses.

The shock he felt added to his delight, to his mounting excitement. "Is that you, Teresa? Have you come back to me after all?"

She stared at him silently with her large eyes. He had always been entranced by her eyes. They called him, made it impossible to stop.

"What a pleasant surprise," he added.

Silence. The girl gripped something between both hands. It caught the light. He drew closer, stepping slowly down the aisle.

"So! *You* are my sweet FlowerGirl? Such a tease! I like that."

"You've stolen the key."

He felt for the leather around his neck and slipped the key under his shirt. The metal was cool on his skin, but he considered it a triumphant cold. "Indeed. Will you tell me now what I'm to do with it? You've been so helpful, my dear. What is that you're holding?"

"I loathe you! I hate what you did to me!" she screamed as she moved from side to side.

Lester saw the gun. "Now, now, let's not be rash."

Teresa backed through the doorway and onto the path, motioning him against a low rock wall on the edge of the precipice. He raised his hands in mock surrender. He knew she wouldn't use it, and this could be quite a nice little adventure.

28

Mont Saint Pilon

KELLY COULD SEE THAT THE TRAIL HAD NOT BEEN KEPT UP. Boulders and sharp shards jutted from decomposing stone, and although the path was wide, the going was slow as they maneuvered for footholds. Her running shoes provided little protection from the uneven trail and she envied their elderly companion's thick-soled boots and walking stick. Daniel's shoes were not much better than hers, laced leather walkers, but he proved to be agile as he followed the old man who moved with a bounce in his step.

They stopped in front of a stone oratory. "I appreciate these resting places at my age," their companion said, laughing. "Built in 1516, they were. Seven of them along the Chemin des Rois, but only four left. Around seven feet tall with scenes from the Magdalene's life. Hard to see the etched pictures on the stone, though. I used to guide folks up here, long ago. So I know the stories. Rather liked being a guide, that I did." He stroked his beard with his free hand, pulling it together to form a point that fell to his waist.

Kelly approached the miniature chapel. A scene had been carved on the lintel, but she couldn't identify the story, the stone so worn by the years. She peeked into the dark interior, but could see nothing. As she peered, she heard once more the alarming wail.

"We need to move on," Kelly said urgently. Something glittered near the oratory, on the edge of the trail, and she picked it up. "Daniel, it's Teresa's bracelet." She recognized the cross, the fish, the miniature church, the medals, all glinting in the pale light.

"She's been this way," Daniel said hoarsely, breathless. "I had a hunch that might be the case. Let's get moving."

The trees and shrubs lining the trail became scrubby and sparse, the stony terrain more strenuous. Kelly watched her footing, nearly slipping on the smooth limestone outcroppings.

The old man glanced at Daniel. "I assume you know the legend?"

"You mean the one about angels carrying Mary Magdalene to Mont Saint Pilon to hear them sing?" He breathed the words huskily, and Kelly recalled his asthma.

"You okay?" she asked him. "Do you have your inhaler?"

"Somewhere, not sure. Okay for now."

"Need to catch your breath, son?" the old man said. "Here's a little something I use occasionally." He pulled a small pump from his pocket.

Daniel regarded the hiker with curiosity. "Thanks." He sprayed into his mouth, inhaling the vapor slowly. "Let's keep going."

"My name's Joseph, by the way. Joseph Adamson. The air can get thin up here real fast. Now you just climb at your own pace."

They introduced themselves and continued to climb, carefully gauging the placement of their feet, holding onto the rock or scrub for balance.

"Is the chapel open?" Kelly asked Joseph, seeing in her mind Teresa facing Lester Sansby, facing her stepfather. What would she do?

They halted abruptly where the side of the trail dropped straight and sheer to the valley below. Feeling dizzy, Kelly moved away from the edge and breathed deeply. When she thought she couldn't go on, she recalled her dream. Somehow the dream steadied her, at least for the moment. She had climbed this way before and it had been beautiful.

"It's not usually open," Joseph said. "Vandals, you know. Always a problem. And theft. A friar let me inside a few years ago. Nice altar and a primitive statue of the Magdalene. Built in 1618, but there were earlier ones before that. High winds here. Dizziness. Some pilgrims have fallen to their deaths, so take care."

They continued up the trail to a flat broad shelf at the top of the ridge and the whitish rock caught the sunlight, blinding them. The wind picked up, blowing their jackets and biting their cheeks, and Kelly gasped at the view before her. The massif sloped away to the south, and on the far end of the ridge stood the chapel, seeming to balance itself on the rocky crest, anchored on the promontory, a stone box with a gabled entry. Far beyond the chapel, the Mediterranean shimmered, a thin band of silver. Behind, from where they had come, below and to the north, Kelly could see the forest, and farther, straight out to the horizon, Mont Sainte-Victoire, a smudge in the distance.

Daniel stood transfixed, bracing himself against the wind and breathing deeply. Then, as though recalling why they were here, he scanned the ridge. "Joseph's gone on. And I don't see any sign of Teresa."

Kelly followed his gaze. Far off, on the trail curving down to the south, below and around the chapel, Joseph's bent figure plodded slowly. He turned as if he felt their gaze, waved with a raised open palm as though in blessing, and continued on.

"Let's check the chapel. I think it was in my dream." Kelly started up the trail that crossed the ridge, quickening her pace, nearly running toward the stone church of Mont Saint Pilon.

*

They drew near, and Kelly could hear Teresa's strident voice, full of alarm. "The police are on their way. They know I'm here. You can't hide now. You can't escape."

"I don't believe you." It was a man's voice, velvety and smooth. "Now come to Papa like a good little girl. You lured me up here, come along now. You told me the key was here and there it was, right in the tabernacle like you said. Such a smart little girl, my little girl."

"I'll use this. Don't think I won't."

"No need, my pet. No need. Come to Papa, just like the old days."

Fear gripped Kelly as she glanced at Daniel. He appeared wary but determined. They moved around to the front of the chapel and its shallow porch. Beyond the porch, a ledge with a low stone wall about three feet high bordered the precipice. Beyond the wall, the sheer face of the cliff dropped straight to the valley floor. Lester Sansby stood with the wall behind him, his hands raised. Kelly thought he was the man she saw earlier, although now he was hatless and unshaven with a rough stubble. He wore dark glasses and held himself easily, his feet planted apart. He leaned forward in a familiar manner, as though playing a game with a child. Teresa faced him, her back to the chapel, and her shawl flapped in the wind. Kelly could see her eyes narrow as she grasped the revolver with both hands, her body stiff with resolve.

"She's got the gun," Kelly said under her breath.

It was barely a whisper, but the two turned toward her. As Teresa took her eyes off Lester, he rushed her, and the gun went off, echoing into the canyon. He grabbed her waist, and she flung the revolver to the corner of the terrace. Holding her tightly, he inched his way toward the gun, eyeing Daniel with contempt.

"Why if it isn't our little duo." He sneered. "Clark Kent and Lois Lane. Nice to see you, Dr. Weaver."

Daniel opened his hands in supplication, in peace. "Let…her…go," he said slowly, as though measuring his words would give them power.

Kelly stood near, her panic mounting. Why couldn't she move? This was what it meant to *freeze*, she thought.

"Let's just talk about this, okay?" Daniel said.

"About what, you little snot?"

"Your argument isn't with Teresa, now is it, Dr. Sansby?"

"You want to ruin me." He glanced toward the gun and crept closer, reaching. He grabbed it and pointed it at Daniel, as Teresa writhed in his grip.

"Let her go," Daniel said. "It's me you want."

At that moment Teresa wriggled loose just enough to fix her teeth into Lester's wrist. He screamed and released her. "You...! What did you do to me?" He stared at his bloody hand.

Teresa ran to Kelly, and they moved to the shelter of the low brush. The girl was trembling, tears streaming, and Kelly held her tight, steadying her.

Daniel turned to Sansby, who still held the gun. "You distort and lie," Daniel said softly, but in a voice like steel. "Why do you do that? Why do you pick on those children?"

"You mean my posts? That's my service to humanity. I set them straight. And they aren't children...well, most of them anyway." He leered.

"You steal from the young. You take away their faith and feed on their despair."

At first Kelly wondered why he was carrying on this debate; then she realized he must be stalling, hoping the police would arrive, hoping Teresa really had called them.

"You fool," Sansby mocked, "you're just like them, a victim of brainwashing. Can't you see I'm setting you free? Now move aside. I don't want to use this. I'm not a violent person. But clearly little FlowerGirl isn't quite as friendly as I'd hoped. Or remembered." He sniggered.

"You beast, you take away their dignity."

"They enjoy it, at least they enjoy the attention, and the freedom granted them, once they come around. *They* think I'm wonderful. *They* think I'm their savior."

"You post photos online in your network of porn."

"They love it."

He was enjoying himself, Kelly thought, even bragging, blinded by his own arrogance.

"They are young," Daniel said earnestly, his voice pleading their pain. "They are innocents, lambs led to the slaughter."

"How dramatic, Dr. Weaver! My, oh my. And not, I might add, in a position of strength." He moved the gun up and down, settling it on Daniel. "Why don't you move along now? Then we can forget all about this. You and the girls are blocking my path, and that is not a wise move."

"Give me the key, and we won't press charges."

"And please, remind me who has the gun? Your rose-colored glasses are growing rosier, my boy. And who would believe you? Your word against mine, a fanatic against a respected academic. Everyone hates your silly creed. Everyone thinks you and your ilk are crazy as loons."

"We're three against one," Daniel said. "And then there's the death of Father Gilbert." He paused, waiting for a reaction. "The murder investigation is still open. The police would like to question you. There may be a warrant out by now."

When Kelly heard her godfather's name, she stepped toward Daniel, a slow rage rising. Teresa had slumped to the ground, moaning and rocking, her arms wrapped around her knees.

Lester's eyes grew wide, full of alarm edged with fear. "You can't get me on that. I didn't do it." He glanced at Kelly nervously.

"Feeling guilty, Dr. Sansby?" Kelly asked boldly as she drew near Daniel.

"Let's have the gun, Lester," Daniel said, seeing Sansby's hesitation.

"Did you do it, Dr. Sansby?" Kelly asked, seeing the direct approach was throwing him off balance. Did she have some power over him?

"It wasn't my fault." Sansby shook his head and threw his arms wide, brandishing the gun that discharged into the air by mistake. He was clearly unnerved.

"What wasn't your fault?" Kelly asked, her tone serious, as though demanding the truth from a child.

"They were just in the way...not my fault...," he howled.

Kelly started, then began to shake, but forced herself to continue. "Who...were...in the way?"

"Your folks, you idiot—an accident—you can't blame me for that, you goody-goody." His face had grown flushed and his voice high-pitched. He rolled his eyes and Kelly could see their whites.

Kelly and Daniel exchanged glances.

"The shooting ten years ago?" Daniel asked.

"Gilbert deserved it then," Lester screamed, "and he deserved it now. The world's better for his going." He waved his gun at them. "Stand back or else."

"He killed my parents!" Kelly screamed. She stepped closer as though to attack. She wanted to strike him, scratch his eyes out, beat on his insufferable chest.

Daniel restrained her with his arm. "He has the gun. Forget him. Stand back."

"But he killed my parents!" Kelly sobbed, her eyes filling with tears. She covered her face with her hands. She could see her mother and father vividly. Her grief surged, her lips quivered, her body shook. She allowed Daniel to guide her to Teresa, to the dry grass and scrub. Her head throbbed as she watched Daniel. Teresa continued to sway, moaning, now eyeing Sansby with increased hatred. Would he kill again, here? How long could they hold out against this man? Where were the police?

"You filthy murdering beast," Daniel screamed, pointing his finger, standing in front of the women as though their protector.

Teresa had grown eerily quiet, her gaze still riveted on Sansby. Without warning she rose, pulling herself up to her full height, and stepped in front of Daniel. She looked to the steely sky, her eyes full of anguish, and she raised her arms in a dreadful keening, her shawl whipping about her in the wind. She turned her eyes upon Sansby. They were large black pools, icy cold. Kelly shuddered.

Teresa charged, her arms in front, screaming, "Aahhgg!" Her head was bowed like a ramrod and she drove her entire weight into his stomach. Caught off-guard, he wavered, dropped the gun, and fell backwards over the low stone wall. Kelly watched with horror as Teresa followed, her body catching on the rough rock. She hung there, her arms stretched out, staring wild-eyed at the gorge below, as Sansby plummeted. Kelly heard him shriek, a death echo in the now howling wind.

The next minutes would forever be a part of Kelly's memory, etched with the trauma. Daniel helped Teresa away from the precipice to safety. Kelly and Teresa followed Daniel into the chapel, out of the cold. They collapsed on the dusty stone floor.

Kelly wrapped her arm around Teresa, pulling her close. The girl wept softly, as though tears could cleanse. Kelly's teeth were chattering and she fought to control her rage, mingled now with relief. The ogre was gone. He murdered her parents. But he was gone. Did he kill Father Gilbert as well? Probably.

Daniel laid his jacket over Kelly's shoulders, gently touched Teresa's head, then turned to Lester's satchel by the door. He emptied it onto the floor, clearly hoping for the key. He sighed heavily and wrung his hands, pacing the small nave, glancing at the stone altar and the Magdalene in the niche above. Kelly could imagine his thoughts. They were safe and Lester Sansby was gone, but so was the key.

"It's over," Kelly whispered to Teresa. "It's over. He can't hurt you ever again." She gazed at the primitive Magdalene who held her jar of sweet-smelling oils. The Magdalene was peaceful and strengthening, gazing upon the altar.

Teresa wiped her eyes with the back of her hand. "He can't hurt you, either. But it will never be over. I'm sorry. The key was around his neck."

Daniel said firmly, "Let's worry about that later. The important thing is that you are all right. That we survived this. Survived *him*."

Teresa nodded, then said, suddenly comprehending the last few minutes, "I've killed a man. What have I done?"

"It was an accident." Kelly saw again his startled expression, his terror as he fell backward. "And he killed my parents. He would have killed us too without a second thought."

"You saved our lives," Daniel agreed. "He had the gun."

Teresa's face went blank, as though dueling emotions had formed a truce.

"Did you really call the police?" Daniel asked.

Teresa nodded. "They should be here by now. Father Bidwell called them."

Soon they heard the whirling drone of a helicopter, muted by the chapel's stone. Daniel stepped through the doorway and turned back to the women. "They're here."

"Let's go." Kelly helped Teresa up. After a glance back to the Magdalene, and the sweet power of her weakness, Kelly stepped outside, her arm at Teresa's elbow. Then she reached into her bag and pulled out the bracelet. "Here," she said, pressing it into Teresa's hand and closing her fingers over it. "I think this is yours."

Teresa nodded understanding, gazing at the Magdalene medal over Kelly's heart. "Thank you, my friend."

They watched the chopper make its vertical descent, fighting the wind. It hovered, rocked, and planted itself, the huge flat blades slicing the air, the motor roaring into the wind.

*

As he fell, Lester screamed.

His insides lurched and icy air engulfed his tumbling body.

Flashes of the girls and the boys, of his daughters, his lovers, his conquests struck his consciousness in rapid succession. He saw others too, his mother and father, his colleagues, his brother. He felt the acrid bitterness of hating and not loving, of taking and not giving, of having and not seeing.

But then he heard a song, a melody, and it hurt his ears, for it was too piercing, too sickeningly sweet. "No...," he wailed. "Stop the singers..."

An icy darkness came over him, inside and out, and he heard a sinister laugh of triumph from far away, as though from another realm, a place he had known and grown to enjoy…a place of pleasure…

The melody returned, plaintive, and with it a light washing out the dark.

"No…," he wailed again. "No singing…no light…"

The cold and the dark returned, this time with its silence, but with a promise of pleasure.

It was all so deviously familiar. "Take me…I know you…I'm yours…," Lester Sansby cried. Lightning cracked and pain, sharp and intense, racked his body, splintering his soul.

It was over.

29

Pierre

KELLY DECIDED THAT THE SMALL WINDOWLESS OFFICE could have been anywhere. But here, in Marseilles Airport Security, she would not have expected to find the circumspect Father Bidwell and the ingenuous Pierre. The two men sat in chrome chairs next to Teresa, Daniel, and Kelly, giving the impression that they had fulfilled their mission in life. Pierre wore jeans and a white shirt, his keys resting upon his heart, and Father Bidwell wore his black cassock. They regarded the *gendarme*, a tired-looking man of middle age, who sat behind a scuffed desk and who seemed impatient, as though hoping to send them away as soon as possible.

The officer glanced at his watch, then turned to a memo pad. "So I am instructed," he said, raising wiry brows over bloodshot eyes, "to witness a transfer of evidence." He glanced up.

Father Bidwell nodded to Pierre, and they stood. "Indeed," Father Bidwell said, smoothing his robe. "Pierre? Could you explain, please?"

Pierre turned to Kelly with pride. "I have found what you desire," he said. He pulled a frayed brown cord from his pocket, and with it, a key with no tassel. Kelly recognized the brown cord. The key was shinier, but still had dark discolored places.

Daniel glanced at Kelly and with that glance she knew that the key belonged to her. As though involved in a sacred ceremony, she stood and opened her palm. Pierre placed the cool metal in her hand. "It belongs with you," he said. As his hand released it, he bowed from the waist.

"But how…" Daniel interrupted, now standing, but drew quiet as though recalling that patience was a major virtue.

"You may indeed ask such a question," Father Bidwell said. "It was Pierre's insistence. When he learned that the body had been retrieved in the canyon, you see, Pierre, our most excellent sacristan, was distressed about the key. It was his watch, his guardianship, you might say. So Pierre found the key." He regarded the young man with fatherly affection.

The *gendarme* rose and cleared his throat. "If I might explain." He glanced at Kelly, then Teresa, who remained sitting silently, staring at the floor with her hands folded in her lap. "It is not a pretty thing to tell, not pretty to tell the ladies."

"It's okay with me," Kelly said, turning to Teresa. "Are you okay?"

"Yes, I want to know," she whispered, determinedly turning to fix her gaze on Kelly.

The policeman nodded soberly, wrapping up his report. "We found the body—identified as Monsieur Lester Sansby—hanging from a pinnacle on the side of a cliff of La Sainte-Baume. It appears it was an accident, as has happened on Mont-Pilon before, alas. He must have lost his footing. But he did not die from the fall." There was a dramatic silence as the officer regarded each of them in turn. "A thong of leather, this thong, to be exact, strangled monsieur by the neck. The key was wedged into his throat. *C'est très bizarre.*"

Shocked, Kelly stared at the key with revulsion. Did she hear the officer correctly? Daniel studied the *gendarme*, then considered Pierre with increased respect.

"Mademoiselle, it is clean," Pierre said quickly, "boiled."

"Thank you." Kelly slipped the key carefully into her bag.

Teresa was studying the floor and twisting her rings. Kelly sat alongside and wrapped her arm around her shoulders. The young woman's ashen face was torn with contradiction.

"And I am told," the officer continued, "Monsieur Pierre paid a visit to the local station. He asked about the key and, *alors,* here you are. So that is all very good and I have witnessed this transference of the evidence. But now, my friends, I have a pressing appointment." He dusted off his hands to signal the end of the interview, stepped to the door, and opened it with a flourish.

In the cold hallway, they said good-bye to the two men, Pierre with his rough handshake and teary eyes, Father Bidwell with his serious and knowing demeanor. Kelly led Teresa to the gate, Daniel following, as their flight for Rome was called. She glanced in her bag. The key remained in the pocket, safe. Considering its recent bloody history, she wasn't ready to wear this around her neck. She was glad she wore her Mary Magdalene medal, and she touched it with affection as she walked along the narrow jetway to the open door of the plane.

30

The Ambry

"THE KEY. DO YOU HAVE IT?" From the Crucifix Chapel, Daniel glanced back into the nave of the church of Maria Maddalena and up to the golden organ loft.

Kelly followed his eye. No sign of visitors, no threat of intruders. She opened her palm and studied the key. It was like a safety deposit box key, she thought, much like those she used when she worked at the bank and matched the key to the client's. Daniel pointed to the keyhole in the ambry, camouflaged in the patterned wall. The Christ on the cross gazed steadily upon them and the carved Magdalene stood silently nearby. Daniel had gently pushed a latch in the wrought-iron gate and it had swung easily open.

Kelly stepped into the small sanctuary, Daniel following. She inserted the key and turned it a quarter turn. She heard a slight click, but the door remained fast. She twisted it again and pulled. Nothing.

But on the third counterclockwise turn, the door sprang open. She felt inside, and for a breathless minute, as her fingers explored the cool metal interior, Kelly prepared herself for disappointment. They had come so far and been through so much, would this be the anticlimax of the journey? Were they indeed on a fool's errand? Her fingers traced the rough inner walls. They touched something long and round and she pulled out a narrow canister. Removing the stopper from one end, she peered inside. Daniel reached for it immediately and replaced the stopper.

"This could be old, a real find," he said, his voice tense with excitement. "Let's keep it sealed and have Father Francis decide how to proceed."

Kelly again reached inside, pulling out a flash drive and a folded paper. She knew that this data device, the size of her finger, contained enough memory to hold a small library. With its USB port it could connect to any laptop. The flash drive lay in her hand, daring her to guess its contents. "What do you think?" she asked Daniel.

"I'm hoping it's Father Gilbert's research. What's the paper?"

Kelly unfolded the sheet. It was as she had hoped. Another of her godfather's letters lay open between her fingers and as she read Father

Gilbert's words, her heart beat faster. Daniel read over her shoulder, his head close to hers. She could hear and feel his breathing.

> My dear Kelly,
> I go soon to our heavenly Father and to your parents. You have completed your quest and I pray you have made a journey into faith, have renewed your Baptismal vows with Our Lord.
> Please give this flash drive to Father Francis. It is my recent research on the wonderful and penitential Magdalene. He will know what to do with it.
> Thank Daniel for any part he played in helping you. May he have my blessing for all time.
> Your legacy will now be released by Father Francis. It shall include a small sum to help with your continued education. I also give to you the rights to my collected works, such as they are, including the material on the flash drive, and this early manuscript. Daniel and Father Francis will help you with these details. Hopefully you should derive a small income from this. Use it for your children, to protect them and teach them the love of God, the nature of objective truth. Teach them the Apostles' Creed and the story of Mary Magdalene and the great and good news told by the early Church, those first Christians.
> All is grace in our Lord Jesus,
> Your loving godfather,
> Keith Gilbert

They stood silently before the crucifix and the Magdalene, rereading the letter. Kelly wiped tears from her cheek. "He's really gone, isn't he?"

"Not forever, but yes, we'll miss him. He was, is, a saint."

Kelly refolded the paper and slipped it in her bag. She left the key in the ambry door. "It belongs here," she said.

Daniel nodded. "Indeed it does."

"Teresa's waiting," Kelly said, and they walked through the nave, under the golden vaults.

They stepped outside La Maddalena, into the bright piazza. Tourists still congregated in front of the restaurant, and taxis maneuvered up the narrow lanes, easing around the pedestrians.

Teresa looked through the open window of the car with her large and serious eyes. "Where to?" She revved the engine. "What did you find?"

"Santa Susanna," they said in unison and laughed. Kelly sat in front, Daniel in back.

As they drove toward the Corso, Kelly explained what they had found. And, as Teresa worked her way through the busy squares of fountains and churches to the neighborhood of Santa Susanna, Kelly read again her godfather's letter, this time aloud. This letter would not be burned, she thought, grateful.

Teresa smiled, and Kelly saw traces of satisfaction on her features, as though she had turned a corner, gone down a new path. She was beginning the rest of her life.

They both were.

31

L'Ancienne Vie

SATURDAY MORNING KELLY SAT BETWEEN TERESA AND DANIEL in the frescoed nave of Santa Susanna. Other conference attendees and members of the press were settling into the long pews, and Kelly could feel the anticipation of the crowd. Papers rustled, and a low hum of conversation echoed in the vaulted space. She noticed many of the attendees wore earphones to receive translations. Video cameras were expertly placed to tape the proceedings, to be aired via radio, cable, and Internet. A podium stood to the far left in front of the chancel. Beyond and above, the stunning apse glimmered over the high altar. It was a curious amalgam of art, faith, and science, and Kelly absorbed the complementary nature of the three, each a part of man's measure. Truly, they could not be separated.

Kelly had woken early that morning from a deep sleep. She had dreamed once again but could not hold on to the images…yet the melody lingered, a soaring song in a major key, or was it minor, delicious in its harmony, a melody so familiar and strange, sung by a chorus so heavenly…

But it was gone. She pulled herself out of bed, raised her window, and breathed the warm air. Summer had come to Rome. It was barely light, but the city was waking, with its early bustle of traffic and shouts and workmen, Roma stretching and yawning like a robust tabby cat. Kelly turned to her dresser where, alongside *Watership Down*, she had arranged her souvenirs the night before, a visual reminder of the flood of impressions of the last few days: her Santa Susanna brochure from Father Francis, her Maria Maggiore icon of the mysterious *Salus Populus Romani,* the Santa Croce crucifix from Brother Sebastian, the Lateran book of glossy photographs, the small carved Magdalene figurine from La Maddalena, the medallion from La Sainte Baume, and most beloved, the last letter from her godfather. She had photos too, which, she thought gratefully, included images of most of Father Gilbert's letters. And the key from Father Paul and Pierre that now rested in its home in the Rome church of the Magdalene.

Kelly moved back to the window and gazed over the city. She decided to start her new life with daily prayer. She focused on the far horizon where the sky held the church domes, and whispered hesitantly at first, but soon with greater desire, "Our Father, who art in heaven…"

Now, in Santa Susanna, Kelly was grateful for this new beginning, this better way of living, this good news. She looked up as Father Francis stepped to the podium. He sipped from a glass of water and opened his folder. He surveyed the crowd, demanding each person's attention, and adjusted his glasses.

"As a replacement speaker for Father Keith Gilbert, I am woefully inadequate. He was not only a scholarly man but a saintly man, and while the purpose today is not to eulogize his life, I must say that the greatest tribute to him, aside from his love for you all, and ours for him, is to read key excerpts from his work and to reveal his recent discovery. It is a great honor for me to do so."

He hesitated, and Kelly, sitting in the second pew, could see his lip tremble and his eyes moisten. She recalled he had mentioned he sometimes stuttered.

"Ex-ex-ex-cuse me," he said as the audience waited expectantly. He sipped again from the glass, wiping his brow. He tapped on the manuscript as though to gain confidence and began to read, at first with hesitation, then more purposefully, then with an easy rhythm as he became immersed in the concepts, lost in this world of ideas, faith, and the quest for truth:

"W-w-w-we all know the debates raging in New Testament Scholarship. Allow me to summarize the accepted findings so far. Since this report will be used in a broader forum than this audience, forgive me for stating what many of you know, first that manuscripts of the early Church were written on papyrus, a kind of reed, made from woven strips…"

Kelly listened to Father Francis summarize the kinds of materials used for these early writings, the papyri, the codices, and the copies made through the centuries. She followed him through the history of persecutions and how this affected the copies and ultimately the final form of the Gospels known today. Fascinated by the development of these early accounts and how we know what we know, she found herself waiting breathlessly for each word.

After clearing his throat, he took a sip of water. "So what can we say?" He surveyed the gathering, then looked to the frescoed saints on the walls, and out to the cameras. "Evidence supports historical assertions regarding early Christianity. What can't we say? There is not enough evidence to give us the historical development of the Christian movement in the first generations. There is not enough evidence for some early assertions made by the first Christians regarding powers, visions, miracles, even the Resurrection."

Kelly glanced at Daniel. Even the Resurrection? How could he say these words to these devout believers? How could he say this to the cameras that would broadcast his statements to the world? To a world of unbelievers?

Francis Fitzroy tapped his manuscript, and continued, his eyes on fire, as though this part of his remarks were a personal grievance avenged. His stutter seemed to have disappeared.

"Yet the search for the historical Jesus that has produced so-called *critical history* has not replaced the traditional Christian narrative. These scholars of doubt can know no more than we scholars of faith. The doubters call the Christian narrative *mythic*, implying untrue, but it is just as likely to be true as the doubters' narrative. What we *can know* and what we *do know* is a little about the lives and beliefs that produced these texts. We *can* know about the world of the first century, their symbols, and their beliefs. The writings do not give us history, but they reflect the movement they produced..."

As she listened, Kelly could see where he was heading and she pondered his words, re-ordering her own vision of early Christianity. He spoke of historical assertions, of converging evidence, of inconsistencies giving even greater credence to those crucial consistencies in the Gospels. She listened and soon felt that a much stronger foundation for her beliefs was being laid in her mind and soul. Perhaps it wasn't clear-cut evidence, but it wasn't a leap of faith. Father Francis spoke of probabilities leading to certainties and the ultimate nature of all historical truth. Never had she felt so certain of the statements she repeated in the *Apostles' Creed* than at this moment. Joy filled her heart like bright sun bursting from a dark cloud. She could *truly* believe.

Father Francis opened his palms, his eyes glinting. "And thus, we see the power of the Christian claim. Jesus, Christianity says, was fully human and fully God, one person in two natures. When He rose from the dead and ascended to Heaven, He remained fully human and fully divine, taking our human nature in its glorified state with Him. The Incarnation is permanent. Jesus is the sinless human being who lives an unfallen life in a fallen world and makes it possible for other human beings to be part of Him and benefit from His sinlessness. We aren't sinless, but we can enjoy these benefits through our sacramental connection in Baptism and the Eucharist.

"We can know history in many ways. The community of Christians of the first century and the ensuing history of the Church all point to the historicity of the Resurrection. We continue that history in this Church community as we witness to the power of Christ! As Pope Benedict stated, 'God enters into dialogue with the people he created, speaking through creation and even through silence, but mainly in the Church through the

Bible and through his son Jesus.' "

A thrill ran through the hushed nave as Father Francis said these words. Daniel glanced at Kelly, nodding, and Teresa squeezed her hand. Kelly did indeed feel part of this Resurrection history, by simply believing, and now believing carried so much more certainty and delight.

The priest spoke quietly about the astounding growth of the Church, the fervor birthed by the Holy Spirit, and the four Gospel accounts that were accepted by the Council of Ephesus. Kelly, for the first time, found herself proud to be a Christian. It was a small pride at first, but it grew. It was a good kind of pride, she reasoned, a glorious and holy pride.

Father Francis spoke now in a more serious tenor, as though leading to the final revelation. "Given this background, we consider Saint Mary Magdalene. We know the earlier tradition of the Magdalene was embellished by medieval historians. We seek the more pure tradition. But what is muddied and what is pure? What is false and what is true? Étienne-Michel Faillon, the nineteenth-century Sulpician scholar, discovered three texts which he contends are tenth-century copies of an earlier text. He calls this earlier text the *Ancienne Vie* and convincingly dates it fifth-sixth century. Such a text would be the purest tradition of Mary Magdalene's life in Provence. Clearly the more copies of this *Ancienne Vie* that are found, the greater the reliability of the primary source.

"It is my pleasure and honor to announce to this gathering that Father Gilbert found a fourth text, essentially identical to the three that Faillon discovered. It too has been dated to the tenth century. Thus, it also can be identified as a copy of the same fifth-century *Ancienne Vie*. In English this document would read roughly as follows:

> With the Apostles at that time was Saint Maximin, one of the 72, a person commendable on account of the total integrity of his morals and famed for his teaching and his gift of working miracles. Saint Mary Magdalene who lived in his company—just as the Blessed Mary Ever-Virgin in that of Saint John the Evangelist, to whom the Lord had entrusted her—devoted herself to the care of this holy disciple.
>
> During this diaspora, Maximin and Mary Magdalene went to the seashore. There they boarded a vessel and, after a favorable journey, arrived at Marseilles. Disembarking there, inspired by the Lord, they went into the Comté of Aix, distributing abundantly to all the seed of the divine word and endeavouring night and day, by their preaching,

their fasts and their prayers, to attract to the knowledge and worship of Almighty God the people of this region, who were as yet unbelievers and not yet regenerated by the waters of Baptism.

The Confessor and Pontiff Maximin governed the church at Aix for many years, attending faithfully to preaching, exorcising demons, raising dead people, giving sight to the blind, curing the lame and healing every sort of infirmity.

Now when the time drew near for Mary Magdalene [to die], she saw that Jesus Christ—to whose service she had dedicated herself so completely—was calling her in His mercy to the glory of the heavenly Kingdom, in order to give forever the food of heaven to her who had faithfully supported Him in temporal life, when He had appeared in human form. She died the eleventh day before the Kalends of August [= 22 July], the angels rejoicing...

Taking her holy body, Bishop Maximin embalmed it with various romantic spices and placed it in a worthy mausoleum. Over her holy body he built a basilica of remarkable architecture. There one can see her tomb, which is of white marble...

And so, after his holy death, he was honorably buried there by the faithful...this monastery is called the Abbey of Saint-Maximin...

"The style of this document is clearly pre-seventh century. Thus we say that it was believed as early as the fifth century that Maximin, one of the disciples sent out by Christ, became Bishop of Aix. It was believed that Mary Magdalene preached with him in the area, and that they were buried in the place known as Saint-Maximin. It was *not* believed—but not disbelieved either—at that time that she lived her last years in a grotto."

Kelly caught her breath and exchanged glances with Daniel and Teresa. She had found the story of Mary Magdalene in La Sainte Baume enchanting, although it was difficult to imagine anyone living in such a dark and damp place. Now she saw Mary Magdalene traveling through the valley below and the hills around Saint-Maximin, preaching the extraordinary news of Christ's resurrection. And this would be something Kelly could visualize with a fair degree of faith that it was true. She turned to Teresa, whose face was unreadable, and Kelly understood that she was still dealing with the trauma of the last forty-eight hours. Teresa blinked and seemed to show a trace of satisfaction that the research had been safely found. Daniel's eyes were wide and attentive, not wanting to miss a single word.

The priest locked glances with Daniel, smiled, and rested an appreciative eye upon Kelly. "I would now like to thank Ms. Kelly Roberts and Dr. Daniel

C. Weaver for their successful search for Father Gilbert's manuscript and this historic document. The scholarly community of Rome will be forever indebted to you. Also I wish to express gratitude to the University of Roma for their verification on such short notice. I understand that Ms. Roberts, now the owner of Father Gilbert's collected works and this historic document, has been most generous in loaning this copy of the *Ancienne Vie* to the Vatican Library."

The room applauded as Kelly and Daniel stood and nodded their thanks.

Father Francis beamed. "We shall now break for refreshments in the Orangerie next door. Thank you all very much."

32

Courting

THEY STEPPED INTO THE GARDEN COURTYARD. Immediately Kelly and Daniel were met with attendees offering congratulations, and Teresa stepped away quietly, moving slowly toward the refreshment table. Some of the attendees spoke Italian, some French, some broken English, and Kelly nodded and smiled and said *grazie*. Eventually she and Daniel joined Teresa, and they filled their plates with provolone, grapes, and bruschetta as Daniel balanced three glasses of wine. They soon found a quiet corner where they could watch the crowd.

A light breeze blew, and Kelly wondered if her French braid was in place. Earlier that morning, a subdued Teresa had braided Kelly's long plaits, showing her how to weave sections and fasten with a band. Two shorter strands were left to fall, softly framing her face. The Provençal skirt, camisole, and shawl she borrowed from Teresa made her feel festive as though she was at an important celebration, and perhaps she was. She was beginning to believe they had truly succeeded in their quest, and she would soon be home with Matt.

Teresa had pulled her own curls high, rolling them tight on top of her head, forming a crown. The style made her eyes appear even larger, although sadness still veiled them. She wore the same black and white skirt, tee, and blue shawl that she wore that day in Maria Maggiore, a day that now seemed long ago. Indeed, Teresa had become both friend and sister, and Kelly's desire to protect her was stronger than ever.

Kelly glanced at Daniel in his blue blazer and yellow tie, his khakis. She was at ease with him beside her, a sweet and unthreatening presence. Once the sexual expectation had been removed, a great weight had been lifted. Why was that? But did she see him as a brother or…a suitor?

Suitor. The old-fashioned word came to mind, a cousin of his earlier word, *courting.* Time would tell. For now she was enjoying his enjoyment.

Daniel pointed out reporters from *Opus Veritatis,* professors he recognized from school in Rome, and several respected biblical scholars who were particularly concerned with methodology and truth, and the education of the young.

"They insist," Daniel said with fervor, "that value judgments should be connected to objective reality."

Kelly saw where he was going. "So if there is only subjective reality, a personal reality, then those value judgments are totally chaotic, without meaning."

He nodded. "Such statements have no connection with natural law, what C.S. Lewis called the *Tao*, something greater than mankind that rules our consciences. Without such an authority, we become beasts, acting on instinct. This subjectivism is a huge lie, taught to our children."

"I understand their worry. So much history is distorted." She glanced at Teresa, who was quietly following their conversation, her eyes moving from one to the other.

Daniel recognized another face in the crowd. "Hannah Farris." He motioned discreetly in her direction. "The redhead. She's promoted five criteria that have long been recognized as yardsticks of truth by historians, but she explains them for the lay person. An excellent journalist who contributes to the Catholic press."

"And they are?" Kelly knew he wanted her to ask. "The five criteria?"

He raised his brows and recited, "Embarrassment, dissimilarity, multiple sources, consistency, and rejection."

"Embarrassment?"

"Testimony would not include embarrassing facts unless they were true, such as Jesus being chased out of his hometown, his disciples questioning or even denying and betraying him. Dissimilarity refers to the facts standing out from the age, new and strange, as is true in many of Jesus' teachings."

"And multiple sources must mean where the Gospels agree."

"Exactly, and they do agree on key points."

"Consistency refers to consistency of character?"

"Right. The Jesus we find in one account should mesh with the one in others, similar in multiple sources."

"And rejection must refer to the crucifixion as well as the many other rejections Jesus suffered."

"A socially ostracizing death, not a hero's death, not a leader or lord's, certainly not *a god's* death. Such things are likely to be true, or highly probable. It would be unlikely that a tale so demeaning and embarrassing would be invented."

Teresa continued in her silence, watching them, and Kelly could see that in her persisting exhaustion she welcomed passivity. She was wounded and she would heal, but she appeared to have aged twenty years in the last few days. Her eyes were red and puffy, and her melancholy was nearly tangible. As Kelly pondered how to help, she noticed Sister Gabriella in her green habit across the lawn. The nun waved cheerily, lifting herself up on her toes. A slim blonde stood next to her, whom Kelly thought she recognized.

"There's Brigitte Durieux," Kelly said, waving to the two women, "with Sister Gabriella."

Gabriella made her way over, a jaunty bounce in her step, lifting her robe with one hand and holding her wine glass with the other, her features bright. Brigitte arrived first, her stride long and graceful. She beamed and kissed them on both cheeks, exclaiming, "*Alors! Bonjour, mes amis! Enchantée!*" Gabriella kissed them too, winking and laughing.

"Brigitte and Sister Gabriella, how good to see you," Kelly said.

Gabriella gazed at the sky. "It is a magnificent day, I should say so, my dears! A magnificent day, one my old papa would be proud of, to be sure, to be sure! Congratulations to you, my wee little Kelly, on your most excellent find. I knew you could do it and I kept you in my prayers, that I did, especially my prayers to the lovely Magdalene herself who no doubt interceded directly to our Lord on your behalf! Directly, no doubt! And congratulations to Daniel as well, who has helped you on your quest. And Teresa, my dear, so good to see you too. But who would have thought such a document should come to light? Who would have thought it?"

Brigitte nodded in agreement as they watched the Irish nun. Kelly was again entranced by Gabriella's words, tumbling like a waterfall.

"Thank you, Sister," Kelly said. "I'm still a little stunned by it all."

"Madame Durieux," Daniel began, with some perplexity, "I have a question for you. There are a few missing pieces to the puzzle of the key. I have an idea that you might be able to help."

"But of course, what is the piece you desire of which to know?" Brigitte Durieux's eyes glittered as though finally she could tell her secret, finally someone asked.

"The key," Daniel said. "Do you know how it got from Rome to La Sainte Baume?"

"But why do you think I would know such a thing?"

Gabriella was watching her friend closely, and Kelly guessed the nun knew parts of Brigitte's story, if not all. "Don't you go a-teasing him, now, little Brigitte."

Kelly laughed, for Brigitte was a tall, statuesque woman, and *très élégante* in her gray silk pantsuit. Even Teresa couldn't prevent a half-smile.

"A hunch, I would say," Daniel said. "You knew Father Gilbert, you lived in the area, and Pierre wouldn't have traveled to Rome."

Brigitte folded her long beringed fingers and nodded as though she was a partner in mystery. "*Oui, c'est moi!* I carry the key to the tabernacle of La Sainte Baume. I carry it many times. Father Gilbert keeps his work safe in the Maddalena ambry. No copies of the key, he said, and no box in bank. He tried that, and papers stolen. *Poof!* I help him with his important secret work. I come to Rome. We open the ambry. He puts in new work. I return the key to Pierre. But, *vous savez, alors!* I did not know a new key was made for the tabernacle of La Sainte Baume. I did not know you search for this key. I did not question. Father Gilbert sends to us many pilgrims. We are happy to help. He is a good friend for many years. He stayed with us when he did his research in Provence."

Daniel nodded. "That explains it." He hesitated, then added, "Yes, he was a good friend. I miss him."

"But, Monsieur Daniel," Brigitte said, her eyes again twinkling, "you have not asked the big question."

Daniel appeared confused. "Another big question?"

Brigitte laughed a light happy laugh. "*Ah, oui.* The big question is Plan B. You are so smart, it is the question to ask, is it not?"

"And," Kelly asked, "what *was* my godfather's Plan B? I assume you mean what would happen if we didn't find the manuscript."

"*Exactement!* But you were right to follow Plan A. To honor Father Gilbert's wishes."

"Tell them," Gabriella said. "Don't go a-teasing again, little Brigitte. Tell them about Plan B." The nun placed her hands on her hips and raised her brows in command.

"Ah, yes," Brigitte said, swaying back and forth and seeming to enjoy the moment greatly, "Plan B was this: Father Francis would force the ambry. But he did not know this."

"Of course," Daniel said, sounding relieved. "If necessary, that could have been done by the right authorities."

"I suppose," Kelly added, thinking of their time in France, "Father Gilbert was serious about my paying attention."

"And you did," Gabriella said. "You sure did." She grinned.

Brigitte grew quiet. "Did the police find the man who is responsible for Father's death? I would like to see him…hang."

"We heard that the suspect went missing." Kelly turned to Daniel. "Did Father Francis say anything else?"

"Only that he left an Internet trail. Went by the name of Fab, short for Fabio, his real name, not terribly original. They're still piecing it together, but it appears he was bragging online that he had tampered with Father Gilbert's medication."

Brigitte gasped. "Digoxin!"

"How did you know?" Daniel asked.

"I buy for him when I visit. I help him. And I know what it is—my own Alain takes it. It slows the heart."

Daniel nodded. "He slipped away quietly."

"Even so, it's awful." Once again, Kelly blamed herself for the years lost. *One cannot turn time back,* she thought. But then he would want her to move on. She had, after all, obeyed his last wishes, and she was glad of that.

Teresa watched and listened, her eyes clouding over. "I miss him."

Gabriella turned to her. "We all do. And Teresa, my dear, we have missed *you.* You have not visited us in a long time. Perhaps another retreat with the sisters might be good? Brigitte comes often."

Kelly observed the three women, seeing their friendships from the past. Rome was, perhaps, a small world, one in which her godfather still lived, for his love wove through them all, connecting them, healing them. She was grateful for his life on earth and knew that in his life in heaven he prayed for them.

Teresa was making an effort to be affable. As though forcing her words to the surface, she said, "Yes, a retreat. A good idea. Thank you." Suddenly her face changed, as though waking from a bad dream. "Sister, we must find Melanie. We have to find Melanie!" she implored, her voice rising. She grabbed the nun by her shoulders.

"Yes, indeed, we shall." Gabriella wrapped a steady arm around Teresa, calming her. "Come and walk with me. Let's talk about Melanie. Let's visit her and see how she's doing. She may like to come home now. Indeed, I do believe she might like that." She glanced at Brigitte. "And I have need of your excellent company on this glorious day."

Brigitte followed them with her long stride, carrying the wine glasses and humming softly.

"Melanie?" Daniel asked, clearly puzzled.

"Her sister. She was unjustly committed to a mental hospital…by Sansby."

"No!" Daniel cried, stunned.

They watched the three women walk toward an orange tree in a far corner near the viewing terrace, Gabriella chatting seriously, Teresa studying the grass under her feet and nodding vaguely, Brigitte gently touching the girl's shoulder.

Daniel inhaled deeply. "Gabriella and the sisters will care for her. Teresa needs a lot of caring. And Brigitte steps in wherever she is needed, I think."

Kelly shook her head. "I hope so. Melanie will need them too. And after what Teresa went through on the mountain…what do you think she intended to do up there?"

"We'll never know for sure," Daniel said thoughtfully. "Perhaps Teresa doesn't fully know or admit to herself. I believe you were right when you said she was trying to trap him in some kind of theft. But her rage took over and she had the gun. She wanted him alone on top of that mountain. I'm glad we arrived when we did."

Kelly relived the scene in her mind. Teresa was no match for Lester Sansby, and only tragedy would have come from such violence. But grace prevailed, perhaps with the aid of a mysterious Joseph Adamson. She and Daniel had arrived in time. A certain sort of justice was meted. Now Teresa—and hopefully Melanie—must heal.

"Teresa told me she was thinking of joining a religious order." The recent conversation in that other garden, the cloister of Saint-Maximin, belonged to another time.

"That's good. I'm glad."

"And you?"

His dark eyes searched hers, warming her. "It's been a possibility, I won't deny it. Not so sure now. Do you think I should join an order? Or become a priest? Or both?"

Kelly felt flushed. What did she think? What could she promise? Nothing, now. "It has to be your decision, Daniel."

"Not weighing in on this at all?"

"I-I-I think…I'd like to see more of you."

"And I, you."

"Are you staying in Rome?" Kelly asked. "With all the excitement of the manuscript and the document, Father Francis must need an assistant. There must be papers to write, pieces for journals and the press."

"This much I've decided. I'm going home to Berkeley on Monday's flight, on your flight. I need to prepare for summer session. And I miss Major and Daisy."

"The dogs," Kelly said, relieved. Another few days with Daniel would steady her, keep her on track. Had she come to depend on his friendship, his company? Or was there something deeper?

She searched her heart and found nothing except maybe need. Was need a kind of love? She thought not. At best, an infantile love.

"I'm glad." She self-consciously touched her glasses.

"And what about you? Any plans for your little nest egg?"

"I'm banking some of the legacy, in a trust for Matt. And there might be enough for me to go back to school and study history, maybe teach."

"And move to a safer neighborhood?"

"We'll see."

"And Saint Mary's?"

Kelly paused, then replied, "I think I'll be a regular there now."

"Me too."

They crossed the lawn to the viewing terrace, and they looked out over Rome, to the domes and the red roofs, the congestion, the haze. Kelly's feelings were all a mix. There was so much of Rome that she hadn't seen.

Daniel sounded wistful. "We never got to Trastevere. The bookstore. Remember?"

It seemed long ago, that conversation as they walked up the Via Torino, spooning their gelato. "I remember. Maybe we can go tomorrow? I wish I could stay in Rome ,and I wish I could be home. It's a wonderful city, and I feel like I've only scratched the surface."

"If that," Daniel agreed. "Rome is never-ending, indeed eternal in its mysteries. There's always things to see and discover, new puzzles and new mysteries. Just the churches alone—over five hundred I believe at last count—are glorious in their secrets. All I can do is promise myself that I'll come back. It's the only way I can leave."

Kelly laughed with appreciation. "I can see that. Me too. I'll look forward to returning."

"Me too." Daniel gazed into her eyes. "And let's go to the Trastevere bookshop tomorrow after church."

"But for now, let's go see Father Francis and thank him again," Kelly said, nervous with the attention.

Cradling their glasses, they walked toward the orange tree where Teresa, Gabriella, and Brigitte had gathered around Father Timothy, who held court in his wheelchair alongside Father Francis.

Before joining them, Daniel touched Kelly's arm, staying her. She turned to face him, realizing for the first time he was a bit taller after all. She waited for him to speak, looking at the ground, then the view, and then into his gentle, curious eyes. The moment held such promise, Kelly thought, as though it dangled before her forever, in some kind of delightful limbo.

A breeze blew her hair, and he touched the strand, smoothing it down. "If I might be so bold, Miss Roberts, I was wondering how you felt about courting?"

"Courting?"

"Getting to know one another…a little better?"

Kelly nodded. "Courting. I like the idea. No commitment, just courting."

"And we'll see how things go, what's true about us and what is not, what God has in mind for us, who we are meant to be, our true identities."

"We'll see what is true."

"We may only learn what is probable."

"A bit of faith involved?"

"A bit of faith."

Appendix

The Apostles' Creed, as translated by the Roman Catholic Church

> I believe in God, the Father Almighty, Creator of heaven and earth; and in Jesus Christ, His only Son, our Lord: Who was conceived by the Holy Spirit, born of the Virgin Mary; suffered under Pontius Pilate, was crucified, died and was buried. He descended into hell; the third day He rose again from the dead; He ascended into heaven, is seated at the right hand of God the Father Almighty; from thence He shall come to judge the living and the dead. I believe in the Holy Spirit, the Holy Catholic Church, the communion of Saints, the forgiveness of sins, the resurrection of the body, and life everlasting. Amen.

All churches and historical sites I have endeavored to describe accurately, and I heartily recommend them to visitors to Rome and Provence.

Chapter Notes

Directions in a church:
For the purposes of clarity, I have used the traditional directions with regard to church interiors: the chancel and sanctuary stand at the eastern end, the narthex at the western end, the transept runs north/south. Even in churches where the building doesn't actually face east, churches still adopt this nomenclature. The tradition of facing East in prayer, mentioned by Saint Basil in the fourth century, is based on Holy Scripture, both the Old and New Testaments, where Christ is identified as the East, or the "Orient," with references to both the Incarnation and the Second Coming.

Sanctuary and nave:
I am using the term *sanctuary* to mean the altar area, usually raised above the rest of the church, and the *nave* to refer to the area where the congregation sits.

Catholic and catholic:
The use of catholic with a lowercase *c* is generally accepted to mean the faith passed through the ages; the use of Catholic with the uppercase *C* refers to the Catholic Church.

Chapter Seven, Father Francis

Art and religious belief:
The author Michael Donley, who has researched the story of Mary Magdalene in Provence (*St Mary Magdalen in Provence, The Coffin and the Cave*), was kind enough to read a draft of this novel. He adds the following comment with regard to the drift away from religious belief:

> The drift away from religious belief actually began with the Renaissance, with the man-centered use of perspective rather than the flat foreground of icons, and also the use of real women as models when depicting the Virgin. Such art is "religious" only in name. The "renaissance" was of course a "rebirth" of classical *pagan* culture.

The Church of Santa Susanna:
The Paulist Fathers and Cistercian nuns staff the Church of Santa Susanna. The English-language library and parish center welcome visitors and new residents.

www.santasusanna.org

Chapter Eight, Susanna

Santa Susanna in the Old Testament:
The story of Susanna is included in the Book of Daniel by the Roman Catholic and Eastern Orthodox churches, but is considered apocryphal by most Protestant churches. Anglicans include the account as part of the Bible but stipulate that it is not to be used for the formation of doctrine.

Chapter Ten, Incarnation

The crèche:
The existence of the crib in Santa Maria Maggiore is reflected as early as the time of Pope Sixtus III (432-440) when this Pope created a "cave of the Nativity" similar to that in Bethlehem, designed, it is thought, for pieces of the cradle brought by pilgrims.

http://www.vatican.va/various/basiliche/sm_maggiore/en/storia/interno.htm

Chapter Eleven, Father Timothy

Dating of the story:
In 2010, the year of this story, the Corpus Christi procession was actually cancelled due to rain; the observances on June 3 were confined to the Lateran Basilica, led by Pope Benedict XVI, and included Eucharistic Adoration and Benediction. In the year prior, 2009, the procession occurred as described, from the Lateran to Mary Major, as it did in 2011.

It should also be noted that normally the basilica would be closed on the afternoon of the Pope's arrival; I have taken fictional liberties with the logistics of Kelly and Daniel's visit on the afternoon of Corpus Christi.

Chapter Sixteen, La Maddalena

The reference to the ambry is fictional, although there is what appears to be a small door in the left (northern) wall of the Crucifix chapel.

Chapter Twenty-four, Antoinette

Gnosticism: Carl E. Olson and Sandra Miesel write in *The Da Vinci Hoax:*

> Gnosticism was exclusive, elitist, and esoteric, open only to a few. Christianity, on the other hand, is inclusive and exoteric, open to all those who acknowledge the beliefs of the faith handed down by Jesus and enter into a life-giving relationship with him. Jesus Christ of the canonical Gospels is a breathing, flesh-and-blood person; he gets hungry, weeps, eats and drinks with common people, and dies. Jesus Christ of the Gnostic writings is a phantom, a spirit who sometimes inhabits a body and sometimes does not, and who talks in ways that very few could understand. (pp. 68-69)

Ronald Nash is quoted in this same work:

> Far too many writers use this late source material (after A.D. 200) to form reconstructions of the third-century mystery experience and then uncritically reason back to what they think must have been the earlier nature of the cults...Information about a cult that comes several hundred years after the close of the New Testament canon must not be read back into what is presumed to be the status of the cult during the first century A.D.
>
> From "Was the New Testament Influenced by Pagan Religions?" in *Christian Research Journal,* Winter 1994, p. 145.

Chapter Thirty-one, L'Ancienne Vie

Notes on Father Francis's speech:
This speech is based on the writings of Luke Timothy Johnson in *The Real Jesus,* D.C. Parker in *The Living Text of the Gospels,* and Michael Donley, Ph.D., in *St Mary Magdalen in Provence,* with suggestions from Paul S. Russell, Ph.D. This fourth copy of the *Ancienne Vie* is fictional. The text

shown is the third copy found by Étienne-Michel Faillon in the nineteenth century, translated by Michael Donley.

Chapter Thirty-two, Courting

The Orangerie: To my knowledge, this garden is fictitious and created for the purposes of the novel.

Hannah Farris: These five criteria for historical truth are taken from an essay by Alice Camille in "The Gospel Truth." (See Bibliography.)

Bibliography

Barzun, Jacques, *From Dawn to Decadence—500 Years of Western Cultural Life, 1500 to the Present* (New York: HarperCollins, 2000).

Camille, Alice, "The Gospel Truth" in *U.S. Catholic,* October 2010, 44+. The five criteria for history. Co-writer of the homily service, "Prepare the Word," and author of *God's Word Is Alive* (ACTA, 2007), available through alicecamille.com.

Donley, Michael, *St Mary Magdalen in Provence, The Coffin and the Cave* (Herefordshire, UK: Gracewing, 2008).

Johnson, Luke Timothy, *The Real Jesus* (San Francisco: HarperCollins, 1996), and *The Creed, What Christians Believe and Why It Matters* (New York: Doubleday, 2003).

Lacordaire, Henri, *The Life of Saint Mary Magdalene* (1859), www.lifeofmarymagdalene.com.

Myers, Ken, "Irrigating Deserts," *Touchstone,* September/October 2010. Speaks of Lewis's *The Abolition of Man* and how education teaches subjectivism to our young to the great peril of our society, denying them the ability to make judgments, since there is no objective reality.

Olson, Carl E. and Miesel, Sandra, *The Da Vinci Hoax* (San Francisco: Ignatius Press, 2004).

Parker, D.C., *The Living Text of the Gospels* (New York: Cambridge University Press, 1997).

Pseudo-Rabanus Maurus, *De vita Beatae mariae Magdalene et Sororis eius Sanctae.*

Russell, Paul S., *The Apostles' Creed* (Berkeley, CA: The American Church Union, 2008), and *Reading the Gospels Today* (Berkeley, CA: The American Church Union, 2009).

Schmemman, Alexander, *For the Life of the World, Sacraments and Orthodoxy* (Crestwood, NY: Saint Vladimir's Seminary Press, 1963, 1973).

Welborn, Amy, *Decoding Mary Magdalene* (Huntington, IN: Our Sunday Visitor, 2006).

PILGRIMAGE

Christine Sunderland

*It was a day
when nothing should have gone wrong…
but everything did.*

Madeleine Seymour will never forget what happened twenty-two years ago in her own backyard. She's still riddled with guilt. Hoping to banish the nightmares that haunt her and steal her peace, she travels to Italy with her husband, Jack, on a pilgrimage. As a history professor, Madeleine is fascinated by the churches they visit…and what they live about the lives of the martyrs. But can anything bring her the peace that her soul longs for?

www.ChristineSunderland.com
www.oaktara.com

OFFERINGS

Christine Sunderland

Jack's haunted by fears of the past.
Madeleine holds a powerful secret.
And Rachelle is running away.

For the last seventeen years, her husband, Jack, and son, Justin, have been Madeleine Seymour's world. Then, during Justin's wedding reception, Jack collapses. Jack needs surgery, and he insists it be performed by the doctor who perfected the procedure. But the doctor isn't reachable, and time is running out.

Dr. Rachelle DuPres, plagued by memories of a deadly failure, flees America to search out her roots in her ancestral village in Provence, France. But as she tries to locate the graves of her Catholic uncles and her Jewish parents, will their roles in the Holocaust bring more angst—or the answers she so desperately seeks?

A poignant story about choices made along the way…
and the miracles of the heart.
Set in the breathtaking beauty of France.

www.ChristineSunderland.com
www.oaktara.com

INHERITANCE

Christine Sunderland

She risked everything to save a life…
But who would save hers?

Vietnamese-American Victoria Nguyen, seventeen, flees to England with a powerful secret…and a determined senator on her trail.

Madeleine Seymour, a history professor, and her husband, Jack, a retired wine broker, travel from San Francisco to London to purchase property for a children's home—and find much more than land at stake.

Brother Cristoforo, a black Franciscan from the Seymours' Quattro Coronati orphanage in Rome, wrestles with demons of his past and present.

Woven through the mists of Lent to new life on Easter Day, *Inheritance* draws the lives of these four characters together to a stunning, unforgettable conclusion.

A poignant story about choices made along the way…
and the miracles of the heart.
Set in the breathtaking beauty of England.

www.ChristineSunderland.com
www.oaktara.com

Hana-lani

Christine Sunderland

*Only opening their hearts will keep them
from plunging into the dark abyss.*

Old Nani-lei lives in Hana-lani, her family home in rural Hawaii. She looks after her grandson Henry, 52, and his daughter Lucy, 6, who have returned to Maui from Berkeley after the death of Maria, Henry's wife. Henry and Maria, both professors, had been working on *A History of Ethics,* and now the grieving Henry struggles to finish it.

City girl Meredith Campbell, 36, fast-paced, self-centered, and beautiful, believes her body will ensure her happiness. After losing her job and finding her lover unfaithful, she flies to Maui, sure he will follow…but her plane crashes near Hana-lani.

As their worlds collide in a natural world both beautiful and dangerous, Henry will be forced to act on his words, and Meredith will come face-to-face with her own life choices.

*A poignant journey that unravels T.S. Eliot's "permanent questions"—
what is goodness, truth, and love?*

www.ChristineSunderland.com
www.oaktara.com

About the Author

CHRISTINE SUNDERLAND, author of *Pilgrimage, Offerings, Inheritance,* and *Hana-lani* (all OakTara) has long been fascinated by the nature of historical truth, particularly in reference to the first-century Christian Church and the veracity of the New Testament Gospel accounts. Her many visits to Rome and southern France have inspired this exploration of the claims of the twentieth-century "historical Jesus" movement and the novels of Dan Brown.

She serves currently as Managing Editor of the American Church Union (*Anglicanpck.org*). She has recently edited for the ACU a second edition of the retreat addresses of Raymond Raynes, C.R., *The Faith,* first edited by Nicholas Mosley in 1961.

Christine holds a B.A. in English Literature *cum laude*. She is an alumna of the Squaw Valley Writers Workshop and the Maui Writers Retreat. She lives in Northern California with her husband and two amazing cats. She writes wherever and whenever she has a chance.

www.ChristineSunderland.com
www.oaktara.com

CPSIA information can be obtained at www.ICGtesting.com
Printed in the USA
BVOW02s0846060913

330299BV00002B/787/P

9 781602 901261